BLOOD RED SKY

BLADES OF GRASS BOOK 3

AUSTIN CHAMBERS

CREDITS

PROOF READERS – Loren Foster and Cheryl Nelson Deariso

COVER BY – Ivan@bookcoversart.com

ISBN – 978-1-7360479-5-8

Published by Crossed Cannons Publishing, LLC
P.O. Box 334
Seabeck, WA 98380-0334
www.authoraustinchambers.com

Blood Red Sky
Blades of Grass Book 3

PROLOGUE

CANADIAN FORCES BASE ESQUIMALT
Victoria, British Columbia, Canada

THE SILVER ROOTS OF THE TALL BLONDE WOMAN'S HAIR would've told a tale to any who had bothered to notice. Fortunately for Navy Captain Marie Darnell, the months since the unthinkable Cascadia disasters and the eruption of Mt. Rainier had taught her to keep her hair French braided for easier placement under her hardhat in the wet, windy winters of the Pacific Northwest. *Pacific Southwest,* she reminded herself. *My first trip to Canada. Well—in an official capacity, anyhow...* The cold January winds coming east off the Pacific and the Strait of Juan de Fuca had not-so-politely removed Marie's hardhat, sending it dangerously close to the edge of the pier before a Canadian shipyard worker had snagged it some thirty-odd feet away. In three months, the hair-coloring had revealed a level of stress few have known in modern times. There was a distinct line where the blonde turned gray.

"Thank you," Marie said to the worker, meeting him halfway to retrieve it. She gave him a warm smile and then used the plastic safety cap's ratchet device to tighten down the inner harness on her head.

"I guess I should've warned you about the wind," Canadian Admiral Joe Copper admitted sheepishly. "The sailors around here call this spot near the end of the point 'Hurricane Corner'." The short, thick admiral turned back to the southwest, joined by the American officer and a handful of others to watch the once-in-a-lifetime arrival.

"We get rocked by wind down in Bartlett, too," Marie said. "This hardhat has seen quite a few bad days in the last three months."

The admiral turned, giving his new colleague a respectful look of awe. "Yes," he said a bit softly. "I imagine so. I know how bad the mega-quakes felt up here. I can't imagine them down there..." His voice trailed off, not wanting to distract his guest as the damaged submarine in her care arrived. The duo was staring at a pair of Canadian tugboats taking custody of an older Los Angeles class United States submarine from two American tugboats. In the distance, a flotilla of privateers known as Jennifer's Navy was providing security. Like her namesake city, the USS El Paso had been through a deathblow of turmoil recently, though not at the hands of the Mexican cartels. Mother nature had been the villain.

In the days immediately following the 'hammer of Tahoma', Marie's annihilated shipyard—the only one on the United States west coast capable of working on nuclear subs and aircraft carriers—had risen through the ashes to stop two near catastrophes. And though her team had proudly sacrificed themselves—a few paying the ultimate price—to save the USS Halsey from taking disastrous flooding in a filling dry-dock, the Chinese PLAN had still seen to the supercarrier's destruction just a few days earlier. Marie's blood boiled just thinking about it. *I hope we kill hundreds of thousands of those pricks with this op,* she thought coldly. *Millions.*

The pair of officers standing near the windy pier and seawall were looking at Marie's other disaster-turned-miracle. On the day the disasters struck, the El Paso had been undergoing a months-long nuclear refueling. A specialized canister containing spent fuel rods was hanging from a crane inside the opened submarine's reactor compartment. The lifting lines on the violently shaking crane snapped, sending the canister and thousands of feet of two-inch thick steel cable piling into the sub. People were killed. And though there was no 'melt down' of the non-working reactor, there had been enough damage and radioactive waste leakage to warrant buttoning up the ship. To make matters worse, the dry-dock flooded almost instantly, filling the ship with seawater through various openings that were in a state of disassembly. Its service life had been reduced to zero. In normal times, she might've been cleaned for years before being scrapped one razor-blade-sized-piece at a time. But times were anything but normal. And with some creativity and courage, the USS El Paso would serve just once more.

Within two weeks of the disasters, as the tensions between China and Russia escalated at a rocket's pace, the Navy decided to make the best use of the worthless hull. Marie and her shipyard workers had been given orders to make the ship whole again. *Just get her to stay buoyant at two-hundred-feet, Captain,* she'd been ordered. *A one-time trip down. That's all you need to know.*

I guess now I need to know, she acknowledged in her thoughts as she stared through the gusts at the once mighty hunter. She and the admiral were there to oversee the El Paso's arrival. The small Canadian shipyard's sole drydock wasn't big enough to accommodate the American submarine. Everything would have to be worked pier side. "Once she's tied up, Admiral, may we go to the armory? I'd like to ensure the accuracy of what Task Force Truxtun reported before the work package arrives."

"Of course, Captain." He was intrigued by his wildest imagination but knew the Americans would share their plans only when ready. The Task Force vessels had spent over two months bringing emergency supplies to the naval facilities in Washington State—and removing sensitive and classified tech and weapons on their return trips. Some of those munitions had been transported via helicopter to the Canadian armory near Victoria. "I must admit that I'm highly curious about the installation of all of those explosives on this dead sub," he teased just a hair. They watched the lead tug pulling El Paso turn east into the harbor, towards the pier they were standing on. "When is your mission package arriving?"

"Tonight, sir. It's being hand-carried. This is just too sensitive, given the levels and sophistication of the Chinese hacking." *Hand-carried?* Marie scoffed at herself. *That's an understatement.* What she knew, and wasn't telling the Admiral, was that a pair of operatives—one from the CIA and the other from the Naval Special Warfare Development Group —were en route from the east coast via a C-130, due to parachute directly onto the base in the cover of darkness in a few hours. Each carried a copy of the mission plans, just in case the other's parachute failed.

"And your other ships and subs?" the admiral asked. "Still trickling in over the next few days?"

"Yessir. I believe the arriving orders will clarify that," Marie lied. She already knew, and the career maintenance officer didn't much enjoy having to play tight-lipped spy. *But orders are orders,* she reminded herself. Marie also knew that things were bound to change. She knew for sure that the USS James L. Hunnicutt, having been rushed through emergency repairs down in Hawaii, was due to arrive soon. She'd been told to expect two surface ships and three additional submarines. All vessels needed her skilled team, with help from the Canadians, to perform a variety of emergency installs. Some of it high-tech, some of it low-tech, some of it simply software or communica-tions updates—all of it highly classified. "And I forgot to say, Admiral, thank you for the barracks for my folks. We've all been living in canvas tents for the last three months."

"Of course, Captain," the admiral said. "Any idea what you all will do after your part of this operation is over?"

"Well, I'm guessing Hawaii. Pearl Harbor fared okay after the tsunami since it's on the south side of Oahu." She was referring not to the Cascadia disaster, but to the giant rogue wave caused by a nuclear torpedo, the one that had finished sinking the battle-damaged Halsey along with dozens of smaller naval ships. It had slammed the northern shores of several Pacific islands, causing hundreds of thousands of civilian deaths. "If," she said with emphasis, "China doesn't take control of it..."

CHAPTER 1

"And in recap, the total number of United States Naval vessels known to have been sunk or sinking over the engagements of the last eighteen hours are as follows," the buzzy and sometimes warbly voice crackled over the HAM radio. "Three aircraft carriers. Four attack submarines. Three Ticonderoga class cruisers. Six Arleigh Burke class destroyers. Nine littoral combat ships. And seventeen ships specific to refueling, supply, or amphibious assault. Entire squadrons of aircraft from all branches of the military have been hacked and are presumed destroyed. There is an unknown number of ships with smaller amounts of damage. Casualties to sailors and Marines are expected to be in the dozens of thousands. Stay tuned for our update in forty-five minutes. The next round of net check-ins may bring in additional facts regarding President Allen's responses to the ongoing unprovoked attacks by China..."

As the American Contingency Radio Network operator provided his call sign to close his transmission, Bob turned the command post speakers down, reducing the buzz to a low hum. Everyone at Acme Ranch, except for most of the kids and the two people on watch up on the hill, was in the converted garage trying to grasp the gravity of what they were hearing. The air was scorching and still. Karen Kirkland realized she was finally hearing her heart pound in her ears, just in time to hear Jerome Washington's wife Robin gasp loudly.

"That can't be right!" Robin proclaimed, shaking her head as the tears that had been building up burst through the full seams at the bottom of her eyes. "Dear God!" she yelled a little louder, looking at Granger Madison... wishing Jerome weren't on watch up on the hill at that moment.

This broke the seal on the emotional vacuum occupying the ranch's principal center for monitoring radios, using maps, and tracking all activities. Soon Karen had taken a giant breath, too, as her body told her she'd been holding it in tense anticipation. Fred, Brad, Donna, Daniel... they were all joining in the most shocking news they'd heard since 9/11—truly the modern equivalent of what their grandparents and beyond had experienced on December 7th, 1941. Karen saw Tracy, Granger, and their guest—a Delta Force operator named Mikkel 'Voo-Doo' Hudson—exchange worried but knowing glances. Like Bob and her Uncle Claude, the men were all combat veterans. Despite that, this news was beyond anything their minds had told them was likely to happen in their lifetimes.

"What's this mean?" Karen asked Granger, who was sitting in a folding chair, still recovering from the cartel IED that had rattled his cage a mere twenty-five hours earlier. The pair were nowhere near being 'a couple', though she had grown fond of their flirtatious small talk.

"I'm not sure..." the Road Runners' leader admitted quietly, under the near din of worried, excited, angry emotions pouring out in the garage. He looked at the special forces master sergeant. "Is this Rampart Edge thing still a go? I mean—this Chinese-Mexican-Venezuelan buildup on the border no longer looks like political theater..."

VooDoo looked at the satellite phone in his hand. The display told him he still had a working network with which to receive calls. "Until I'm told otherwise, yes," the hardened graying soldier said. "It would seem we are suddenly behind the eight ball. If anything, the need to align capable civilians just became a thousand times more urgent." He eyeballed the scarred, retired-firefighter and former Marine before him. "But you're in no shape to go, bro. I'll handle it."

"Too bad Lucky Charm took off for L.A.," Granger said. "I might've taken you up on that. But you need to either take me or Tracy. No way am I letting you roll without someone to watch your back."

"We can decide that in a few hours," VooDoo said, scanning the Casio G-Shock on his wrist. "I'm going to grab a few Zs before this phone rings." He made his way past the pair and the wall shelves filled with freeze-dried food and into the house.

Karen heard the commotion dying down. She could see Claude and Bob seated at the bench on the far wall, both with headsets on, each working a large HAM radio to try finding new signals and learning new information. Tracy had just wandered over to her and Granger. "Wheeewww..." was all he could say to his friend.

"I think I'm still heading north with VooDoo in the morning," Granger told his younger buddy. He caught ranch owner Donna Wolf's attention and gave her a request to come over with a small wave. "Tracy will be in charge of security while I'm out on the recruiting mission," he told Donna. "You said something about caves to the west?"

"Yes," Donna said, affirming with a quick nod. "About three miles. Technically on state-owned grazing land. But we and one other ranch are the legal users and custodians of the twenty-one thousand acres. Why?"

"I think that Tracy and Karen should spearhead a mission to scout those caves—and start setting them up as a bug out location."

USS Lyndon B. Johnson DDG-1002
    Northwestern Pacific Ocean

"What's the status, XO?" Navy Captain Millie Goldberg said smoothly, voice releasing just a fraction of the tension into the handset of the ship's sound-powered phone. She was on the LBJ's bridge, taking a rare respite from her feet in her Skipper's chair on the starboard side. The bridge was about halfway up the smooth, angled surface of the unique vessel's lone structure above the main deck. Built for stealth and superior wave-cutting, the long slender hull had helped the nearly brand-new ship survive the nuclear-torpedo-caused tsunami that had wiped out a large portion of the northern fleet, including the mighty supercarrier, USS Halsey. LBJ and her crew were attempting to thread the fine needle of balance between rescuing fellow sailors from the freezing ocean and searching for Chinese threats.

"Less than one minute, Captain!" Executive Officer Commander Agwe Bailey hollered into his handset over the roar of the January Pacific wind and rain. His accent always present, the native Jamaican had spent an entire career working to perfect his English for just such a moment. The muscular 41-year-old was almost always smiling, despite his role as the ship's number two officer. The XO role was one akin to a motorcycle club's enforcer, always ensuring areas were inspection ready and sailors who lacked discipline were kept in line. But the events of the previous two days had driven the smiles and positivity out of every surviving soul. The incredulous feeling that war was breaking out with China remained. It was the Captain and XO's roles to keep people performing their jobs. "The last survivors are moving into the hangar bay. We're pulling the Jacob's ladder up right now!"

"Copy, XO. Sea Snake 21 is reporting that the group of rafts to the southwest are empty. I'm suspending the rescue and recovery for the night, and there's a good chance we're being re-tasked sometime in the next several minutes. Have the 1st Lieutenant take over the intake of survivors. Get yourself dried and fed and be in the CIC in thirty minutes." *I think we need to get that helo back on the deck, pronto,* she concluded silently. *Better get to the Combat Information Center.*

Millie didn't even wait for the acknowledgment. She cradled the black plastic phone and stepped back down off the swiveling stool, left knee creaking and frozen with arthritis and pain. "OOD," she said, calling the Officer-of-the-Deck over, who had just finished taking a report from the ship's Damage Control Central on a different handset. "I'm heading to CIC. The rescue detail will be reporting stowed for sea shortly. When they do, make your heading 115 at twenty knots."

Millie worked her knees a bit as she departed, barely hearing the OOD repeat the orders and call out to the bridge team that the captain was departing. She proceeded aft down the short centerline passageway and zigged left up the inclined ladder to the next deck. Moving aft once more, she ended at the closed door. They were much too high off the waterline for needing watertight hatches at this point. She twisted the knob, realizing that the space might need to go back to 24-hour protection. At sea, the only persons on board were presumably the crew. But ever since she'd heard about the Chinese special warfare assault on the Russian fleet, the possibility of such an event happening to them was not too far back in her thoughts.

"Ops," she said as she walked into the dark space, shooting a quick left and then right past two blackened panels meant to keep hallway light out. Everyone working in the CIC was kept at near-night-vision to enable longer and easier durations of staring at electronic screens.

"Aye, Cap'n," a very tired Lieutenant Commander Dennis Bates called out in the dark, responding to the nickname for his role as the Operations Department Head.

"Flight ops," Millie announced as she squinted and made her way toward her Ops Officer. "Let's move the rescued to the mess decks and the infirmary. I want Sea Snake 21 back on deck in twenty, if possible."

"New orders, ma'am?" the mid-level officer asked. The secure comms center was part of the overall tactical brain buried in the ship's upper structure. Even though the top-secret message had been sent straight to the captain, he knew she'd be briefing him shortly.

"Just a warning order," she advised. "We're going to progress east-southeast and keep our eyes and ears peeled until the new orders arrive. On a separate note, let's start locking the accesses to all the sensor spaces like we're in port."

The bulb turned on over Ops' head. "Good thought, Cap'n" he mumbled, not able to stifle a yawn as he spoke. "Sorry, Ma'am."

"Of course, Ops. We can't sustain this pace without risking a greater catastrophe. We undoubtedly will be engaged at some point. I'll be addressing the crew shortly. We'll be going to a port-starboard rotation soon." The crew would remain in a modified battle-ready condition of General Quarters, with half of them being allowed to go eat and take naps. Dennis Bates went to make Millie Goldberg's orders for the helicopter come to life.

She took a fresh look at all the tactical data the ship was taking in —known or suspected contacts under, on, or over the ocean... Radio and satellite transmissions... Input from their drones and military satellites, not to mention the ship's own long-range cameras. The last known positions of the Chinese subs, combined with the amount of time that had passed, led her to be gravely concerned. The only recompense was that the artificial tsunami had been just as damaging to their own craft. Then there was the space threat. So far, China had shown no restraint at lobbing devastating tungsten slugs from space. Team LBJ literally had to scan continuously in all possible directions for the next attack. Millie cracked her own yawn and headed toward the exit. *I should go down and see how these Halsey survivors are doing,* she thought.

USS LYNDON B. JOHNSON DDG-1002
Northwestern Pacific Ocean

CARMEN MARTINEZ WATCHED THE CHAOS IN THE LBJ'S
hangar slowly become more organized. Various sailors from the
destroyer's crew were barking orders and performing tasks. Blankets
were being handed out. Corpsman and the ship's doctor were working
with engineers to frisk the crew for radioactive particulates. As the
once mighty warship had split open from missiles, internal explosions,
and crashing after the giant wave sent their bow skyward, the two
nuclear reactor compartments could no longer contain their Pandora.
Radioactive coolant water had mixed with the cold, salty sea, covering
some of the sailors with various levels of contamination. A decision
had been made to decontaminate all the survivors, regardless of readings. Wash-down shelters had been constructed out of tarps and
folding frames, set over tougher plastic tarps to catch the water. It was
destined to be thrown back into the sea, but it needed to be kept from
reaching every crack and crevice in the helicopter bay.

"Next!" Carmen heard a female corpsman yell. "You! Name!"

"Mar-Martinez," Carmen stammered, still shivering. Ten hours in
the round orange covered raft had been more than enough cold expo-
sure for her. *I'm never going in the ocean again,* she'd thought a
hundred times. "C-C-Carmen. DC3," she added, letting the person
know she was a third-class damage control specialist.

"Step into the cofferdam," the corpsman told her, pointing as if
explaining to a five-year-old.

Carmen didn't mind. Between fighting fire and flooding, jumping
off the sinking ship, and floating in the life raft, she did not know
when the last time she'd slept was. *I just wish I could wake up from this
nightmare,* she thought, reminding her of months earlier in Washington State when she'd had a similar thought. She stepped over the lip
to the temporary pool and moved in next to another sailor, a male, who
was mostly undressed. The LBJ's crew just didn't have the space, mate-

rials, or manpower to worry about something vain like mixing the genders in the wash-down.

"Strip and throw all of your garments into the chute!" she heard a male sailor order, voice and face muffled by a full-face respirator and a full set of rubber rain gear. During the horrendous experience, her mind wandered once more to watching her friends—most of them—unable to escape the tilting aircraft carrier. *Where's Dustin? And Cobra?* she wondered. Those were the two men from her life raft that she actually knew before the tragedy. She felt the healing powers of warm water from a rubber hose and nozzle cover her from head down.

"C'mon, shipmate," she heard the voice behind the mask once more. He was not unsympathetic. It was just the tone of a tired sailor with a long night ahead of him. "Toss the uniform. We have coveralls waiting for you." He had a long-handled brush and was dunking the hard red plastic bristles into a bucket of soapy water.

Carmen felt the burn of feeling returning to her frozen hands as the warm water ran over her. She fumbled through the process of doffing her uniform and undergarments. *After the SOBs in Washington had their way with me, how bad can this be?* she asked herself. In the last two months, she'd used a strict workout regimen as her post-rape therapy. Between that and Cobra's Jiu Jitsu classes, she'd made her petite frame hard. Almost buff.

She felt the bristles as the sailor begin to scrub her head and scalp, joined after a moment by the brush of a second sailor. "Keep moving forward," she heard a different voice say. Through the soapy foam and mere slits of her eyes, she could see the male survivor ahead of her stepping out of the cofferdam up ahead. She moved into his spot as the sailors kept scrubbing. No place was too private in the attempt to remove from her skin any contamination she may have swum through.

When ordered to, she stepped out of the cofferdam into the open towel being held by a female officer. "Step through the forward center-line hatch and head port," the woman instructed. "You'll be led into the air detachment maintenance office."

Carmen did as ordered, continuing the procession as one of 137 survivors that LBJ had picked up from her sunken ship. She'd been guided through the process by LBJ sailors all along the way, receiving a set of coveralls that had been donated by a crew member. More radioactive readings, another recounting of her name and rank, and she and the others ultimately found themselves on the ship's mess decks. The smell of the space had been nearly identical to the Halsey's, instantly bringing back a flood of memories. Sandwiches had been prepared. There were personnel specialists assigning Halsey sailors a place to go sleep via the old-school 'hot rack' method. LBJ crew members just going on watch for the night would not need their bunks. It wasn't a great solution, but it got the Halsey crew members out of the way while the destroyer's crew went about the tasks necessary to find the enemy before it found them.

Carmen found herself in the berthing compartment for female sailors near the head of the ship. It plowed up and down through the waves and rocked port-to-starboard a lot more than she'd been used to sailing on the carrier. She found the correct rack, and after a trip to the bathroom, planted herself behind the blue privacy curtain. *Will try to find Dustin later,* she decided. The tough Latina fought back the well of tears building behind her eyes as the emotional toil caught up. *God. I don't know how much more I can take...*

CHAPTER 2

NORTHEAST, MARYLAND

U.S. AIR FORCE COLONEL LOU CALDWELL STEERED THE DARK blue mini-van with government plates off the I-95 corridor and past the Flying J gas station, headed east toward his old hometown of Northeast, tucked into the corner of Maryland. His mind was occupied with so many threads—tasks for his new job, disbelief that the U.S. was actually at war with China, not to mention all he'd been through in the previous few months—that he was driving on instinctive autopilot. He'd not even bothered figuring out what radio station the unfamiliar vehicle was set on, turning it off two hours earlier when he'd left the Pentagon. He felt Rusty's breath on the back of his neck in a small huff.

"Almost there, boy," he told the German shepherd. Ears perked, his new companion had sensed the speed shift off the interstate, unusually still, even for nearly 9 p.m. It was only the second day since Lou had been told he'd be taking over the task force by Colonel Ryan Jackson. Like most of the Pentagon, they were all shifting to a variety of secure backup locations around the country. Lou was destined for Pennsylvania's Raven Rock Mountain Complex, commonly called 'Site R' in movies and conspiracy circles, so a detour to his brother's house was in order. "You'll get to play with Kyla soon," he told the dog, hoping he'd understand.

The military-issued phone in Lou's pocket buzzed just as he was maneuvering the awkward walking brace on his right foot over to the brake pedal for the slow drift into the town's main street. *Better check this before I get there,* he thought tiredly, his eyes dry from staring too long in the winter night drive. The small summer boating-town nestled on the north end of the rivers that formed Chesapeake Bay was mostly darkened, the few restaurants and taverns still open in January closing for the evening. Lou braked to a stop on the small main drag's right side, pulling the phone out of his right bomber coat pocket.

Emergency Alert! All hands seek shelter in a secure facility. NAD. Lou stared for a second at the last acronym. *Not a drill,* he reminded himself. Something caught his attention out on the dark, wintry lane. Employees and closing patrons of the local crab-house were just past the building, gawking and pointing toward the south. Lou opened the van door and was blasted by the near-freezing air. Zipping the lined collar up around his neck, he told Rusty, "C'mon, boy." The eager companion didn't need to be told twice, bolting through the warmth of the driver's seat and to the street. Using a cane to lean on as he walked, Lou led Rusty toward the end of the restaurant's scenic wooden street side covered deck toward the four people. *Uh-oh,* he thought as he saw one woman put her hands to her mouth in reactionary horror. "What is it?" the colonel asked the strangers as he approached.

"Not sure," a man in his late 20s answered. "I'm betting they nuked D.C." he said smugly, trying to display a nonchalant tone that his voice betrayed.

Lou whipped his head and saw the orange glow to the south. *Nope,* he knew immediately. *These people would all be blind. The entire sky would be as bright as the sun,* he remembered. "Not a nuke," he said, trying to calm the small crowd as they all stared down the Northeast River in the general direction of Baltimore and Washington.

"Then what?" a middle-aged woman asked, not trying to conceal the concern, voice cracking slightly. The brilliant glow looked like sunrise, distinctly outlining the horizon in red, orange, and yellow before fading to blue, purple, and black high in the sky.

That's a great question, Lou thought, already headed back toward the van, slapping his leg to get Rusty to follow. He followed the dog out of the cold and back into the warmth of the idling vehicle. He used his fingerprint to cue up the phone past the lock-screen and punched the small icon for the supposedly secure messaging app. Lou then started to read the full warning, half mumbling out loud as he did. "... planes hacked in Operation Boomerang..." He paused. *That must've been the return strike I was hearing whispers about,* he realized. *Sending bombers over the pole to pay them back for the carriers...* A painful pit formed in Lou's gut. He pushed his eyes back onto the screen. "... space-based MAHEM..." he mumbled once more. "Chinese space-based response expected for any or all USNORTHCOM strategic and tactical locations. Seek shelter immediately."

Rusty whimpered from the passenger seat, head cocked to his right and ears perked as he felt Lou's tension. Lou looked up at the dog, reaching over and placing his hand just behind the dog's head and neck, giving him a good rub of assurance. "Seems like we made it out of town in the nick of time, pal," he said as yet one more unbelievable event had stacked up on his conscience. He placed the van back into drive and pulled out onto the barren street without remembering to check for right-of-way. In ten minutes, he'd be parking at Foster's house. *So if I read that right,* he clarified in his mind, preparing to be bombarded with questions from his family, *China hacked our bombers, and now each of us has used spaced-based molten-metal weapons to wipe out surface targets on the other...*

GARDEN GROVE, CALIFORNIA

"MA! PLEASE!" ALEX NGUYEN SAID LOUDLY AND WITH irritation in English, before switching to Vietnamese. "Why do you have to make a big scene with every meeting?" The 32-year-old hotel owner-turned-organizer had desperately wished his parents would stay in their room for the neighborhood watch meetings, to no avail. The original hotel owners, his parents had escaped Vietnam long before Alex or his three siblings were twinkles in their eyes. Like most families from that culture, multi-generational families and overbearing mothers were an accepted norm. But unlike most natural born Americans, the naturalized Nguyens knew what true oppression and tyranny were. Despite knowing the importance of the meetings, though, it couldn't stop Alex's mother from trying to direct who sat where or complain that they weren't serving enough for their guests.

Originally hosted in the living room of the family home two blocks away, the neighborhood watch meetings had moved to the hotel. In fact, most of the group's members, now calling themselves the 15th Street Posse, had moved into the hotel for mutual defense. Smack in the middle of the metro area southeast of Los Angeles, this hotel had been the proving ground for his impromptu band of guardians. The '15SP,' as they'd taken to calling themselves, had originally formed to protect each other's homes as society continued to unravel. But when an armed gang had taken over the hotel, the melting-pot unit had banded together and taken it back in a daring and surprise operation with little more than crossbows, baseball bats, and a couple of shotguns. This had garnered the attention of Marine Corps Captain Brandon McDonald and his task force.

The Rampart Edge program had sprung up in the same short timeframe as the 15SP, born out of a mission initially comprised of just Brandon and Lou. The men had shared a unique and quiet assignment, traveling America and ascertaining her readiness, both militarily and in the civilian populace. They'd found that anywhere they went, people had maintained the very same spirit that the nation had formed under—*we'd rather die a free-people on our knees than live one moment as a subject. We just need help learning what to do.*

And while Lou and Brandon certainly couldn't do it all, they could organize a new military unit that could make a big impact. Starting with a list of people they'd met in the months since that big natural disaster in Washington State set the new order in motion, Rampart Edge had begun to send experienced operators and agents into the communities of America to help spread that exact knowledge. Two evenings earlier, Alex had been escorted to a meetup at the famed Chinese theater in L.A. where he'd been told he and his posse were exactly the kind of people the military was looking for.

"Please take a seat, everyone," Alex tried to nudge politely. Except for some of the younger or older family members and a few folks standing watch up on the roofs of the hotel's three buildings, the small, stale conference room was packed. As the din quieted down, Alex introduced his guest. "This is the man you all have been hearing about. Sergeant?" he addressed the man standing next to him at the room's end.

"Hi, folks. I'm U.S. Army Staff Sergeant Patrick McBrogan," the 5' 9" redhead introduced himself. Though not tall, the muscular soldier had an air about him that only the most clueless of predators wouldn't pick up on as a threat. The junior member of his Delta Force unit, McBrogan had been sent from Arizona to join the L.A. mission just a night earlier. The rapidly deteriorating condition of the coming world war had forced him and his team to part ways. There were just too many units around the nation wanting this training. And too few Special Forces or Delta Force teams were available to provide it properly. Those along the border and to the west would get top priority, as China had shown their hand. Their own amphibious ships, along with those they'd captured from Russia, would have to land somewhere... and most of the American west coast was far too rocky and mountainous or isolated. They would need to land troops somewhere near a populace to reduce the chance of WMDs be deployed against them.

Hence, Southern to Central California was getting top priority in defense measures. "But if it is easier, ya'll just call me Lucky Charm," the Louisiana native said with Southern grace.

"Lucky Charm?" Lauren Duarte asked with a small smirk that concealed a slightly defensive posture. "As in 'magically delicious'?" Had those in the room not known Lauren—or the fact that she was sitting right next to her wife, Jessie—they might've mistaken it as flirtatious. The former correctional guard had been the largest distributor of knowledge to the shaky watch group when they stood themselves up several weeks earlier. Though she shirked the leadership tag onto Alex, she felt a sense of ownership for the accomplishment thus far.

"We go by radio handles for security reasons in my line of work," Lucky explained with a smile. "I'm just glad I'm not any shorter." He scanned the small, dated conference room in the 1970s era hotel. "Let me get down to the brass tacks, everyone. From what I understand, y'all did a bang-up job retaking your property from a vicious and violent gang. Alex just spent the last hour walking me through your operation and showing me what you all did. I don't want to piss in your Wheaties, but the reality is that some of y'all shoulda been killed."

"Yo!" Roman Lopez said, somewhat annoyed, as he pointed to his arm wrapped in a makeshift cast and slung to his body. "This bullet graze ain't exactly a paper cut mister cereal man..."

"I get that," Lucky said without offense. "That's the perfect example. A simple three inches over and that bullet would've hit you in the chest at the angle Alex said you got hit. Look, ya'll," he said, scanning the room once more. "I'm not downplaying your courage or tenacity. You all are a lot smarter than the average gang bangers, and you leveraged that. That's perfect! I can work with that. But I also won't sugarcoat it—some of us are going to die in the coming weeks." The murmur arrived on cue as Lucky Charm took a breath and started reading faces. He was already getting a feel for who had come to terms with the coming reality.

"Just what exactly are you doing here?" Alex's brother Henry asked. "Besides spreading this BS doom and gloom?" The 27-year-old was less pragmatic and more prone to irritation than his older brother. "Is the Army going to be providing aid? The power outages were bad enough when they were rolling! Society is unraveling right in front of us. What do you expect from us?!"

Lucky Charm weighed his words as he deciphered just how much the group was still in the dark. "I get that the local government and FEMA have been withholding some of the shocking truth from you all. I don't mean to scare you, but we're at war with China. It is a matter of time before Chinese military vehicles will roll right down Westminster Avenue," he said, pointing toward the door to the room. As the remaining stale air sucked out of the musty space, he looked Henry right in the eyes. "I expect you to fight."

ACME RANCH
Southeast of Tucson, Arizona

"I THINK THAT'S GOT IT, UNCLE CLAUDE!" KAREN YELLED toward the partially submerged greenhouse's door. The roughly twenty foot wide, forty-foot-long custom house had been dug into the hard Arizona dirt many years earlier by the original ranchers. It had 'gone to pot' with non-use, as time had allotted sun and wind a chance to take over. About four feet below the grade of the ground, it had been dug out to have several tiers on each long side. At the top—ground level—a row of cinder blocks had been installed and formed the base for a conversion to lumber that carried a basic pitched roof. The roof itself was made of clear polymer corrugated panels, attached with gasketed sheet metal bolts. Earthen steps, capped with flat stones, led in and out of one end. Karen and Claude had taken on ownership of the project to fix the structure back to a usable asset. At that moment, they were trying to see if the several photovoltaic panels near one corner of the roof would put out any electricity by plugging a small heating pad into one of the two outlets attached to the old battery and inverter system.

Claude clumsily squeezed his large frame back down the narrow opening steps and into the unique greenhouse. "Ugh! This is almost as bad as the tunnels in 'Nam," the old wobbly veteran declared. "Not that I was small enough to fit!" he sheepishly laughed, walking up to the first of a few load-bearing legs that ran down the middle of the space's dirt floor and giving it a confirmation shake. "I need to go through the whole solar array and clean it up. I think we have some dielectric grease and shrink-wrap with the radio gear. That'll help me protect the connections," he explained. "What are we starting again?" he asked his niece. "It's only January."

"Let's see," Karen said, looking up instinctively as she searched her thoughts. "Broccoli, cabbage, greens... onions, I think... There are several cool season veggies we can get started now here in Arizona." She moved farther down the area to the blue barrel under the vent in the gable. Small metal troughs along the roof collected the tiny amount of precious Arizona rain and sent it through PVC pipes to the barrel. "Bone dry," she told Claude as she pried the lid up a bit. The filthy greenhouse roof, covered in the reddish-brown dirt of the ranch, made it hard to inspect in the barrel.

"I'm sure the pipe is in need of replacing," Claude advised. "If," he said, emphasizing that word, "we can safely get to a hardware store, there are some much better UV-resistant options we could replace it with. But for now, we'll probably be able to patch the leaks. I'll get some pond water and run some tests."

Karen led her uncle up and out of the sunken greenhouse and started back up the quad trail through the Arizona sage toward the nearby fenced garden area and back of the main home beyond that. She could see one of the quads to the west, coming back down the trail that led up the hill toward the property's main OP, or observation post. It rounded a switchback curve and disappeared from view. "Must be noon," she thought, knowing that someone had just relieved someone else on watch.

"That would be Tracy coming back," Claude confirmed. He and Bob Salvage, the other original Road Runner 'old-timer' were the primary organizers for the ranch's Command Post, so he was familiar with the watch bill. Keeping an eye on the property had become even more imperative after the shootout with the cartel near Sierra Vista a few nights earlier, not to mention the building Chinese and Mexican coalition along the border. And now Granger had taken off with a Delta operator, looking for more capable groups to train. Though the group possessed several experienced competition shooters, Tracy was the last truly battle-tested fighter other than the elder radio shack vets. Claude's grizzled face suddenly softened as he looked at his pretty niece. "Your mama sure woulda been proud of the woman you've become," he admitted of his sister. "Especially after dumping that dog-turd you married."

"Oh, come on, Uncle, David wasn't that bad at the beginning. We just—"

"CP, this is Popeye!" the radio on Claude's waist crackled, cutting Karen off. "I—I've... help!" Tracy's voice was clearly distressed and in pain, the radio signal crackling.

The pair craned their heads, looking for any signs of dust the two hundred or so meters away where he should have exited the trail. "He should've been back in sight by now!" Karen exclaimed, moving down her own trail toward the house rapidly.

Claude hobbled along as quickly as he could, pulling the radio off his belt. He could hear Bob take over for one of the teenage CP trainees, trying to respond to Tracy. "Go on, Karen!" Claude called ahead. "Don't wait on me!"

The forty-three-year-old CrossFit instructor took off at a near-full sprint, hoping that the quad's gear would be findable while opting to run up the west-bound trail once she'd reached it. She rounded a curve near the base of the hill, passing a standing dead mesquite tree. She saw dust hanging in the air and sprinted for another twenty seconds. It seemed Tracy had taken a different switchback too tightly, causing the quad's right-side tires to grab too much soft dirt on the hill. Both machine and man went rolling down the hill, crossing over the trail once more and continuing another thirty feet.

Karen saw Tracy, who was trying his hardest to keep his pain limited to grunting. The Navy vet was covered in dirt from head to toe and his face twisted in agony. Karen could see immediately he'd dislocated his shoulder but feared that might be the least of his injuries. She reached him, radio still being squeezed tightly in his left hand. "Tracy!" she practically screamed. Panic set in. She'd taken plenty of basic medical classes, and seen plenty of gym injuries, but the reality of being the first on-scene to an aggravated accident was setting in. She took a deep breath. *Medical kit!* She screamed in her head. *Where's the quad?* All she could hear was her pulse pounding in her ears. *There!*

She ran almost forty feet away, doing a rapid squat and gripping the top of the quad's seat, now resting firmly on the ground. With her deadlift capabilities, rolling the heavy machine over enough to change her grip and continue pushing it was easy in an adrenaline-fueled surge. It slammed with a thud onto the ground, mangled and unusable. The heavy canvas bag was still tethered to the machine's rear stowage rack. She unzipped it and found the tan roll of medical gear that they'd all been trained to use was there. Grabbing the roll and the blanket, she sprinted back toward Tracy, taking deep breaths as her heart was fully engaged in fight or flight.

Tracy's nostrils were flaring as he tried to breathe wildly and rapidly through them. "I think my jaw is broken!" he tried to mumble through pain and clenched teeth, bloody lips barely moving. He was laying at an odd angle due to a misshapen right shoulder.

Karen could see blood oozing out of his mouth. *Don't get focused on the mangled shoulder!* she told herself. Everyone on the ranch had been practicing medical training, with Robin Washington as the lead, based on her years as a clinical nurse. "M!" Karen yelled out loud at herself as she thought of protocols. "M-MARCHE!" she exclaimed as she started to look over Tracy, anxiety and stress nearly as bad for her as it was for him. "Massive hemorrhage!" she yelled at herself, not caring how ridiculous it sounded. The training was working, coming back to her through her voice, trying to overcome her panic and stress. After looking for major bleeding, she was assessing 'A'—Airway—as the acronym had taught her. Not seeing an obvious bleed, she unrolled the medical bag, grabbing the scissors to start cutting off his clothes, hands shaking nearly uncontrollably.

"Unh-uh!" Tracy grunted, painfully trying to move his head in the 'no' fashion.

"You don't think you're bleeding?" Karen nearly screamed, not realizing how loud she was. "Uh—uh—Airway!" she remembered once more. She took a good hard look at Tracy's head. *Why doesn't anyone around here wear helmets on these things?* she wondered as she looked. Tracy's breathing was severely distressed, and she worried about any jaw or mouth bleeding causing an airway issue. "I want to roll you onto your left side!" she announced as she patted his arms and legs through intact clothing.

Tracy nodded yes, and she moved him into the recovery position as his grunting morphed into an open-mouthed scream that lasted a few seconds. Karen never even heard two horses rushing up the trail and stopping a few feet away. Pedro del Sur and Daniel Monitor hopped off two of the ranch horses and ran into the brush where Karen was continuing to look over her patient. "Where's Robin?!" she demanded, wanting the real medical professional to relieve her of duty.

"Brad'll bring her!" Daniel explained excitedly. "He's coming back from the northern pasture with the ute," he said, referring to the ranch's one side-by-side off-road utility vehicle.

Pedro wanted to crack a joke to cheer up Tracy, but he knew immediately that this was a much worse situation than a wisecrack could help. "Damn, bro..." he mumbled as he spread the blanket over his friend. He looked anxiously at Karen and Daniel, wondering what to do.

"Grab the shemaugh in the med bag!" Karen ordered. "We can try to stabilize the shoulder and be ready when they get here!"

Pedro snapped out of it, digging through the bag to find the large, heavy square cloth. "Uh... what do I do?" he asked in confusion.

"Make a triangle, idiot!" Daniel snapped a bit testily.

"Right!" Karen agreed before shooting Daniel an agitated look. "You need to calm the hell down," she growled at Daniel, who exchanged angry glances with her. "Carefully sling his arm. Then we'll tether it to his body somehow." She looked at Tracy, whose eyes were clamped shut like his mouth as he continued to breathe heavily through his nose. "Hang in there, Tracy! It's going to hurt, but we're gonna get you taken care of!"

CHAPTER 3

USS James L. Hunnicutt, SSGN-93
Four-hundred miles West of Oregon

"Awww snap! It's COB!" Master Chief Darren Jorgenson heard as he sped into the high-tech submarine's mess deck to investigate the commotion. It was but one of a few whispered murmurs which signaled the impending doom of his arrival to the scene of the fistfight. He discovered a few petty officers trying to hold two sailors apart, one of the senior first-class POs already scolding the culprits.

"Turner! You guys break it up!" he was trying to enforce without an actual yell. All seasoned submariners, particularly this crew, were fully aware of the dangers of transient noise. The emergency repairs to the submarine that had been damaged escaping the Chinese People's Liberation Army Navy attack just ten weeks earlier were so fresh that some of it hadn't even been painted properly. As the new war broke out in the recent days, the urgency of this ship's new mission had been unprecedented. "Get to the AMR! Now!" Petty Officer Mitchell growled at one of the culprits. With anger and disgust on his face, young Turner stood himself up as the two sailors holding him loosened their grasp. He grabbed his dark blue coveralls, yanking them down at the front to straighten his collar, giving his rival a grimace and stare as he made his way out of the mess deck.

"What the hell is happening here?!" Darren commanded. He was the submarine's Chief-of-the-Boat, the senior enlisted person. He worked directly with the ship's Executive Officer to keep a tight rein of discipline for the one-of-a-kind U-boat's crew. Though technically outranked by any officer, he answered only to the boat's Commanding Officer. He turned his gaze to the other junior sailor involved in the scuffle. He was a new shipmate to the crew, not one of the seasoned veterans who had barely escaped the East China Sea with their lives. Darren had just welcomed a handful of replacement crew aboard in the last few days before they left Hawaii. "Atlas, is it?" he recalled the young man's last name. *Torpedoman's Mate,* he remembered. The young sailor was a new member of the recently revived rate, the specialized job brought back from the responsibility of the Machinist Mate's as a naval morale-boosting decision. "Follow me," he said calmly and with complete command authority, giving the 'come here' with one finger. "Let Chief Bianco know about Turner," he ordered Petty Officer Mitchell, though he knew he didn't have to. By one minute after a fight, eighty percent of the crew on a submarine knew. In another minute it would be one hundred percent.

Darren turned and plowed through the tight passageway, taking a tight zigzag left and right, heading down a very steep set of stairs, called an inclined ladder, and continued to drag the junior sailor forward by an invisible leash. He took a right as he opened a door and led young Micah Atlas into Lieutenant Commander Carla Gingery's state room and office. He and the Executive Officer had an arrangement for Darren to use her space for 'counseling' when it was needed. On a surface ship, the master chief would have his own small office. Submarines offered no such luxury. "Close the door," he calmly instructed as he took a seat in the bolted, swiveling desk chair.

"I-I'm sorry, COB," the slight young man stammered as he turned after closing the narrow metal door. One of the XO's coats was hanging on a hook on the interior side. It caught the young man's shoulder as the door closed, falling to the floor. "Oh geez!" he exclaimed, trying to squat to pick it up. "S-sorry!"

This kid is about to burst into tears, Darren realized. There were times in his life when he would light-up a grown man for being a baby. He was far removed from being that impatient farm boy from Iowa. Leadership over the course of his career had taught him to be patient when trying to learn why a kid acted the way he did. The navy's newest sailors were even younger than his own adult children. *This kid is barely growing peach fuzz.* "Calm down, Atlas," he said. "Mitch, is it?" The majority of folks in submarines went by last names most of the time. A first name would help bridge the emotional gap between him and the skinny, short youngster standing in front of him.

"Y-yes, COB. I-I'm the new TM," he said.

Darren chuckled at the kid trying to explain who he was by explaining his job designator. "I know. And you guys are without a Chief right now. And your LPO will probably knock on that door any minute. But she can wait. What was the fight about?"

"That's just it, COB! I have no idea!"

"None?" Darren asked skeptically.

"No, si—" the youngster caught himself as he was about to say sir, which would've been a big no-no. "No, COB," he repeated. "I don't even know that guy. I bumped into him as I was getting into my seat to eat. I think he spilled his bug juice!"

Darren knew that Turner was a lackluster sailor. *It probably is just that simple. But this is the first festering sore, a warning of a bigger issue,* he realized. The crew had been forced through emergency repairs in Pearl Harbor, unallowed to return to their homeport on leave. Not that it was an option. The submarine was based in Slaughter County, Washington, which had been rendered nearly completely unusable by the unprecedented natural disasters that had triggered all the world's current hostilities. The Navy had been sending task forces up there non-stop ever since to evacuate critical weapons and other resources. But the married sailors in particular had been upset that they couldn't be allowed to travel home. *There is no way to get there!* Darren and the rest of the ship's leaders had emphasized. *There are no air or seaports operational!* The ship's morale was the lowest Darren had even seen in his career. And now they were back at sea and headed toward a Canadian naval base. The Hunny was operating under a limitation to not dive below 400-feet because of the emergency nature of the repairs. That limited their maneuverability in the event they encountered a Chinese submarine. Their sub had been outfitted with a set of towing rings on the very outboard side of their rear horizontal stabilizers, the fixed structure that held the aft-end dive planes. Commanding Officer Brody Woodward had decided to hold the current mission a secret until the last moment. Only Darren, the XO, the onboard SEAL team, and the other officers knew exactly where they were headed and why.

"Where are you from, Micah?" he asked, prying into the young man's past for some answers. Just then, a set of knuckles rapped themselves on the far side of the tiny stateroom's door.

Expecting it to be Micah's Leading Petty Officer, he instead heard his XO's voice. "It's me, COB."

"Head back to the torpedo room," he instructed Micah. "I'm coming down in a while to continue this. Go let your LPO know."

"Yes, COB," Micah said a bit more calmly. He turned and opened the door. Carla Gingery gave the young sailor a polite half-smile as he slid out of the space and headed back down the tight passageway.

"He's a sensitive one," Darren said as he stood while the XO entered her own stateroom.

"Sorry to interrupt," she said. "What was the fight about?"

"That's just it. Nothing. Turner is a jerk. If it were normal times, I'd say he was flexing. But I think it's a tension thing," Darren said worriedly, wondering if this crew could hold it together for the impossible mission that awaited them.

USS LYNDON B. JOHNSON DDG-1002
  Northwestern Pacific Ocean

"STANLEY! IT'S ME! WHY WON'T YOU SAY ANYTHING?" MILLIE said, her voice raising in concern. Her husband of 24-years was just ignoring her. He gave her one last look and went around the corner of the building. It didn't belong here. *Wait—I don't belong here,* Millie thought. *Where am I?* She ran for two seconds, but when she rounded the corner, Stanley was gone, replaced by a panda bear. *What the—*

"Captain!" she heard. She turned and looked but saw nothing. She looked back and the panda was lunging at her, jarring her out of the deep slumber. "Captain Goldberg!" she heard again. "Sorry to startle you, ma'am!"

Millie shook herself out of the very-short, long overdue sleep, eyes burning as if filled with sand. *Unnnghh,* she groaned in her mind in the realization that she was still dead tired. "What time is it?" she politely asked the young male sailor trying to awaken her.

"0310, Ma'am," he replied. "Ops says he needs you in CIC immediately." The sailor retreated to the door to the captain's stateroom, turning to see Millie just barely stirring. "Ma'am?"

"I'm up," she said. "Tell him I'll be there in three," she ordered as the door closed. *I won't be any good to anyone if I don't splash some water on my face and take a pee,* she told herself. She had taken to staying in socks and coveralls during the crisis, needing merely to don her boots in an emergency.

Just under three groggy minutes later, Millie was entering the Combat Information Center, heading right to the center. Fortunately, the passageways in the ship's superstructure were kept lit with red lighting in the night hours, making it much easier for her eyes to adjust to the dark space. The blue hue of electronic screens bounced around the room, reflecting off the faces of the various women and men staffing the sensors. She weaved her way around a bench of consoles with sailors sitting at screens and made her way to her Operations Officer. "What do you got, Dennis?"

"Sorry, Skipper. I really wanted to let you sleep until 0400. Towed array is picking up a submerged contact, definitely not one of ours." The AN/SQR-20 passive sonar array was trailing on a mile long cable that played off the ship, enabling it to hear through much quieter water that the mid and high-frequency sonars built into the ship's hull. "We're getting plant and screw noises. The computer says it is probably a Chinese AIP..." He was referring to the subs that operated on air-independent propulsion. Not as noisy as nuclear-powered submarines, they could easily sneak into attack range.

"Range and bearing?" Millie asked, eyes glossing over the screen in front of the sonar technician.

"Forty-three thousand meters, Ma'am," the young lady replied. "One-seven-five relative."

"When was our last course change?" she asked her Ops officer.

He scanned his G-Shock watch. "About twenty-two minutes ago," Dennis told her.

So they're almost directly behind us, Millie realized. She took the nearby sound-powered phone handset off of its cradle and dialed the bridge, desiring to speak directly to the Officer of the Deck. "Lieutenant, we're going to force this sub to play his hand. Increase speed to twenty-five knots and make your bearing 1-1-0. In ten minutes, make it 0-1-0. Copy?" After waiting for the officer to confirm her orders, she hung up the phone and scanned all the status boards, intaking all known contacts on the surface and in the air. She analyzed the ocean condition reports, contemplating the option of sending the helicopter up. "I want to—"

"Captain to the radio room!" blared over the speakers in the Combat Information Center, interrupting Millie. It had come over the ship-wide 1MC system, meaning it had just woken the one-third of the crew out of their precious little sleep.

Shock crossed the faces of several sailors, spooked by the eerie break in protocol. Millie's face wrinkled in tired worry as she made her way to the nearby space, crammed with all the gear for old-school radio and new-school satellite communications. She opened the door and there was a whirlwind of activity as three operators were busy decoding a variety of transmissions. Each had a headset on, one of them with one ear peeled off to hear a second communication coming over a desktop speaker.

Dennis Bates had been a step off her heels the entire way. "Senior?" he barked at the senior chief electronic technician on behalf of the captain, clearly displeased at the outburst.

"Sorry, Ma'am," the senior chief apologized directly to the captain. His bloodshot eyes were wide with fear. It was then that Millie noticed one of the sailors was crying while doing her job. The senior NCO handed Millie a clipboard.

She scanned the decrypted message. *Whuh... what?* She looked at the senior chief, then at Dennis, handing him the clipboard. "Get back to CIC," she told him.

"The Pentagon is... gone? Our Pac-Fleet headquarters, too?" His face turned pale before Millie's eyes as he looked up. He shook himself out of it and began to follow her order.

"Have the bridge take us to GQ, Ops," she added. "And let's do a full sensor sweep. We're making a speed run to Canada."

ACME RANCH
Southeast of Tucson, Arizona

"SO, WHO ALL IS GOING THEN?" DONNA WOLF ASKED IN LOUD concern. "And what's that leave us for our own defenses?"

"I think it should be me, Brad, Pedro, and Robin," Karen said to the group, most of whom had flocked to the ranch's parking area in front of the main house.

Jerome and Robin Washington's large SUV had been moved up to act as an ambulance. Tracy was in the back, laying as comfortably as he could. Someone had retrieved the remainder of an old pain prescription from their belongings, but Robin had put the kibosh on the idea. "He has a jaw injury. We don't know the state of his digestive system," the nurse had explained. "If his stomach is injured, then putting pills in there is the wrong move." She had just taken another blood pressure reading to monitor for shock and left the rig to find out why the group was bickering.

"No way!" Jerome said. "If Robin goes, I go!" the man announced with authority.

"The kids, baby," Robin tried to soothe her husband. "You need to stay here…"

As they stepped aside to have a quieter marital debate, Karen addressed the rest while pointing at Robin. "However that plays out, Robin should go since she's a nurse."

"He's stable," Daniel argued. "What if someone else here needs her help?" he said with just snide enough of a tone to challenge Karen's leadership.

"Tracy doesn't have time for us to debate this, Daniel," Karen said, trying to maintain her calm. "Granger would agree if he were here."

"But he isn't. And Tracy was in charge of security," Daniel countered. "And since he is now incapacitated, it should probably be me or Fred!"

"This is still my ranch!" Donna Wolf interjected. "What makes you think you or Fred should be in charge now?"

"Of security, I mean," Daniel explained. "Because we have the most practical shooting experience."

"Leave me out of this," the older Fred Bowers mumbled.

"—And this trip to town definitely needs to have security considered!" Daniel concluded.

This fool is going to be a pain in every decision, isn't he? Karen thought.

"I'll go!" Pedro said as he threw his hat into the ring. "Tracy is my bud. He sponsored me to this group. I owe him." He looked at Jerome as he and Robin were still debating off to the side of the group. "I got her, bro. With my life."

The look of a husband who was losing an argument crossed Jerome's face as the realization that their kids would be at the ranch all alone finally plowed itself into his reasoning. "Thanks, brother," he acknowledged Pedro.

"So that's me, Robin, and Pedro," Daniel announced. He looked at Donna's brother Brad. "And you?"

"Brad stays here!" Donna interrupted. "I've already lost my husband to this cartel. I'm not losing my brother, too!"

"Sis, it's okay," Brad said softly. "I'll—"

"I'm going," Karen said matter-of-factly. *And I don't owe you an explanation why,* her stern glare told Daniel quietly but clearly. "And Uncle Claude is in charge of security," she announced as she looked at Donna Wolf. "He is a Vietnam combat vet, after all," she explained. "As well as being an original Road Runner."

CHAPTER 4

NORTHEAST, MARYLAND

"BUT THIS CAN'T BE HAPPENING!" BARBARA CALDWELL proclaimed. "It—it just isn't possible!"

"Well, it is," Lou told his sister-in-law. He didn't sound as matter-of-fact as he was going for, the stress of the unfathomable events betraying his voice. His cane caused the old home's wood floor to creak as he made his way from the entryway to the couch that had been his bed in the early days of healing from his gunshot wounds obtained in Mexico.

"Why?" proclaimed Kyla. The teen was already coping with the trauma from the near-death abduction. The reality that the landscape of her country, and indeed the entire world, had just changed forever was too much to process. "What does it mean, Uncle Lou!" the young lady more barked than asked. Foster, her father and Lou's brother, had been quietly waiting for his family to get through the shock that Washington less than 100 miles south had just been obliterated by a Chinese space-based kinetic weapon. As had many other strategic locations throughout the United States.

Lou plopped onto the couch while Rusty headed for Kyla and sat right on her feet where she stood in the transition space that led to the kitchen. The German shepherd was protective of her and could sense her stress. Lou looked at his brother. "You need to get it out, too?" he asked in a flippant tone that resembled the angry drunk Lou from the time after his son's suicide.

Foster moved to his easy chair and fell into it. He looked for a beer that wasn't there. He hadn't had beer for two weeks, as the supply chain and high fuel prices had made the small selection left on the shelves ridiculously expensive. "I'm beyond words. This thing with China has been brewing for years, if not decades," the older Caldwell declared, glancing at his wife's worried face.

Barbara was too tense to sit. "Shouldn't we be doing something?" she asked. "What do we do?" The question oozed the strain it was loaded with. "It's not like we have a bomb shelter!"

Lou could see the tears starting to overflow from the corner of her eyes. He scanned the rest. Kyla's brow was furrowed, face flush, but she was not about to cry. *At all,* Lou realized. *This girl has definitely been primed for a new world view the last few weeks.* His brother's face carried the same burden as his wife's, a burden of worry compounded by confusion. "The same thing you have been, Barb," Lou offered as rationally as he could muster. "Conserve your resources. Get to know the neighbors better..." He drifted in thought. *What should they do?* he asked himself, thinking. His eyes drifted toward the back of the house. "Start gathering anything you can to plant a garden in spring." He looked back at Foster. "You got any spare materials? Lumber? PVC? Plastic sheeting?"

Foster looked a bit confused. "Y-yeah..." he offered. "You need to bury a body or somethin'?" he almost guffawed.

"Start a greenhouse in the garage or shop. Get some seeds and start planting."

Barbara's eyes shifted. The small idea was a simple nugget of hope. It wasn't much, but it was enough. "We have some seeds!" she declared, happy for the simple distraction.

"Just flowers, Mom," Kyla said.

"No!" her mother corrected her quickly, turning her head toward the know-it-all. "I've had some cucumber and tomato seeds saved. You don't know everything," she reminded the eighteen-year-old. She turned her head back to Lou. "I have some seeds."

"Good," Lou said, nodding in approval. "The point is to start making every decision based on a new set of ideals. No longer think in terms of 'What should we watch on TV?' Start thinking in terms of what you're going to eat. How you're going to get fresh water. How—"

"We have the pool!" Kyla interjected excitedly.

"True," Lou said. "And I guess you guys have some pool shock stored up?" He looked at his brother.

Foss had been lost in thought, half listening as his mind raced around the same types of questions. "Huh? Yeah. Some. Suddenly it doesn't seem like enough..." he mumbled.

"Get on YouTube. Tonight!" Lou ordered Kyla. "Before it goes away forever. Start looking up how to filter water, how to make homemade bleach out of pool shock. Stuff like that. You find a video you like, try downloading it. A lot of them have transcripts, too. If you can't save those, then at least screen shot the most important parts. Then print them before the power goes away." The Caldwell family was starting to evolve as their plan unfolded. They were becoming... 'preppers' suddenly.

Kyla gave Rusty a reassuring scratch behind his right ear. She headed for the stairs, the inherited dog following. "On it," she said. "Holler up anything else I should be looking up," she said as she ran up to her bedroom.

"I... I guess I can start figuring out how to make a simple green-house in the garage," Foster said. "I'm kinda worried about the shop getting broken into. We live in the sticks, I know that. But—you know —there are still thousands of people a couple of miles away. Do we have enough soil?" he asked his wife.

"I have some potting soil," she admitted. "Not nearly enough, but it's a start!" She sounded almost excited, but the reality of what was happening had slipped back to her forethoughts. "Is all of this going to matter?" she asked Lou. "What if there's a nuclear missile headed here right now?" The stress reappeared on her flushed face.

"It isn't," Lou assured her. "They know they can't win that game. Based on things I know they've been up to, I'm guessing they want to leave America relatively intact."

"For what?" Foster asked, confused.

"For themselves," Lou said. He could see his brother and sister-in-law just weren't getting it. "To invade."

"Can they do that?" Foster almost yelled. "What about the Navy!"

"The Navy has taken huge losses in the last two days." Lou explained, confused. "It's been on the news..."

"I heard something, but I guess I wasn't paying enough attention. I thought our carrier hit a reef or somethin'..."

Lou held three fingers up. "We're down three carriers in the Pacific. And a bunch of ships were wiped out by a giant tsunami caused by a nuclear torpedo." Barbara shrieked. "Thousands dead," Lou said sullenly.

Foster stood up and went to kneel by his wife at her recliner, who was now openly sobbing. He took her hands into his large paws. "What're you gonna do, little brother? Do you have a job anymore?" The chubbier bearded Caldwell almost choked on his words as the gravity that World War Three was beginning had hit him fully.

"I think I need to borrow Sheila again," Lou said, referring to the black Springfield Hellcat his brother had lent him for his trek to find his missing wife. "I'm heading down to the Proving Grounds to catch a chopper." The base at Aberdeen was less than twenty miles south. "There are contingency locations for the military to head towards. I'll be trying to make my way to Pennsylvania."

GARDEN GROVE, CALIFORNIA

"COVERING FIRE!" ALEX YELLED WITH THE CONFIDENCE OF A pimply nerd. He watched most of the members of the 15th Street Posse lean out much too far from their pieces of cover.

Lauren Duarte was the most adept by far. The former correctional officer from Ohio had moved to the Los Angeles area just nine months earlier to be with Jessie, a woman she'd developed a strong bond with while socializing in their favorite zombie sub-Reddit. The coming war had halted their plans to marry, but it had only affirmed in her mind that she was meant to be in Garden Grove to protect the one person on the planet she felt truly knew her. She held her rifle sans magazine and ammunition up to her shoulder, trying to get a proper sight picture on the flip up iron sights.

The well-worn M4, one of several Army surplus units that had been provided by their Army trainer just an hour earlier, looked the most natural in her hands over any other of his neighbors in Alex Nguyen's opinion. He wasn't trying to downplay the rest—Roman Lopez had proven quite handy with his shotgun, after all. And Ned Manner was a Coast Guard veteran who demonstrated courage over fear despite a lack of infantry training. Alex and his neighbors had won the battle against the gang who confiscated his motel by a combination of fortitude, luck, and good planning. If he'd had any delusions that they were an effective combat unit, the previous hour had dispelled them.

"Stop!" Patrick McBrogan, aka Lucky Charm, called out loudly. "Everyone pause where you're at. I'm gonna come 'round and show y'all what you're doing wrong," the Delta Force operator said through a thick Louisiana drawl. He motioned for Alex to join him and started with Lauren, who was kneeling next to the corner at the breezeway between the motel's two northern buildings. "Good work. Just tuck that support elbow in a bit. You a lefty?"

"No, I was just trained to switch shoulders on left corners in my old job," she explained.

"Oh. Cop?"

"Jail guard," she corrected.

"Okay. Stick with that. If we had time and a propuh range, I'd show you that that whol' thing is a myth. Play with it," he advised. "You'll see. Nice work, though. Good wide base on your knees." Alex was following their trainer as he moved down toward a corner near the office door. The main parking area of the motel was inside a courtyard of all the buildings, accessed by driving under a covered overhang near the office. The buildings provided a very natural barrier to anything in the parking lot on the north, west, and south sides.

"I'm sorry!" Sissy Lopez explained sheepishly as Lucky and Alex walked up. She was tangled in her sling, unsure of how to hold the rifle.

"That's okay," Lucky said. "This is why you all will be getting homework to help each other dry practice anytime you're not doing anything else. But tell you what. See how you're standing in the open? You'll be dead in an actual fight, miss."

Sissy groaned, understanding the importance of the training but not really desiring it. "I obviously wouldn't be standing out here like this if bullets were really flying," she countered.

"Aight," Lucky replied. "Just remember you train like you fight," he cautioned. "If you have to step away from a wall or car to fix it now, that's what you'll do under stress." He made his way toward the office.

We are hosed, Alex thought. He appreciated that they'd been recognized for their notorious resistance fight a few weeks earlier. Just a week or two before that, he and his brother Henry had taken shelter in the office as a pair of police were ambushed and assassinated a mere fifty yards farther up the street. The gravity of the state of things wasn't lost on the 32-year-old. But the reality that the Army was trying to train them to—*What? Play soldier?*—right in the middle of Garden Grove wasn't lost on him. And on both major streets to the north and west of the hotel, people were traveling like herds of bison. Fuel and food were becoming scarce. *The only thing keeping them from taking the hotel like the gang did is our armed barricade at the front,* Alex thought.

He and Lucky made it to Micah Benson, a notorious story in and of himself. The 17-year-old homeless youth had a rough life and the street smarts of someone twice his age. Unlike most Americans his age, he was not trained in tactics by video games. But he'd seen enough people get hurt, maimed or killed in his actual life to know that the state of things was no joke. And though Alex was fully aware of the kid's unfortunate story... and had extended a certain amount of trust and leeway because of it... the street-rat had grown accustomed to answering all criticism with anger and sarcasm. "You think this is a joke?" Lucky said as they approached the youth, rifle still slung to his back, as he leaned against the corner and smoked.

"Yeah. I do," he said defiantly. "I know how to duck. I know how to crouch. All this," he said, waving his hand at the others across the parking lot. "Just a waste of time. We should be out shootin' these gats."

The hardened Delta operator just stared at the youth, unimpressed. The pair locked eyes for four seconds before the kid finally averted his gaze to Alex. "Sorry, Alex. You know it's true, brah..."

"I know I would've thought the same thing at your age," the short motel owner said. "But my folks came here from Vietnam on a raft, man. They have impressed upon me that we have to be ready to fight! Don't slap the hand that's trying to help us, Micah!" He'd become the kid's surrogate father figure in the preceding year. There was always a fine line between respecting Micah's genuine struggles and letting him be a jerk. At the age of seven, Micah started a two-year fight against brain and spinal tumors. At thirteen, his mother died of a fentanyl overdose. At fifteen, Micah had to stab his own father with a letter opener to keep the drunkard from strangling him to death. *Listen, dude,* Alex had told him one day after finding him scrounging food out of the hotel dumpster. *Just come in every night and I'll give you a sandwich. But quit yelling at my customers.* That was eleven months earlier.

"Pfffttt," Micah spewed. He gave Lucky Charm one last glare before he unslung the rifle and took a knee for cover behind a stranded car next to the curb.

Lucky just gave Alex a look and moved on out to the center of the parking lot. "Everyone on me," he called out loudly. Those he'd addressed and the others strolled over, some in a variety of misfitted tactical gear. Soon there were a dozen folks standing around the soldier and the business owner. Lucky had placed himself so that they would all semi-circle around him with their backs to the west.

"Turn around," was all he said.

Confused looks joined a few whispered 'Huh?'s as the small group of wannabe citizen defenders were confused by the simple command. First Henry and Lauren complied, which led to the others eventually following suit. Micah was leaning against a minivan nearby, refusing to play along.

"See that mass Exodus?" Lucky Charm asked. Visually, the group could look west under the motel's covered front drive and see Brookhurst Street. On it was a steady flow of people on foot and bicycle streaming by. Most didn't even acknowledge Roman and Ned standing armed guard at a makeshift barricade—though some did. They would study the men, sizing up the hardness of the potential target. "Most of those people are just a few meals away from killing you for your food and water." That made Micah look up. Most of the others turned back around. "Do you all think that kicking the gang out of this hotel was a one-time event?"

"This ain't just a hotel, anymore," Lauren called out, standing behind the shorter Jessie and wrapping her arms around her girlfriend. "It's our home." She scanned the group. "And those few of you that haven't moved here from 15th yet are bound to regret that eventually."

"What's your point?" one of the others asked Lucky.

Patrick McBrogan had a harsh truth to share, but he was still searching for the words. He let out a deep breath. "The delivery of guns and food this morning. It's just the start." He reached for the back of his head and neck, giving them a quick rub as the tension was getting harder to get rid of each day. "Ya'll have heard the news. Some of our ships and bases were attacked. That's just the start."

"What're you saying?" Jessie asked. "The power outages, the riots, the supply chain issues. We know. Things will get really bad before they get better. We get that."

"I don't think you do," Lucky said. "Normally there'd be a dozen guys like me here training you. But you seen all the battles with the cartels the last several weeks. We're kinda busy lately. I'm not training you to be a military unit. There's a massive invasion comin'. We'll be hundreds of miles behind enemy lines. I'm training ya'll to be guerrillas."

TUCSON, ARIZONA

"I THINK WE'RE BEING FOLLOWED!" KAREN SAID AS SHE steered the big green SUV. The Acme Ranch group had been forced to take Tracy to one of the two Banner University medical facilities. As Operation Venom Spear had unfolded, the military had taken both St. Joseph's Hospital and the Tucson ER and Hospital under martial control. The former had become nearly overrun with refugees from throughout the city, displaced by the growing intensity of the fights between the combined military and police forces and the cartel gangs. Many folks weren't even injured—they just had nowhere else to go. The latter had become the primary location for trauma from those same battles.

The evening before had been entirely consumed by making their way through a variety of checkpoints. Most were by the government forces, though a detour through one neighborhood had forced them to pay a "toll" to a local gang. Money was no good. They had brought some of the more obscure hunting cartridge ammunition to trade off in just such an occurrence. It was near midnight before the university facility would finally take Tracy into their custody. The hospital security made it perfectly clear that they were not allowed to wait. After yet another tense debate between Karen and Daniel, the foursome had found a consensus to park at a nearby Catholic school and try to sleep in shifts. Karen's idea of waiting for daylight had resonated with Pedro and Robin.

"That truck back there pulled off the curb a block behind us when we left the school," she said as the rig plowed south through littered streets in the rising dawn. "And they're catching up slowly." She pulled her eyes off the big side mirrors just in time to catch a gray SUV come sliding from the left into the intersection ahead. Her mind raced as she recognized the shapes of rifle barrels pointing out.

"H-hey!" was all Daniel, sitting to her right, could manage to yell. He felt his head slam into the closed window as Karen jerked the rig to the left. It took a hard bounce up the slight slope into a boarded-up corner convenience store as she tried to steer and maintain speed, maneuvering around the defunct fuel island. They slammed their heads again as she bounced the rig out the other street's entrance.

"Sorry!" Karen yelled. The older vehicle had a loose suspension and tossed its occupants around inside as she veered, trying to regain control. She looked in the rearview mirror, but it was too small to see anything in the early morning hours. Scanning the side mirror, she saw the rig turn around and start giving chase.

"Look out!" Robin yelled from the seat behind Karen's. "To the left!" The original vehicle had moved a block over as soon as Karen had started to evade. They were now flying up the parallel road at an extreme rate. Karen hit the brakes, quickly back up three-hundred feet, and pulled up a side street into an older neighborhood, barely missing being rammed by the rig, which was screeching to a stop.

"What're you doing?!" Daniel yelled. "You should've rammed them! Now those others are right on us!"

"They would've hit us if we'd kept going!" Karen yelled back. "Not the other way around! Granger said to always keep moving when ambushed! This street was the only way to keep moving!"

Pedro was getting thrown around as he scrambled over the rear bench to the spacious back. "Can you open this back window?" he hollered up to the front as he pulled his rifle over the bench after him while bracing one hand on the ceiling.

"I-I don't think it opens while we're driving!" Robin said tensely.

"Sorry, Robin!" Pedro yelled as he tried to kick out the safety glass.

"T-turn there!" Daniel commanded.

"That puts us back onto the main road!" Karen argued. "They'll see us!"

"Do you have any idea where this neighborhood ends?" Daniel yelled back.

"I think we'll come out onto Broadway!" Karen said, laying on the horn to drive a group of teenagers on bicycles back out of the street. "There's got to be a military checkpoint there!"

"One of those kids has a gun!" Daniel countered. "Just turn!"

Everyone lurched right as Karen slammed the wheels left and onto a different street. She looked up in the rearview mirror, only to see Pedro finally clearing the rest of the broken sheet of safety glass from the rear cargo door. He began to fire at the chasing truck, missing wildly because of the bouncing. But it was enough to get them to back-off a bit. The sound and smoke of his rifle fire assaulted their ears and nostrils, adding to the confusion.

Karen hit the brakes as she once more tried to turn onto a main southbound avenue. As Pedro braced his rifle with his support hand in the corner of the window frame, he was able to get a good sight picture through his red-dot and control his muzzle from bouncing. The chasing rig came flying up rapidly, not expecting Karen's slowdown to turn. Pedro poured shots into where the driver should be behind the morning glare. As the Acme Group started heading south, the vehicle failed to turn, slamming directly into the other chase rig that was already on that road. "I think I got 'im!" Pedro yelled to the front.

"Let me drive!" Daniel ordered as he scanned over the rear bench and past Pedro to confirm. "After you've gotten some distance."

You can go screw yourself, Karen thought as she went back to scanning the road ahead.

CHAPTER 5

CANADIAN FORCES BASE ESQUIMALT
Victoria, British Columbia, Canada

MASTER CHIEF DARREN JORGENSON STOOD ON THE PIER staring not at his own submarine, but the USS El Paso. The older defunct U-boat was covered in topside guardrails with an erector-set style frame and a heavy vinyl tarp roof. It offered a level of rain coverage, for sure, but the primary purpose was to protect the happenings from the eventuality that foreign spy satellites would figure out she was parked there. On the pier was a temporary scaffold barn with its own roof. It had been constructed as a large tunnel for semi-trucks to pull under. During very specific periods of time, forklifts and cranes hurried through the process of unloading torpedoes and other high explosives from the trucks and placing them into the old sub via a roof covering that ran from the pier, up the gangway, and into the ship's weapons loading hatch.

This will probably be the pinnacle op briefing of my career, Darren thought. *Of all our careers,* he corrected himself. *And the final one* he realized with gloom. He'd found his way over from his own ship's pier with just one other person. His CO and XO were tending to a multitude of tasks. "Can they really wire all of those warheads to blow up?" he asked Navy SEAL Lieutenant Angelo Cusimano. "Or will it all just go off because one thing blew up?"

The short, wiry commando had been in the Teams for most of his nine years in the Navy. He was the officer-in-charge of the eighteen-member platoon assigned to the Hunny. A nearly new SSGN, the lead ship in the specialized class of submarines carried a complement of forty-eight Tomahawk cruise missiles, six per each of the eight missile tubes. It also had two LOCs, or lock-out chambers, meant for rapidly deploying the on-board SEAL team to conduct underwater operations. Each LOC, located between the sub's conning tower and the missile tubes, had mounted on top of it a large chamber designed to carry the mini subs for the operators. It gave the vessel the appearance of having two babies hitchhiking on its back. At 500-feet long and thirty-eight feet in breadth, the sub was shorter and skinnier than the granddaddy SSGNs that had been converted out of old Ohio-class missile submarines. Like the spy subs of the Cold War, the Hunny had been fitted with deployable thrusters and specialized sensors that enabled her to maneuver in tight waters that submarines normally couldn't. She was a creature meant for both gathering intel and then laying non-nuclear waste to an enemy. Lt. Cusimano and his team were new to the sub's crew, replacing those SEALs that had been aboard during their action in the Northern Yellow Sea. "I'm sure all of this will be wired together," he replied.

"Gotcha," Darren said.

"KISS method," Angelo continued. "This dead sub will need to rely on batteries for this final trip. I'm guessing our sub will be able to send some data back via the towing connection, but for the most part, this Trojan Horse will have to be fully independent. And that means keeping things simple."

"Makes sense," Darren said.

"Now maybe you can answer a question my men and I have concerns about," the officer hinted.

"Whatcha need, Lieutenant?" As a senior enlisted NCO with over two decades of career, Darren knew that anything sensitive he was privy to, this special warfare officer was allowed to know.

"The rumors. About them sinking subs just by hacking... I mean— hacking surface ships? Sure, I buy that. But what's to stop them from planting a bug in Hunny's computers that will just send us to the bottom like a crumpled sardine can...?"

"Skipper has alluded to Australia and Great Britain saying it has happened to them. To my knowledge, we've not lost any subs like that. Yet."

The pair turned and started walking back to the head of the pier. "That's not a very comforting way you put that, COB," Angelo admitted.

"Aye," Darren said in Navy slang. "But we've tightened up the systems and computers we're accessing now. Very tight. Skipper or the XO have to approve all electronic comms—in or out. Why do you think your team wasn't even allowed to bring cell phones on down at Pearl?"

"I guess I just thought that was an abundance of paranoia."

"It isn't paranoia if they're really trying to kill ya, L-T," Darren said glibly.

A drizzle was turning heavy. Darren scanned his eyes south as they made the slow trek, not able to see his homeport state of Washington, but feeling saddened by being so close none-the-less. *I wonder how my girls are managing,* he thought. Darren was not prone to worry, as he realized it provided no value in his already stressful occupation. He'd forced himself to be content that at least he knew what had happened to them. At least he knew they were safe as part of a camp and impromptu community at his local gun club. Many of his crew had received tragic news—or no news at all, which was worse than tragedy in its own way. He heard Angelo sneeze and forced his thoughts back to the present. "Let's pick it up, Lieutenant," the Hunny's senior enlisted member advised as he wiped the rain off his glasses. "We'll have plenty of chances to be wet and worried later. Especially you."

ACME RANCH
Southeast of Tucson, Arizona

"KAREN... WAKE UP..." KAREN'S SUB-CONSCIOUS MIND HEARD. It pulled her out of REM with a start, her eyes stinging when she opened them. The deep slumber hung heavy over her as the daylight filtered from the bunkhouse window through dust and to her waking face.

"Unnn... What time is it?" Karen grunted at her Uncle Claude, still exhausted but feeling like she'd had enough sleep to be ready for... whatever.

"A little after five in the evening," he answered, handing her a steaming black coffee after she'd swung herself up and planted her socked feet on the wood floor. "Wanna tell me about the ambush?"

"Wha—?" she asked, confused. "We already did, I thought," she countered.

"Now tell me the rest, niece. While it's just you and me..."

Karen reached out and took the life-giving nectar, gazing at her sole remaining family member in Arizona. "Waddya mean?" *What's he getting at?* she wondered. "We pushed through it, they wrecked into each other... we got lucky and escaped." She scanned the old veteran's face. "Oh—and Pedro shot one of them, probably."

"What about Daniel?" Claude asked.

Karen's veins turned cold as she realized where Claude was going with this. *But why?* "What's that arrogant twit saying?" she asked, voice instantly going defensive.

"I'm trying not to read too much into it," Claude admitted. "But the more I listen to that guy talk, the more I think he's a snake. He's trying to make it sound like you almost killed them with your driving... that you were frozen with panic. That it was lucky he was along to tell you where to turn…"

Karen's anger lit up. Coffee crossed the rim of the mug as she stood up to face-level with her uncle. "That son of a—"

"Now calm down, Kare Bear," Claude said as he raised his hands. Karen handed him the mug as she brushed past him, trying to get to her boots at the foot of the bunk. Claude spun. "Wait! If you go storming in there upset, all you did was prove him right. Right?"

"I'm just fed up with men lying about me!" Karen screeched at her uncle, the memory of a vile divorce welling up in her mind. Her fire was lit. "I was the one who drove us out of it! If I'd listened to him, we'd all be dead. That conniving, condescending jerk couldn't plan his way out of a wet paper sack!" She took the mug back from her uncle and headed toward the dining table in the middle of the ranch bunkhouse, plopping her head into her hands after she sat.

Claude sat down across the dusty oak table from her. "I figured it was somethin' like that," he admitted. "But you need to not fall for this guy's trap. I've seen guys like this my whole life, even in 'Nam. Play the slow quiet game. Let 'im dig his own hole."

Karen let that sit for most of a minute before speaking. "I know I look tough and act tough," the CrossFit instructor told her uncle. "But something happened in high school…" Her eyes moistened just enough for Claude to see them get glassy. "And I've been paying for it ever since by letting men say whatever they want about me." She sniffed as she wiped her eyes with the back of a hand.

"I'm sorry to hear that Kare Bear," her loving uncle said. "I've always known that under your strength is something you fear." He paused and took a sip off his own coffee mug, looking around at bunks and empty coat and hat hooks to choose his words. "Not to downplay that, but we all have something that scares us buried inside. Even that jerk in there," he motioned toward the main house. "But if he's going around and talking like that in front of me and the rest, we need to let it play out. Keep an eye on 'im. I'll bet my right nut that he's going to try to build an alliance."

"You mean—like... that stupid game show out on the island?"

Claude snorted a quick chuckle. "Somethin' like that!" he smiled. "If he's half the snake I think he is, he won't be able to help it."

"But Granger and Tracey and the others..." she asked aloud rhetorically. "A bunch of them know him from their gun club..."

"Doesn't mean they truly know him, honey. Some of the most notorious snakes in history were charismatic. The best thing you can do is let your actions speak for you... and let his speak for him. The truth will eventually surface." The sun's angle through the windows continued to decrease, its rays eventually completely disappearing as Claude continued to counsel his niece in the subtle art of not giving a crap what people think about her.

THE PROVING GROUNDS
Aberdeen, Maryland

"CAN YOU POINT ME TOWARD THE FASTEST ROUTE TO THE airfield?" Lou inquired of the gate guards. Sandbag vehicle traps had been added to the arterial that led into the base on both the inbound and outbound sides of the thoroughfare from Maryland Boulevard. The water-filled, bright orange plastic barricades were still present as well. Lou had passed a large sign proclaiming that the security status was 'Alpha', an attempt to deter any unnecessary traffic. The R & D base was home to multiple tenant commands, employing several thousand civilians and active duty. The national state of emergency declaration by FEMA to every phone and email that the NSA had ever collected had done a good job of keeping unnecessary folks off the bases. Nobody wanted to be on the next one attacked.

The trip down started for Lou at 1:00 AM, after a bite to eat, a nap, and a tearful goodbye to his family. There was already a traffic jam of people clogging I-95 and any westbound roads out of Cecil County. State Highway 40 had fared little better, but as he was headed south, it wasn't as bad for Lou. Most people heading south were turning off for the large chain stores, searching for groceries and supplies. Though still in the wee hours, crowds were building at the stores. *I wonder if these crowds will just decide to open the stores for themselves?* Lou had traveled the route from Foster's many times for his physical therapy after his battle injuries. On a good day, it would be about a half-hour trip due to long traffic lights every couple of miles. This trip had taken over two hours.

The soldier, decked out in full battle gear, gave Lou's identification a very thorough physical examination before even bothering to insert the chip end of the card into her handheld scanner. Ignoring Lou, she watched her partners at work. One MP was walking a dog around the government issued van. Rusty was on full alert, but was only chuffing, taking assurance from Lou's soothing hand on his nape. Another MP was walking along with a rod, the bottom of which was a mirror. He was checking the bottom of Lou's van. The wireless scanner's LED turned green. "Thank you, sir," she told Lou. "You'll turn right just past the golf course. Phillips Field Road. Can't miss it."

"Thank you, Sergeant." Lou knew the gates were probably stressed and decided not to pepper the guards with questions they couldn't answer. Once the hydraulic posts keeping him from driving retracted into the ground, he proceeded over them, feeling the slight bumps as he slowly sped up. In less than two minutes, he was making the turn. The orange hue from the southwest toward Washington DC was still there, though several sets of large floodlights were dimming it some-what. As he approached the normally quiet Army airfield, Lou could see some sort of impromptu command post set up near the one hangar and admin building on this side of the airfield. Just past that building was a sole control tower, much shorter than one might see at a major airport.

Before the van could get to the small driveway from the road to the building, Lou was being directed by an orange flashlight. One small cone of light, a soldier barely visible behind it because of the airfield backlighting, was held still and horizontal, pointing at the other as the operator waved it in a repeating semi-circle. *Guess I need to park in this field,* Lou realized. *Makes no matter. I'll probably never see Maryland again,* he realized with a deepening sadness he was trying to suppress.

There was a growing collection of vehicles in the field, some government, some civilian. Though no helicopters or planes were in the air, Lou recognized the high-pitched whine of a small plane being warmed up somewhere out on the tarmac. He grabbed his stuffed duffel and placed his arms into the awkward bag's shoulder straps. It always amused him that despite every advance in military technology over the recent century-and-a-half, the Army still relied on the world's most painful design for non-combat gear carrying. He decided to leash Rusty, so he had to keep a hand on the nervous dog with the cane hand and carry his handbag at the same time. "C'mon, pal," he told his new buddy. They'd started bonding in the short time Lou had rescued him from the dog's post-kill quarantine.

Rusty scanned nervously, looking and listening with perked ears in all directions. He stayed as close to Lou's right leg as possible as they made their way in the grass past the other vehicles. Lou slowly made a bee line for the building, seeing the occasional truck or HumVee speed by on the road proper. The official parking area was packed with mostly military vehicles. The closer he got to the hangar and admin building, the more he could see "hurry up and wait" on full military display. The one lobby area was packed with people, some in uniform, others not. It was obvious that a few of the higher-ranking had brought wives and children with them, looking for... *Where?* Lou thought in annoyance. *Where do these people think they're taking their families?*

The slight colonel with the cane and the dog made his way into an organized chaos inside the building's primary space. Whereas the facility on the far side of the longest and last remaining operational runway was geared towards the movement of small loads of material and the conducting of tests, this one acted as a hangar and a support facility for visitors. There was no permanent staff for the airfield aside from a maintenance crew. The front lobby-type area was packed with people, most waiting and making small talk. It was near standing-room-only. Lou and Rusty politely moved through the mix of active duty and civilians and made their way to a counter. The building was being staffed by soldiers from CECOM, one of the other commands that used space on the Proving Grounds. Their specialty was deploying to remote locations to set up mobile command posts. They'd basically deployed two miles to the airfield to facilitate the influx of emergency air traffic.

"Colonel," a tired looking First Lieutenant said, recognizing the full-bird insignia on Lou's dark blue 'piss-cutter' cap. "What can I do for you?"

"Looking for a local hop, Lieutenant," Lou stated. "Hopefully you can hook me up with a helo to south central Pennsylvania."

"Just might be able to find some MNG to help with that, sir," the young officer said, clacking on a computer keyboard below the counter both men were standing at. "Anything flying in and out of here is local anyhow. Runway is too short for the big planes."

Lou used to be a pilot of such craft. The thought of anything but small craft here was silly to him. But he realized the communications officer across from him had been dealing with a lot of panicked people on a sleepless night. "You think the Maryland Guard will be coming in?"

"Oh yeah," the young man nodded. "We've had a few of theirs come in for various high-rankers a couple of times tonight. Are you on orders, sir?"

"Nothing official," Lou explained. "I'm with the Pentagon." Just saying that made the young officer's face go pale. A few of the surrounding conversations suddenly went static. Lou could almost feel the stares on the back of his head. "I was already up here," he explained.

"Alright sir, we'll get a message over to the local guard most ricky-tick. Pennsylvania, huh? They're going to want to know where."

"Near Blue Ridge Summit," Lou said. "A little complex called Raven Rock."

ACME RANCH
   Southeast of Tucson, Arizona

"KARE BEAR!" KAREN HEARD DONNA CALL OUT ON THE RADIO. She was enjoying the post-dawn morning trying to make progress on the sunken greenhouse project, having been relieved from the night watch at the observation post on the hill just an hour earlier. The beautiful hues of blue, purple, and red had falsely predicted a glorious day arriving. "Come to the main house! It's Claude!"

Upon hearing the urgency combined with the name of the one man she truly trusted, Karen grabbed the radio and bolted up the trail. In less than a minute, the athletic woman was running into the house, discovering commotion noises coming from the enclosed garage. Some of the older kids were hovering in the entry and family area, staring at Karen with grave concern when she entered. She made a left at the wide-open kitchen and progressed up a hall that led to the door to the former garage. When she entered, she saw Claude laying on a blanket in the middle of the floor, pale and ashen.

"Wh—what happened?" Karen gasped as she watched Robin Washington and Pam Bowers tending to her uncle. They'd just rolled him up and gotten the blanket under him and were in the process of covering him with another.

"It seems like his heart!" Donna said, angst dripping off her words.

"He's still conscious?" Karen asked, seeing Claude appear to be moving his head as she knelt down near him. "Uncle!"

"He is," Robin said as calmly as she could, looking around in time to see Kaitlin, Donna's oldest daughter, running back into the ranch's command post with a large plastic box. The fancy tackle box had been converted into an advanced medical kit similar to what an ambulance would carry. The teenager let it hit the floor next to Robin with a thud. "You still with us, Claude?" she asked as she began unlatching the split apart lids.

"Rosher that," Claude weakly mumbled through barely moving teeth and lips, cold sweat beading on his head.

"I'm gonna give you some aspirin," the nurse said as she popped the top off the pill container. She knew better than to use the words 'mild heart attack' to the patient. "Give him this," she ordered Pam as she handed her the pill and water bottle. She pushed the button on the battery powered sphygmomanometer cuff to get another blood pressure reading.

"You need to take this pill!" Karen ordered her ailing uncle as she knelt at his head, helping to pick it up while Pam put it between his lips. "You're not allowed to go anywhere, Claude!" she ordered. "You hear me?"

CHAPTER 6

"COPY. HEARING YOU FOUR BY THREE," BOB SAID INTO THE microphone mounted directly to his headset. Karen, Donna, and a few others were in the command post, listening to Bob's scratchy and warbled conversation with an AmCon radio operator located in Texas. He'd flipped a switch to power the sole speaker in the former garage once he realized he'd had an audience. When 11-year-old Chandler Wolf, one of the children radio trainees, realized the gravity of what they were hearing, he went and fetched his mother. From there, word had trickled out via the small ranch radios that something was brewing on the border.

"What does all of this mean?" Donna asked Karen as she scanned Bob's quickly scribbled notes. What he'd been hearing was coming much too fast to use a standard 'fill-in-the-blanks' radio report. On the pages were the frightening and incomprehensible reports of military activity on the American southern border in Texas and eastern New Mexico. Whereas China and Venezuela had been landing troops south into Monterrey and Chihuahua Mexico, it was apparent their status as advisors in Mexico's ongoing grievances was growing. The United States' anti-cartel operations and attacks on Mexico's side of the border had been the inciting incident that allowed China to seek and support a new ally. Columns of a variety of tanks, troop carriers, and other heavy equipment were starting to move north and position themselves strategically at border crossings and other places that the U.S. military had been staged in the preceding weeks.

Coupled with the attacks on the U.S. Navy and Air Force and the Pentagon, the meaning was more than obvious to Karen. She scanned the room, seeing a few of the children. Daniel Monitor and both Fred and Pam Bowers were trickling in. "I think we need to excuse the kids," Karen suggested to Donna.

"What's up?" Daniel asked, his tone confident and friendly. Karen wasn't sure if she was over-reading it, but she felt the air around Daniel was rife with assumption of his status as some sort of leader.

"Chandler, get the little ones back into the playroom," Donna ordered her son. "Yes—you can come back," she cut him off before he protested.

Bob held up a hand with a finger raised, causing Karen to shoosh the room. He pressed his headset onto his ears until the ear pads were flat. They were listening to some static and a mostly poor signal. The numbers and unit designators being relayed by the civilian patriot radio operators were actually coming from a variety of sources. Bob kept one hand on the headset and began to scribble again. He would occasionally reach up to the radio and push a button, trying to dial in the signal.

Ignoring Daniel's question, Karen suggested, "Maybe we should fire up the local bands and start trying to listen in to the local nets? Bob can't do it all himself," she said to remind the room that Claude was ill in bed, effectively cutting their radio monitoring in half.

"What's going on?" Daniel repeated, this time with a slight agitation that he'd been ignored.

"Troops are moving to the border along Texas," Donna answered in a hushed tone.

"Oh," Daniel said. "Karen's right—we should start listening in on the 2-meter and 70-centimeter bands," he said with a Tom Cruise smile while making eye contact with her. "Good thinking, Karen."

I know what you're up to, weasel, Karen didn't say. Ignoring the compliment, she said, "Sounds like you know what you're talking about." She was trying—and failing—to hide her true feelings for him from her face. "Is that something you can do?"

Daniel guffawed. "Whuh? Me? No, I was thinking more like the older kids or Robin... or you..."

"Because we're women?" Karen fired, causing Donna to give her a surprised look.

"Uh, no—because you all have the least firearms training," Daniel explained with a laughing grin. He was calm, with an almost smug tone. "I mean, Pam's a woman, and I didn't mention her because she's a competitive shooter."

"He's got a point," Donna suggested, trying to defuse the tension.

"You also didn't mention Brad," Karen countered without reminding them that he wasn't a trained shooter, either.

"Would you all take this conversation elsewhere?" Bob suddenly burst as he turned and stood. He pulled the headset off. "I'm going to get on the other radio and start talking to locals. You all figure out how to get me more manpower... somewhere else," he said bluntly as he shook the back of his hands to wave them out of the room.

Both Daniel and Karen followed Donna's lead, not just out of the command post, but across the large ranch home's main living space and out the back sliding door to the pool area. Straight out from the door were two tables with chairs and umbrellas. To the left was a large plastic storage closet which contained a variety of pool implements such as toys, floats, masks, and snorkels. Rounding out the area was a large propane grill to the right. "Listen, you two, I don't know what the beef is, but this little game you're playing isn't a good way to make a lasting impression on me," Dave Wolf's widow said.

"Yes, I agree wholeheartedly," Daniel said. His stare and fake smile pierced Karen's shields. "I have no idea why you're so hostile towards me..."

"Don't you?" Karen just asked with her own fake smile. "I will not dignify him by playing his game," she told Donna directly. "But since Tracy has been hurt, I feel like there's been a certain... void... in Granger's absence." She looked back at Daniel with her own smug smile.

"That's true," Donna acknowledged. "I'm not going to lie—we need you two here at the ranch just as much as you need to be here. But I'll kick you both out if this bickering festers into something more poisonous. This is my children's home—and both of you are guests. I won't have... whatever this is," she declared as she waved her pointer finger between the two of them.

"I'm sorry, Donna," Karen said. "I'll work on my attitude towards Daniel." She looked at her foe.

"Me, too," Daniel stated. "Whatever I've done to anger you, Karen —I'd love an opportunity to account and apologize for it."

I bet you would, weasel, Karen thought as she held a sincere gaze. *And here I am looking like the angry one. Just like Claude said would happen.* "Great."

"Perhaps we can work on the greenhouse together," Daniel suggested just as the loud repetitive slapping of air started to crescendo off the hills to the west. "Since Claude is ill, it'll give... us..." The thwapping of heavy rotor blades was unmistakable. "... give us..."

"Contact!" Pedro called out on the radio each of them possessed. "Helicopters rapidly approaching from the northwest! I mean—they are bookin'! Right for the LP/OP!"

A split second later, three Army Blackhawk helicopters blasted over the Listening and Observation Post on the hill in a southeasterly direction. A few seconds later, they drifted from a wedge formation into a single column, with the first chopper leading the other two in a counterclockwise circle around the large ranch. The three ranch residents were joined by several others as the powerful birds-of-prey shook the house in an unmistakable fashion. About a minute later, with one full loop completed, the lead helicopter continued to circle the ranch while the other two peeled into the center. From due south, they slowed and descended into the field between the main barn and arena and the highway several hundred yards to the east. Even in the decay of January, there was enough sand and grass to envelop the two beasts in clouds of dirt and debris as they settled in to land in the field out past the stream.

"Vehicles coming in! From the highway!" Pedro screamed excitedly through the radio speakers. The noise and distraction of the giant warbirds had covered the arrival of several military Humvees and trucks. They had turned off the highway and were headed up the ranch's driveway as if they owned it.

CANADIAN FORCES BASE ESQUIMALT
   Victoria, British Columbia, Canada

CAPTAIN MILLIE GOLDBERG, HER EXECUTIVE OFFICER, AND her Command Master Chief were the last to arrive at the Maritime Forces Pacific Headquarters building. Home to the various commanders of Canada's West Coast Navy, they were using Admiral Copper's most secure conference room. Like the Fleet HQs of their American counterparts, the Canadian headquarters was adorned with flags, photos of ships, and inert large caliber gun shells wrapped in decorative twine, called 'piping.' Millie's team was greeted by a junior officer in the building's 'quarterdeck,' or lobby, and taken via elevator to the third-floor meeting room. Most of the room stood from their seats as the trio arrived.

"Welcome, Captain Goldberg and Team LBJ," Admiral Copper said with a subtle smile. "We've saved you three a spot just here to my right," he said as he made a slight gesture from his place at the end of the long wide conference table.

Millie made the typically mundane pleasantries by introducing her Executive Officer and Command Master Chief. In exchange, she learned who the other command teams were. There was the USS James L. Hunnicutt, as the primary submarine. There were three attack-specific SSN teams representing the American subs USS Scranton, USS Illinois, and USS Key West. And there was another surface ship, the USS Bunker Hill. "You're the Captain who started Venom Spear, correct?" Millie asked Patricia Cooper.

"Team Bunker Hill at your service, Captain!" Patricia replied.

It wasn't lost on Millie that counting herself, Patricia Cooper, Carla Gingery as XO of the submarine James L. Hunnicutt, and Marie Darnell in charge of upgrades and repairs—that women had come a long way in a male dominated naval environment in her career. After a few minutes explaining the harrowing details of surviving the nuclear-torpedo-incited massive wave and picking up survivors, the meeting finally started moving to the details of the top-secret response they were to carry out.

Amongst various American and Canadian staffers of the highest levels were a pair that stood and took their places at the head of the room. "Gentlemen, the floor is yours," Admiral Copper announced as he rolled his chair a bit to his right and in alignment with Millie's.

"Thank you, sir. Greetings all. I'm Commander David Yanda from Development Group." It was assumed that no explanation was needed, as most everyone in the room had full knowledge of the group otherwise known as SEAL Team 6. He looked at his counterpart, who was key in providing the intelligence for this Hail Mary operation.

"And I'm Agent Craig Booker from the CIA. I'll be providing the intel for this brief, as well as interpreting the updates as the mission unfolds."

Millie scanned the room once more as the two men spent a few additional seconds on the history of the mission planning process. *Five ships and subs,* she thought. *A CO, XO, and Master Chief from each, all in one room. In an age of space-based weapons. DEVGRU... The CIA... And a dead useless submarine. Not to mention the shipyard commander and her senior leaders from Washington State. We must be involved in something... unprecedented.* She tuned her ears back in for the rest of the opening remarks.

"... Captain Darnell's team also installed additional batteries as she buttoned up the engine room and reactor compartment and welded the El Paso's hull cuts back into place." SEAL officer David Yanda motioned his hand toward Marie Darnell as he spoke. "It's important to remember a few things as we get into the nuts and bolts here. El Paso is just dead weight—a big slug in the water that will maintain a neutral buoyancy at about one-hundred seventy feet of depth."

"That's a very ballpark estimate," Marie interjected. "Our engineers are the best there are, but we've had to make some SWAGs when calculating this." She was referring to perhaps the Navy's oldest tradition— the 'Scientific Wild Ass Guess.' "There are just too many variables and no way to conduct trials on this."

"Understood," David acknowledged. "And it isn't Captain Darnell's team that are wiring up the munitions you're about to hear about. I've got my own experts working on that." He nodded at his partner, who started passing out secure packets, but only to the five ship and sub commanders. "Agent Booker is handing out the full mission plan, along with primary through tertiary contingency scenarios, communications strategies, and the like.

"Operation Flea Flicker..." Millie heard another officer say as she opened her folder. She recalled from introductions that he was the CO of the USS James L. Hunnicutt. *Didn't you all hit the sea floor escaping Chinese torpedoes?* she thought. One thing she was sure of, though, was that it was the Navy's newest and most high-tech sub—and she was glad the Hunny would be involved in this mission.

"Yes. Aren't the admirals clever?" Craig quipped. "Present company excepted, of course," he smiled as he glanced at their Canadian host.

"The op name will make sense as we pour through this. What I will preface this with is that once we deploy—"

"We?" Millie heard the skipper of the submarine USS Key West ask. The submarine had a history with the USS James L. Hunnicutt, having claimed a combat kill while saving the spy boat from a PLAN torpedo attack.

"Ahh, yes. Agent Booker and I will be along for this... in the Hunnicutt," David explained. "There's a lot of moving pieces, and we'll take monitoring all five vessels' progress off the list of stresses Commander Woodward will have to deal with."

"Before we get into the operation befitting a Hollywood blockbuster, I want to impress upon you just how dire things have become," Craig Booker said. "In addition to their own sizable fleet and air force, China was able to capture a fleet of Russian amphibious ships in a special naval operation. Via submarine insertion, their commandos used rubber rafts to approach and board one ship in a convoy. After eliminating most of the crew, they drove the ship long enough to take on a few hundred paratroopers. One by one, they boarded and hijacked over a dozen ships, each capable of hauling thousands of troops and hundreds of tons of tanks and hardware." He let that thought settle for a minute. "We've cracked their most secure communications, just like they've done with ours. We believe that smaller fleet is bound for the coasts of Oregon or Northern California."

"Or both," David added.

"Or both," Craig Booker repeated. "But our target is the much larger fleet headed toward central and southern California. As you all know, they and Venezuela have been landing thousands of troops and hundreds of tanks in Mexico, who they've managed to turn into an ally. That buildup, the attacks on our fleet and now Washington D.C. and key bases... There's no way the approaching fleet doesn't invade at this point."

"Not if, but when," Millie said, wondering if her uniquely designed destroyer was just as key to this operation as the submarine James L. Hunnicutt. The USS Lyndon B. Johnson wasn't just a long, tall slender wave cutter. It had the latest in radar-repelling engineering and technology.

"Precisely," Craig said. "China has been knocking out satellites for two weeks, not just ours but the Brits and the Aussies, too. Their hacking has sent hundreds of our newer planes crashing. Our older tech seems to be more resistant to their cyber-attacks. It is imperative each of you stick to our comms strategy and maintain strict signal emissions control. We're talking zero emissions. You can't even turn on your weather radars."

What? Millie thought, not sure if she was believing what she heard. *They want us to sail into battle blind?*

"The lives of your crews depend on it," Craig said. The CIA agent's face was as deadly serious as he could make it. "But to get to the main point, we have aerial and satellite confirmation of at least one-hundred and ninety amphibious ships, aircraft carriers, submarines, and surface combatants in the main battle group. They're carrying an estimated four-hundred-fifty-thousand soldiers and sailors. With their own and the captured Russian planes, they could easily send another one hundred thousand paratroops." Someone let out a shocked low whistle. "And that's just wave one, and it doesn't include the smaller northern fleet," Craig reminded. "They have nearly thirty percent of our entire population in their military—nearly one hundred million."

The gravity of that number hit the group like a giant Newton's apple. "We... we have to stop them..." one of the junior officers along the room's edge mumbled louder than she had intended.

"I must impress upon you one thing, my American friends," Admiral Copper suddenly announced. "Some of my bosses are taking a lot of heat from my government leaders. There are those in Ottawa that feel more of an allegiance to Beijing than to Washington. A minority, for sure—but a vocal one."

"Noted," Craig said. "We know Canada will be our allies when and where it really counts. Back to this. We haven't knocked out all their satellites, just like they haven't ours. We know they know you're all here in Victoria. They've most likely seen the El Paso transit up Puget

Sound to here. And that will most likely be going to drive them crazy."
He paused just for a few seconds to check faces. "But not as much as
when they see Hunnicutt towing El Paso out to sea."

"Finally," Brody Woodward said, albeit with a grin. "They installed
those tow rings at Pearl. Do the people behind this scheme realize that
we have a depth limit of four-hundred-feet?"

"Yes. And we've leaked about your speed limit of eighteen knots
since your repairs, too," Craig said.

"We—we don't have one of..." the sub's commanding officer
started before he caught the sly grin on the CIA operative's face. "Ah.
Misinformation. Duh."

"Correct, skipper," Craig said. "We don't want them to know how
truly fast you can still be." He looked at the other three subs' leadership
teams who were quietly perusing the handouts in front of them. "All is
not as it seems in this operation."

"We're getting a retrofit, too?" the captain of the Virginia-class sub
USS Illinois asked.

"It starts tonight," Marie Darnell said. "Just as soon as the cranes
get some of our welders and their gear on-board."

"Correct," Craig added. "Like Hunnicutt, you guys have superior
speed because of your enclosed propulsor. That will be key in the
subterfuge we're selling them."

"What's this?" Millie asked in concern. "We're going to make
ourselves targets for them to board us like they did the Russians?!" The
petite redhead could turn into hot lava when she needed to.

"Keep reading," SEAL David Yanda said as he stood back up.
"You're just the bait. We'll be there. They'll never expect what's
coming..." Millie took the suggestion and kept reading, falling quiet as
she continued to learn more. "Some of the east coast fleet is trying to
get over here as quickly as they can. Washington won't dare choke
them up in the Panama Canal, which means you're waiting for a
couple of more weeks before they get here to join the fight. As you all
read and get to the point where we hit the invading fleet, just realize
that the remaining subs from Hawaii, Guam and San Diego will be

attacking, too. They're being told to hold off until the stated date and time we commence. Then, like hounds on a fox, they'll attack in such a way as to drive the carriers and largest amphibious ships directly where we want them."

"Flea Flicker, huh?" Millie asked as she made eye contact, first with her own team, and then with the command teams for the other ship and three subs. "How exactly do we run this play?"

"Right up the middle," David Yanda answered directly.

ACME RANCH
Southeast of Tucson, Arizona

"YOU REALLY HAVE TO LEAVE AGAIN?" KAREN ASKED Granger Madison and Delta Force Master Sergeant Mikkel 'VooDoo' Hudson. "You guys made such a flashy entrance yesterday afternoon..."

"Won't usually be like that," VooDoo promised with a very slight grin. "Not anymore." The pair of men had linked up with the U.S. military commanders at Camp Navajo in the northern part of Arizona while on their scouting mission. Though still assigned to the Rampart Edge mission, VooDoo's leadership in arguably America's best Tier 1 Special Operations Unit always gained him respect and privilege amongst any allied troops.

When the general in charge of all Arizona Army and National Guard forces learned how the operator and the former Marine came to be working together, he was intrigued by the former Joint Chief Chairman's non-linear thinking. *I always liked General Montgomery,* he told the pair. What was supposed to be a two-minute meet-n-greet turned into sixty. At the culmination of it, he knew he had to see the ranch and Road Runner concept with his own eyes. *And I'm even headed to the border already!* he had declared.

Knowing an opportunity when he saw it, Granger made the spot-decision to give the blessing for the visit, not that a lack of permission would've stopped the flag officer. He and VooDoo flew down with Brigadier General Walter Forbes, who was visiting the two Brigade Combat Teams that had established armor, artillery, mechanized infantry, and air cavalry from New Mexico to California over the preceding week. He felt the ranch on the small highway southeast of Tucson might be an excellent place for a potential basecamp for some of the battalion commanders. From there, they could control operations at the border crossing at Nogales but also be ready to evacuate Fort Huachuca if necessary.

After thundering in impressively the evening before, Granger spent some time smoothing things over with Donna. He knew he needed to ensure she knew something—an invasion was imminent. "You want the Army here," he'd told his best friend's widow. "Without the air defenses they'll bring, this ranch wouldn't stand much of a chance." The next morning, he and VooDoo were trying to sneak out early. The National Guard would be arriving in large numbers by 0700, and they didn't want to get stuck in the commotion. There were still a couple of organized groups on Lou's list that they needed to check out and potentially get linked into the patriot-army marriage. But Karen was the earlier bird.

"We've got a HumVee waiting for us down by the highway," Granger told her.

"Look—I know we briefed you on Tracy last night. And Claude. And the fact that we've learned the hospital isn't taking any new patients. But I didn't get the chance to tell you about... someone else."

Granger stopped stuffing a couple of items back into his large gear bag and gave her his attention. "What is it?" he asked, concerned.

"How well do you know your pal, Daniel?" she asked.

Granger turned to VooDoo. "I need to take five. Let's go for a walk," he suggested to Karen.

It took closer to fifteen minutes as they paced off less than a hundred feet. Granger listened and gave consideration to what her concerns were. VooDoo walked over about halfway and pointed at his watch face. The ANG and Brigade Commanders would be making a mess of the highway shortly. Granger slowly led his friend back toward the truck tailgate they'd been using in front of the main house. "I have something for you," he told her in one last attempt to bolster her self-confidence. He dug into a large parachute bag he used as a case for hauling tactical gear and found what he was looking for.

"This was mine when I was in Force Recon," he said as he handed her a Kabar knife in a worn, light brown leather sheath.

Karen wore a shocked look under her dark hair and ponytail. "I—I can't take this," she whispered.

"I want you to have it. Keep it on you at all times. And when you see it—remember that I believe in you."

Karen was at a loss for words as she took the gift. Donna Wolf came out of the house and approached the two.

"Bob says they're about ten minutes out," she advised.

"Listen, Donna—it's your place. But if I have any say whatsoever, it is my advice that Karen here be the deciding vote on any security related decisions."

"Well, I—"

"I—I'm sorry, D," Granger told her. "It's not about tactical experience. It's about having a level head. And I think Karen does. I'd have Jerome do it, but he'll turn into a raging bull the moment his wife or kids are threatened." He looked at Karen. "And... well..."

"I don't have kids," Karen said, still a little embarrassed by that at the age of forty-three.

"I hate to drop this on you without a conversation," Granger apologized to Donna. He scanned at the antsy VooDoo. "But I'll feel better knowing Karen can override any stupid decisions."

"O-okay," the normally confident ranch owner said as she watched Granger turn, grab his heavy bags, and start double-timing with VooDoo down the main driveway toward the highway.

CHAPTER 7

RAVEN ROCK MOUNTAIN COMPLEX
Pennsylvania-Maryland Border

RUSTY HAD FINALLY FALLEN ASLEEP BETWEEN LOU'S FEET AND those of the man across. He'd kept a close eye on the other dog in the helicopter, also a German Shepherd. The twin-bladed CH-47 Chinook was loud, cramped, and hot, which all served to lull Lou's new best friend to sleep despite his concerns. The dog had grown up in a home-made junkyard in the mountain foothills of southwest Virginia. He was still adjusting to his new life as an untrained service dog.

We're circling, Lou realized. *Finally.* He picked his left leg up and straightened it over Rusty to stretch, repeating the process with his damaged right leg. The recovering alcoholic longed for a drink to help with the pain where his kidney had been shot. He twisted his shoulder back as nearly as that of the men on either side would allow, trying to see out the circular window behind him. Twenty passengers and crew were crammed into the flying workhorse's belly, seated on red fabric benches sewn to aluminum frames. All were active duty military or highly important civilians. Lou caught a partial glance out of the window, craning his eyes past the edge of the tan outer airframe paint job.

The craft was circling to its left, putting Lou on the downhill side. He recognized the two red and white radio towers on top of the mountain from photos. *Raven Rock,* he thought. *Site R. This is the one everyone knows about, he remembered. I bet POTUS is somewhere else, though...* The loud craft straightened out once more, heading northwest and just a bit deeper into Pennsylvania before another banked turn aligned it with the heliport pad. The turbine engines and heavy blades both picked up in volume as the pilots slowed the craft and carefully eased down on the collective. Rusty's head perked, brows wrinkled with worry. Lou reached down and pet the dog's nape twice before covering his ears with both of his hands.

Moments later the craft settled, kicking up the top layer of January snow as it did. The pilots reduced the throttle, and the enormous engines and blades took almost five minutes to wind themselves down to a stop. This allowed the aircrew to exit and conduct a wheel chocking and a few other post-flight checks. Once completed, they allowed their passengers to disembark. Rusty stayed at Lou's left leg, a behavior he was forced to learn because of the cane Lou used. The heel was still recovering from the gunshot and surgery. They followed the crowd down the stern ramp and south toward the main road. A motorcoach was waiting, as were those folks and their baggage who were taking the same helicopter back to Camp David. It was the final stage in a chaotic two days of travel to four different bases for the pair. On any given day, Lou could've made the drive from Elkton to the nearby town of Pen Mar, Maryland in less than three hours. *But only the invited get to come here,* he knew.

Built in the early 1950s, the Cold War complex known as Site R— Raven Rock—was one of three military complexes for the emergency preservation of government publicly acknowledged by Washington. Along with NORAD at Cheyenne Mountain, Colorado and the Mount Weather Emergency Operations Center in Virginia, Raven Rock had become a sort of Yeti in movies, novels, and pop culture. While visions of vast underground cities danced in people's heads, the truth was less exciting—though still an impressive feat of engineering.

Site R had four large tunnels, or 'portals', that full-sized trucks could drive into to reach the center of the underground complex. They all eventually converged on a small key hub, comprising a few roads full of several interior buildings, most two to three stories tall, and all built on giant shock absorbing mounts meant to defend against the detonation of nuclear bombs on the mountain above. There were two power generating stations and two water reservoirs—one for drinking, and a much larger one for industrial use. All of this centered exactly under the antennas on top of the mountain.

"Good to see you, Colonel," Lou's former boss, Ryan Jackson, said. "I take it you were out of the Pentagon when they hit?" The Marine colonel had relinquished command of the recently stood up Rampart Edge program to Lou and had just started to take some personal leave with his family. Jackson had been one of the dominos to fall in the political aftermath of the Joint Chief sending planes and helicopters into Mexico pre-maturely as part of Operation Venom Spear. But despite that, General Judah Montgomery and his aides that took the metaphorical axe were still held in high regard by the Allen administration.

"It was a fluke," Lou said. "I was taking him to see my niece," he added with a nod toward Rusty.

Ryan Jackson took custody of Lou's two bags, leaving him to carry just his briefcase. The pair moved toward the crowds passing each other at the bus's entrance. "Sometimes we just don't know why God works the way he does," he admitted. "Just look at you," he joked with just the slightest of smirks. Ryan had never hidden his contempt for Lou, failing to understand why General Montgomery had been sponsoring the alcoholic wreck. But Lou had proven his tenacity and commitment, and Ryan was slowly coming around to him.

Lou took the slight jab off the chin not with retort but reflection. "I'm still not sure God exists, Colonel, but with all I've been through— you're right. It does make me think I've been helped along for a reason..." He decided to change the subject. "I'm dying for some information—and some sleep. Any idea what's going on with these attacks?"

Colonel Jackson glanced at his G-Shock watch. "We're headed straight for Monty's office," he said as he tossed Lou's bags into the under-coach storage and moved into line behind those boarding. "He's got plans for you two," he said as he looked down at Rusty. "Just be patient."

Six-tenths of a mile down the road and several hundred yards into the mountain, Lou found himself staring at a set of stairs leading up the outside of a three-story dorm building. *So frickin'* weird, he thought, trying to look past the building's roof to see the manmade cavern. There were just too many lights causing a glare. It was an odd sensation of being in a perpetually dark and never-ending night. *NCO Barracks – Second Floor. Officer's Barracks – Third Floor,* he read. *Are you kidding me?*

"Sorry, sir. Your dog needs to report to the kennels," an MP walking down the stairs said as he stepped onto the main floor.

"He's not a working dog. He's a service animal," Lou explained.

"I... don't think that matters..." the Air Force sergeant said, unsure of himself.

"It's okay, Sergeant," Ryan explained. "If your CO has a problem, just tell him to call Colonel Jackson.

The sergeant knew he would not win against two full-bird colonels. "Roger that, sir," he said as he started to leave.

"Uh, sergeant," Ryan added. "Could you do us a solid and take the colonel's bags up to the barracks? We're on the way to a meeting." All three knew it wasn't a question.

The look on his face says it all, Lou thought as he watched Ryan transfer custody of the bags. *He's safe here, but will the price of admission be to be the officers' errand boy all the time?* "Thanks," Lou told the enlisted man.

Two 'blocks' over, the pair and the dog walked into a first-floor office. It gave the appearance of most standard American offices, minus the decorations. It had desks, computers, chairs, and fake paneling on the walls. *Fake plant,* Lou noted as he looked around. *Pictures of helicopters and aircraft carriers on the walls. Pretty typical.* Gone were the personal touches that one might decorate their permanent cubicle with—family photos, Keurig machines, little rubber duck collections...

The floor was two-foot-square panels, a false floor that covered miles of fiber-optics and other services and fire extinguishing systems. The room had over two dozen cubicles, the short kind that barely covered the height of the computer monitors. There was a slim aisle between the two rows. As Ryan led Lou and Rusty down the center toward the room at the far end, Lou's cane made an odd hollow clunk on the false floor. Ryan scanned his access badge at the RFID reader next to the door.

"Lou!" an exhausted looking General Judah Montgomery said upon seeing the pair enter. Unlike his plush office in the now-rubble Pentagon, the generals and admirals that had made it to Site R were sharing a space much like the one Lou had just walked through. The key difference was the giant screens on the far wall. Past the various desks, several chairs had been arranged in front of a bank of monitors. There was a tense hubbub of activity in every corner of both offices, but nothing cued up on the main giant screen at that moment. By the time Lou was done scanning the space, the general had made his way over. "So glad to see you, son," he told Lou warmly.

"Likewise, sir. Colonel Jackson and I were just discussing how fortuitous it seems that we were all out of the Pentagon."

Judah led the pair over to his desk and pointed them to a pair of chairs to drag over. "Well, some of us made it out of the Pentagon thanks to an early warning from the intel agencies," he admitted.

And yet, they couldn't give the citizens a moment's notice, was Lou's first cynical thought. "And continuity, sir?" Lou asked, wondering about the state of the government.

"The Allen administration, a large portion of Congress, four of the Supreme Court Justices... All safe and sound, spread out amongst five sites in five states. And technically, I'm still the Joint Chief since Congress had not yet confirmed my replacement—whose helicopter crashed from being hacked, by the way." Judah looked at a bank of clocks on one of the walls, representing several time zones around the world. "I'm sorry to be curt, Lou. But... what of Rampart Edge?"

"I had a good piece of it with me here in my briefcase when all this went down, sir," Lou answered. "I'm sure it's still in the servers, too, right?" he asked as he looked at Ryan for a quick glance.

The general shook his head. "A lot of our middle-grade data was compromised or flat out deleted by their hackers. Not to mention the destruction of servers and satellites. But you're saying you have some idea of the status? Who has been deployed where? Civilians we've vetted? That kind of thing?"

"Yes, General," Lou said, a look of confusion crossing his face.

"Good... good..." Judah said, his eyes lost in thought for a moment. "I'll be making some calls and decisions about what to do with that tonight. Get some rest and meet me here at zero-five-hundred tomorrow morning. Is there anything you need?" he asked, looking down and letting a patient, lying Rusty sniff the back of his hand.

Lou looked down. "Maybe a come and go pass for him from the kennel and dog handlers," he admitted. "But really what I'm missing out on, sir, is—what the hell happened?" he asked in earnest. "Are they insane?" He held up his work-issued smartphone. "This thing quit working this morning, and it wasn't the battery."

Judah took a deep breath and asked Ryan with just a look.

"I figured you'd want to tell him, sir," the other colonel said in reply to the raised brow.

"Last night the power grid went down everywhere. All three of them, including Texas. It wasn't an EMP—we figured they're using trojans and AI so that the physical infrastructure remains intact."

"Well, that's something, sir," Lou said. "If they turned it off, we could turn it back on, right?"

"Once we take out their hacking centers, yes," Judah said. "But they have several of them, and Allen is trying his level best to not use nukes. And as you know, we lost a large portion of bombers and fighters to the same hackers!" The general reached for a cold coffee and took a swig. "The U.S. Government still exists," he continued. "We and our allies all faced multiple attacks. Key bases and command centers were targeted with space-based kinetic bombs. The 'rods from God' we've all heard about? Plus MAHEM."

"Yes, I saw that in the emergency alert," Lou admitted. "MAHEM?"

"Magneto hydrodynamic explosive munitions," Judah said. "Hacking to take over and crash aircraft and ships. Satellite-based missiles that took out our missiles. And two very large invasion fleets headed our way, augmented by the ships and planes they took intact from Russia, whose economy has been crashed, by the way. Trillions of dollars and crypto have disappeared. And the United Nations did an overnight evacuation out of New York. They're headed to The Hague in the Netherlands."

"No big loss there, sir," Lou quipped. He stood up and gave Rusty a slight pull on the leash to get him to stand up. "I'm sure you have plenty to do, and I'll hear plenty more in the barracks. And thank you for getting me approval to come out. It's like the wild west out there." He turned to leave.

"How's the, uhhh... leg, Lou?" Judah asked.

He means my drinking, Lou knew. "Fine, sir. I still struggle in my head... but all I have to do is think about that man who died saving me from being beaten to death..." His face started to cover itself in shame and remorse.

"Good to hear," the general said. "We're drastically short of pilots. I expect you'll be brushing your wings off, soon."

USS LYNDON B. JOHNSON DDG 1002
  Canadian Forces Base Esquimalt

. . .

"THE IRONY, HUH, CAPTAIN," COMMANDER AGWE BAILEY SAID with his usual grin, interrupting the Navy captain's quiet contemplation. The pair and others were watching a crane swap out one of the two large barrels out of its box mount. One near the long skinny ship's bow was to remain as constructed. The one closer to the bridge and ship's primary structure was being replaced to align with plans abandoned years earlier.

"Military intelligence," the short redhead said with a smirk. She, her XO, and Shipyard Commanding Officer Captain Marie Darnell were watching the action from the comfort of the high-tech bridge. The row of windows low in the ship's main superstructure was one of the few traditional features on the unique combat platform, tattling to those that would care exactly where important people might stand. Though a long, slender, and tall ship, most of the surfaces were far smoother than her counterparts. This gave the ship an extreme advantage, called a 'multiplier', in terms of radar cross section. The three Zumwalt class destroyers had also been designed with floodable ballast tanks, not unlike a submarine. This allowed the ship to increase her draft during combat, which was the amount of her under the waterline, thereby improving the already impressive stealthiness.

Both Marie and Agwe snickered at the age-old joke. Marie's team wasn't just in Canada to work on the secretive El Paso. Her skilled machinists were there to supervise their Canadian peers on the important combat and communications upgrades to both surface ships and all three submarines. Equipment—and in the LBJ's case, specialized munitions—had been brought from the United States to Canada over the preceding several days.

When LBJ's two sister ships had been constructed, the Navy had installed the AGS, or Advanced Gun System, a 155-millimeter cannon that fired rocket-propelled rounds. But with LBJ, the intention had been to convert the box mounts to a more high-tech railgun. In typical military fashion, both programs were scrapped for cost after commitments had already been made. While the two older ships were complimented to use the existing stock of shells, LBJ's railgun mounts had been retrofitted to fire smaller 127-millimeter hypervelocity projectiles. On that day, the forward mount would remain the same, and as much of the ammunition for it that would fit was being transferred from the aft mount's magazine. The aft mount, located just forward of the bridge structure, was being converted back to the railgun. Though the program had been scrapped, almost 200 of the one-million-dollar tungsten and titanium slugs had been constructed and purchased.

Unlike traditional cannons, which required an immense chemical reaction to explode the shell out of the barrel, the railgun was designed to shoot slugs at speeds of near Mach 7 using only electromagnetic energy. And it would take a lot, so the engine rooms were beefed up with two Rolls Royce gas turbine and generator sets capable of putting out seventy-eight megawatts. The high-speed slugs could travel with deadly velocity and accuracy on a much lower angle of trajectory, giving it the ability to shoot targets hundreds of miles before those targets could shoot back. The ship also had vertical missile launchers built into the decks along the sides of the ships both fore and aft. She was carrying a mix of several dozen Tomahawk cruise missiles, along with some rocket launched torpedoes and smaller self-defense Sea Sparrow missiles.

"I think if this longshot plan actually works, we're going to be extremely glad we have this railgun," Agwe said, his smile fading a bit as his face reflected his concern for their survival. "I just wish we could know for sure it works."

"Me too, Commander," Millie admitted. "I just don't think we can chance the Chinese or Russians finding out about this upgrade. And I think wasting even one shell would be something we would egret once we're in battle."

"I could find a couple of our mechanics to volunteer to go with you," Millie offered. "A large percentage of my workforce are Navy vets. They wouldn't be a detriment to your crew."

"Thank you, Captain," Marie said, looking at her accomplished equal. "But we already have several dozen extra sailors we picked up from life rafts. It's a bit crowded."

"They're not going back to San Diego?" Marie inquired with a slightly puzzled look.

"Norfolk, actually," Millie corrected. "With the loss of three carriers here in the Pacific, some are going to Norfolk. A few back to San Diego. And those with injuries are staying here in Canada. But with the attacks on D.C. and the fleet HQ, I think that these sailors have been forgotten about..." After a pause to think, Millie added, "And that's okay. I've chatted with them. Most of them are ready to dish out some payback. I want them around to remind my own crew what's at stake on this suicide run."

CHAPTER 8

KAREN AND DANIEL DISMOUNTED THEIR HORSES AFTER THE climb up the trail to the west observation post to give the animals a breather. The ranch's second quad—the one wrecked by Tracy—was in the ranch's maintenance building. Someone from the Army promised they would send a transportation operator, also known as an 88 Mike, to see if they could repair or fabricate the tie rod parts needed to get the rig moving again. The sole working quad was being used by the oncoming and off-going watch stander. The ranch's three axle utility vehicle wouldn't round the sharp corners on some switchbacks and needed to go a couple of miles around a large hill to get up to the post. Pedro del Sur was looking west with his binoculars as the quiet pair walked the last hundred yards.

"Tell us again from the top," Karen said. "The radio signal was horrible."

"A large plume of dust, like from a vehicle, caught my attention," Pedro explained as both Karen and Daniel started using their own binocs. "Look northwest, down the edge of that mountain's north slope. See where that deep crag kind of looks like a nose? Now move your eyes straight north from there until you're looking at the flat desert. There's an old road and gate on the DNR property."

"I got it," Daniel announced.

Karen was still not seeing it. "Not yet, but what'd you see?"

"A truck. Not a semi. Not a pickup. Something in between, like a work truck. But it was hauling a trailer."

All three of them lowered their spectacles and exchanged glances. "I suppose we should ride over and check it out," Karen said.

"Without a doubt," Daniel said.

I wonder if he doesn't even realize he sounds arrogant, Karen thought. *Maybe it's just that simple.* "Thanks, Pedro. Keep an eye on us. Not sure what's happening with these cheap radios, but I expect we won't be able to get the CP, even with the repeater."

"Maybe the MCV is sending jamming signals," Pedro suggested. That's what the chatter on the HAM bands had taken to call the Mexico-China-Venezuela coalition amassing on the border.

"We'd know if that was the case," Daniel said.

Karen and Daniel made their departure, heading north to the top of the trail they'd just come up. They passed it and found themselves on a continuation of the quad trail that made a slow descent to the north-west. Forty minutes of forced small talk later—they were both trying to 'get along', after all—they were approaching the gate through the lowland sage and cactus. "OP, this is Martin Riggs," Daniel called into his radio. "Comms check." Like everyone else, Daniel had selected a handle for himself on the air.

"I hear, ya," came a relatively clear Pedro. "You guys are scratchy at best."

"Copy. We're approaching the objective. Cover us," Daniel replied.

The pair slowed the horses and dismounted. *Martin Riggs? Comms check?* Karen mocked Daniel in her head. *Objective?* As much as she found Daniel detestable, in her mind she knew she was lagging in things like how to properly conduct a security check or use the radio.

Snap out of it, Kirkland, she scolded herself. *You're better than this— and him. Regain some control.*

Karen handed Daniel the reins to her horse. "Cover me while I check it out."

"Yes, Ma'am," came the overly polite reply and salesman grin.

Daniel unslung the AR platform rifle that was on his back and moved it to his front. Karen's had been on the front the entire time, the adjustable sling cinched up as tightly to her bosom as it would go. She looked all around, including behind where she saw Daniel scouting out the horizon with his binocs. *I should've thought of that,* she admitted to herself. *He knows how to do this stuff. I'll give him that.*

She moved around the gate and surrounding area, finding that the entire metal box-cover for containing the heavy recessed padlock had been cut off with a torch. There were a variety of tire tracks and a few old crusty cow patties. She moved back to her partner. "I think someone has been out here trying to steal cattle. Or at least scout that possibility. I'll cover you while you check it out," she said. "You're good at this stuff—you might see something I missed."

"Holy cow! A compliment?" he said, smiling.

"I see what you did there, Daniel," she said, forcing a smile back. "Don't be too long. I think I figured out where these caves we're supposed to go look for are."

Daniel came to the same conclusion as Karen. They agreed their isolation out in the wilderness meant trying to track a rig without backup wasn't a good idea. Daniel called the information to Pedro at Karen's request. He also let the overwatch know that they were moving west around the foot of the next mountain to scout the caves. They rode for another half-hour, passing into the next small valley. They'd been gaining elevation, though in passing by the next slope west were still in a bad position for radio traffic.

"I think I see the cavern," Karen called back to Daniel, whose horse was about five lengths behind. She headed up the slope to the south-east a bit and rounded a big mesquite tree that partially obscured the entrance. Karen looked around before dismounting. The rocky outcroppings peaked both on the east and west with the valley they were in, moving south for a few hundred yards before veering southeast where it rose and crested a depression, called a 'saddle', in the horizon. *I bet we can go that way and be west of the south pasture that the Army is using,* Karen thought. There were signs of rockslides in several spots, something that concerned her. She heard Daniel's horse finally round the mesquite.

"That's a decent sized opening," he said. "Let's go have a look."

They tied the horses to a mesquite branch and walked the last ten yards up. The mouth was more of an overhang, the desert floor extending under for several yards before the walls finally choked closed. Other than a slight descent of less than three feet, the cavern was relatively flat. It was narrow for several feet before opening up. Daniel pulled a pocket flashlight out and started to adjust it to the brightest setting when he fumbled and dropped it. It settled in a small crag close to where Karen was standing. They both reached for it.

"I'll get it," she said as her hand picked up the small device. Daniel stumbled in the dark as he was stooping and reaching and put his hand onto Karen's hip for balance, touching close to her rump. A jolt of alarm surged through the fit woman. *Oh, hell no!* she thought. "What the!"

"Sorry!" he said, sounding sincere as they both stood and regained balance and posture. "Seriously, I just tripped." Karen gave him a shocked look as she handed the flashlight back. He used its clip to mount it to the bill of his ball cap. "Wow, this really opens up!" he said, trying to change the subject.

Still keeping her peripheral vision on her travel partner, she glanced around, playing it casual as she fought the near overwhelming desire to run for the horse and bolt. "I think we need more people and bigger flashlights," she said. "But yes—we could definitively tell the others this is a place to move some of the food and supplies to. Let's go see about the outer defenses," she suggested. *I need the hell out of this cave.*

They retreated to the horses and looked around. "A new OP on one or both of these hilltops," he pointed. "And see where that saddle dips? We should put some foxholes above it on both sides."

Karen's mind drifted as 'Martin Riggs' continued to show off his tactical prowess. *Tracy, why'd you have to go and get hurt?* she wondered. *And how long until Granger gets back?*

GARDEN GROVE, CALIFORNIA

ALEX'S FACE WAS POURING SWEAT AS HE HAULED THE LAST two full sandbags from the older building's trapdoor roof access to the corner facing toward the major intersection of Brookhurst and Westminster seventy yards to the north. Several of the others were filling them from dirt along the edge of the parking area and moving them through the building to the access. Alex had opted to have Micah and the one other former 'street kid' in the group help him. They were establishing low walls on the two perimeter corners of all three of the motel's buildings. As the task wore on through the warm but overcast day, he was starting to regret his choice of workmates. Both had a vested interest in moving more slowly than their leader.

"C'mon, guys," he pled. "I'm in my thirties. You two should be smoking me in these laps! Less rapping and more moving."

The pair ignored him and continued to chat as they carried but one sandbag at a time. It was obvious to Alex that Micah had the hots for Sassy Sasha. A former street kid herself, Sasha was nineteen and two years older than her would-be suitor. The self-proclaimed 'beat-boxer' was beautiful enough to make most men and women take a second or third glance, even without the makeup, lashes, nails, and weaves that most young ladies in the greater Los Angeles area used to lure their 'prey'. Half black and half Vietnamese, she had been clean of her fentanyl addiction for seventeen months. And before the Chinese had knocked out the power grid entirely, she had fled her halfway house as soon as the rolling blackouts had grown from hours to days a few months earlier. She'd been staying with a cousin, but that option dissolved when they packed up to move to Nevada a few days earlier. *No more after her,* Alex had told Micah when asked to bring her in. *We can't house everyone here, you know.*

Alex let one of his sandbags fall and land on the torch-down asphalt roof and shoved the other in the middle spot of the fourth row. The fighting positions were behind the very low parapet walls on the older motel. Lucky Charm had instructed them to be as tall as a person squatting plus one row. The bag-wall was slowly adopting an elbow shape. He turned toward the lagging teens. "Seriously. If you two aren't going to pick up the pace, then you're not pulling your weight as far as I can tell..."

"Easy, dad!" Micah said with a smart tone.

"Naw, he's right," Sasha said. The handle 'Sassy' was a holdover from her drug days and one she used while promoting herself as a rapper. She was smart enough not to bite the hand feeding her. "Sorry, Al. We'll pick it up," she said as she placed her sandbag on the small wall. "Whoa..." she added with a sense of awe. "Looks like a zombie movie set..."

The trio were staring at two veins of foot traffic. Though Brookhurst Street's north-south flow was divided by a grass and palm tree strip, both sides were filled with foot traffic headed north. They all craned their necks past the tire shop next door and saw the flow blending in and heading east with a much larger horde. The fires and smoke that had become common to see coming from L.A. to the north-east seemed to have moved much closer.

"What the hell, yo!" Micah said. "Where they all think they goin'?" As he spoke, a fistfight broke out amongst four people at the intersection. After getting thrown to the ground, a man pulled out a small pistol and shot another. People began to run and scream.

"Get down!" Alex said instinctively, squatting and trying to pull the others down.

"Mannn—why you trippin'?" Micah asked, yanking his arm back from Alex. But once he saw Sasha get down to one knee and crouch, he followed suit.

Alex smirked when he saw that. "It's a matter of time before that violence comes here to the inn," he explained. "Again." The sound of automatic rifle fire reverberated from another fight to the west to drive home his point.

"Friendlies incoming," they all heard Lauren say on the small family radio clipped to Alex's pants. So far, their Army trainer, Lucky Charm, hadn't had any luck providing his potential insurgents with radios. Micah had managed to trade off a recurve longbow one of the others had provided for a set of four radios at a street market. Every hour, everyone knew to add three clicks to whatever channel they were on and move up. The next day they would go down four every hour. There was no way to have secure comms, but it was hoped that the small effort of having to hunt for their conversations on moving channels would deter the lazier criminals.

"Yeah, we see 'em," Alex responded. They watched the crowd barely part as a convoy of three military vehicles turned left from Westminster and head toward them, right past the still bleeding victim in the street. The presence of the belt-fed machine guns on top of the leading and trailing HumVees was enough to keep the vast majority of travelers moving along. The convoy stopped in front of the hotel, and half of the residents along with Lucky Charm exited the rear of three Stryker vehicles and headed under the cover over the access driveway. "Let's get going," Alex advised as he stood and picked up the other sandbag he'd carried over. A book slipped out of his back pocket and hit the roof.

"What's dis?" Micah asked, picking it up. "Gu-ey... Gwayyy..." he struggled to read the title.

"Guerrilla," Sasha said nicely to her friend. "Say it like the animal."

"U.S. Army Gorilla Warfare Handbook," Micah slowly drawled. "What's this?" he asked again.

"Something Lucky Charm advised I read," Alex said. "Something we should all read."

Micah handed the book to Sasha to look over. "I'm just glad there be pictures in it. I don't read good," he explained.

Sasha flipped through it. "What's it for? Why's dude even here?" she asked.

Alex started leading them toward the access hatch. "To teach us how to defend ourselves, I guess." *I don't really want to explain to these kids what an insurrection is,* he decided. *Or who we're supposed to insurge against.* He moved along quickly, not caring if they kept up. "Coming down!" he yelled into the hole. He descended the ladder into the janitorial closet on the third floor and bypassed two people that had been roping up the sandbags from the parking lot. The small manager stepped out onto the covered exterior walkway and saw the group filtering into the parking area inside the perimeter formed by the buildings and fence. Alex made his way down the stairs and caught up to Lucky Charm as he was heading into the motel's meeting room-turned-command-post.

"How'd it go?" Patrick McBrogan asked. "Anything happen while I was gone?"

"Another shooting out on the street," Alex said. "Nothing happened here directly. How'd your trip go?" The soldier had secured transport and took half of the 15th Street Posse to go sight-in the rifles he'd provided them.

"We got them dialed in, but I don't think we're going to be able to score another trip. It's getting too hairy out there."

Alex felt like Lucky had stopped himself short of saying everything he wanted to, but he didn't press the matter. "What about supplies?" he asked earnestly.

"Well, just by us driving up we've made this place somewhat of a target," Lucky said. "We'd definitely be on everyone's radar if we started unloading boxes and boxes of food. I'm still working on the logistics," was all he said.

What's he not telling me? Alex wondered.

USS James L. Hunnicutt SSGN-93
   Canadian Forces Base Esquimalt

The conning tower of America's premiere spy submarine had the usual crowding associated with leaving port and preparing for sea. Sailors in foul weather gear were poking out of the rectangular hole like misaligned toothpicks out of the top of their box. Some were in fall protection harnesses, sitting up on the 'sail' structure itself, using binoculars to scan the distance. This wasn't for enemy threats, per se, though that was certainly a possibility. Their task was to watch for navigational issues, whether a pleasure craft, a commercial fishing boat, or simply a giant log to be avoided. Several of the electronic radars and antennas were elevated, doing their jobs. At that moment, though, the sub was 'dead-in-the-water.'

Executive Officer Carla Gingery had control of the submarine's conning tower, keeping the sub as still as possible during the intricate evolution. On deck back aft, Chief-of-the-Boat Darren Jorgensen and Commanding Officer Brody Woodward were overseeing a slew of sailors doing the normal departure process—stowing the poles and fiberglass rope used for the topside lifeline, stowing the ships mooring lines, and performing last minute checks. A CO wouldn't normally be out there. But it was the tugboat activity behind the ship that had captivated everyone's attention.

"How do you think we're going to handle, hauling the El Paso behind us?" Darren asked his skipper.

"Like a wounded pig, COB," Brody admitted. "What concerns me most is when we stop. What happens if the SEALs don't get it disconnected in time?"

"Aye, sir. I've been pondering that question myself."

The shipyard in Pearl Harbor had welded two very hefty towing rings to the stern, one each on the outboard side of the vertical stabilizers. Those were the structures that provided a stabilizing force on the outer edge of the ship's rear dive planes. Where the rudder steered the ship port or starboard, the fixed vertical stabilizers helped keep the ship from wanting to spin under the torque of the propulsor. The modern shrouded submarine propellers were more akin to a modern jet turbine—they didn't twist the ship along its center axis nearly as much as their predecessors. But the vertical stabilizers also provided the housing for the sub's towed sonar array and trailing antennas to clear the propulsor as far out from the ship as possible, greatly reducing the possibility of them entangling. The tugboats and divers were attaching the tow cables to the connection points on the Hunny while two other tugs held the El Paso in place. The EP, as the crew had taken to calling their wounded sister, was being held afloat by a series of buoys that would be remotely disconnected when it was time to dive, as were the heavy lines connecting the two vessels.

"What time is your briefing to the crew, sir?" Darren asked.

"Within an hour of diving, COB. This crew has been tense enough as it is. I want them to understand why the timing of this monkey-and-football exercise is so critical."

Darren took a glance south once more. *I wonder if we would be able to see home if we were tall, like a ferry or carrier? It would've been nice to see her one last time.*

CHAPTER 9

ACME RANCH
    Southeast of Tucson, Arizona

EARLY THE NEXT MORNING, KAREN LET THE QUAD DRIFT UP the trail toward the ranch house. She eased off the throttle and took in two contrasting scenes. The orange of the morning sun reminded her of calmer, more peaceful days when she and some of her CrossFit clients would drag the equipment to the park next to the shop and do group workout circuits in the growing dawn. *I need to start running and working out,* she told herself. *I always feel more confident when I've killed a fitness challenge.*

The other sight was the up-before-dawn Army, moving actively in the south and east fields. She saw a virtual city of tents, modular portable buildings, and shipping containers spring up. On the hill a mile or so south of their own LP/OP was a mobile truck radar, part of the Integrated Air and Missile Defense System. The Army had been working for close to twenty years to replace the aging Patriot missiles, slowed by politics and lack of funding. And though most of the batteries located in the valley at the ranch's southern boundary were the aged but reliable Patriots, the National Guard had received a few active Army technicians and two box launchers full of the experimental replacement missiles.

Also on that hill was a growing collection of radio antennas. *It's looking like we've already been invaded,* Karen quipped to herself. Not that she'd ever wanted to live in a commune, but up until the Army had shown up it had been quite lovely and peaceful at the bug out location—*aside from the jerk,* she reminded herself. And though the rapidly decaying behavior of society at large, such as the trip to the hospital, reminded her of a number of zombie and post-apocalypse movies she'd watched on streaming services, the reality was far different. The presence of the Army and the space attacks on the American ships and bases were horrifying milestones—*there really is an invasion getting ready to happen.* At a few hundred yards away, she wasn't hearing most of the morning activity of the Army, but rather the ranch house's main generator. They were running it and shutting it down in cycles to save fuel, mainly for freezers, charging batteries, and attempting to use the internet.

She throttled up once more, heading up the trail toward the main house, noticing several folks including a soldier out by the pool as she rounded the large structure. Parking at the garage, she shut down the engine. "Morning, Bob," she said to the radio operator, who had one of the car bay doors opened to get some fresh air. "How's Claude?" She'd needed time to think, unable to sleep after the weird event with Daniel in the cave. She'd just spent the entire night on watch at the OP as a way of avoiding the bunkhouse—and dealing with her insecurity.

"Same ol' gruffy mule," he quipped about his friend and fellow Road Runner. Bob was flipping through the manuals for some new digital handheld radios the Army had given their hosts. Though the Road Runners had been using Bluetooth antennas and apps such as ATAK to text each other in the field, they had not made the time to upgrade the ranch's communications other than with the stuff they had brought with them.

"I'll go see him in a bit," Karen said. "What's happening out at the pool?" she asked as she plugged her radio into one of the several docking ports. *Might as well get it charged while the generator is running.*

Bob stood and stared at her blankly, thinking. "Oh—a water class. Filtering, sanitation—that sort of thing. I pointed out to Donna that we will not be wasting fuel running the pool filters, so she may as well use the pool for drinking water."

"Oh," Karen said. "Makes sense." She moved back out of the garage, opting to travel around the house. She could see Donna and her two oldest kids, along with the Bowers and the Washingtons, listening to a soldier lecture on making bleach. As she approached, she thought she saw Pam Bowers' face turn to stone. *Did I just imagine that? What'd I do to you? It's just your insecurity, Kirkland,* she chastised in her mind. *It's not always about you.*

"... so, really it just becomes a math problem at that point," the young female soldier was saying. "Since this pouch of pool shock is only fifty-six percent calcium hypochlorite instead of seventy, you add more."

"How do you know how much?" thirteen-year-old Kaitlin Wolf asked.

The soldier smiled at the young lady. "We divide the small number by the big number to find out the percentage. In this case, our pool shock is only eighty percent of what the ratio we're working with is. So instead of the eight tablespoons we would use, we'll use ten tablespoons."

"And this makes bleach?" Jerome said with a slight laugh. "I mean —what the hell is 'other'?" he asked as he stared at the ingredients on the packet he was holding.

The soldier laughed. "The ten tablespoons in a gallon will make roughly six percent household bleach," she said. "Once you've made the solution you can use it to treat a larger volume of water with the bleach ratios we discussed earlier. And the other ingredients are sedimentary and will settle. The only thing I advise is to make sure you're not using shock with perfumes and clarifiers added."

Sounds like I missed an excellent class, Karen thought. She didn't want to disrupt their group dynamic, so she headed toward the sliding patio door. *I'll go see how Uncle Claude is doing.* After opening and entering, she gave one last glance at the group by the pool as she closed the door. Both Fred and Pam Bowers were staring at her with Pam's hand to Fred's ear, covering her mouth as she spoke.

USS Lyndon B. Johnson DDG-1002

"Martinez! Hold up!" Carmen heard as she was transiting through the ship's mess decks. She recognized the voice of a friend from the USS Halsey before she even turned.

"What's up, Cobra?" she said somewhat seriously. Like everyone the LBJ crew had saved from the ocean after the carrier's tragic sinking, neither of them were in a place emotionally to even fake being in a good mood. While grateful to be alive, the carrier sailors that hadn't been given orders to Norfolk or San Diego while in Canada were not happy to be back at sea. For Carmen, it was just one more knock in life added to the growing chip on her shoulder. *First the earthquake and volcano! Now this! What's a girl gotta do to get home!* She thought every night as she tried to catch a few hours of sleep in a borrowed bunk. One of her more religious shipmates on her new crew had made the mistake of asking Carmen if they could pray together. *God?* She screamed incredulously before filling the air with a typically colorful sailor monologue. *What kind of cabron God would allow this stuff to happen to people?!* What little faith Carmen might've learned from her hard-working Huntington Park mother had long dissolved.

"You working with the damage control division here, yet?" Jimmy Jiang Feng asked. A Master-at-Arms by training, Carmen had started taking Jimmy's Brazilian Jiu Jitsu classes several weeks earlier. Between that training and a renewed dedication to fitness, Carmen was trying to ensure that the next slimeball biker who tried to rape her was going to have to fight for his life instead. Out of all the carrier survivors onboard LBJ, Jimmy and a fellow damage control specialist were the only two Carmen truly knew and liked.

"This morning," she said. "I'm still pissed that they wouldn't send me home. But I can't sit around the mess decks and stew about it, or I'll go loco."

"I get it," Jimmy nodded. "Listen, I'm going to start classes again. This ship has a couple of grapplers, but no true BJJ instructors. I'll be in the cop-shop. Come by after afternoon quarters," he said as he turned to head aft.

"Where's it at?" Carmen called after him.

"This way," Jimmy said without even turning. "It ain't the carrier!" he half-joked. "You can't walk very long without running out of ship!"

Ain't that the truth, Carmen thought. The long skinny destroyer cut through waves like a champ when facing them head-on, which was hardly ever. The side-to-side rocking and the bow rising and plunging in the open ocean were much rougher than the carrier sailors were accustomed to. *Getting my sea legs after leaving port takes like a full day.* She continued forward up the starboard side passageway until she found the correct side passage. She followed a newly learned path through a hatch, down a ship's ladder, and ultimately toward the center into a space called Damage Control Central.

She entered the space and waited for a chief petty officer and a first-class petty officer to quit speaking. Once she'd caught sight that Carmen had arrived, Chief Amber Jazuk finished up her instruction to the person she was directing. She sported a ship's ball cap that was identical to the standard uniform cap in all ways but one—its bright red color made sure everyone who was talking to her knew she was the ship's fire marshal. "Alright, Martinez. All done at Personnel?"

"Yes, Chief. It's a little hard for them since we couldn't exactly get our records as we abandoned ship."

"Yeah... about that..." Chief Jazuk said before looking at the peer she'd been talking to. "Jeff, I'll be back in ten. Walk with me," she ordered Carmen. The two women started heading back up to the main deck the way Carmen had just traveled. "I need to go check a hot work permit," she explained. "Listen—I can't even begin to imagine what you women and men endured," she led in with her New Hampshire twang. "But I've got bad vibes," she confessed. "This war—this mission... whatever lessons-learned you have for damage control and abandoning ship, I'd like to hear them. That okay with you?"

"I—I guess, Chief. I don't really feel like there's anything to say..."

"There is, Carmen. I'll prep some questions. I can't expect you're just gonna sing like a canary, you know what I'm sayin'?" she said with a slight laugh. The pair were almost to the helicopter hangar. "But if you think of anything—anything—" she repeated in emphasis. "—Let me know."

"There is one thing," Carmen admitted. "This morning after quarters... I don't know their names. The tall skinny white dude, and the shorter Latino guy..."

"I know who you're talking about," the Chief admitted. "Campbell and Sopa. They're basically two halves of the same mentally challenged brain. Everyone calls them Soup 1 and Soup 2. What about 'em?"

"I hate to sound like a snitch. But they pissed me off pretty good..."

"Go on, Carmen. If it's nothing, you wouldn't have brought it up."

"Jokes," Carmen said. "Not any one thing in particular. Nothing bad. Nothing even really against those guys." She started to clam up. "I don't know, Chief... forget I said anything."

"Sorry, Martinez," Chief Jazuk said as she scanned the welding paperwork in her folder for a job in the hangar bay. They were welding what essentially looked like a set of shark cages to the one corner that would fit them. "You ain't gettin' off that easy." The grizzled NCO said. "Spit it out."

"It's the attitude," Carmen said. "It makes me wanna bust them in the mouth. They act like they're going to the mall later. My ship literally cracked open from battle damage and exploding magazines after that wave hit us. We had huge fires and flooding beyond what anyone on this ship can imagine. I had friends—" Carmen cut herself off as she detected her voice rising in a mixture of anger, fear, and sorrow. She had developed a tight bond with her friend RaeLynn, and the sight of seeing her fall back into the sinking ship would forever haunt her nightmares.

Chief Jazuk just looked at her newest team member for a moment in silence. "Roger that, shipmate," she said in a little more subdued tone than she'd been using. "This is exactly why you need to debrief the crew on what you went through."

89ᵀᴴ AIRLIFT RESERVE SQUADRON, WRIGHT-PATTERSON AIR Force Base
   Dayton, Ohio

"NO WAY!" THE AIR FORCE COLONEL, FACE NEARLY PURPLE, yelled at Lou. Rusty sensed the tension emitting from the man and let out a throaty growl, pulling on his leash, which Lou was keeping very short. The man glanced down at the dog and then back at Lou.

It's obvious he thinks his eagles will protect him from dog bites, Lou thought, regarding the man's rank insignia. "Look, Col—"

"Colonel..." he started, looking at the name placard on Lou's bomber jacket patch—"Caldwell. I don't know you from Adam. You can't just waltz in here and demand a jet. Especially," he growled with emphasis, "now! Every squadron on this base lost planes to the hacking before we were able to shut down all receivers that carried digital—wait a minute!" The angry man's face turned sour with realization. "I know you..."

Uh-oh, Lou realized.

"You're that Lieutenant Colonel that got grounded for being drunk!" The man looked at Lou's uniform in disbelief. "The one that was flying the Beast a couple... of..." He looked up at Lou, the anger still present, but taking a back seat to confusion and disbelief. "Not a chance." The man looked at the young first lieutenant who had been quietly observing from a standing position near her own desk in the squadron office. "Call security if he doesn't leave on his own, Lieutenant!" He started to turn.

As she acknowledged the order, Lou calmly said, "You won't want to be doing that, Lieutenant." He was already pulling a paper from his briefcase, made somewhat challenging because he did not want to lose any of the tight leash he was holding. The colonel spun on his heels, but Lou cut him off. "You're going to want to read this before you say another word, Colonel."

The angry officer snatched the letter from Judah Montgomery out of Lou's hand and started reading. His lips stopped mumbling. Lou watched the man start over and re-read the letter more thoroughly. Like most of the remaining U.S. military, he was fully aware of the quagmire of confusion that the attacks had caused. One thing he was clear on, though, was that Montgomery was still, in fact, the Chairman of the Joint Chiefs. He threw the letter back at Lou, spinning back toward his office. "Get him whatever he needs, Lieutenant," he ordered two seconds before his slamming door knocked an office photo of a C-17 off the wall.

Lou turned and saw the stunned look on the young lady's face. She looked at Lou, then Rusty, then Lou again. "I—I've never seen him get that mad before..."

"If you think that's bad, you should meet my wife," Lou joked. *Julia,* he instantly thought. *It's actually been three days since I thought about you.* He was a bit shocked at the sudden realization, wondering if it was from moving on emotionally, or just the tragic events of the war. *Maybe a bit of each,* he decided. "Would you mind holding Rusty, here, while I dig out some records?" he asked humbly.

"I thought you'd never ask!" the woman said. As a reservist, she had been forced to flee home for the military with little chance to mentally prepare for the dark reality ahead of them. "I have an Irish wolfhound at home that I miss so much!" she said. She took the dog around to her chair and started scratching behind his ears.

After Lou handed her the leash, he hobbled over to a padded chair on the other side of her desk and sat, pulling his briefcase up onto his lap. He looked at his dog, who was lapping up the attention. "You're just a whore, aren't you?" he joked at the dog. Rusty cocked his head for a second before lying at Angie's feet.

"When was the last time you Flew, sir?"

Lou flipped open a black binder and scanned his flight records. "Nineteen... almost twenty months," he answered her. "But I don't think these are normal times, Lieutenant..."

"Angie, sir. Knecht. Call sign Connect 4," she grinned. "And normally we'd make our reservists spend some time in the simulator, but the base is trying to conserve power, so those have been tagged out of service."

"I have..." Lou looked up, trying to scan memory, then looked at his logbook. "Well, I guess I could go and do some math... But about 4,400 hours in the Globemaster. I think I'll be fine."

Angie was busy typing up a set of orders for Lou. "Will you be needing one of our pilots to co- for you, sir?"

"You know, now that you mention it..." Lou hadn't been given much time to think about it. It had only been one day since he made it to Raven Rock, and here he was in Ohio suddenly flying again. Only this time, he was the pilot, and the missions would be directly supporting his special task group with Operation Rampart Edge. "I guess I will. But this isn't a simple hop. It will need to be someone who is open to constantly changing orders, ground missions in between flying..." *Getting shot at by the Mexican cartel.*

"Excuse me, Colonel? Did you say cartel?"

Lou felt his ears turn hot. "Huh?" *Did I?* His eyes grew a bit wider.

"Cartel, sir?" She couldn't tell if she was being punked.

"I—I'm sorry, Angie. I guess I was mumbling my inner monologue. Just ignore that," he said in embarrassment.

"And the loads, sir? Where will you be receiving? Deliveries? I may as well get some of the flight plans filled out for you..."

"Thank you, Angie. I'll be able to bypass some of the logged planning process based on who I work for and the need for security about what I'm doing," he informed her. "The drop-offs will vary." *And some will be airdrops,* he didn't add. "But I'll be heading to Pope first." She did not need to know that his cargo would be a bunch of Special Forces Green Berets. "Who is watching your dog, Angie? Husband and kids?"

"Oh, no sir!" she said with a smile. "My parents. They're near Richmond, Indiana. No spouse and kids."

"Why don't you be my wingman, then?" Lou asked. "You can't possibly be as annoying as my last one." *I wonder how the World's Grinniest Marine is doing.* He'd not been able to speak with Brandon McDonald, but Ryan Jackson vowed to help Lou recall Brandon and the others involved with their program from the West Coast as soon as they could locate and communicate securely with them.

"Me, sir? I—I'm like the most junior pilot in the squa—"

"Even better," Lou said. "I'm damn sick and tired of stuffy frat boys. First off, how many hours you got?"

"Barely a hundred, sir," she said. "Other than flight school and qualifying, I mean."

"Perfect! You'll be an expert in the Globe by the time we're done. And you can see my dog every day!"

That got the young brunette thinking. "I—I..."

"It's a done deal, Angie. You can type your name on the orders, or I can go get Colonel Pouty-Lips in there..."

The young pilot showed a pretty smile. "I suppose you'll want me to find us a loadmaster, too, sir!"

CHAPTER 10

ACME RANCH
Southeast of Tucson, Arizona

THE PATRIOT MISSILES LAUNCHING WERE SHOCKING, IF NOT anticlimactic. The batteries were too far away, and missiles too small, for it to be an earth-shaking experience in the main house. But the noise and the bright light of launching was enough to draw the attention of everyone on the ranch. Closer to the Army command post, alarms had sounded. An alert on their mobile PA system had warned them—*incoming missiles!*

The radar station on the southwest hilltop had detected the rapid accelerations and radar profiles of CJ-10 missiles being launched off of large mobile launchers a mere thirty-seven miles away. The surprise attack happened along the border almost simultaneously from California to Texas. The targets were exclusively airfields and anything with a surface-to-air missile battery.

Karen had been visiting Claude in one of the main house bedrooms when the noise and light from the launches caught her attention. "Wh

—what's happening?" she exclaimed in shock at the bedroom window. "Is it starting?" she asked, face fraught with fear.

"Come here, niece," Claude said, voice weaker than she was used to hearing, scratchy from days of light use and illness. Karen moved back over, having a hard time keeping her eyes off the window. She saw her uncle's open hand drifting slightly off the edge of the mattress. She put her hand into his. Tears began to fill her eyes. "They're still days away from invading," the old Vietnam veteran told her through rapid shallow breaths. "This is just testing the waters, so to speak. Seeing if they can catch the Army with their pants down. Getting in a few lucky hits is a bonus. What they're really doing is looking for holes in the radar coverage."

"What if one of theirs gets through here?" she worried. "How're we going to move you? Maybe we should start moving out to the cave we found..."

"In due time, dear," he said with a slight cough. The pale skin under his new gray beard—a by-product of water-rationing—stood out in the room. One candle danced in the corner, sending flickers of light and long shadows onto the walls. "Tell me what is bothering you. It's written all over your face."

"It's not important, uncle," she said with a forced smile, trying not to worry him with her inner fears. "You just need to get stronger and quit fretting over me!"

Loud distant booms, like thunder, reverberated through the walls and windows. "Sounds like they got 'em!" Claude said with mild jubilation. "If you don't want to talk about it, then at least bring me up to speed on the cattle thing..."

"Like I told you yesterday, Daniel and I found signs of possible cattle rustlers. Today, Brad and Donna were able to determine that at least fifty head are missing. Thing is... I think they think the cattle went missing last night—while I was on watch."

"You said you pulled a double-shift last night?"

"Yeah..."

He looked hesitant as he asked his next question. "Is... it... possible you fell asleep?"

Karen let out an enormous sigh. The worried look on her face amplified. "I don't think so. But I guess it could be possible. Plus, even with the NODs, it's nearly impossible to make out detail at that kind of distance at night."

"True, true..." her uncle concurred. "In the end, it just doesn't matter, Kare Bear," he said with reassurance, squeezing her hand.

"It's just—I... I just wish Granger and Tracy were here to deal with all this," she admitted with another sigh. "Nobody would be talking about them behind their backs!"

"And that's happening to you?" he asked, voice picking up in volume a bit.

"I don't know... Maybe."

"Karen, dear. I don't know most of these folks very well. They seem pretty solid—on the outside. But none of us can see a man's heart. I trust the Road Runners. I trust Donna. The rest? Time and their deeds will tell you more about their characters than their words ever will..." The sound of more explosions off in the distance caught the attention of both mentor and disciple. Both of them let their heads drift toward the window. "That'd be the debris impacting somewhere south of here," Claude said. "That's the unforgotten rule in combat—for every action there are both intended and unintended consequences. You have to be prepared for both." He reached up and pulled his niece's tear-streaked cheek and face, still aimed at the window, to look at him. "That's true for most of life's problems..."

USS JAMES L. HUNNICUTT SSGN-93

. . .

THE HUNNY HELD TWO KNOTS OF SPEED, THE BARE MINIMUM that Commanding Officer Brody Woodward insisted on for the unprecedented evolution. The last thing that he or the SEALs outside the sub needed was for the dead El Paso to drift into them. Forward momentum was a must, and though two knots was slow, the intricate piece of this part of the operation was going to take at least a couple of hours. The divers would effectively need to swim four nautical miles in open ocean to keep up with the subs while performing the tasks.

Chief-of-the-Boat Darren Jorgenson was in the Tactical Operations Center, watching them work on the submarine's external cameras. The vast majority of submarines did not keep cameras on the outside. Their missions just didn't require it. But this submarine had been designed to deploy divers—not just special operations forces, but technicians— along ocean floors for the installation and recovery of spy equipment. This occurred in foreign harbors, near enemy naval bases and other strategic locations. The average American would never believe the risks taken, and where, by the crews of intelligence gathering subs. And every president since the start of the Cold War prayed they weren't the politician on duty the day one of these subs was caught in the act.

It's bad enough we're towing this wounded pig, Darren thought. *But the proximity of the Illinois in all this ups the chance for Murphy to screw with us incredibly.* The Virginia class submarine was dangerously close to the Hunny's starboard side, trying to maintain the same two knots. The two subs were far faster than their older Los Angeles Class cousins. They had places to be as quickly as possible in the coming raid on the ocean-bound horde en route from China. And like the Hunny, the Illinois needed gear attached outside the sight of satellites. That left the SEALs, led by Lieutenant Cusimano and the visiting DEVGRU SEAL Commander Yanda, to perform the installs. They'd departed a full day ahead of the surface ships and the other two attack subs.

Darren saw the divers deflating the air bags that had been installed on the various pieces of cable and equipment for neutral buoyancy. Watching them wrap up caused a subconscious sigh of relief in the

TAC, not just by Darren, but from everyone in the tight room. The space reeked of Copenhagen, cold coffee, and body odor. Despite a good climate control system in most spaces on the sub, the multitude of computers and screens coupled with the stress of the previous couple of hours had led to more than one set of sweaty pits in the room.

"Just between me and you, COB," Lieutenant Commander Carla Gingrey said, "I'm more than happy that Illinois is taking on this part."

"Me, too, Ma'am," Darren agreed as he followed his XO back out of the space. With the other sub pulling away and the SEALs heading for the Lockout Chambers to enter the James L. Hunnicutt, the pair would be needed back in the sub's main control room. "I prefer a straight fight to all this sneakin' around," he said, wondering if he'd ever get to see his favorite movie again.

USS Lyndon B. Johnson DDG-1002

In the thirty-one hours since leaving Victoria and the Strait of Juan de Fuca, the USS Lyndon B. Johnson had been barreling at thirty knots on a south by southeast course. Traveling at her publicly known top speed left a little wiggle room in the tank for her actual classified max speed. And it was simple for her submarine companions to keep up—*Most of them,* Millie reminded herself. She'd even managed to catch four hours of sleep, once again having a foreboding dream of her disappearing husband. She chalked it up to the worry of the unknown. All but one of her children were adults and living their own lives in Virginia, where she'd spent the bulk of her career. Before she deployed in the Pacific several weeks earlier, her husband Don had taken their teenager back to his folks' place near Traverse City,

Michigan. Knowing they were deep into the upper Midwest brought Millie a small amount of comfort.

She sat in her captain's chair to the right of the state-of-the-art bridge, reading the mission package for an eighth time under the light of a dim red reading lamp attached to the bulkhead. She could see all of the eight forty-two-inch plasma screens that were displayed in a semicircular arch around the main bridge console. That console housed the chairs for two operators, surrounded by a bank of smaller displays, keyboards, and other controls. Unlike older Navy ships, this new design drove via joystick. Called "fly by wire," it was rapidly responding digital technology.

Millie stood and stretched a bit, switching off the red LED lamp and leaning toward a window. Cupping her eyes with her hands, she tried to look out at the ocean and night sky. Both were so black, there was no way of telling where one ended with the other's beginning. *Dear Lord, please keep the moon at bay for us. Please.*

"Captain to CIC," she heard her Operations Officer's voice say over a speaker mounted in the bridge's overhead. Millie gave up her scan for the horizon and departed the bridge, heading to the ship's combat brain.

"Got any news, Dennis?" she asked Lieutenant Commander Bates.

"Two submarines have signaled the fleet that two Chinese submerged contacts fit the profile of those that hijacked the Russians," he said. "Here." Dennis pointed at a horizontal touch screen that was built into the top of a belly-high counter. The area was a mere six-hundred-forty miles north-northwest of southern California.

"They're sure?" Millie asked. "Yuan class?"

"Yes, Ma'am. Report says the sound signatures match the ships in the intel package." Every submarine had its own unique characteristics that made it identifiable to a computer and highly trained sonar operator. Reactor plant cooling machinery, propellers, and the sounds of taking in or expelling water from the ballast tanks all played tattle-tell on a sub's identity. One primary mission of attack submarines was to tail and record other submarines to capture such data. They could then program the fleet computers to positively identify other submarines. And a major goal of navies was to make their own submarines so quiet that there were little of their own noises to be recorded in return.

Millie let out a sigh. *Dang it,* she thought. "I must admit, Commander—I was really hoping we could skip this part. I'll have the bridge plot us a course to approach this grid from due north."

"Shouldn't we slow down some, Ma'am?" he asked, confused. "Try to at least make them work to find us?"

"That's the real humdinger, Dennis," Millie said. "We want them to find us."

OVER SOUTHEAST KANSAS

"HOW MANY NIGHT LANDINGS HAVE YOU DONE?" LOU ASKED his co-pilot, Angie Knecht.

"Only three, si—I mean, Lou." She was having a difficult time relaxing with the first-name routine Lou insisted on when it was just the five of them. Though they hadn't yet painted their newly chosen aircraft name—*Lady Liberty*—on the fuselage, they had already started bonding as a team.

Besides the pilots, Lou had commandeered two enlisted personnel. Technical Sergeant Gray Saylors, age thirty, was the loadmaster. His responsibility was for calculating the fuel loadout and weight distribution of the load, which was plane, fuel and every thing or person inside. This included planning accordingly if they were to land on very short runways or even fields and deserts. The C-17 Globemaster III was a very capable aircraft, given the correct weight and fuel loads.

The fourth human member was Master Sergeant Travis White. At thirty-eight, he was nearing the end of his career, spent entirely as a mechanic. He was certified in many of the airframe and power mainte-nances that would, with Gray's help, keep the aircraft flying in between the much more extensive needs when they could park for several days. Not normally needed as part of the crew, Lou thought enticing a mechanic on short notice might not happen. But given a chance to go help distribute payback for the attacks was all he needed to mention. The fifth member of the team was Rusty. In the thirty hours they'd been together, they'd already flown to North Carolina and picked up two Special Forces 'A' Teams—twenty-four men—and a dozen pallets of equipment and supplies for each of them.

The destination for the first team was a small farm in a corner of The Sunflower State. Lou would get a chance to visit not one but two new-old friends, something he was stoked about. But more impor-tantly, there was a movement brewing there... Exactly the kind of drive and leadership they'd been looking for in the Rampart Edge program. The people he was visiting had each suffered a tremendous amount of loss during the preceding Venom Spear months. They, too, were itching for payback, and the new China-Mexico alliance only gave them all the more drive to defend America.

Lou had spent the long monotonous hours regaling his new team with tales—not only how he came to own Rusty, but the events before —all of them. He owned up to his continuing fight to stay sober, and how his depression for his son's suicide had cost a Good Samaritan his life. He told them he and Brandon were literally right there as the cartel carpet bombed El Paso's city hall and other buildings with drones. And he told them all about the mission that cost him a kidney —and nearly cost Judah Montgomery his position as the nation's top general.

He told them about the fears and hopes he'd found in his travels across America, and how those findings had helped develop the Rampart Edge program they were now all a part of. Lastly, he told them about his partner, Brandon McDonald, and how the surrogate son he'd found so annoying at first had inadvertently taught him it was okay to love another human again.

Lou glanced at the nightscape below them, taking in the various generator-powered lights aglow in Wichita fifty miles ahead. They couldn't take the chance of firing up the onboard GPS and navigation systems only to be driven right into the ground by a seventeen-year-old hacker in China. It was old school for them—maps, stopwatch, known speed, and compass. That was how aerial navigation was happening in 21st century warfare. "I think you should take this one," he told his new partner. He scanned back. Travis was napping in his right-side seat behind Angie, holding Rusty's leash. Lou craned harder to his right in the multi-point harness holding him in his pilot's chair on the left. He saw nothing where Gray's right knee would've been. *He's up and doing the pre-landing checks,* he thought. *Good.*

"Let's swap lists," Lou ordered. He and Angie reversed roles as pilot and co-pilot, which included the pre-landing lists. In 2009, a crew had made a landing without the landing gear deployed at Bagram Air Base simply because they'd failed to use the landing checklist. Lou had been by-the-book by that point, lucky to be flying after running his A-10 out of fuel in Afghanistan in 2007. The two traded clipboards.

Angie contacted the controllers at McConnell Air Force Base to verify runway and approach instructions. Lou began to scan his responsibilities as co-pilot. In the back of his mind, he'd hoped that all of this was worth it—that the battle-hardened friends he was visiting would be up to the challenge of growing a large civil defense force, just as he'd made the Special Forces he was hauling believe.

CHAPTER 11

USS James L. Hunnicutt SSGN-93

THE CONTROL ROOM OF THE SUBMARINE WAS QUIET, AS WAS the entire boat. No sailor wanted to make any unnecessary noise. This was not the time to drop a water bottle. They were rigged for ultra-quiet. The modern vessel's sensors converted their data into a three-dimensional display with accurate scale, distance, and depth. They could "look" at themselves in relation to any other vessel for several dozen miles, more as they accepted a degree of inaccuracy. But for anything within six miles, whether surface or submerged, it was considered undeniably correct.

Darren was impressed with the layer cake of activity on the screen. He was maintaining his place of authority over the steering and diving station, a task that required fewer people and oversight than on older submarines. Carla Gingrey had control of the ship while the Captain, along with Commander Yanda and CIA Agent Booker, was personally reviewing the details of the dangerous mission with the SEAL team back at the Lockout Chambers.

"Sonar, everything still the same?" Carla asked her operators.

"No new contacts, Conn," the lead sonar technician reported. "Contacts Yankee-1 and Yankee-2 still making revolutions for five knots at periscope depth, bearing one-seven-five, directly in front of contact Zulu-1."

"ETA for when Zulu-1 will cross over them if they don't change course and speed?" she asked.

Which they won't, Darren thought. The CO and XO briefed the officers and chiefs on every detail of this mission—excluding their own bleak thoughts on the probability of survival.

"Approximately one hour, Conn."

"Bring the display out to seventy-thousand yards," she ordered one of the control room techs. The digitized display changed in scale, showing Zulu-1—the USS Lyndon B. Johnson—at the top. Several layers of dim grid lines provided scale for position and depth. The two Chinese submarines were indeed directly ahead of LBJ's course.

Just like the CIA said, Darren thought with a slight cough. He made some spit in his mouth to wet it, an old trick to avoid reaching for that droppable water bottle when silence could mean life or death. *These clowns really are going to try and take her down like they did the Russians.*

The other piece of intel the sensors were displaying—the part that the Chinese obviously didn't know based on their lack of panicked activity—was the Hunny one kilometer behind and below them by an additional depth of one-hundred-and-fifty feet. They were traveling seven knots and trying to time it so that they would slow down to match speed as they crossed under the Chinese when they began their diver operations.

Subs that were hovering at slow speed—especially older subs like the adversaries above them—needed to constantly adjust the list and trim of the ship to keep the required depth and attitude. The sonar operators were growing sleepy, listening to the ships above them continuously filling and emptying smaller tanks located in the front, middle, and central areas of the vessels. The thing that worried the

Americans the most was those ships not being on their game and drifting down in depth enough to hit their own conning tower.

The SEALs were about to deploy themselves out of the ship, ready to plant explosives on the steering surfaces and seawater valves on the enemy U-boats. Torpedoes made noise, and that gave the Chinese an opportunity to radio details of the attacking Americans' location to their satellites. The planted explosives, on the other hand, would detonate on a timed delay. Even if the hulls weren't breached, the damage to the valves behind the screens would invariably mean uncontrolled flooding. The damage to the dive planes and rudders would mean they had no way to control their direction or even their descent. The subs would sink themselves slowly until reaching a depth in the cold black nothingness that was too much, imploding them like a beer can. *It's kind of a cold-hearted SOB thing to do to other sub sailors,* Darren thought. But a split second later, he remembered how many Americans had died in recent days, and any empathy evaporated.

Lastly, the SEALs were being tasked with following their Chinese counterparts up to the surface. The LBJ was briefed and supposedly ready for the intruders, but Commander Yanda wasn't going to take any chances. Thirty-two highly trained Chinese special forces might just be too much for the regular sailors to handle.

Over Darren's career, he'd heard rumors of some of the daring and unbelievable operations of submarines in the Cold War years. He knew that what they were doing would go down as legendary in the annals of the U.S. sub sailors' close-mouthed club. *If we survive to tell the tale,* he remembered.

ACME RANCH
Southeast of Tucson, Arizona

· · ·

THE SOUND OF THE EXPLOSION CAUSED EVERYONE IN THE bunkhouse to fall or jump out of bed. It was pitch black except for the security lights of the Army basecamp nearby slicing through the high windows.

"What the hell was that?" Pedro was the first to yell.

Who's on watch? an exhausted Karen wondered as she turned on the little portable radio. After it beeped to indicate it was powered up, she caught a report already in progress. *Bob must've already hopped out of his rack,* she realized. He'd taken to sleeping on a bunk in the CP until he was confident some of the teenagers and Donna could finally handle all the radio, mapping, logbook, and relay responsibilities.

"—really bright flares slowly drifting down!"

Fred Bowers, Karen realized. *Not Bob.* She looked down into the dark of the bunkhouse and could see Pam just starting to rouse herself from her slumber. Fred's next words were interrupted by the staccato sound of automatic machine gun fire, both on the radio, and drifting in through the walls.

"Hold on!" he yelled into the radio. "I don't know what they're shooting at, but they're really lighting something up about a mile to the southwest!" Bob took advantage of Fred's slight break in transmission to start peppering him with questions.

"Everyone, get your packs and rifles and get to your positions!" Karen called out as someone finally brought an LED lantern up to a usable level of lighting. Bodies were starting to scurry. Karen was still in her one set of tan cargo pants. She slipped into her boots and grabbed her rifle, coat, and pack. She arrived at the bunkhouse door just behind Pedro. The others were still scrambling.

The two prospective Road Runners both ran down the southerly trail toward the main barn. Pedro kept going as Karen peeled off on the arterial trail to the below-grade greenhouse project. She passed it and hopped into a two-foot-deep foxhole, reinforced with a two-foot-high berm that faced south and east. She unslung the rifle and propped it on the berm. Doffing the pack, she reached into the top pocket and pulled out a small pair of cheap binoculars. She started scanning for the bright glow to the southwest. *Must be some kind of parachute flare,* she thought as she watched a pair of mortar-launched white phosphorus flares slowly drift back to the earth under small parachutes. They finally passed behind the crest of the hilltop, which was muffling the gunfire from the Army's perimeter security farthest to the south.

She turned her attention to their small city, barely able to see past the lights that pointed out in all directions, including back at the main ranch. The long shadows and bright lights made for an eerie and stressful sight, even as the sounds of gunfire slowly dissipated to nothing.

About twenty minutes later her radio earpiece crackled to life. "Kare Bear, CP, you copy?"

"I hear you, B—" she caught herself before fully saying Bob's name. "Sorry!"

He ignored it. "I've been given a SitRep from our guests. Things are stable."

Damn! She thought as Bob went silent. Deep inside, she'd wished he'd have advised her about what to do next. *But they expect me to make a decision!* she fretted. "Okay. Everyone but the OP fall back to the command post," she announced.

Karen put her pack on and grabbed her rifle. She walked back at a normal pace, scanning in all directions. When she'd finally made it to the garage entry near the main house's front, she saw a small group collecting. *Donna, Pam, the Washingtons...* she thought as she started scanning. Pedro was just behind her, and she saw Daniel Monitor coming off the trail next to the backyard pool from the direction of the west trail to the OP. "Looks like about everyone?" she half asked Bob as she walked up.

After another minute of excited nervous chatter, Donna finally spoke up. "Bob, go ahead and tell us what you know, so we can get the kids back to bed."

"My liaison with the Army said they weren't attacked," he announced. "They discovered a Chinese special operations team on long-range patrol doing recon." This caused a few audible gasps.

"Dayummm," Jerome said quietly.

"The firefight was about here, I'm guessing," Bob said, pointing to a topographical map of the ranch and its surrounding area. "They described it as a wash between two gentle slopes. They wouldn't tell me over the radio what grid coordinates. But it was a long-range fight. They don't expect casualties. They have a patrol element out hunting for them, but my guess is they're long gone." He paused. "If they're even half as good as the Viet Cong were."

"What's that mean for us?" Donna's brother Brad was the first to ask.

Bob looked at Karen. "I know we're short of manpower, but Fred is up there all by himself. We should double up the watches."

"I think you're right," Karen said. "Does any—"

"I'll go," Daniel announced. He looked at Pam and they exchanged a knowing glance.

"Alright, then. Thanks. Bob, is there any way you can get hold of Granger and get him back?"

"VooDoo left a few names in Tucson we could try to relay a message through, but he didn't seem real confident about it when he told me," Bob said.

"Let's give it a shot first thing in the morning, anyway, okay?" Karen suggested. "Let's try to get some sleep," she told everyone else. Over the next two minutes, the group broke apart and drifted back into the house or toward the bunkhouse. Brad gave Daniel a ride up the hill on the quad for him to finish the night watch with Fred Bowers. Karen passed the large trees opposite the driveway parking area and headed for the cowboy bunkhouse, seeing Pedro waiting for her by the corner of a horse fence.

"Did you see what I saw when we were all getting up and getting boots on?" he asked as he started walking next to her.

Shadows... Karen thought. *A lantern...* "I guess not," she admitted. "I thought we did okay. Nobody had to be shaken awake. They all got moving, even if they were slower than us."

"I guess I should rephrase," Pedro said. "It was what I didn't see."

He stopped walking as they neared the Washingtons and Pam who were entering the bunkhouse.

Karen stopped and faced him. "What, Pedro? What am I missing?"

"Daniel," Pedro said. "I'm not much for talking trash, but... he is, and it pisses me off!"

"What about him?" Karen said, eyes drifting up as she searched her memory.

"He wasn't there," Pedro said. "He wasn't on watch. So why wasn't he in his bunk at three in the morning?"

YUAN CLASS TYPE 039A SUBMARINE CHANG CHENG 333

THIS ONE PROBABLY WON'T BE QUITE SO EASY AS THE LAST ONE, Ma Nan thought as he worked. He and the rest of Squad Two were pulling the inflatable from its storage compartment over the rear main ballast tanks. Squad One was performing the same feat just a bit forward. He thought he could just make out the chemical lights and bright LED headlamps of the two squads doing the exact same thing on Submarine 032 just forty meters to the starboard. There was an inherent amount of fear in the back of his mind as they worked in the cold eastern Pacific. His thoughts helped his mind think about anything other than getting lost in the black abyss. *The Americans are aware we're at war, unlike when we ambushed the Russians.*

He saw one of the others waving his chemical light in a series of rapid circles. *We're ready.* The diver collected everyone's lights and secured them in a bag in the same compartment the boat had been stored in. They couldn't risk any light being seen once they reached the surface. They all adjusted their air level on the buoyancy compensating vests by adding air from their tanks, allowing them to float just a bit higher. Each was trying to position himself over the raft, a task not so easy without swim fins. A lesson learned from the last time was that they'd wasted precious seconds trying to pull those off and ditch them. They weren't surfacing a mile away and motoring in—this was a one-time shot, perfectly placed and timed. All eight men released a bit of air just a few feet over the deflated raft, their weapons and other tools tethered to it with a variety of quick-release nets. *Now we're just waiting.*

Each man was getting a good workout, treading in a slight forward swim. The subs were moving ever so slightly. The red lights atop the submarines' conning towers and rudders flickered, signaling that the USS Lyndon B. Johnson was a minute away and still on course to pass right over the middle. *Here we go,* Ma thought excitedly. He was eager to test himself in a true combat scenario. *The Americans have become so fat and lazy.* Confident, Ma wasn't so naïve as to think this was going to be a cakewalk. He just believed in himself and wanted to serve his family and country with honor.

One of the others pulled on the rope, triggering the air cylinders to start inflating the cells on the three-meter rubber craft. Within seconds, it attained a positive buoyancy. It hit the divers and paused, slowly winning the fight against their added weight as the cells continued to fill with air. Once the boats and divers were a mere ten-meters from breaking the surface, Ma could hear the powerful five-blade, eighteen-foot propellers chopping the water. One of the others secured the air tanks filling the craft—the air already added would continue to expand as they rose.

Suddenly, their boat started bellowing air out of both sides in a loud and violent fashion! Their ascent stopped. Ma felt another soldier grabbing him. *Who is that?* he wondered angrily. *What's happening? Training, men! This is why we practiced relentlessly.* He reached for the bottles to crank them back open in the hopes that it could out-fill their leak. *We need our gear and rifles!* But then Ma's own training kicked in. *If we can still get on the ship, we can use our backup weapons!*

Ma pulled the pistol out of his thigh rig and triggered the light mounted forward of the trigger guard. He couldn't believe his eyes. *What are those!* He could see dark shapes pulling his teammates into the dark. The small beam only cut through the ocean about two meters, which added to the eerie event. There were bubbles everywhere, and the now loud rumble of the giant ship next to them stopped. His mind was racing when his own regulator suddenly stopped working. He was awash in a curtain of bubbles as his scuba hose, cut into two pieces, leaked air all over him. Suddenly powerful hands grabbed him and started swimming him straight down!

Ma started to panic, tightly holding his breath. The shock of getting yanked down by... whatever it was... had made him drop his pistol in the dark depths. He tried desperately to shake out of the grasp of the unknown leviathan when he got hit by one of its flippers. *That's— that's a diver's fin!* Ma reached down to his ankle, lungs on fire as he struggled to keep the precious air in before whoever it was drowned him. He could feel his inner ears in pain, almost like something was trying to poke through them, as the depth increased. *There it is!* He pulled the knife off his calf and gave the hand on him a sharp stab. The grip released!

Ma shot for the surface, mask tight to his face as he didn't dare waste anything in his lungs trying to add pressure to it. He could feel himself getting lightheaded, not knowing how much farther he had to go. Any thought of getting a case of diver's bends from the rapid ascent was long gone in lieu of certain death. As he broke through the wave, he took a giant gasp, inhaling saltwater as he did, coughing wildly. A loud staccato sound of explosions rung his ears, assaulting his dizziness even worse. He ripped his mask off. *Where are the others?!*

Expecting a firefight, he saw only a one-sided slaughter, as the fifty-caliber machine guns sticking through the open access covers on the very slick side hull of the USS Lyndon B. Johnson were filling the area of Squad 1's raft with hundreds of rounds of 619-grain bullets. Every fifth round was a tracer, giving off a burning red metal and oxidizer that gave the scene an even more ominous gloom. Still gasping, Ma couldn't even scream in horror. The machine gun fire covered the sound of the small boat, a larger rigid-hull inflatable that had deployed straight out of the back of the American warship.

"Halt!" he suddenly heard behind him. Spinning around in the water, a spotlight came on and blinded him.

Ma took a few deep breaths. *Never, you capitalist whore,* he thought with a scowl. *A couple of good deep breaths and I'll try to get down to—*

Ma never heard the butt-stroke from the American SEAL treading water behind him. And had he realized he would become the first prisoner of war in World War Three, he might've thought twice about shooting for the surface.

CHAPTER 12

The old gray Huey helicopter passed over the small prairie town with the same loud thwapping noise Americans had come to associate with it when watching Vietnam movies. The single-rotor, two-blade UH-1N utility chopper was still proving a workhorse while the men and women who first flew it were now moving behind walkers and sharing war stories in veteran retirement homes. Unlike in the Vietnam movies, the preferred mode of travel in the un-air conditioned beasts was with the sliding doors closed—especially in winter. Those didn't prevent Lou from glancing below as they began a loop around the town. He looked forward, able to see the small map clipped to a flat board strapped on top of the right-seat pilot's thigh. The man was scanning it, looking back and forth at the map and down at the ground through the helo's plexiglass windows by his feet.

"Almost there," Lou silently mouthed to Angie immediately to his right. They were in the center of the four-person bench that faced forward. Outside of them were the officer and senior NCO from the first 'A Team' they were deploying. The craft's crew chief and assistant airman occupied the sideways-oriented seats on the sides behind their center-bay bench. Though they were all wearing bulky headsets for communication, the loud rumble of the twin engines reverberated through the body, including the tiny bones of the inner ear, making listening to speech a chore at best.

Angie nodded in understanding, leaning into Lou unintentionally as they banked and descended south of the main town. They paralleled South Santa Fe Avenue for just a few moments before banking once more and settling in a field between a pond and Toto's Revenge, a local nursery. As they settled, the craft gave one final bounce and stopped moving as the pilot cut the throttle. The engines powered down slowly, and the pair of crew members pulled levers and slid the two side doors to the rear. Lou, Angie, and the two Special Forces soldiers all got out of the craft, subconsciously crouching their necks just a bit as they walked away. Lou was the last to catch up, his cane getting stuck in the cold Kansas mud. *Glad Rusty stayed back with the guys,* he thought, not relishing the thought of trying to keep his pal clean during the coming days.

"Want to try the house first?" Captain Jun Yong "Don" Ho asked Lou. The crew made their way the four-hundred-feet through the winter dead grass toward a well-maintained home that was between them and the nursery.

"Looks like we've got company already," his Army comrade said. Sergeant Major Rowan Byrnes was the senior sergeant in their ODA, or Operational Detachment Alpha Special Forces team. He used his eyes and a slight nod to point toward a young man and woman approaching the group from the field farther south to their left, behind a fertilizer business. They wore a mix of hunting clothing and had small packs with rifles slung across their chests.

Lou looked south and a smile turned itself up slightly at the corners of his mouth. As he turned his head back toward his Army comrades, he noticed a few adults coming around the house to their west, obviously curious about the helicopter that landed in their field. He thought he recognized a figure in that group as well. "I think we've found the right place," he said as they continued to move toward the house at Lou's pace.

As they approached the group standing on the back patio, Lou heard a woman's voice cry out in pleased surprise. "Lou?" Rosie Ortiz questioned as she started moving toward her forever buddy. "Lou!" she screamed, her walk turning into a sprint.

"Hi, Rosie!" Lou smiled as he braced himself for impact. Rosie moved right into his open arms and embraced him around his neck, feeling her savior's embrace around her low back. The former undercover cop kissed him on his right cheek twice and began squeezing him again.

The pair in the field to the south started jogging over as the rest of the patio group moved out into the grass with puzzled smiles. There were four adults, including one that made Lou do a double take as Rosie finally released her grasp. "Morris?" he asked, knowing his eyes were deceiving him.

"Marvin," the young man said casually. "The bum you're looking for is right there!" he joked as he pointed. Lou turned a bit and finally recognized the man he'd befriended on a bus ride many weeks earlier. "I'm his brother."

Lou looked back at Marvin. "In the Army, right?" he asked as he recalled the lengthy conversation.

A perplexed look crossed Marvin's face. "I... I was... I mean—my end of service date passed, but when I made it back from Korea, they told me to take some leave and report back. Then the attacks started, the power went out... I'm still figuring out what to do next."

Morris Dooghan and Jordan Croft, his college friend, finally made it to the group, with the accelerated breathing of someone who just jogged for a minute. His smile, a rare commodity in recent weeks, spoke volumes. "Good to see you, Lou!" The young good-looking man gave the colonel a quick bro-hug. He shook his head in mild confusion. "Wha—what brings you all out here?"

'Here', was a small piece of land in the southeast corner of Kansas, just south of the area's Walmart and on the edge of a small town of

eight thousand people. That was over half the entire county population. To say they were 'in the sticks' was not an understatement.
Morris' parents had come from their Roeland Park neighborhood to his
aunt's house to escape the rapidly deteriorating condition in the
Kansas City metroplex.

"We'll get to that," Lou said. Rosie grabbed his head and gave him
yet another kiss on the other cheek. Introductions started, as Lou
finally met Marvin's parents, LaTanya and John. "I see you and your
sister are doing okay," Lou directed at Rosie. Weeks earlier, when she
was done with the debriefing with the Texas Rangers and federal
government about her cartel undercover work, she and Angel needed a
place to set up a new life for their own safety. Rosie's developmentally
challenged sister needed full-time care. Rather than an obvious facility
that would make finding them much simpler for the cartel, Lou had
suggested another idea. With one phone call, the Dooghan's and John's
sister had lovingly opened their country home to a pair of strangers.

"We're very blessed to be here," she replied.

"Bee and I have been out here a while," Morris said. "We're cold!
Let's move this inside!" he suggested.

The huddle loosened a bit as people started moving toward the
house. "Might I suggest the greenhouse?" Janet Pierson asked. The
widow was Morris' aunt and owned the property and business.
"There's not much for customers in there and plenty of space."

A few minutes later, they were all settling into a mix-match of
folding and camping chairs under the fiberglass roof of the large nursery's rear area. A few more minutes of small talk finally gave way to
Lou being put on the spot for what was at play.

"I'll start with saying once more how sorry I am that you and your
friends were affected by the unfolding of Operation Venom Spear," Lou
said. Morris looked down as his usual anger and depression, which
had been on reprieve since the helicopter landed, returned. Lou could
literally see Morris' stature deflate at the shoulders. Next to him, the
younger Jordan's face turned to ice cold stone. The violent deaths of
their friends nicknamed 'ThatNub' and 'Goldi' were still very raw to

think about for the youths. The rest of their college paintball team had drifted back to their hometowns in the wake of the university finally shutting down indefinitely.

"And in our couple of conversations since then," Lou stated, trying to be ginger with his wording, "you mentioned putting together a security team here in town?"

Morris looked back up as his mother declared passionately, "Against my strongest objections, he sho' did!"

"Ma," Morris' brother Marvin said, trying to calm her down by grabbing her hand.

She continued her rant. "Don't you people know when to let these kids alone? Leave 'em be!"

"Mom!" Morris said. "Please!"

"I feel ya, Mrs. Dooghan," Lou said, thinking of his deceased son Terrance. "But your son has a talent for organizing. And these men—" Lou motioned toward the respectfully quiet soldiers sitting in the circle of chairs. "—represent just two of an entire team here to help you all stand up an actual civil defense force."

"A—a team?" Morris asked, and a look of understanding crossed his brother's face. The soldier was a member of the Army's 46th Transportation Company and had already guessed that the camo-clad men in attendance were Special Forces.

"An A Team, to be more specific," Lou said. "Captain Ho, why don't you tell these folks what all you do." Lou motioned for Morris and Angie to follow him as he stood. He led them up the main aisle of the nursery.

"Colonel?" Angie asked, slightly perplexed by the sidebar conversation.

"You need to learn just what it is I do besides fly, Lieutenant," he said. "Just in case."

"I don't know what you expect, Lou," Morris admitted. "We're just a family trying to get by, led by a cop with PTSD and two college airsoft players."

"What have you accomplished here in Chanute?" Lou asked.

"Uhhh, Bee—you know, Jordan... and I had joined a local gun club to keep up on skills. We kind of bring that average age of those members down to about forty," he joked with a slight grin. "But once Marvin arrived, and they found out he's active duty, it kind of opened them up to us a bit. They don't have too many folks that look like me and him 'round here!" the half-black man smirked. "But we've been meeting up with a bunch of them a couple of times per week. Even though he ain't infantry, Marvin knows enough Army stuff to teach these Fudds a thing or two..."

"That's my point, Morris," Lou said. "Wherever you go, people flock to you. You have a certain charm, with your model looks," Lou smiled as Morris squirmed uncomfortably. "Am I right, Lieutenant?" he asked Angie.

"I'm overwhelmed with passion, sir," she said with flat monotonous humor, which made Morris laugh out loud as they strolled.

"Alright, alright. I feel ya," Morris admitted. "But why the operators?" he asked in reference to Lou's companions.

"It's what they do, son. There's ten more of them on the way here right now."

"What?" Morris asked, surprised and instantly worried about what his mother would say.

"They're outfitted with a lot of gear, my friend," Lou said. "They'll be able to take the ten or whatever you've started training and turn them into a hundred. You just help them recruit the bodies."

"To what end, sir?" Morris asked. "It's not like we're going to the border to fight the Chinese."

"Understood," Lou said. And though he knew his next statement would be a bit melodramatic, his recent events with the relatives of Julia's new boyfriend taught him that the enemies could be local criminal dirtbags just as easily. "But what about when the Chinese move the border to Kansas?"

ACME RANCH
   Southeast of Tucson, Arizona

THE ARIZONA SKY WAS A LIGHT BLUE WITH HIGH STREAKS OF
clouds as the winter sun peaked midday to the slight south of overhead. "Sounds like the quad is coming up the trail," Pedro said,
checking his watch. Karen remained quiet, still deep in thought about
Daniel Monitor. *What is that guy's agenda?* she kept asking herself. The
gas engine's muffled noise increased as it broke through the trail
opening to their left, coming into view. Brad steered toward the OP
with Jerome riding just behind.

   The machine came to a stop a few feet from the OP, crunching
gravel under its tires. Karen and Pedro had scavenged dead branches
with a pruning saw from nearby trees over the course of their shift.
They'd worked on laying them to appear as an old pile over the dug-in
hole of the observation post, an attempt to provide concealment and
maybe a hair of cover, too. "Nice!" Jerome said as he scooted himself
off the machine.

   After the usual turnover procedure and small-talk, Karen and
Pedro hopped on the quad with her on back and made their way back
down the hill. She felt a pit building in her stomach, as she was finally
going to get a chance to talk to Daniel about his mysterious absence in
the middle of the night prior. *I've always hated talking to arrogant men
when I know they're going to disagree,* she admitted to herself as they
bounced down the dusty trail. Upon arriving at the ranch proper, they
made a detour toward the shop to top off the quad with fuel from the
one-thousand-gallon, crank-operated gas tank. It was one of four such
tanks—two for gasoline and two for diesel—built under a framed and
aluminum three-wall structure.

"What're you gonna say to him?" Pedro asked, reading his partner's thoughts.

"Still thinking about that," she admitted. Over the preceding six hours, she'd let Pedro in on some of her history of abuse and how it had affected her esteem over the years... why it fueled her workouts and made her want to become a fitness coach. She held the nozzle in the machine's fuel tank as Pedro cranked. "Good," she said when the fuel was near the top.

Four minutes later the pair were parking near the main garage. Karen walked off, and after greeting Bob and two of the teenagers, headed into the house. She found Robin Washington and Donna conducting reading lessons with some of the younger children in the living room. "Do either of you know where Daniel is?" she asked.

"I think he said he was working on the sunken greenhouse," Donna said. She stood up to follow Karen to the front entry, following the security leader out of the house. "Listen, Karen," Donna said. Karen stopped and turned. "We need to talk sometime soon. I've been hearing some things."

"Me, too," Karen said with just an air of rudeness that she didn't intend. "In a bit. I need to find Daniel first." She spun back around and started across the ranch. *I need to rip this Band-Aid off,* she thought. Leaving her host speechless, Karen marched at a determined pace past the main corral, down the southerly trail, and found herself at the greenhouse a pair of minutes later.

"Daniel!" she called out as she approached, seeing his figure moving around inside the structure through the semi-transparent corrugated fiberglass roof panels. A moment later, he strolled up the few earthen and rock steps to ground level.

"Hi, Karen," he said with a certain biting air in his tone.

"Hey," she started. "I'm not sure how to approach this, but—"

"Hold on," he said coldly, hijacking control of the conversation. "I've tried being nice to you."

Karen found herself on the defensive, which made her angry. *You damn smug prick!* she thought. *What makes you—*

Even her thoughts were being cut off rudely as Daniel pushed his aggressive stance. "First you totally freak out coming back from the hospital—"

"What?" Karen almost yelled.

"And then you grabbed my crotch back at the cave—"

Karen was seeing red, at a loss for composing a complete thought. "You lying mother—"

"And you let the cattle get stolen!" Daniel continued, getting slightly louder each time he cut her off. "I'm sorry," he said as he de-escalated his voice and broke out his snakish grin. "I finally had to say something to Donna this morning..."

"You WHAT?" Karen screamed.

"And she told me things have been disappearing, too," he calmly continued. "It seems there's a thief skulking about."

"Yeah, and it's you!" Karen yelled. "This morning when the missiles shot off. You weren't even in the bunkhouse!"

"I was dropping a deuce at the outhouse," he countered. "Pam will confirm I'd just left my bunk a bit before that. I dropped my flashlight and it woke her up," he said with a self-satisfied air. "The real question is... why did the cattle get stolen on your watch?"

Karen let out an enraged screech and spun around. She stormed farther south down the trail, toward the ranch's hay barn and beyond. *I need to go cool off!* she thought angrily. *What a lying sack of manure!*

"Hurry back!" Daniel called after her. "Donna wants to talk to you!"

CHAPTER 13

USS LYNDON B. JOHNSON DDG-1002

MILLIE WATCHED AS HER LEAD ENLISTED CORPSMAN installed an I.V. into one of the three POWs in the cage. She'd just returned to the hangar from watching a sailor wash blood off the deck with a fire hose. There were two prisoners in the other cage that had been welded to the deck and bulkhead, one in each forward corner of the ship's helicopter hangar. "How are they Senior Chief?" she asked, watching the shivering men deny the offered blankets with the one hand not cuffed to a cage bar.

"Core temps are in the low 90s, Ma'am," he answered. "They're all young and fit. They'll bounce back after these warm fluids."

Defiant looks, Millie thought. *On most of them. But you... you would kill me right now if you had the chance. Wouldn't you?* "Let them know that they won't be mistreated," she instructed Master-at-Arms James Jiang 'Cobra' Feng, one of the rescued carrier sailors.

Born in Austin to immigrants from Taiwan, Jimmy was an avid rock climber and Jiu Jitsu instructor. His father, a professor at the University of Texas, foresaw the need for his children to have at least a working knowledge of Mandarin as they aged. Jimmy spoke it well enough to be an adequate translator and relayed Millie's words.

I wonder how this would've played out if the SEALs hadn't sabotaged these guys from below? she wondered. The American naval special warfare operators helped round up the survivors and count bodies. They estimated that there were seven to eight men per squad. Eight had been drug down until they drowned. There were nineteen bodies floating, all ripped apart violently by the machine gun fire. The SEALs had found no identifying tags of any kind. The LBJ crew rounded them up and photographed them, both individually and as a group, on the helo deck. After, she had the chaplain provide a small prayer. Without ceremony, but also without disrespect, the Chinese forces were sent back to the sea to become one with Davy Jones' locker.

The USS James L. Hunnicutt had sent a message the old school way—by using morse code via a signal light mounted to the top of the periscope mast. *PLAN subs destroyed.* The message was a nice confirmation, but unnecessary. The LBJ's own sonars had already picked up the good news. About the same time the ship's boat was helping the American operators scoop up dead bodies, a series of explosions occurred all over both of the enemy U-boats. American sonar operators listened in fascinated horror as the sounds of the enemy subs flooding reached their ears. It had taken a mere forty-eight minutes for the first one to fill and sink to its crush depth. The other hung on and fought for survival for nearly ninety-one minutes.

After yet more dead silence, Millie quipped, "What'd he say?" triggering a small smirk from the Navy cop. In addition to Jimmy, Millie, and three corpsmen, there were two armed guards in the hangar bay. *I'll reduce that to one after this is settled,* Millie decided. *The roving security patrol can back up the guard. We need everyone at their stations where we're headed...*

ACME RANCH
    Southeast of Tucson, Arizona

NEARLY THREE HOURS AFTER STORMING DOWN THE TRAIL AND
into a grove of trees near the stream, Karen found herself walking into
the bunkhouse. "There you are," a concerned Pedro said. He moved
toward his watch partner from the table where he was quietly reading
an ARRL book on amateur radio principles. He nodded his head
toward the door.

Karen scanned the room and saw Daniel, Fred, and Pam all in their
bunks, trying to get naps taken before their watch started at 1800
hours. She'd set up teams of two or three people to provide round-the-
clock overwatch at the observation post in six-hour shifts. Her theory
was that people would have an easier time on a six-hour shift versus an
eight-hour one. Additionally, she knew nobody wanted to be the
person stuck out there all night, every night.

She made eye contact with Pedro as he closed the distance toward
her. Turning, she led him out of the bunkhouse and started to head
toward the main house. "Not yet," Pedro said as softly as he could.
"Follow me."

Not fully sure if he was an ally or not, Karen turned and followed
Pedro down the main driveway for a slow trek toward the highway.
"Why all the secrecy?" she finally asked. "I know Donna wants to talk
to me. And I know Daniel has been spreading lies."

"Then why'd you disappear?" Pedro asked. "I know the dude is a
weasel, but you didn't do yourself any favors." He plucked a piece of
tall grass from the pasture and began to chew on it. "Donna is starting
to buy into his BS."

"That's a tad disconcerting," Karen said. "And you?"

"I've always been a good judge of character, I think," the short
Latino man said. "My feeling is that he's jealous that he's not in charge,
and you're the person in his way. And—he's a manipulator, too. He
gets off on getting people to do what he tricks them to." He paused for

a quick moment, searching for a smooth way to say the rest. "... But I also think you're being sensitive about him for some reason. You need to defend yourself. Calmly! But still... you have to say something. But before I can back you fully, just tell me—why'd you disappear? Where were you?"

Karen studied her acquaintance. Having spent time on watch with him and knowing that Tracy had sponsored him into the ranch group, she knew she was at a point to either trust him or completely lose her mind. "I went to sit in the thicket down south. I was so livid that I got a migraine. I closed my eyes for a few and woke up ninety minutes later." She studied Pedro's face. "I know! Donna's not going to believe that!"

Pedro saw her tearing up a bit. "Look. We all got things we're dealing with. And now that you've shared some of the abuse you suffered in the past, I can see plain-as-day that they've undermined your self-confidence. Granger trusts you. So do I. But you need to trust yourself..."

Karen stopped and turned. She stooped a couple of inches and gave her friend a hug when he faced her, stunning him. "You're right," she agreed.

They turned and moved at a slow pace down the long driveway, stopping at the main gate and turning back. She continued to expand on some of her past traumas which she'd already shared. By the time they'd made it back to the main house, nearly an hour had passed on the slow stroll.

Donna stepped off the covered front porch with a serious expression plastered on her face. "You finally ready to talk?" she asked, though Karen doubted there was but one answer.

"Yes." She looked at Pedro, who nodded reassurance as he headed back toward the bunkhouse. "I know there's some stuff I need to clear up," she said, preparing to follow the ranch owner back into the house. "I'm sorry I ran off earlier. I'm starting to learn that—"

"Donna!" they both heard a familiar voice call out. The two women spun and saw Daniel Monitor passing a very confused Pedro at a quick jog. Walking behind as rapidly as they could keep up were Fred and

Pam Bowers. "We found something you should come see!" he proclaimed with all the faux confusion of a professional grifter. "We found the stolen goods!"

HOLLYWOOD BOWL
　　Los Angeles, California

THE STRYKER VEHICLES PLOWED THROUGH THE TRASH STREWN street as it turned left up Pat Moore Way, parting the angry crowd that had been amassing as more military vehicles continued to arrive at the outdoor amphitheater thrice graced by The Beatles. The crowd was being held in place by a combination of Army reservists and California National Guard. A series of trucks and Humvees were forming a mobile gate and fence across the primary drive up the hill. One of them moved as the mine resistant vehicles approached, allowing them to pass through. A voice on a loudspeaker was barking instructions to the crowd—"... not distributing food at this location..." Dozens if not hundreds of angry voices could be heard yelling back.

"That doesn't sound fun," Lauren Duarte leaned over and said to Alex Nguyen. They, their Delta Force guide Patrick 'Lucky Charm' McBrogan, and two other similar soldier-civilian teams were crammed into the hot loud rig, bouncing the final few hundred yards in what had been a slow trek to the Hollywood Hills. Anything less than a convoy of military vehicles carrying belt-fed machine guns on top was quickly becoming a suicide run to make. Though the gangs and cartels had largely gone back to hiding in light of the Venom Spear roundups, they were far from gone—and rapidly being outnumbered by a larger fearsome group.

"Hungry, thirsty people are by far the thing that makes me lose the most sleep," Alex agreed. "There's just too many people here in SoCal." The lines of worry had grown immensely on the young motel owner's face as he worried about how to protect his parents and sister. *My lazy brother,* he thought. *He'd better step up or face the consequence.* The loud diesel engine's whine started to decrease in volume as they made another left while slowing, moving at parking lot speed. After another minute, they stopped. *Thank you,* Alex internalized as he dabbed his head with a sweat rag. He'd been fighting the need to puke for most of the trip.

They joined the sea of strangers and soldiers moving toward the amphitheater, a ragtag looking group to say the least. Most civilians were in a combination of dirty jeans and hoodies or outdoor coats. But there was a large variety of other players, too. *Characters,* Alex thought. *They all look like they're Cos Players.* The most common group he saw were those tactical mall ninjas in a variety of camo-patterned trousers and tops, some sporting their tactical harnesses and gear. Others wore football or hockey gear. *Like friggin' Mad Max,* Alex almost laughed to himself... almost. He secretly coveted some form of padded protection for his own shoulders and appendages, jealous that he could not shed the social norms in his mind to not care what others thought.

Is that... an Indian headdress? he almost laughed until he realized that the man wearing it was indeed a Native American. Under the beautiful chief's adornment was an older man, still spry and strong looking for his age. Other than the ceremonial feather crown, which was trailing hawk and eagle feathers down to his lower back, he was wearing a normal coat and faded jungle fatigue pants. Like almost everyone, he was armed with a rifle. As Alex continued to look around, he started to lose his cynicism for those around him. Then one uniquely attired fellow drifted into his line of sight.

"Dragon!" he called out, not recalling Dacso Sarkany's actual name. The man in tan pants tucked into combat boots, black turtleneck, and flowing tan trench coat slid through the crowd, his custom AK slung to his back.

"Goot to see you egain," he drawled through his thick Hungarian accent, offering a closed fist to bump.

"You, too!" He caught Dacso eyeing Lauren. "This is our best fighter, Lauren," he introduced. The reserved Hungarian just nodded. "What do you think they're going to tell us?" Alex asked. Dacso shrugged as the three were part of the much larger crowd being choked into a heavily guarded entry control point. "He won't tell us jack squat," he said, pointing at Lucky Charm.

"No good," Dacso said. "Neever good," he added as he waved around at the crowd amassing. A veteran of the Hungarian military, including a combat tour in Afghanistan and wounded as a U.N. peace-keeper in Kosovo, he knew what all veterans across the globe had learned—when they gathered the troops en masse and unplanned, things were about to become worse. After they'd made it through the checkpoint, the crowd was flowing toward the large amphitheater's seats and benches. Dacso drifted toward the small collective of people he'd arrived with.

"Later, Dragon!" Alex said as he and Lauren instinctively started to follow Lucky Charm.

"You guys can go chill with your buddy," Lucky said. "I'll find you." It sounded a lot like an order to Alex, who looked at Lauren.

"Roger," Lauren said. The former jail guard found it easy to slip into the military lingo. She nodded at Alex to follow her as she scurried to go find them seats near their known ally.

A few moments after they sat, Alex said, "I've never actually been here." He scanned the entire scene ahead of him. Rows of plastic indi-vidual seating comprised where they were, in the lower seven sections closest to the stage. The famed 'clamshell' over the stage was far from original, the latest in a string of replacements in the century-plus old facility's history. The gentle slope of the benches behind them, along with the tall hills to the north and northeast, formed the bowl to which the location was named. And though they were too close to the stage to see it from their chairs, Alex had noted the white Hollywood sign, tran-sitioned from wood to steel in 1978, in the hills as they walked in.

"Me either," Lauren said. "But then—I haven't lived here very long."

"Do you regret coming out here now?" Alex asked, redirecting his gaze from the hills to her eyes.

"No!" she almost laughed. "I mean—does it suck, now? Sure. But Jessie is here. She's my everything. I'd rather die here with her than live fifty more years in Ohio without her."

"I get that," Alex said. "I've never had a chance to look for that kind of love. Vietnamese mothers expect their sons to marry girls they've grown up with. She doesn't seem to comprehend that her kids are American." He finished with a disgusted grunt disguised as a chuckle.

"What's with the Dragon dude?" Lauren asked, looking to the odd European's group to their left. "How'd you meet him?"

"From when they gathered us all together a couple of weeks back."

"And his name?" Lauren prodded.

"I don't recall," Alex admitted sheepishly. "Dax? Dack? It's Hungarian. But they call him Dragon because he burnt down a cartel stronghold with a flame thrower."

"Really?" Lauren said, whipping her head toward Alex to see if he was joking.

"Yeah," Alex nodded. "There was some other reason they call him that, too, though I don't remember."

The pair cut their chatter down, as did most of the crowd, when a set of military members joined the few on stage with a determined pace to their stride. As the crowd quieted, the sound of a large military diesel generator could be heard rumbling off the hills. A tall, young, muscular man in a Marine Corps uniform moved to the microphone.

"Thank you all for being here," he said. His opening words coursing through the speakers caused the last few talkers to finally shut their yaps. "I'm Captain Brandon McDonald, the point of contact for the various special operations forces you've been working with for the last several days. I'm joined by leading officers of the various elements of Operation Venom Spear, as well as other units from the National Guard." Brandon looked at his note cards and cleared his throat. The Christian believer kept his head bowed for just another moment, asking for wisdom to speak tough words.

"I... I don't quite know the best way to say this," he started as he raised his head. "But the situation is even more dire than we'd hoped when we met just a week-and-a-half back. As bad as the loss of power and internet services has been... with the ongoing operations to round up the cartels... and the giant spikes in violent crime..." He paused for a second, sipping on his water bottle. "Something even worse is on the way."

"Spit it out already!" a loud voice deep in the crowd hollered out, triggering a slew of murmurs in the process.

"There's a massive invasion fleet of Chinese warships on the way."

Alex's stomach turned to knots when he heard that. He felt Lauren grab his hand in support.

"The damage to our Navy and military has been catastrophic. Many of our older jets have been retrofitted back to older technology to make them immune to the AI-assisted hacking that China has perfected. We will fight them off. But I'd be lying if I said we could guarantee success." The crowd started to erupt into emotional outbursts, many calling out in disbelief. It took Brandon thirty seconds of pleading for them to quiet down enough to continue.

"Where's the Army!" one woman demanded.

"The U.S. Military has been staging itself in the central and southern California valley as well as along the southern border for the last two months," Brandon continued, pushing straight through the rantings of a few others. "The remnants of the Navy will not be able to stop them. They're headed for the beaches from here to San Diego. They'll be able to take the Port of Long Beach. We know they've had cells of civilians—many of them lifelong residents of the United States —infiltrating every level of government, education, and business. And this isn't purely ethnic. Many of their cells are not of Asian heritage. Many of those cells have been instrumental in the fall of our power grids and commerce systems, enabling key protective measures to be bypassed at critical moments." The crowd had grown eerily silent.

"We can expect to see Chinese forces on the ground here in three days," Brandon finally confessed. The raucous roar of the crowd echoed out from inside the clamshell structure he was standing under, making hundreds of people sound like twenty thousand, all of them angry. It took nearly ninety seconds of his silence to bring the volume down, with several dozen of the civilian troops storming off in rage.

"The United States military will continue to support you to the best of our ability. For their own safety, and for national security reasons, we're recalling most of the operators who've been helping you stand up your civilian protection units." Feet started stomping, making the hill shake, as the angry voices ramped up once more.

Alex looked around for Lucky Charm. He and Lauren both stood, the taller woman scanning for him, too. "I think we should make our way back to the rigs that brought us," he suggested. "I've heard enough." The Marine officer on stage was still trying to talk, though the irate group around them was starting to put off a mob vibe.

As the pair made their way toward the growing number of people leaving, Alex heard his name behind him. "El-ecks," the thick accent yelled. He turned to see Dacso waving, trying to get him to stand fast. Alex and Lauren exchanged glances. The Hungarian caught up, with four others standing guard around him. "Ceety no longer seff."

"I know it isn't safe, Dasco!" Alex said as he just missed properly recalling the former henchman's forgotten name. "But we—" he said, pointing back and forth between himself and Lauren, "represent several families of people with nowhere to go!"

Dacso pointed east past the Hollywood sign. "Zoo," was all he said. He saw a confused look on Alex's face, but Lauren picked it up.

"The old Los Angeles Zoo? What about it? It's probably got a thousand drug addicts living in the old cages and pits..."

Dacso shook his head. "We teck eet over lest few deys," he said, pointing to his own armed comrades. "Strong!" the strange Hungarian exclaimed. "Soopplies," he added as he pointed around at the various Army members. He moved his hand to his mouth to imply food.

Alex looked at Lauren. "Whaddya think? Round up the 15th Street Posse and head for the zoo?"

As Dacso began nodding in affirmation, Lauren said, "The old cages and animal traps up there would make great bunkers."

"Ja! Yes!" Dacso said as he leveled his right hand and sliced the air in a cut-off motion, ending the conversation. "Eet ees well..."

CHAPTER 14

AS THE EVENING SUN MOVED BEYOND THE CREST OF THE nearby hilltop, the growing dusk hid the transitions Karen's facial skin tone was going through. In a matter of seconds, she'd gone from her normal tone to ghost white, finally landing on an angry red, almost resembling the same rosy cheeks and nose of a lifelong drunk. In front of her was the spot she'd woken up just two hours earlier—a random tree she'd never been to before. Next to it was a fresh mound of dirt and a large pelican case that was just dragged out of a hole by none other than Daniel Monitor.

"I was concerned when Karen hadn't come back from storming off very angrily in this direction earlier," Daniel explained. "What with the Chinese commandos out here sneaking around and what not. I came down here to see if she was safe and found a freshly dug spot." He popped open the waterproof case's hinged lid. Inside were two radios, two bottles of alcohol, several boxes of ammunition, a pistol, three knives, and an assortment of food and cash. "Is this where you came, Karen?" he asked in mock shock.

"Not cool, bro!" Pedro defended his partner.

"Easy, Peter," Daniel said. "Sorry. Pedro," he corrected himself. The misnomer had the desired effect of putting Karen's ally on the emotional defensive. "We all know you two have a thing." Pedro's jaw nearly hit the dirt. "Which really makes me wonder why she came onto me in that cave..." He faked a new revelation coming to mind. "Ah, yeah... Granger isn't here..."

"You're the one who tried to touch me!" Karen screamed at nearly full volume. "Donna! You're not—"

"Quiet!" Donna called out with authority, like a 'mom-voice' on steroids. She rubbed her temples with both hands as a headache started to form. "Everyone back to the garage! Now!" she yelled as she stormed up the trail. The ranch owner fumed over what she knew for sure and what she suspected on the angry march north. When they made it to the converted command post, her tone had calmed little. "Bob! Kaitlin! Go see if Claude can make it down the stairs!"

"What's goin' on?" Bob started, not wanting to move his ailing friend without a significant cause.

"Just do it," Donna ordered. "Please." She looked at Karen. "I want the truth! Who did you let come steal our cattle?" she barked.

USS James L. Hunnicutt SSGN-93

Chief-of-the-Boat Darren Jorgenson slipped into the tight space where he bunked with five other chiefs and senior chiefs. Two of the other five were in the space, and though it was about time for breakfast, he'd been up the previous forty hours and needed a nap.

In recent years, U.S. submarines had returned to operating on true 24-hour days, a shift in the 18-hour doctrine that had dominated the silent service for most of the previous one hundred years. As such, the ship tended to run the lights so that they assisted with traditional sleep patterns. "Anyone seen my sleep mask?" Darren asked, eyes encircled by dark bags, as he scanned all around his feet and in between the tight corners between bunks and lockers. His two peers were also preparing to skip a meal in favor of some rest.

"Sorry, no," Senior Chief Carlos Alford replied as he was propping up the bunk top. The hard metal lid to the coffin locker, along with the thin mattress on top, swung up on hinges. A simple prop arm could be raised to hold it up at an angle, allowing the user to access the eight-inch-deep storage under their sleeping quarters. Three of these bunks, jokingly called 'racks' by the sailors in ironic reference to medieval stretching devices, were stacked on each side of the small room tucked between the outboard side of two missile tubes. Between the two racks on the far wall was a standup locker unit divided into six high-school style lockers for hanging garments. Carlos reached into a specific spot in his coffin locker to find his shower gear. "Any confirmation of the scuttlebutt about Pearl?" he asked.

"I think the skipper will address the crew at zero-eight-hundred," Darren said. He opened his standing locker and started moving around items stacked on the bottom below his hanging khaki uniform shirts, still on the hunt for his missing blackout mask. "But yeah..." he added with saddened disbelief. There was a well-known culture amongst Navy chiefs that anything said in confidence always stayed between each other. "Hawaii is under invasion. The Air Force and Marine fighter squadrons have been putting up a fight, but the military is taking a beating there."

"What?" Chief Dean Clark exclaimed in disbelief.

"Seriously," Darren warned without raising his voice. "This stays here in the goat locker until the old man speaks." The irony was that Darren was five years older than his skipper. "The PLAN destroyers are taking losses, but there's so many of them that Sub Squadrons One and

Seven are taking a beating. Not just at sea, either. The North Carolina was destroyed in drydock at the shipyard."

"And here we are, sneaking around at eighteen knots a hundred miles off the continent!" Carlos practically yelled. The normally subdued nuclear power plant operator was just as tired as Darren.

"Not forever," Darren promised. "Get some food. Take a shower. And a nap." He scanned the stunned faces of both chiefs. "There're almost two hundred ships headed for L.A. And it's up to us and just a few others to stop them."

ACME RANCH
    Southeast of Tucson, Arizona

"WHAT IS ALL THIS NONSENSE?" CLAUDE ASKED THROUGH wheezy breaths as he stepped into the garage radio shack from the house. Donna's daughter Kaitlin was supporting him from the front, arm poised under his arm and around his back. Behind him, Bob had a hand on both of Claude's hips, trying to feel for any unstable steps with as much notice as possible.

Karen wore a wrinkled brow on top of her anger. *If Claude's health tanks because of this, I don't know how I'll react,* she thought with buried worry. She scooted toward the small group when she saw Claude, guiding him toward one of the folding camp chairs around the map table in the middle of the room. "I'm sorry, Claude!" was all she could say, feeling slightly guilty for also feeling grateful that he'd made the trip out of bed.

Claude went into a bit of a coughing spell as he sat, prompting Robin Washington to finally say something. "You people shoulda let a sick man be," she chastised as she walked toward the door. "I'll be back with a stethoscope, Claude," she announced before departing.

"What's... all the... drama... about?" Claude finally said. He was pale and pasty, his breathing heavy and labored.

"I am so sorry, Claude," Donna said as she pulled a chair over and sat across from him. "You were one of my Dave's inner circle," she said. "But I've got some concerns about your niece's... emotional stability," she said.

"I—" Karen started to say, but stopped when her uncle raised a wrinkled, weak finger.

"Specifics," was all Claude could mumble after the exhausting trip across the large house.

"Theft," Donna said point blank. "Attempting to sexually harass someone." That comment drew a doubtful look from Claude. "Possible cattle rustling. And the anger issues. I don't know if I can have her here, Claude."

Karen was seething, practically chomping her tongue off, waiting to speak.

"My... niece..." Claude was interrupted by Robin's re-entry into the garage.

"Ya'll need to wait while I check his lungs," she said bluntly. She had a small oxygen cylinder in a bag over her shoulder. She cracked open the valve and set the flow to two liters-per-minute. After she'd put a nasal cannula under her patient's nose, she had him lean forward and started listening to his lungs.

"Who?" Claude asked. "The... assault thing..."

"Daniel," Donna answered. A few heads turned as the entire ranch except Jerome and Brad were watching the stressful drama unfold.

Claude slowly turned his tired head. "Him?" he asked incredulously, almost laughing as he choked on the word. He looked back at Donna. "My Karen... would never... touch someone... the wrong way," he said. "Especially... him." The sound of detestation practically dripped off the final word as Claude glared at Daniel, causing the younger man's feet to shift in uncomfortable silence.

"Cattle were stolen," Donna explained. "On her watch. The night after, she was the one who supposedly discovered it was happening. I know this is painful to hear, Claude. It's due to my respect for you and your years working with Dave that I brought you down here to hear it all firsthand. And a cache of missing items was just recovered from a spot she was at an hour earlier."

Karen couldn't help it. "That's total BS, and you know it, Daniel!" she bellowed.

"You planted that stuff when we went for a walk," Pedro added.

"No, he didn't!" Pam Bowers said, as she shot Karen a condescending look. "We found it with him!" Fred sat silently, mulling over what his wife had said.

Claude leaned forward, coughing wildly, which triggered a reaction from Robin. "I think you have pneumonia, honey," she said to Claude. "We need to get you back to bed."

An uncomfortable silence started when Claude was done coughing. "I... I can't wait until Granger gets back to help with this," Donna sighed with exasperation. She looked directly at Karen. "You need to get whatever you brought with you and leave at first light."

CHAPTER 15

ACME RANCH
Southeast of Tucson, Arizona

"CLAUDE!" DONNA WOLF CALLED AT THE FEEBLE MAN AS HE headed across the house with Karen's assistance, leaning with one arm draped across his niece's shoulders. It was the crack of dawn and Karen wasn't going to spend another second where the group trusted the wrong person. They were almost at the front door. The original Road Runner ignored her, under enough duress as it was with his weakened, ailing heart. Karen opened the door. "Karen!" Donna finally said. "Don't be ridiculous!"

Donna was right on their heels as they traversed across the terra cotta tile covered porch and out into the main parking area where Karen's charcoal gray Elantra was warming at idle in the chilly dawn air. "Claude! You're not well!" Donna voiced once more.

The Vietnam vet stood. Using his niece as a support column, he turned to face his buddy's widow. "How far back... do we... go... Donna?" he asked under fast and shallow breathing, his face ashen.

"Blood's thicker..." He turned back toward the car and began his descent under Karen's help.

Robin Washington came out with a small medical bag, concerned for the man's health. "This ain't right, Claude," she scolded. "You need to get yo' butt back to bed. And you—" She pointed a mom-finger at Karen and Donna. "You two should go sit down an' talk this fool stuff out before some real damage happens." With that, she pushed her way past the two women and knelt down between the open car door and her patient to check his blood pressure.

"Don't worry, Donna," Karen said. "I'll respect your decision. And I tried to get him to stay. But I will not beg him to. We're family." She headed back toward the house to grab Claude's bags of clothing and gear but stopped short when she heard Donna call out to someone else.

"Not you, too!" she said to Bob, who was hauling his own radio gear and bags from the garage and heading toward the car's trunk.

Karen turned from the front door and followed Donna down to the rear of the car. "Bob. What're you doing?"

"Claude's my brother, Karen. Not a real one. It's a veteran thing." He looked at Donna with a disappointed but resolute face. "If they go, I go." He set his boxes on the ground since the trunk hadn't been opened yet and headed back toward the garage, Donna in tow.

"Wait, Bob! You don't have to go! Who's going to run the command post?"

Bob spun around. "Open your eyes, Donna! You've known Claude an' me for years! And he's known Karen her whole life! There's no way she's pullin' the shenanigans you accused her of. Somebody's done hoodwinked you in a bad way!" He headed for the garage once more.

Pam Bowers had found her way from taking some of the kids to feed the chickens and fetch eggs—just in time to catch the scene. Her husband Fred and Daniel Monitor were up at the observation post. Two horses could be heard coming up the main trail from the larger barn, as Jerome and Brad had been tacking up for an all-day patrol to look for more signs of intrusion. When they saw the commotion, they moved their steeds over toward the car and house. The audience was building.

Donna called out to Bob. "Have you been able to get hold of Granger yet?" she asked with slight desperation. The prospect of losing all her late-husband's friends over this incident was starting to dawn on her.

"Been trying," Bob called out a few seconds before re-emerging from the space with another armload of communication gear. "Not sure if any messages have gotten to him." He pushed past the worried ranch owner. "Karen, dear. I'm going to need you to open that trunk. I'll take the shot-up SUV from the hospital run, but I don't want this gear sittin' in the back with no rear window. We need to get into town and grab Tracy. There's just a whole lotta tension on the airwaves as everyone is buggin' out of Tucson." Karen reached for her fob in her pocket to hit the trunk-pop button.

"Everybody just stop!" Donna yelled. "I need to think!"

USS Lyndon B. Johnson DDG-1002

RED AT NIGHT, SAILOR DELIGHT, Captain Millie Goldberg recalled the old adage. Though the air was a crisp cold breeze that accompanied the mood of the rough twelve-foot swells, the dark red sunset had been refreshingly clear and beautiful. She was back on the ship's stern, at the aft end of the helo deck. Any traces of enemy blood had been long washed away by salt water, first from fire hoses and then by the uncaring but consistent spray of the ocean. The typical salty crust had formed in the small, star-shaped holes used for tying the helicopter down while it was on deck. None of it was any saltier than the tracks of her tears as they dried on her cheeks.

Millie had just received word of the battles in Hawaii. She'd taken a few moments to get away from people—a minute or ten to catch her breath... to compose herself... to hunt for the words that would inspire and inform her crew while simultaneously breaking their hearts. The same transmission mentioned retaliatory strikes against the faux Chinese island-bases in the South China Sea by the Australians. *At least somebody is getting bloody along with us,* she fretted to herself.

The red was slowly changing to purple as night swallowed day. *Red in morning, sailor warning,* she remembered the other half of the phrase. *A storm is coming.* Millie turned from the starboard side, heading toward the personnel hatch on the forward bulkhead, just a few feet to the side of the larger hangar doors. Suddenly over the ship's loudspeakers, or 1MC system, the Boatswain's-Mate-of-the-Watch started ringing the ship's bell repeatedly and loudly.

A fire? was Millie's first thought. *No! Not now!* She started running for the hatch.

"Security alert! Security alert! All hands stand fast! Now muster the Security Alert Team at Damage Control Central! Backup Alert Force, muster on the mess deck!"

Why not at the armory?! Millie was wondering as she transited into the hangar. The answer revealed itself in a mere moment. The armory was very near, and the Officer-of-the-Deck had chosen to muster the team at the DCC, one of two other locations on the ship with a weapons locker—and the only one with people already there. That locker was not compromised.

"What happened?" she demanded, seeing a sailor with his pistol drawn, holding one of the POWs frozen on his knees. Another sailor was lying on the deck, motionless. One of the cage doors was open, the port cage which had housed three prisoners. She shot a look at the other cage. Both POWs were alert—still cuffed with one hand to a bar. And both, shoeless and wearing only plain navy-blue coveralls, were obnoxiously yelling at their loose comrade. In the open cell, three pairs of handcuffs were still attached to the cage, laying on the deck. *The other two must have escaped while this one was still freeing himself,* Millie concluded.

One of the helicopter mechanics was checking on the guard on the deck. "I—I think his neck is broken!" she said in shock.

"I'm not sure, Ma'am," the roving patrol finally answered his captain. "I found him like this and had to wait for someone to come in! I was too scared to move once I got this guy to kneel!"

"He... he is dead!" the other sailor repeated, her fear getting the best of her.

"If he tries to get up, kill the SOB!" Millie ordered. She headed toward the hatch on the forward bulkhead. At that moment, the only sailors that would be moving in the entire ship were those assigned to respond to the threat and their backups heading to muster at the mess deck. The security team would be issued weapons, and the officer in charge would assign teams to investigate the ship in sectors. *They know this started here,* Millie reasoned. So they'll clear the aft end first! She decided to wait, lest she get shot by a nervous sailor—or attacked by a Chinese commando.

But Murphy wasn't done. Like the character Mayhem from those car insurance commercials, havoc once more broke out. The ship's bell broke the tense silence again. "Fire! Fire! Fire! Fire at 2-tack-126-tack-3-tack-alpha—the port storeroom! This is not a drill!"

Acme Ranch
   Southeast of Tucson, Arizona

THE QUAD CAME SKIDDING TO A STOP NEAR THE WEST observation post. Karen and Pedro hopped off and started heading toward the branch-covered dugout that had been built to look east at the main property and southeast toward the Army's outpost, which was a beehive of activity. Daniel came out of the hole while Fred approached from the direction of a slit trench that had been dug a bit to the south to use for relieving the bowels and bladder. "What're you still doing here?" Daniel asked in genuine surprise.

"Things changed," Karen said, giving him an icy glare. "But there's more pressing issues right now!" She picked up the binoculars hanging around her neck and started scanning toward the border. "I think we're too far away to see..." she told Pedro.

"There's been a ton of thunder coming from that direction," Fred said. "But it must still be a ways off. I can't seem to see a dark system moving in."

"What are you looking for!" Daniel demanded. "This is why nobody likes you, Karen!" Pedro shot a pissed-off look but had learned to let Karen fight her own fights in the lengthy conversations while they were on watch together.

"Artillery," she answered. As if on cue, several jets flew from the northwest from the direction of Tucson, headed toward the border. "Bob says that the Army has started spreading out to cover the entire border and the Chinese have started lobbing shells at them."

"Let's get going," Daniel said to Fred. As the pair were moving toward the quad to take it back down the dusty trail, the sounds of gunfire could be heard erupting to the southwest.

All of them started scanning that direction. Karen ran farther west to get a better view into the next valley. "Aren't Jerome and Brad still out there?" she yelled back.

"Yeah!" Daniel said. "Their radios haven't been able to reach the CP. They've been relaying to us." He scanned his wristwatch. "Their last check-in was almost an hour ago." The sounds of gunfire were picking up in intensity. A small unit firefight was fully involved.

"That could be the Army's perimeter security," Pedro suggested. Suddenly, all four of their radios crackled to life.

"OP, this is Rover-1! We're under attack! Is there anyone who can back us up?" Jerome's voice was panicked.

"Rover, this is the OP," Karen said as calmly as she could as she eyed Daniel and Fred, already gunning up the quad. "A backup team is en route. Which canyon are you guys in?"

"We're a good mile-and-a-half down the second canyon, way past the cave!" Jerome screamed into his mic. "Brad's been hit! And so have the horses!"

Karen could feel the blood pounding in her ears as the adrenaline was in full swing. "Is it an armed gang? Cartel?"

"No, OP! These cats are in uniform! Real pros! I think they mighta been enemy commandos moving in on the Army post or somethin'!"

GARDEN GROVE, CALIFORNIA

"BA! SAY SOMETHING TO HER! HELP ME CHANGE HER MIND!" Alex begged his father in his parents' native Vietnamese.

"Alex is right, Chi," sixty-five-year-old Lahn Nguyen calmly told his wife. "We of all people should know what the Chinese are capable of."

"I don't care!" the old woman yelled, emotion practically spraying off her words. "I can't do this again!" Tears started to flow, the memories of nearly drowning and dying of thirst on a salty raft nearly fifty years earlier crisp like she'd just lived them. "We've worked too hard! We did what we were supposed to! We built! We saved! We paid our taxes! We became Americans! That was supposed to mean something!" The old woman broke down sobbing. She flung herself face down into the double pillows of her motel bed.

Alex was shocked. He'd never seen his mother so out-of-control before. Always the strict authoritarian, she was the glue that held the family together, other than his oldest sister who moved to New York with her husband. Chi was the iron fist that normally guided and protected the family. For the first time in his life, Alex felt something other than resentment for the tiny, overbearing woman. He felt sorry for her. "Ma. I know how much the inn means to you. But none of these friends and neighbors will go if we don't." It was two mornings after he'd heard the unimaginable news. "We have to go—now. They'll be here tonight or tomorrow."

Most of the 15th Street Posse had heard and heeded his and Lauren's pleading advice to flee for the old L.A. Zoo. Most had packed lightly until Lucky Charm showed up for one final goodbye the following day. He'd brought with him more weapons and supplies— and the advisement that he'd arranged for an Army convoy that would come get them in the middle of the night.

She continued to weep into her pillow, pulling the second one tighter over her head to cover her sobs. Alex's small radio crackled. "Al, you might wanna get up to the roof, bro," he heard Micah Benson say. Alex had never heard that tone in the young but life-hardened youth before.

"Go, son," Lanh said. "I'll get us ready to leave." The old man shooed his son out of the motel room with his hands. Alex left and made his way to the third-floor supply room and roof access. Moments later, he was standing near Micah and Sassy Sasha and a few others.

"What do you make of this?" Sissy Lopez asked as Alex looked up to the late afternoon sky. In the light blue California airspace, streaks were rushing at high altitude and rapid rate. "Missiles? Contrails?"

"There's no flames," her husband Roman injected his thoughts immediately.

"Yeah, I don't know..." Alex agreed. He was trying to count them. He craned his neck south, seeing they were spread out along most of the horizon. "The slower ones could be jets, I guess. But some of those things are just bookin'!"

"Could they be planes?" Sasha asked. "The paratroops we heard about?"

"If they are, then they's early," Micah complained.

"I don't think they could jump at that speed," Alex said. "And they're like… wayyyy up there."

"Not all of them!" Roman interjected. "Look!" he screamed as he started pointing to the northeast. High in the sky, they could see rapidly approaching contrails—dozens of them. California Air National Guard F-15s and F-16s rocketed on afterburners. The approaching American fighters began to split off in pairs, moving around in dangerously fast loops, trying to get above and behind their enemy. Missiles filled the sky.

Micah let out a string of choice words for the entire group—nobody could believe what they were seeing. Smaller groups of contrails broke off the main tracks from the westerly approaching strike force, as Chinese fighters intercepted the American defenders and launched missiles. At all costs, they would protect the bombers moving west across North America. As for the high-level gravity weapons, they were moving much too fast for anything other than missile batteries to engage. As the later afternoon winter air turned from blue to orange to red, the white streaks and yellow explosions of aircraft over southern California turned the sky into a tapestry of patriotic death and destruction.

CHAPTER 16

USS Lyndon B. Johnson DDG-1002

The destroyer was in chaos. Sailors who were supposed to stay put were now running to their repair lockers. Security alert aside, fire reaching a weapon's magazine, fuel tank, or engineering space would certainly kill many or all of them. Carmen was still learning her way around the new vessel. By the time she reached her repair locker near the ship's middle, the leader of that locker had designated two hose teams to go investigate the storeroom. There was a definite haze in the air coming from the center port area of the ship.

"Fredericks! Take Martinez here and—"

"All repair parties, Damage Control Central!" Fire Marshal Amber Jazuk said directly on the 1MC system. "We're getting reports of a second fire in the R-Division berthing compartment!"

After another moment, the repair locker's sound-powered phone talker called out, "DCC says we need to assign one of the hose teams to go investigate! They're sending a two-man security team to escort us!"

"Damn it!" the petty officer in charge said. "I've already got two teams at the other fire!" As if on cue, two sailors in black ballistic plate carriers and battle helmets, armed with M4s, arrived to escort someone to the starboard side fire. "Hold up!" the leader said. "Martinez! Man the plug for Teams One and Two! Fredericks, you're with me!"

The two firefighters and two security members made their way through the hazy cross-passageway that traveled 'athwart,' or across, the ship and disappeared in the light smoke. Carmen grabbed a spare set of sound-powered phones and made her way aft to the plug in the port passageway near the personnel office. She could see fire hoses from both fixtures at the hose station flaked out in the hallway, both leading through the same hatch. Dark gray smoke was billowing out of the hatch. As Carmen plugged the phones in and donned the headset, she heard the clunking of legs pounding their way up an inclined ladder. Kneeling at the open hatchway, a sailor crawled out under the smoke in full firefighting gear. Through a masked face, he yelled, "What's the mother-loving hold up?!" He was waving his arm in a rapid circle. "Charge the damn hoses!"

Carmen could hear a set of heavy footsteps pounding from a cross passage behind her. "I'm on it!" she yelled aft toward the firefighter. The firefighter pulled the lever on the large ball-gate valve in a slow controlled fashion, trying to fill the hose slowly so as to not 'hammer' the nozzleman on the other end. She then un-pinched some of the hose where he was standing and then followed the water back down the flight of stairs, disappearing from view. "Hey!" Carmen said, turning and getting ready to report that the hose team was attacking the fire through the headset. As she turned, she looked down just in time to see a bare foot above a blue coverall leg coming straight for her chest. *What the—!*

The foot connected, sending her into the valve she'd just turned from. Her back screamed with pain from hitting the heavy metal flange and large operation lever. She fell to the mess of hose on the floor, and the closer of two Chinese POWs came moving in with a look of rage in his eyes. He raised the same right foot that had sent her flying over her face and went to stomp. Weeks of Cobra's BJJ classes suddenly kicked in. Carmen rolled in at the man's other leg and reached up to grab the one that was stomping, catching him by surprise.

The man was lightning fast, and though small and lean by comparison to her American rolling partners, extremely powerful. He squatted down on Carmen, sitting on her with all his weight straddling her like a bully pinning her to the ground. *Not again!* the rape survivor screamed in her head. He tried to pummel her with blows, but most of them were only hitting her arms, which she held as tightly as she could to her body, forearms covering her face. She heard the other one yelling at her assailant in their own tongue. The distraction was all she needed.

The man took his eyes off her for just a split second. She used her planted feet to make a quick hip thrusting motion, which sent him off weight just enough that his hands hit the deck on either side of her head. She reached over his right arm with her right. Grabbing her left hand, she was able to trap his arm. When he struggled for control, the white belt student grabbed his right arm above the wrist and pulled it toward her center while slamming the man's right elbow, which was bent with her left hand. Simultaneously, she trapped the man's right foot against the back of her own thigh by bending her left knee and hooking her heel outside of his. The ultimate move was to use her bent knees and strength to make a bridge with her body. She threw the man off to her left as she did so, rolling over on top of him. The pair were up against the bulkhead opposite the one with the hose station, still struggling for control in the complexity of loose fire hose.

Carmen reared her right arm back and with an open palm, crashed it down on the man's nose. Almost instantly, she went woozy as something crashed into her head, sending her falling off her opponent. *There's two of them!* she remembered. *Just like back then!* The thought of those horrible days after the Washington earthquakes, when evil men started doing anything they wanted to young women, was almost too much to bear. Carmen's head throbbed as she saw the second one grab the first's hand and help him up. Blood was shooting out of his nose. "Where do you think you're going?!" she yelled as she stood.

The second commando was urging the bloody one to follow him back into another hiding spot, but the wounded one wasn't through. He yelled something back at Carmen as he took a step, getting ready to square off. Carmen could see a third one approaching through the smoke past the second. *Why?* she pled in her mind with a God she no longer believed in. The space behind her assailants turned a bright yellowish white twice in less than a second, as the farthest Chinese soldier exploded the second one's head with two well-aimed shots. The small tight passage filled with the thunder of gunshots. The one closest to Carmen stopped his wind up for his next attack, spinning, blood flinging off his face as he did.

"Halt!" Jimmy Cobra Feng yelled in Mandarin, his rifle up at eye level and still oozing smoke. "Live or die—I don't really care!" And though Carmen didn't understand them, they were the sweetest words the woman warrior had ever heard.

ACME RANCH
Southeast of Tucson, Arizona

"NO! WE CAN'T RISK IT IN THE DARK!" KAREN ARGUED WITH Daniel in the ranch house's main living room. "You guys barely made it back! Jerome's wounded. Brad's dead! The war is starting! And on top of everything else, Bob says the hospital in Tucson is transferring their staff and patients to Phoenix and Albuquerque. If we don't get up there—tonight, mind you—we may lose track of Tracy for good! We can't dump this on Donna right now!"

Two hours earlier, Fred and Daniel had found Jerome, badly shaken and seeking refuge behind a fallen desert willow. He explained that the presumed Chinese commandos had broken contact. A mere eighty seconds after the backup duo had arrived to assist the roving patrol, a pair of Blackhawk helicopters arrived in the area and deployed a squad of infantry. After a tense few minutes under their guard, the Rangers were able to establish that the four men were on the ranch access list. One of the helicopters had been shot down by a shoulder-mounted missile after it had picked up the enemy retreating a kilometer away. While the other had been engaging their foes, the soldiers helped the three recover Brad's body and escorted them back to the ranch's house. Dusk had turned to dark by the time all of that had transpired. Karen had shut down the observation post for an emergency meeting.

"You know as well as I do we need to start bugging out our food and people to the cave we found!" Daniel countered. "At some point, the Army compound down there is going to come under attack, and we're all gonna die when it does."

Donna and her children had taken to her bedroom for some time to grieve the loss of her brother. Claude was convalescing in the recovery bedroom. All the remaining dysfunctional Acme Ranch group and Road Runners were deliberating the sudden tragedy and inevitable reality that war would break out in the thirty-five-mile span to the south once the MCV coalition came across the border.

"Brothuh, please!" the dirty and exhausted Jerome exclaimed. "Some of us got kids in here!"

Daniel stood and moved into the center of the sunken living room from the steps to the dining area, taking the stage. "I'm sorry, ya'll. I don't mean to frighten. But a harsh dose of reality is what is needed right now! And leadership," he added as a jab while he looked in Karen's general direction.

"Cool heads are what we need in this dialogue," Bob corrected in a flat but annoyed tone. "Not word play and grandstanding."

Ignoring the jibe, Daniel continued as he moved slowly in a circle around the room, trying to make eye contact with each adult. "You all know I'm right. The cave will be much safer because we won't be in the line of fire from stray bombs that overshoot the Army units. It'll offer overhead cover and concealment. And that valley leads straight out to the west gate past the northwest pasture."

"That may all be logically debatable," Karen said as she stood from the sofa seat next to Robin Washington. "But tonight we need to make a run to Tucson to get Tracy. And moving to the cave would be treacherous at best in the dark. Especially with two of the horses shot dead."

"Tracy shouldn't have gotten himself hurt!" Pam Bowers chimed in with a sneer.

Daniel pointed at her as if to agree with her as he continued to slowly circle the crowd like a hawk on the hunt. "That's right," he said coolly. "If he hadn't been hot-dogging, he'd—"

"Now hold on just a mother-lovin' minute!" Bob said. "That man has been a Road Runner and dedicated member of this team a lot longer than all of you! And he's solid. Not for a second do I believe he got himself hurt 'hot-dogging' it, as you claim! He's always acted responsibly, whatever he's doing!"

"Look," Daniel said. "I didn't mean to accuse—"

"Yes, you did," Karen said point blank, piercing Daniel with her stare. "It's what you do. And the two of you," she added as she pointed at the Bowers. "Your entire game is about sowing discontent. You're a snake." Robin made a slight gasp behind Karen as the tension began to ratchet. "Maybe not everyone sees it yet, but some of us do. Let's take a vote." Karen scanned the room as she began her own circle. "Who thinks we should send a team to go get Tracy?"

She held up her hand and saw the same 'yea' votes from Pedro, Jerome, and Bob. "And opposed?" She saw hands from both Bowers, Robin, and Daniel.

"So... a tie," Daniel said. "But based on my conversations with Donna, she'd vote for everyone staying put so we can all safely move to the cave at dawn." He saw the look of disbelief cross Karen's face, rivaled only by the look of anger mounting on Bob's. "We can get her down here to vote if you all don't believe me!"

"The same could be said for Claude," Bob countered before Karen could.

"A tie, then," Daniel said. "This is ridiculous. We'll never get anything done by committee! This is why we need a decisive leader!"

"We have one," Karen said. "I get a tie-breaking vote, as per Granger's instructions. We're going to get Tracy—tonight."

"What?" Daniel almost yelled. "You don't get to rule that way!" His face turned red.

"Actually, I do. And Donna can verify it. But we can get her down here if you don't believe me. But don't worry—you won't be going on the run. Decisive enough for you?"

USS James L. Hunnicutt SSGN-93

"Highlight the Illinois," Commander Brody Woodward, captain of the Hunny, ordered. "Panoramic view." On the semi-circle of eight displays spread around the control room, the view switched from the main seventy-two-inch display showing all contacts in all directions, to displaying only the view in the frontal half of the submarine. The contacts popped up on the correct display left to right in relation to the bearing angle from the sub. Depth was still displayed through the stack of nine grids on the screens, with the middle one representing the Hunny's depth, currently two-hundred-fifty feet. When the CO wanted a more three-dimensional feel for which direction vessels were in relation to themselves, it was the future of submerged tactical display.

The bulk of the figures on the forward and starboard screens cluttered the uppermost grid—the one representing the surface. At up to two hundred miles out, the scale showed every vessel as nearly a tiny dot. If the skipper ordered, the technician could highlight any one vessel, or a square of several, and be provided with a list of the type of ship and its capabilities they were looking at. The dots colored red were known to be merchant ships, whether American of foreign. When the computer confirmed contacts were enemy, the icons were green. White were unconfirmed and blue were American or allied warships. *Way over there,* Master Chief Darren Jorgenson thought as he looked to the two most port screens. There were three contacts on the displays—one blue and two green. The green were both moving toward the coast of America and the blue one—the USS Illinois—was cruising ahead of Hunny, parallel to the continent in a southeasterly direction, only nineteen miles offshore.

"They undoubtedly know about their approaching enemy," the captain said. He was watching the same displays.

"The Virginias are quiet, sir," Executive Officer Carla Gingrey advised. "But we are more so. Are you thinking of providing a phantom for them to chase? Give Illinois some breathing room?"

"I am," he told his XO. "There's a reason we have all this fancy hi-tech crap, right Carla?"

The XO smiled. "Aye, Skipper!"

The CO reached for a phone set and dialed the growler crank on the side of its box. "TAC, Conn, I want you to program a fish for... oh... let's say the USS Wyoming. Send it toward bearing three-zero-zero at fifty knots. Give it a half-hour delay before it slows down."

"Aye, Conn. Any particular noise you want?"

"I think if you just amplify the screw and reactor plant coolant pumps, that'll do. Give it a dropping tool, too, just in case they can't pick it up. And have it disappear once it detects they're onto it. Remember—it needs to sink, not swim. Conn out." Brody placed the handset back on its cradle.

"The Wyoming, sir?" Darren asked. "That's an east coast boomer..."

Brody smiled. "Yes, it is, COB. And it'll drive the bastards crazy wondering why it's over here."

Daren gave a tired grin. "Very clever, Skipper."

In the Tactical Action Center, orders were being input into a special computer, which in turn was relaying them to a UUV, or Unmanned Underwater Vehicle. While also performing the duties that civilians knew of, like mapping the ocean, they had a set of martial capabilities that most weren't aware of. There were versions that were meant for simply mining a harbor. And then there were decoys, capable of transmitting sounds. Once the devices were done with their programmed duties, they would normally float themselves for salvage and reuse. But with wartime programming, the sailors wouldn't risk letting the enemy find it. The small torpedo looking robot would sink to the bottom of the ocean and turn itself off.

While several of the later subs had the capability to push these out of the torpedo tubes, the Hunny didn't need to use precious space in her torpedo room. As a spy submarine meant for diver operations deploying and retrieving equipment, there was a floodable tank at the bottom of the sub. They could simply let the 'fish' swim out of the special compartment once it was flooded and the pressure equalized.

Darren looked at the other displays and could see the blue icon representing USS Scranton due west to starboard about twenty-one miles away. *And the Key West?* he wondered. *Oh, of course—she wouldn't show up here on the frontal view given her assignment, would she?*

CHAPTER 17

The C-17 Globemaster III used its reverse thrusters to assist in braking on the short municipal runway one mile south of the high desert town. Lou had handled the landing, despite enjoying teaching his young apprentice pilot and watching her become more confident. Since he had been grounded with the understanding that he'd never fly for the Air Force again, the chance to make a short runway landing and takeoff was too good to pass.

The large workhorse of a plane could vent thrust in the forward direction—"reverse" of normal. This aided in not only slowing the craft on short landings but enabling it to actually back up on lonely desert landing strips. They came to a smooth slow taxi-speed several hundred feet shy of the 5003-foot runway's north end and continued to taxi to the paved turnaround ahead of them. Lou turned the craft into the open area on the off chance that some smaller local plane would be using the maintained and paved landing surface.

"Nicely handled, Colonel," Angie said as she began her half of the post-taxi shutdown procedures.

"I must admit, Angie—it feels good to still 'have it.' Doesn't it, boy?" he said to Rusty as he shook the dog's head. Rusty smiled and cocked his head, waiting for the post landing scooby-snack he'd become accustomed to. Lou retrieved one from the small pouch he kept tethered to his flight clipboard and gave it to his buddy.

Still holding the leash, crew member Travis asked, "Are you taking Rusty with you for today's drop off?" This would be the fourth Special Forces team they were dropping off in just a few days. The tired crew was using wartime flight rules to fly many hours more than they would've been permitted, catching naps in the air. This was the third drop off. Unlike in Kansas where they could take two teams, this drop and the one before in West Texas had required the loading of vehicles for the team to use. With that added to the loadout of supplies, gear, and ammunition that the team would use to train irregular forces, there just hadn't been room for taking two on each trip.

"I'll take him for a walk, but I won't be able to haul him to my meet on a bike. And I know this lady, so I think we'll be out there for several hours."

"Roger that, sir. Good to hear. If we are going to be parked here long enough, I have a few planned maintenances that will take several hours to complete. The fuel filters and the hydraulics are both overdue."

"Do you need help with that?" Angie asked as she removed her headset and turned her head to see the master sergeant. "Gray had mentioned wanting to get off-plane on this leg if he could."

"Sure thing, LT," Travis replied as he turned to depart the flight deck. "Many hands make light work."

The two pilots and one man's-best-friend stood and slipped out into the front end of the hold where they could all take a proper stretch. Lou looked at a soldier exiting the lavatory door. "It's been a bit since we serviced that," he said, trying to recall what day it was and how many places they'd been in the short week. Things had been hectic at every base, preparing for the inevitable. He'd even started to wonder about the reality of flying so close to the border without a fighter escort. At four hundred miles north, they were still in a position to be ambushed in just a matter of minutes. "I'll find a bush. Gonna save room in the hold tank for fertilizer."

Lou kept Rusty leashed while Gray and the soldiers began to unload the craft. He opened the port forward access hatch, sliding the door straight up toward the hold's overhead and triggering the hydraulic folding stairs to unfold from the hull and stop just above the tarmac. They exited the craft and walked around its nose, looking at the airport access road and Highway I-25 just a few hundred yards to the east. *Not much traffic,* Lou thought as he saw one curious pickup pull to the shoulder. A driver got out and stared. *But then again, fuel is a very precious commodity way out here in the desert. Never thought I'd be coming back here,* he admitted to himself.

Unlike the other drops, Lou had managed to make email contact with today's intended patriot. The Gold Star mother, whose son had been killed-in-action in 2009, and Lou had met when he stopped in the small town several weeks earlier. Together with others from the area, they'd dropped what they were doing and stared at a freight train of soldiers and equipment headed west. Small talk had led to a discussion in which Lou learned her son had died in Afghanistan in 2009. That had led to another hour of discussion as her fourteen-year-old son and four-year-old granddaughter waited for Gramm to get done talking to the traveling stranger. They'd swapped phone numbers and emails. Lou had reached out to the woman twelve days earlier as one of the first actions when he took over the Rampart Edge program. She had confirmed things from his recollection of their conversation—that she and many of her fellow farmers and ranchers had formed up a mutual support collective, centered around American Legion Post 0092. Two days earlier, he'd gotten another email from her out of the blue, wondering if he could provide any information to her on the power outage and border hostilities. "I'm starting to really have to stretch the generator fuel," Kimberly McKenzie had explained.

Lucky your email hit a satellite, Lou thought as he turned back to see a Humvee slowly driving down the ramp of the plane. *I bet you and your Legionnaires aren't going to believe your stroke of luck.* In addition to two of the rigs and pallets of several supplies and gear, the team had brought a pair of enduro motorcycles. Though it had been several years, Lou had plenty of experience riding. He'd talked the team officer into allowing him and the senior NCO to take the bikes to go meet his contact while the rest of them off-loaded and prepared for their friendly invasion of the small mesa town. Lou saw two of the soldiers rolling the bikes down the ramps. He looked at Rusty, who had finished peeing on a clump of rough bear-grass. *They're far enough away,* Lou decided about the onlooker at the highway. He started to relieve himself on the same grass tuft. *This plane and my little pecker will pale in comparison to the things they'll see in the coming months.*

TUCSON, ARIZONA

"I'M STARTIN' TO THINK YOU'RE A GENIUS!" JEROME SAID TO Karen, who was riding shotgun in the beat-up SUV. It was nearly four in the morning, and they were on the trip back from the hospital in Tucson. Based on lessons learned from their first trip, Karen had suggested a slew of upgrades, not just to that vehicle, but to the shot-up ranch truck that they scooped up Granger with when the cartel IED had nearly taken him out. It had been staged at a key point between their planned primary and secondary routes once they'd started to approach the thickest vehicular traffic. The permanent power outage, near constant looting, and looming invasion had all but guaranteed non-stop crowds and gridlock traffic around the clock.

First, they simply removed the dome lights. Other improvements included the taping over of all the exterior lights and reflectors. Karen was kicking herself for not having thought days earlier just to remove them. They also used several cans of foam designed to spray into the tire's air nozzle—not a guarantee of running while flat, but it could possibly slow some leaks. They also broke out the front windshield on the SUV and were riding dressed in a variety of winter clothing, face masks, goggles, and neck gaiters. With the rear window having been shot out by Pedro on the last trip, the night wind tore right through the rig and froze them out. They had loaded a large tough Otter Box with six whiskey bottles half full of gasoline, some rags, and a lighter. Another item that Karen had wished they made time for was to install phone books or scraps of lumber on the interior of the door panels for at least a marginal amount of ballistic protection. There just hadn't been time.

As they'd checked Tracy out of the hospital and loaded him into the middle of the SUV, an angry mob of close to four hundred people converged on the facility in search of whatever wasn't nailed down or guarded under gunpoint. They'd barely made it clear of that mob when a looser collective of people roaming the streets began to filter out through the stopped cars of folks leaving the city. Clad mostly in dark hoodies, they began pulling people out of cars and beating them with bats, pipes, and chains. Gunshots had already been echoing throughout the area. They'd suddenly become very loud and close to the ranch team. Jerome had decided to leave the four-lane city street and cut through a nearby low-income neighborhood, only to see the road blocked by barrels on fire. Unsure of what he'd find on the other side, he stomped on the gas, sending a local gang scrambling for the sides of the road.

"Watch out!" Karen yelled as a Toyota land cruiser, with no lights on, sped out of a house's driveway and stopped right in their path. Jerome veered right and banked into a front yard, driving across two lawns and plowing through a child's pool and play set before coming back out onto the road on the other side of the attackers. Karen used her headlamp to study the worn paper Tucson map, intently in the swaying rig.

"Get us over to Broadway!" she yelled.

Behind her, Tracy was trying to scramble into the cargo hold to join Pedro as tail gunner, but his splint and the pain from surgery were too much. He let out a string of cussing in frustration. "Sorry! Best I can do is try to shoot out a side window!"

"Broadway's not close enough to the highway!" Jerome countered. A former firefighter, he knew the Tucson streets quite well.

"I have a plan!" Karen said. Both of them instinctively ducked as rounds zipped past the rig. The sound of Pedro's return fire filled the space with mind-numbing noise and the smell of gunpowder and lead styphnate.

Jerome continued to press hard on the pedal, only letting up enough to punch the parking brake and drift the big beast around corners. "Whew! This is way easier than in a fire truck!"

"Pedro! Throw a cocktail at them on my command!" Karen yelled back. He stopped shooting and began to stuff a rag into one of the bottles. Jerome took two more turns over the next seven blocks and hit a hard left, expertly gliding the rig onto the proper street. "Light it!" she called out next. As they passed a major intersection, Jerome made another left, banging and scraping cars that were barely moving. He laid on the horn as he drove the wrong way up the street, but so few were driving into the city that he didn't have to dodge but one car. "Now!" Karen yelled.

Pedro tossed the Molotov cocktail out the window, causing a small ball of fire to erupt, which sent the trailing land cruiser careening into a mess of cars trying to flee town. Jerome hit one more right turn and started to punch the gas once more.

"Hit the brakes!" Karen commanded. "Back up and go up the wrong way on Toole Avenue!"

"What?" her driver yelled back.

"Trust me!" Jerome did as he was told, and just after making a sharp turn up the curve of a one-way off-ramp, Karen ordered, "Right across the median! See the train tracks?"

Knowing where they'd staged the ranch truck, Jerome screamed elatedly. "I told you you's a genius, Kare Bear!" He guided the rig gingerly down the slope and into the large grass divider, cutting toward the right to drive up to the train tracks at an angle. Slowly they made it onto the open railway, and everyone started rattling as he drove along the rocks and timber ties as fast as he dared, the left wheels in between the two tracks.

"I-it-it's a-a-a g-o-oood thi-i-ing I do-o-n't ne-e-eed to pi-i-isss!" Tracy called out with a pained and bumpy voice from all the jostles of driving on the tracks.

Karen watched her map closely. Pedro assured the team that they were no longer being followed. They went three miles southeast before leaving the tracks as they approached the primary freight yard south of Highway 210. The area was brightly lit as the U.S. Army continued to offload tanks, track-driven bridging equipment, and mobile artillery. "Whoa..." was all Pedro said on behalf of all of them as he leaned out the open back window frame to see.

Jerome drove the battered vehicle through a less-active neighborhood south of Tucson until he reached their rally point and Granger's truck. Karen hopped out a block shy of the pickup. She took a few minutes to kneel next to the dark vehicle. Jerome slipped out and covered her while she slowly approached the truck, suppressed rifle at the low ready. After circling the vehicle and scouting in the bed and cab, she entered and fired it up. Less than thirty seconds later, the two rigs continued the pre-dawn journey back to the Acme Ranch.

CHAPTER 18

USS Lyndon B. Johnson DDG-1002

THE DARK ONLY HELPED, THE MOON A LOW SLIM SLIVER, almost non-existent. Tensions were high. With the sole living escaped POW back into custody and the fires extinguished, Millie had given her crew the most important speech of their lives fifteen minutes earlier... of her life.

"The mission must go on," Millie told her crew over the 1MC system via the interior speakers. "The Bunker Hill will provide air cover with her surface-to-air missiles. But she has to keep her distance. We have submarines engaging the enemy subs all over the Pacific. Our port and the ships in San Diego have taken heavy damage from space-based kinetic weapons. Our port and ships in Pearl Harbor have been engaged in battle by sea... air... land..." The entire ship was pin-drop quiet. "Bunker Hill and the subs in this operation need us. America... needs us..." Millie took a drink of water to moisten her mouth.

"Nobody except our sister Zumwalt ships comes close to our radar-defeating design and technology. It's up to us. Our eighty launch cells contain sixty Tomahawk cruise missiles, four ASROC torpedoes, and with four per cell, sixty-four Sea Sparrow self-defense missiles. We have over two hundred kinetic rounds for each of the two sizes of rail guns. Admittedly, we've never fired either. But we have to try, ship mates."

"We're only eighty-five miles off the coast. There are almost two-hundred surface ships bearing down on the central and southern California coast, in a battle group almost five hundred miles wide. There are another forty-six ships headed toward northern California and southern Oregon. Overhead, fighters are protecting two hundred bombers and cargo planes full of paratroopers. The airborne invasion has started, and the beach assault will be happening in less than two hours. And I'll lay the scuttlebutt to rest... we're almost to the middle of the surface group."

Millie paused for a few seconds, sure that some of the sailors were hearing all of it for the first time and in shock. "This is why we were on you all so hard about maintaining light discipline at the hatches. We've been sailing at perfect zero emissions, based on passively receiving photographic input from our remaining satellites. We're turning east in a few moments, driving right up the middle of the pack. I'm ordering General Quarters. All hands man your battle stations. Now let's kick their asses!"

The ominous electronic GQ gong began bleating over the interior speakers, driving any sailors who were asleep or still in shock from the news into action. They'd already been at Condition Three, maintaining a minimum level of staffing in all spaces and keeping all watertight hatches shut except for passing through. Sailors began to fully staff repair lockers, engineering plants, and weapons and sensor panels. Hatches were verified shut. Ventilation systems that were critical were ensured to be on. Others, which connected with the outside of the ship, were shut down to be ready for a gas attack. The long, slender, radar-deflecting ship plowed through the seas, bow parting cold black waves at a speed of thirty knots. They were making headway in the battle group that was traveling at twenty knots to accommodate its slowest ships.

Millie scanned south from the bridge windows with the night-vision feature on her binoculars. *One... two... seven?* she counted. It was difficult to make out shapes of any ships too far away, something she was banking on would help LBJ if they were visually spotted themselves. At the low height of the bridge, she could see about thirteen miles before the horizon dropped off due to the spherical shape of Earth. "XO, you have the bridge, and you'll maintain it. I'll be back and forth to CIC," Millie announced.

"Aye, Captain," Agwe Bailey concurred. "I have the bridge," he announced to the bridge crew for standard confirmation.

Millie left the binoculars draped around her neck and proceeded aft to the Combat Information Center. She went right to the main center console where her Operations Officer was staring down at the horizontal screen. The screen was an electronic picture, the latest intel they'd received from the sole passing satellite eighteen minutes earlier. A small electronic icon overlayed the image representing LBJ's approximate position. The icon was slowly creeping itself past center and would eventually move off the still photo.

"Have the image moved west on the screen to account for the minutes at twenty knots for them since this photo was taken," Millie ordered.

While a sailor complied, Dennis Bates said, "The rail guns, Captain. They're so fast. Won't they miss most ships past the horizon by flying over them? I mean—the projectiles will have so little arc. They're going to be dozens of miles down range when they hit the water at that speed."

"I've been thinking about that, Ops," Millie said. "We all know these railguns were meant for land attack. And I realize we'll need to turn on all the radars and fire-control systems for the best picture. But see how these ships are aligned?" Millie used her arm as a straightedge.

"Brilliant, Captain!" Dennis said. "Put a round through two ships, three if we get lucky!"

"That's the idea, Ops," she agreed. "Though at only twenty-three pounds, I'm not sure how well the projectiles will fly after passing through an entire ship. But Mach 7? And that much kinetic energy? I guess we'll find out. As will they."

"And we expect ten rounds per minute rate of fire per mount?"

"That's what the labs said, Dennis," Millie said with a smirk. "So, I expect six, hopefully. In between shots, I want you to target ships at the outer perimeter of the southern side of this invasion force with our Tomahawks. Fire off three to four per cycle."

Millie made calls to the gun mounts and engine rooms. She wanted to ensure the Gunner's Mates were ready to hand load the feed tubes down in the magazines. She didn't trust the untested system. And the ship would need to increase its electrical output to 25 megawatts per gun to ensure it had as much efficiency as possible. Electromagnetic rails would cycle a pulse of energy, pushing the projectiles down the barrel with a force so violent it would shake as badly as a traditional cannon. The original mount was using tungsten slugs. The newly installed barrel on the mount closer to the bridge would be firing plasma slugs. The heated friction of the shots would ignite the molten metal cores of the slugs, which would incinerate whatever it hit at 13,000 degrees. Her last call was to ensure that hose teams were in place to spray down the barrels. They would stay inside the ship's flat superstructure until the forward missiles were all fired. *This is unprecedented,* she knew. *Nobody ever expected us to fire these things, let alone hundreds of them in one battle.*

Millie glanced down at the display. "You can pull the map, Ops," she decided. "When I get back to the bridge, we'll be going live. Wait for my order," she said as she moved back out of the space.

A few steps forward and she was back in the dark bridge, looking at the silhouettes of her shipmates being cast by screens turned down to five percent brightness. She strode to port and scanned, searching her memory of the last glance at the intelligence photo. Millie could feel her heart starting to beat faster. An image of Don crept into her mind, making her smile for just a moment. *Lord, please take care of my family.* She moved across the wall of windows to the starboard, continuing to scan.

"Mr. Bailey," she said, her calm voice masking the nerve ball building in her stomach.

"Aye, Captain," the friendly Jamaican replied.

"Tell CIC to light us up." While the XO relayed the command, Millie grabbed the handset near her fixed captain's stool and cued up the 1MC. "All hands, prepare for battle. May God bless us all!" As she hung up, the data from the freshly powered radars, radios, and positioning systems populated the displays. The small whir of cooling fans for dormant computers suddenly came to life. Millie knew that at that moment, in dozens of Chinese warships and planes, the combat centers were reacting in confusion to the unknown source of radar transmission in the dead center of their fleet.

Millie took a quick glance at the displayed enemy positions on the screens overhead and grabbed her handset. "CIC, Bridge. See that line of frigates to the starboard?"

"Copy that, Bridge," Dennis' voice replied.

"Mount One on them. Mount Two hit that amphib to the port forward about seven miles out."

Millie watched in the dark, barely able to see the cowling on the large boxy structures slide up and rear, revealing the long barrels. The heavy, shock-absorbed cannons lifted one foot out of their cradles. The forward-most cannon moved to the starboard, while the one closer to the bridge moved port. In the mounts, small gyroscopes relayed the ship's movement as it rocked and plunged its way through the dark ocean, sending slight corrections to the gun mounts. The barrels were adjusting automatically to ensure their aim was true.

"Fire at will!" the adrenaline filled short captain practically yelled into the phone. Without the traditional fireball of naval artillery, the cannons shook none-the-less, as they spilled their violence toward the invaders with 32 MegaJoules of energy. In the tiniest of fractions of the next second, two ships to the starboard were hit with the slug, one at three miles distance, the other at twelve. The round hit the ocean thirty-two miles down range and skipped along the surface like the world's deadliest tumbleweed, barely missing a third ship.

Both ships caught fire as the intense friction and heat radiating off the round ignited a fuel line on one and passed through a torpedo loaded in its deck-launcher on the other. Explosions ensued. Millie ran to the port in nervous energy, seeing that the targeted amphibious ship full of enemy soldiers was starting a series of recurring explosions. As she ran, the missile hatch covers to the port and starboard bow opened. Four Tomahawk cruise missiles all shot with a bright glare, achieving several hundred feet of altitude before their guidance systems were able to correct them. They rapidly picked up speed, heading south.

Millie jerked the phone on that side of the bridge out of its cradle. "CIC, Bridge—let me know the moment you detect enemy fire control radars!" *They know where we are now...*

USS JAMES L. HUNNICUTT SSGN-93

THE SOUND OF THE ACTIVE SONAR PIERCED THE HULLS OF THE Hunny and the sister ship trailing behind her like electronic nails on a chalkboard, squeaking like a hi-low siren. The sonar technicians had warned of explosions coming from multiple contacts. In the confusion, and in the memory of a strange intelligence report of one damaged U.S. submarine towing a different non-functioning one, the panicked fleet admiral ordered the destroyers to take action. They launched their helicopters, each armed with two torpedoes. And they began active sonar pinging, trying to find the Yankee Imperialist infiltrators to relay positions to their own submarines.

"The source was contact Juliet-one-seven!" an overly nervous sonar technician announced before being asked. The loud electronic active sonar came with its own set of pros and cons. While telling the sender exactly where the submarines were, it also told those who got hit by the bouncing sound wave who actually 'rang the bell.' It wasn't much of a negative attribute to surface ships, as it was presumed the subs already knew where they were. In the state-of-the-art submarine, the sonar operators were no longer confined to their own tiny sound-resistant room. The CO ignored the outburst as he studied the screens ahead of him, and Darren walked over to put his hand on the young lady's shoulder in reassurance.

"Just calm down, Martin," he said calmly. "We're all nervous as hell..."

"Aye, COB," she said apologetically.

"Alright! Here we go!" Commander Woodard, the captain of the ship said in tense anticipation. "All ahead two-thirds! Right full rudder, bearing two-two-zero. I want forty-five knots as soon as we can get there! Let's show these commies what we can do!"

As Darren repeated the orders to his pilots, he watched the digital gauges in front of them to ensure the orders were being followed correctly. He heard Brody continue to give orders.

"Give me the full three-sixty view on the main screen! Highlight the four-mile grid around contact Charlie-zero-one! Put all submerged contacts on Screen Two! XO!"

"Aye, sir!" Carla called out in the tension.

"Call the TAC! Make sure they have the correct surface targets to the north ready to go for the missiles. We'll be sitting ducks during the volley. No wasted seconds. And make sure they have some decoys ready to go. It seems like our chemical countermeasures didn't do jack squat a few months ago."

"Aye, sir."

"Sonar," he called out next. "What's our little sister doing behind us?"

"Key West is increasing speed and peeling off to the south, Captain!"

USS ILLINOIS SSN-786

DAYS EARLIER, IN THE COLD BLACK OF THE NORTH PACIFIC Ocean, over a dozen Navy SEALs worked feverishly for two hours, swimming to keep up with two submarines. Moving one tow cable at a time and under spotlights built into the spy sub, they transferred the towing of El Paso over to USS Illinois, the other ultra-fast propulsor driven submarine in Operation Flea Flicker.

As China used active sonar to find the USS James L. Hunnicutt and the decoy ship behind her, they made the mistaken assumption that the wounded duck, bogged down with an enormous burden to tow, was going to be easy pickings per their false intelligence. The sonar technicians on the Illinois reported the ruse was up... that Hunnicutt and Key West were moving to flank speed and engaging.

"Very well," the calm smooth Annapolis graduate CO replied. "Continue on course, decrease speed to fifteen knots. Prepare to blow the tow pendants."

As the PLAN hunter killers swam under them, Illinois moved over the crisscrossing of warring U-boats at a shallow two-hundred feet, towing a dead submarine packed full with hundreds of torpedo warheads and thousands of other explosives. The Key West would join the Scranton in taking out the enemy subs. The Hunnicutt would start attacking surface contacts with torpedoes and missiles, in an attempt to force the invaders to take evasive action right over where Illinois would plant the largest non-nuclear bomb ever built.

USS LYNDON B. JOHNSON DDG-1002

MILLIE RAN INTO THE COMBAT INFORMATION CENTER. "What's the problem, Ops?" she called loudly.

"Mount Two, Captain," Dennis Bates answered amongst the dark room full of Operations Specialists and Fire Control Technicians monitoring the variety of sensors, radars, and weapon control systems. "The chief engineer is looking into it. He thinks that the intense friction and heat are overloading the system. They're trying to cool and reset it now."

"Decrease rate-of-fire to two per minute on Mount One," Millie ordered. "We need it to stay up!" She was moving directly over to the sonar panel. "How many submarines are you tracking, both ours and theirs?"

The technician looked at the secondary screen next to her main display. "We're still showing at least twenty-seven of theirs, Ma'am." After a slight pause to check further, "And nine of ours." The young man looked at his captain with tears in his eyes as he pulled his headphones off his ears and rest them on his head.

"What were the numbers when we started?" Millie asked, trying to evoke calmness with her manner despite her own fear.

"They had forty and we had thirteen," he said.

He reminds me so much of Peter, she thought. And the resemblance to her son-in-law made her think once more of the family she feared she would never see again. *Snap out of it!* she scolded herself. "I don't want to lose track of the submerged threat," she reminded the first-class petty officer. *Their helicopters and destroyers will start taking even more of ours out.* "Speak out as soon as it looks like one is on to us."

"Yes, Ma'am," she heard as she moved toward the sailors monitoring the air. She silently scanned the screens over them, looking at three waves of airborne assault headed for California, along with fighter escorts. *Where's the counterattack?* she worried. The mission package promised we'd get some land-based air cover. She headed back to the main table-screen and looked down.

"I've lost count, Ops. How many Tomahawks do—"

The impact of the 105-millimeter round exploding just shy of hitting the ship's stern violently interrupted Millie. The ship shook, reminding them all that their high-tech destroyer wasn't completely invisible. Like a bolt of lightning, Millie ran out of CIC and back to the bridge, which was already a beehive.

"It came from the south, Ma'am!" Agwe Bailey said from the starboard side of the bridge, his own binoculars pressed hard into his face, phone to CIC already in his hand.

Millie scanned the bridge's displays, information being sent to them from CIC. "Contact Echo-one-one!" she guessed. The pair both saw the muzzle flash in the distance. "Right rudder!" she yelled. "Flank speed! Make your bearing one-nine-zero!"

As the mighty ship started turning toward the starboard and south, she lurched over to port. Another shell came crashing down immediately in front of the bow. The Chinese Type 053H frigate was adjusting fire. *As soon as they connect, they're going to give our coordinates to all the rest!* Millie realized.

"Flood the ballast tanks!" she ordered. Yet another unique feature was that the ship had the ability to lower its own draft in the water, decreasing its profile in the sky by another eight feet. It was a dicey decision—if they took damage and flooding, then they would be that much closer to sinking entirely.

Mount Two had made its final adjustments and sent one of its lethal rounds back at the frigate. The Mach 7 bullet hit the hull low, entering the gun mount magazine. The ship exploded in a back-breaking fireball. Millie knew that not all her rounds and missiles were connecting. Some were missing within the margin of error for sending ballistics across the rocking ocean. Tomahawks were being shot down by defense systems. But she could no longer count the growing number of fires flickering to the east and south in the gray, pre-dawn sky.

CHAPTER 19

THE LARGE RUN-FLAT TIRES AND DIESEL ENGINE OF THE M-1083 truck blocked out all the noises of the frightening caravan as it proceeded north on Brookhurst Street, headed toward highway I-5. The woodland camouflaged tarp had charred burn holes in it on its roof and left side, scars from heavy use ferrying National Guard soldiers in and out of various firefights with cartel strongholds in recent weeks. Alex, his brother, and parents, and several of their neighbors were riding in the covered bed. The rest of his group were in a second truck. Each rig was towing most of their supplies and gear in a covered trailer. Lucky Charm had made good on his promise to transport the 15th Street Posse north toward the building stronghold at the old L.A. Zoo. *He never said it would be a comfortable ride,* Alex admitted to himself.

Escorted by a sole armored Humvee, the two vehicles were wasting no time on this mission. The lead rig had plowed through a variety of crude barricades and abandoned vehicles. So many Los Angelinos that had waited far too long in the crisis to flee had simply run out of fuel—

or been murdered for what they had. Trash and fires dotted every block along the way. Alex's thoughts were rudely interrupted by the sound of machine gun fire as it exploded from the top of their escort a hundred feet north.

"What is that?" Roman and Sissy Lopez's twelve-year-old daughter Serena cried out. Ned Manner's dog began to whine.

Alex scooted his butt off the left-side bench just a bit so he could turn his head and look out of a baseball sized hole. His eyes grew wide. He whipped around to his brother, sitting to his right. "Help me cut a larger flap in this canvas!" he ordered.

"Dude, I was just falling asleep," Henry said in Vietnamese. "Go away." He refolded his coat into a pillow and leaned his head back.

Alex made a fist and backhanded his younger brother in the gut. "Now, Henry! Let me see your knife!"

With a ticked-off scowl, Henry made a fist, his middle finger's main knuckle protruding a bit. He hit Alex's forearm square between the muscles. The impact caught a nerve just right, sending lightning down the rest of his arm. "Don't hit me, jackass!" he yelled before pulling his folding knife out of his pocket and handing it over.

Alex rubbed his arm and then took the tool. He flipped the blade open and turned back toward the fabric wall behind him. Roman Lopez watched out of boredom and curiosity. "Cut it like a smile, not a frown," he advised.

"Huh?" Alex said as he plunged the blade into the covering.

"Cut it so the flap folds from the top, not the bottom. That way, it'll not be a gaping hole from now on."

"Oh," Alex said. He complied with the commonsense instruction and refolded the knife.

Roman stooped and slid over behind his neighbor on his knees. He reached in behind Alex and helped him push the new, two-foot wide opening up and out so they could see out. Looking left—west—they could see various hordes of people along the road. Some were fighting with a variety of clubbed weapons. One was openly raping someone else. There were three laying in the road, bleeding profusely out of freshly installed holes courtesy of the escort vehicle machine gunner. The flames and smoke of various buildings burning were not enough to hide the most truly shocking event—something so unbelievable that Alex almost thought it was part of Tinseltown's latest movie production.

"Holy shitake mushrooms," Roman mumbled as his face joined Alex's to take in the horror. "They're—they're everywhere!" he cried in disbelief as the two of them started pushing their heads out as far as they could manage, scanning above... to the south... in all directions.

The blood red sky from the rising sun turned to pinks and purples as it crept west, revealing a sky full of Chinese and captured Russian planes. Though there were some American jet fighters attempting to knock them out of the sky, they were outnumbered and heavily engaged by China and Venezuela's defending fighters. Between them and the small, battered convoy, in every direction their eyes could see, were paratroopers at various heights. Some were close to the ground. Others were just dropping out of their planes, the static lines pulling the chutes out of their packs like unfolded bed sheets. All were under the control of gravity with but one mindset—invade America and perform their duty with honor—to the death if needed.

USS James L. Hunnicutt SSGN-93

"Torpedo in the water!" the chief sonar technician called out. "It went active the second it hit!" The mild pinging of the device's active sonar was hitting their hull about every eight seconds.

Darren heard the captain let out an explosive metaphorical dictation about what the Chinese were supposed to do to each other's mothers. They were forty missiles deep into a volley of sending all four dozen toward the enemy fleet. *Out of nowhere. It must've been dropped by helicopter,* he thought.

"Range!" the skipper demanded.

"Thirty-two-hundred yards! Speed sixty-five knots!" The Hunny was cruising at missile launch depth at five knots. Each of the eight tubes contained six of the cruise missiles. As the flooded tubes emptied, the hatch was being re-shut. They were strategically firing from all the tubes to try to keep the boat's list and trim as level as possible. Though most of the missiles had been fired. The remaining eight still occupied six tubes.

"TAC, Conn!" Brody Woodward screamed into his handset. "Suspend firing! COB—make sure we get the green!" he ordered Darren. "Make your depth four hundred! All ahead full!"

Darren relayed the orders to the pilots while he was monitoring the missile tube hatches position on a string of lights. Slowly they turned from red Xs to green Os. "We're in the green, Captain!" he relayed. He felt the ship start to respond to her new orders. Darren started counter-leaning in the rear direction to maintain an upright position. The ship's hull began to compress, but the depth change was so slight that they wouldn't make much popping noise for the torpedo to track.

"Sir, we should stay shallow!" Carla Gingrey said. "There's so much noise from the surface war, we might get lost in it!"

"Good thinking, XO! COB?"

Darren was already relaying the instruction, and the submarine leveled out. "Depth two-oh-two and holding, sir," he said calmly. The electronic pinging from the torpedo was getting louder, the signal occurring every six seconds. *It's still coming,* was the fear that dominated every mind in the submarine at that moment.

The CO was intensely scanning his battlefield displays. The little icons were moving more quickly as they picked up speed. "Highlight grid Alpha fourteen!" he ordered.

The main display zoomed in on the intended area. "Make your bearing three-one-five!" he yelled. "Put us right in between these two ships! Adjust course as you need to, COB!"

Darren ordered the pilots at the control station and pointed at their screen. "Right in that one's wake! I mean you really need to shave it close, Witt!" he insisted.

"Depth one-zero-zero!" the captain ordered. "ETA until impact?"

Darren had his team pull up on the dive planes as the fast submarine gained speed. The torpedo's gain had slowed. "Fifty seconds!" someone called out.

Everyone who could see a screen was trying to do the mental math on when they might pass behind the enemy corvette. They weren't going to make it at that speed. The captain got on the phone with his engine room. "We need the full output on the reactor, Eng!" he said, using the Chief Engineer's nickname, pronounced 'Inj.' Not a soul in the room dared crack a Kirk and Scotty joke at that moment.

Darren continued to monitor the speed. *What about the sonar dome and ballast tank repairs?* he worried. *Are those going to hold?* The submarine's modern design elements, from the propulsor to the sleek curvy cowling at the bottom of the conning tower, to the shape of the planes and stabilizers—all were meant to give her superior speed. With more torpedo tubes than most older classes, and greater speed than any other class of submarines ever built, the theory was that she could cover more ocean and targets if she ever needed to perform an attack role—or evade a torpedo in the open ocean. The mighty vessel was starting to shake as she pressed through the sea at nearly fifty-five knots.

As they approached the gap behind the corvette and the destroyer one mile behind it, Darren's pilots made a slight adjustment. "Range four-hundred yards!" one of the tech's called out.

"Right rudder!" the CO ordered. "Come around the corvette! Put us just under periscope depth!"

As the Hunny slowly made the turn back to the east, the trailing torpedo curved to follow suit. It misinterpreted the noise from the enemy vessel and exploded with enough force to break its keel and send the front and half pieces ten feet into the air. The water all around the ship turned a bright teal green as it filled with heat and gas bubbles. The shockwave rippled through the ocean and impacted the James L. Hunnicutt only three hundred yards away.

The submarine danced, throwing every item and person inside around like rag dolls. Alarms and sensors screamed, and electronic systems flickered and blinked before resetting themselves. Darren, who was standing and facing the starboard where his pilots sat, was thrown backward. He slid to a stop by running into a console on the other side of the control room. He felt the XO slide into him. His ears rang from the noise, head pounding with a concussion headache. "Are you okay?" he asked his XO loudly. He could hear her moan and groan. "Carla!" he insisted.

"I—I'm okay, COB," she said slowly. Both gingerly climbed back to their feet. The pilots, sonar operators, and most of the rest of the conn team were belted into chairs. "Where's the captain?!" she asked excitedly.

Ignoring the blaring sirens and looking farther aft, they saw the answer. Near the inclined ladder at the aft port side of the space, they saw their commanding officer lying unconscious, a growing pool of blood around his head.

ACME RANCH
      Southeast of Tucson, Arizona

THE APPROACH TO THE RANCH WAS BUSIER FOR DAWN THAN any of the crew who brought Tracy home from the hospital would've ever guessed. The two-lane state highway led south past nothing but ranches and grazing land until reaching one town, called Sonoita. Once there, the road branched to other towns west and east. But many of the other arterial roads were clogged as the U.S. Army continued to spread along their front line. Residents had nowhere to go but north, and though many were without an ultimate destination, they still found themselves bugging out on the beautiful Thursday morning. As the two trucks slowed to turn west up the ranch's driveway, they were passed rapidly by car after speeding car of families seeking safety.

"The balloon must've gone up," Tracy said, breaking a long silence amongst the tired friends.

"Sorry," Karen squeaked as loudly as her dry and strained throat would allow. "I guess we could've tried the radio on the trip home. Didn't even think about it..."

Jerome turned up the access. Once past the open gate, he immediately had to pull partway off the drive, hugging the pasture fence closely as Army trucks and equipment were moving to the road. He came up to a military police officer and stopped. The young man took their identifications and checked them against the very short civilian access list. Two minutes later, they'd been cleared and finished the drive to the main house.

"Something's wrong," Karen said.

"Yeah, I bet the invasion has finally started," Pedro said as he gingerly reached down out the back window frame and found the handle to pop open the hatchback.

"No, I mean here," Karen explained. She watched Bob get out of a lawn chair near the open door to the converted garage.

As Pedro and Jerome assisted Tracy with exiting, Karen headed over, concerned about the look on the old Road Runner's face. Though he hadn't been crying, he may as well have been. "What is it?" she asked, unprepared for the answer.

Bob stepped up to her and placed his hands on her shoulders. "I'm sorry, dear..."

Karen knew instantly, causing hot tears to well up in the puffy bags under her eyes. She slowly leaned into the man's gentle but determined pull, landing her chin on his shoulder. "Claude...?" was all she could manage to say.

"He passed about an hour ago," Bob said, holding his surrogate niece tight to him.

Karen started to sob and wrapped her arms around Bob's neck. *Oh, Claude!* she thought. *Why here! Why now! Why'd you have to leave me all alone out here?*

Pedro and Jerome tried to escort Tracy into the house, but he saw Bob's face and headed over under his own power. After giving his older companion a fist bump with the arm not in a sling, he asked, "What happened?"

"Claude had been ill," Bob explained. "His heart. He passed just a short while ago."

The former Navy man fumbled for words. "What? Oh... wow... ohhh..." His face wrinkled in emotional pain. "First Mick and Wolf. Now Claude!"

"Have a seat, brother," Bob said, nodding toward his unused lawn chair. "It's good to have you back."

Inside, after hugging his wife Robin, who had grown attached to Claude as she became his nurse, Jerome the former EMT took custody of the situation. He had Fred go tack up a horse to the ranch utility wagon. Pedro and Daniel assisted Jerome in moving Claude to the front outside the house in a heavy-duty, nylon fold up litter with sewn on handles. Bob held Karen as the men loaded Claude as delicately as they could into the wagon.

Daniel stepped down from the back of the wagon. "My deepest condolences," he offered Karen with a nod and a sincere expression. Karen nodded back and wiped her eyes, though she said nothing. Bob gave Daniel a look that would've knocked a buzzard off a manure cart.

"Guys..." Donna Wolf said as she came out of the house holding something in her clutches. She moved over to the wagon and handed a triangular flag up to Pedro. Its blue field and large white stars were obvious.

"No—Donna, that was your husband's!" Karen said.

Donna nudged Pedro to keep it and walked over to Karen with tears rolling down her cheeks. She gave the woman a hug and then pulled back, keeping one hand on Karen's arm. "Not the one from his funeral," she explained. "The one from his shadow-box from when he left the Special Forces. He's practically screaming at me in my mind that I need to give it to Claude!" she half laughed. "Please take it! I know Dave wouldn't have thought twice about it."

"She's right, Karen," Bob agreed, squeezing her with the one arm still around her shoulders. "She's one thousand percent right—that's what any of us original Road Runners would've done."

"Absolutely," Tracy said from the chair.

Karen nodded and gave Donna another hug in return, a fresh set of tears flowing down her rosy cheeks.

Suddenly, sirens began to play out on the loudspeakers at the Army compound to the south. The ranch group moved past the trees on the opposite side of the parking area, toward the fenced field in front of the main barn. They could see vehicles and people scrambling. Missiles suddenly launched from the defensive batteries a kilometer to the south. One by one, twenty streaks of flame shot out leaving a smoke trail behind. They went in different directions though all were southerly in nature.

A series of loud booms exploded overhead as several jets rocketed by faster than the sound barrier. "Those are Chinese!" Bob called out. Four more jets rounded right around the ranch as they looped from a southerly heading to westerly, trying to get in behind the invading jets. The ranch team all stared in awe, watching the jets slowly peel apart in a tangled web, as the American F-22s started to stray from each other, hot on the tails of the enemy J-10s and J-20s.

Daniel called out to Fred, "Fire up the quad and meet me at the bunkhouse!" before sprinting off to grab his tactical kit.

Donna looked at Karen and Bob. "Should we let them go up to the OP?" she asked in concern.

I don't really care at this point, Karen thought. *I'm just too drained to keep playing games with that clown.*

Sensing that, Bob answered. "It'll be okay," he nodded. "A couple o' sets of eyes up there will probably be good." By then, the sounds of the defensive missiles exploding a few miles off had finally made their way back to the ranch, as did the loud distant rumbles of artillery and tank cannons. The noises added credibility to the building sense of doom and foreboding arising in the pits of everyone's stomachs as they watched a dogfight unfolding in front of the rising Arizona sun.

CHAPTER 20

USS James L. Hunnicutt SSGN-93

The ship's doctor wasn't a doctor at all, but a highly trained corpsman certified for independent duty, like a paramedic. Trained mostly to deal with trauma and any minor medical issues that might befall younger and healthier people, she knew immediately there was a major problem. Though there were minor injuries throughout the USS James L. Hunnicutt, the CO's head wound was by far the worst injury after taking the initial damage control reports. By the time she'd arrived with a couple of repair party firefighters in tow, the conn team had grabbed the nearest first aid kit and applied a pressure bandage.

"We need to get him to sick bay!" she said after only a cursory look. "Grab a litter," she ordered one of the firefighters. She palpated the neck and exposed scalp, checking for signs of fractures.

As much as the conn team wanted to watch, Darren snapped them all back to their jobs. "Sonar, are there any other torpedoes?" he said with authority.

"Not in the immediate vicinity, COB," the chief told him. "We've got filters applied, but between the exploding ships and torpedo shootouts in every direction for a hundred miles, it sounds like an over-the-top video game out there..."

Carla took Darren's lead and snapped out of her own mental funk. "Highlight the Illinois!" she ordered. Most of the systems had rebooted, and alarms were silenced by the equipment operators. At first glance the Hunny had not suffered any noticeable damage.

The main screen zoomed in on the sector farthest to the east. "Sensors picked her up two minutes ago in this location, just for a quick second," the chief said.

"She's got two attack boats between the fleet and her," Carla noted. "Where's Key West?"

"Ten miles southeast and engaging contact Sierra-four."

"And Scranton?"

The crew held bated breath while the sonar techs worked their keyboards. "Thirty-nine miles northwest! She has Two Song class and one Ming class on her! Torpedoes are tracking her... looks like a range of eight thousand yards!"

"Left full rudder!" Carla exclaimed. The ship, still moving at mind-blowing fifty-five knots, banked hard as the control surfaces fought their way to the proper positions under the command of the pilots' joysticks. "Decrease speed to forty-five knots! Make our depth three-fifty, COB!"

Darren continued to relay instructions to the pilots, including once again ensuring that the ballast tanks flooded with the proper volume of seawater to help gain negative buoyancy. The ship shook as she responded to the high-speed demands of combat.

"Torpedo room!" Carla called into her conn handset. "Make sure the fish are set with the proper kill-box on Tubes one thru four. Set tubes five and six for snapshots!" She hung up without even waiting for the concurrence reply.

"Good call, XO," Darren agreed, as he watched the screen adjust itself in relation to the ship's turn. "At the speed we're entering this shootout, we might find ourselves right up on one of those Songs..."

"Conn," the chief sonar tech called out. "Two small explosions from the Illinois! She's moving to flank speed."

Darren gave a knowing glance at Carla. "They've just blown the tow pendants on El Paso. It won't be long now. At least we're already headed in the right direction."

"But what about the Key West?" she countered, her voice racked with doubt. "They're probably too wrapped up in battle to notice! They'll get caught in the aftershock!"

"I get it, XO, but Scranton needs our help, too! And so will the LBJ and the Bunker Hill! Northwest is the right call, Ma'am!"

"But we owe them, COB!" she practically yelled, causing the entire team to freeze for a quick moment. Nobody wanted to go back toward the giant bomb Illinois had just lit the fuse on. "They saved our bacon back in the China Sea!"

"I know... Carla..." Darren said with as much fatherly mentoring as he could. As the XO's partner and the senior enlisted man, he knew he could break decorum with her, and it would be okay. "They're doing their duty. And we're doing ours. We can't save them. But we might save the others..."

The conn remained quiet. Darren saw Carla's eyes turn red with emotion, and he let his follow suit. He wasn't ashamed to let the crew know it was okay to be scared in the face of death—as long as they did their jobs. "Continue course and speed," she finally agreed.

"Turn! Turn, dammit!" they both heard the chief sonar technician yelling at his console.

"What is it, Chief?" Carla asked, eyeing the screen for the positions of the three Chinese subs in the waters ahead.

"Scranton!" he said. All three sonar operators suddenly ripped their headsets off. They'd had the dirty duty of listening in as the enemy's Yu-6 torpedo zero in for the kill. It exploded along the starboard engine room, flooding the space and reactor compartment with seawater as the two-inch thick steel hull peeled back. The submarine immediately began sinking, dropping tail end first though still with its momentum from trying to escape. The sonar technicians put their headphones back on, now that the explosion a dozen miles ahead was over. "Contact Mike-zero-five is coming around!" he yelled. "Right for us at depth six-fifty!"

This damn dive limit! Darren thought. *They've got us trapped on the ceiling!*

"Make your course three-five-five, COB!" Carla ordered, triggering him to direct the pilots. "We're going to swing wide and then come in under them when they try to keep up with the turn." She scanned the screen. "Sonar, do you concur on the range being twelve-thousand yards?"

"Range is good, Conn!"

The Hunny rolled as they turned right just a bit. After fifteen tense seconds, Darren and Carla saw the enemy sub trying to turn to its port in an attempt to cut off their path. "Now, COB! Left full rudder! Bearing two-four-zero! Increase speed to fifty-five! Make your depth six-fifty!"

Darren spent one second giving her the 'seriously?' stare. He repeated her orders loudly and with no further delay. "Six-fifty, COB?" the pilot asked in grave concern.

"You heard the order, shipmate," Darren affirmed.

The USS James L. Hunnicutt protested. As she turned hard and dove, the hull began to make the standard popping noises. Roughly every one-hundred feet of depth added forty-three pounds-per-square-inch of pressure. As she strove to reach deeper water, the hull was being squeezed and compressed, causing the metal to groan. "What're you SOBs gonna do now?" Carla yelled.

The Hunny shot back up to a speed that the PLAN Navy wasn't prepared for. "Range eight-thousand!" sonar called out. "They're diving! They'll be passing on our left!" Another short but lifelong pause. "Her tubes are flooding!"

"Snapshot tube six!" Carla called. The officer seated at the torpedo control station flipped a safety interlock up and over, revealing the flashing red 'Launch' button. He pressed it. The torpedo tubes were offset at an angle, shooting the torpedoes out to clear the ship. The outer door rolled open, turning the smooth fairing of the ship's skin into a muzzle. The inner door opened, the water in the tube having been matched pressure to the ocean. Pressurized water from a separate tank shot the torpedo out several dozen feet, its propeller pushing it farther. It screamed up to its maximum rate. A thin wire played out of the device, allowing the weapons operator in the conn to steer the device. Had it not been for the sound of pushing it out, it was likely the Ming would've never heard it coming. If the guided wire were to break, the torpedo had both passive and active systems to guide its 647-pound warhead to its target. There were no safeties installed on this shot—the torpedo was a threat to anyone in the area, including the Hunny.

"Torpedo in the water!"

"Right rudder!" Carla said. "Make your course three-three-zero. Depth four-zero-zero! Port side countermeasures!"

"Contact Mike-zero-two is opening outer doors! Range ten thousand, bearing three-four-zero!"

"Very well," Carla said. "Launch torpedoes two and four." The familiar sounds of two more Mark-48s being launched two seconds apart were heard and felt. The torpedo team was busy reloading the empty tubes.

The chief sonar operator reminded his team to pull headsets. "Direct hit on Mike-zero-five," he said as the explosion started. After a few seconds, he donned the set again. "Sounds like their shot went after the countermeasure. It isn't following." He held up a finger to ask for a moment. Finally, "She's flooding. I can hear the hull breaking up..."

"COB, maintain course. The 48s will take care of that sub. I've got a feeling that LBJ will be needing us up there."

"Conn!" another one of the sonar operators called. "It sounds like —like—"

The chief took over. "I'm guessing it was the Flea Flicker, Ma'am.

Twenty-five miles east by southeast." He listened a bit more, adjusting some dials and switches. "I heard an explosion like I've never heard... and multiple ships sinking." All three of them were clacking on their keyboards. "Not you, Dan. Keep your ears on what's ahead," he mumbled to one of his subordinates. Suddenly, he looked up with worry. "The ships in that area are getting up-ended like they're in a giant bathtub."

Darren and Carla exchanged glances. "It was a pretty big bomb, XO," he said. "Something like four-hundred torpedo warheads at seven-hundred pounds each. Plus other stuff?"

"There's not much we can do now, COB. Put us down to eight-zero-zero. That wave will probably damage or sink every ship for fifty miles."

Darren gave her a grave look, seeing that she was fully aware of the major risk involved to the repaired sub. "Aye, Ma'am," he finally said before repeating her commands.

ACME RANCH
Southeast of Tucson, Arizona

KAREN WAS JUST GETTING THE HANG OF USING THE JOHN Deere 5R's rear-mounted bucket by the time she'd finished the grave. The irony of placing Claude's resting place near the same tree that Daniel had tried to frame her for stolen goods was not lost. Before that happened, the spot had meant a bit of peaceful solace in a trying moment. Since then, it had represented the initial step of a new trans-formation—of becoming a woman who would no longer allow venomous men to control her mind. Jerome had driven the machine, which had been part of Donna's ranch purchase, down the trail and showed Karen how to use the levers. Knowing that she didn't want to bury a body too close to the open stream to the east, she'd chosen the spot as a way of telling her uncle that she was growing, evolving... that she was... moving on.

"I'll dig it for you, if you'd like," Jerome offered.

"I got it, J," she said with a fragile smile. "I need to be alone." She looked over at the horseless cart, the gifted American flag covering her sole family, tucked in and under Claude along the sides. "I'll call you on the radio when I need some help." In the ninety minutes since, she'd dug the hole and spent some time meditating. Not sure if she actually believed in God, she hoped that there was one—hopeful that Claude knew how much she loved him, something her angry family rarely conveyed to each other.

Am I alone? she contemplated. *Maybe I should just slip out quietly.* She continued to think. To Plan. To wonder. *I don't need the drama. I don't need any more Daniels in my life.* For several minutes she thought about where she would go... how she would eat or sleep out on her own as a war was starting... She wept some more, missing her mother who'd passed from breast cancer eleven years earlier. She thought about traveling to Florida to find the father she'd not talked to for nineteen years. She thought of those at the ranch she'd started to bond with, such as Pedro, Jerome, Tracy... Granger. The thought of the scarred firefighter and Marine instantly brought about the usual heart flutters. They'd shared more than one spark. *I told him I would lead the security decisions, didn't I? But Tracy is back, wounded as he is...* At one point, three deer startled her as they fled north. After stopping and engaging Karen in a staring contest for a timeless moment, they took off sprinting again, sensing the south was no longer safe.

After a long while, and a decision to stay in the hopes Granger would return, she called Jerome on the radio. The sounds of war in the distance had continued steadily, though not at the feverish pace of earlier. More air-defense missiles fired out of their box launchers to the south, snapping her out of her reverie and deep cerebration. She was ready to close the chapter and move forward through the daunting period before them all. Jerome showed up with Bob, Tracy, and Donna. Despite Tracy's wounded arm, the five of them were able to gently move Claude to his final resting place on earth, softly removing the cloth litter and flag. Bob and Jerome folded it up, not quite getting the perfect alignment of three stars on the hypotenuse with the final fold and tuck.

"Thank you," she told Bob as he handed it to her and gave her a warm peck on the cheek. "I've had my final words and prayers," she explained to all of them. "I—I don't even remember the last time I slept! Do you think you could—" She started to weep a bit as she looked at the pile of dirt that still needed to be moved.

"We got it, Kare Bear," Jerome said.

"C'mon," Tracy said. "I'll walk with you."

"Yes, we got it," Bob added. "You don't have to be alone, young lady. We can carry this burden with you."

OVER EASTERN ARIZONA

LOU STOOD IN THE SMALL ACCESS BETWEEN THE COCKPIT AND the empty cargo hold, staring at two of his team members and one German Shepherd. Gray was sacked out across three of the cargo hold jump seats, trying to lie down for his nap. He tried to step quietly back between Rusty and Travis to retake his seat on the left. He'd just taken a satellite phone call from Colonel Ryan Jackson on behalf of General Montgomery. The ringing phone had surprised them, startling his tired co-pilot to alertness. After ensuring she was awake enough to monitor the flight, he'd stepped back to take the call. The plane had been en route from New Mexico to Marine Corps Air Station Pendleton.

"It's too hot on the coast," Lou told Angie once he had his headset back on and five-point harness re-buckled. "Their airborne assault has started in support of an amphibious landing expected to start within a few hours. What planes of ours that weren't successfully hacked are defending as best as they can but are outnumbered two-to-one."

Angie's face turned fraught with worry. "What're our orders, Lou?" she asked, taking advantage of her new boss's preference for informality when they weren't around others.

She didn't have to say what Lou was already thinking—*We'd be sitting ducks.* "The Marine Raiders we were to pick up are taking choppers out of California. Their orders have changed, and there are now four fourteen-man teams. It'll be dark by the time we land where they'll meet us. It's another lonely desert muni runway."

"Where's that?"

"Beatty, Nevada," Lou answered as he pulled maps out of a slot on the side of his seat. They were still navigating the old-fashioned way for fear of hacking. "Right on the state border northwest of Vegas."

"So lemme get this straight," she snorted. "You're going to hit a desert municipal landing strip you've never been to in a valley at dawn, with no controller, and Lord knows if there'll even be runway markers?"

"Uh... no—you are," Lou said nonchalantly. He smiled to himself, almost feeling her glare burn the side of his face. He turned to face her. "I believe in you, Hot Dog. It's time you do the same."

"Hot Dog?" she asked, afraid of what Lou was about to say.

"You said those reserve weenies wouldn't give you a call sign, right?"

"In the name of all that's holy, Lou—please! Anything other than—"

"Oh, c'mon, Hot Dog," Lou interrupted. "It could be a lot worse." He started to fold down the parts of the map he'd finally settled on.

"Please, sir!"

"Do me a favor, would ya'?" Lou said. "Go roust Gray and bring him up to speed. He needs to re-calc the fuel to make sure we can land, takeoff with a bunch of Jarheads, and land again." He continued to approximate his needed turn angle to bypass Las Vegas to the south as she slipped out of her seat and stepped past Rusty. "Hot Dog!" he laughed out loud to only himself, wondering if they would live to tell anyone they knew about his little prank.

CHAPTER 21

"BRIDGE, CIC! WE'RE GETTING FLASH TRAFFIC FROM THE Fleet HQ! The El Paso has detonated! There's a rogue wave heading toward us!"

Millie let the binoculars fall to her chest as she grabbed the phone handset. "ETA?"

"Twelve minutes, Ma'am!"

"What's the status of those Improved Kilos, CIC? Have we reacquired their positions?" It wasn't as if the wave was the only threat. It was fully dawn, and the black-turned-blue sky was glowing red on the horizon. Fires littered the ocean in every direction. Columns of smoke were noticeable wherever Millie looked. And the long slender destroyer would be much more visible with each passing minute. Millie had been changing course, trying to remain as unpredictable as possible. The helicopter-launched torpedoes had been dreadful news for her American submarine protectors from Hawaii and Guam. And though the PLAN submarines needed to work as a pack to sink the

American subs, a surface ship in the middle of battle would be easy pickings.

"Not yet, Captain."

Millie had turned her ship, moving westerly for several minutes, and then turning south. The news of the wave meant they needed to turn east—to drive into it for survivability like they had just a couple of weeks earlier. *I don't suppose we have time to verify with the UAV,* she decided. "Very well, CIC. Is Mount Two up, yet?"

"They're reporting it will be reset and recharged within the minute, Captain."

"Very well, CIC. Be ready to line up a new series of targets. We're heading east again." She hung up the phone, not waiting for a reply. "Make your bearing one-zero-zero, XO. Maintain speed." She headed over to the Boatswain-of-the-Watch near the back bulkhead. "1MC, Boats."

"Aye, Ma'am." The young sailor turned and flipped a switch and handed the 1MC microphone to the captain.

"Team LBJ. All hands brace yourselves and your spaces for another giant wave, like from before. ETA ten minutes. We'll sound the collision alarm when it is a minute out. Keep up the fight. I—"

"Bridge, CIC! Incoming missiles!" the bridge speaker blared. "Bearing one-four-five!"

Millie un-keyed the microphone and tossed it at the Boatswain, scrambling over to their radar display. *One... two—four? YJ-21s!* The anti-ship missiles were extremely maneuverable and hypersonic for the entire trip. They would likely be on them in less than a minute. "Increase to full speed, Mr. Bailey!" She moved over to the starboard windows and scanned. *Nothing!* In the CIC, the team was rapidly providing the final permissions for the ship's automated combat computer to launch as many RIM-7 Sea Sparrows as it thought it needed to.

Millie looked down and saw sailors in firefighting gear scrambling off the bow. Once their bow Tomahawks had been launched, they'd been cleared to go provide cooling water on the barrels. *Oh no!* she screamed at herself. She watched in horror as the heavy doors on two of the 4-missile Sea Sparrow cannisters swung open. "Hurry!" Millie yelled at the glass. Over the course of the next few seconds, just as the sailors cleared the danger area, four of the short-range defenders rocketed out of each cell and headed up and east. Streaks of smoke arose from the bow of the ship in the breaking dawn. The sound of the chaff launchers could be heard. Angled tubes near the top of the ship sent charges filled with thousands of pieces of metal three hundred feet into the sky in an attempt to make itself a better target than the ship's radars for the missiles' radar-tracking systems.

"There's a second wave coming, Bridge!" Dennis Bates' voice squawked over the speaker once more.

Millie watched the Sea Sparrows detonate themselves less than a mile away. The warheads sent metal rods fashioned together like a large expanding accordion ring outward, growing in size and meant to rip through whatever was a threat. Three of the YJ-21s detonated themselves in the ensuing explosions. The fourth moved for the chaff, exploding above and to the side of the ship. The warhead's shrapnel and fireball peppered the starboard side, leaving the hull pock-marked and blackened along the side.

Four more of the Sea Sparrow missile cells opened, launching sixteen missiles at twelve that were inbound, this time from the northeast. As they left in a streak of flame and sound, naval artillery fire roared across the LBJ's stern from the south, exploding just over one hundred yards past the ship. Another shot hit the water immediately aft, exploding and ripping steel fragments into the stern small-boat hatch. LBJ twerked violently in her aft end. Millie was scanning the flaming ships to the south and saw the stern of a ship passing westerly not two miles away. *You sneaky sons-a-guns!* The gun mounts wouldn't be able to swing that far aft.

"Mr. Bailey! Right full rudder!" Bailey repeated the order as the ship's helm-team complied, sending them all lurching toward port at the high-rate of speed. "Pass that burning corvette on its east side." She grabbed the phone and moved the few feet over to clearly see the contacts on the screens over the bridge windows. "There's a destroyer masking in the smoke just past Contact Bravo-one-three! Hit them with both barrels!"

The ship's turn had put the enemy on the port forward quarter. A fireball erupted from its gun once more. Mount one sent a slug toward them a second later. The trajectory was so flat that the projectile screamed over the enemy destroyer's bow when it dipped in a wave just a few feet. *Damn!* Millie thought, watching the repaired Mount Two finish its agonizingly slow turn and fire.

Three seconds after firing, the enemy's slower round caught the LBJ below the helicopter deck, hitting the vertical launch cells along the side that had been emptied of missiles just a half-hour earlier. LBJ shuddered for a split-second from the impact before the explosive in the round detonated in the non-occupied berthing compartments and storerooms. The shuddering intensified as the explosion sent every person flying into whatever was nearest to impact. At that moment, Mount Two had fired, its round shorting the two-mile gunfight by several hundred yards because of the shaking. That meant little, as like a kid skipping stones in summer, the low and flat, high-speed shot may as well have been hitting concrete instead of water. The energy had been bled some, but not enough to stop the mass from slamming into the thin hull of the enemy ship. Even without a warhead, the hard fast object ripped through frames and bulkheads right at water level and directly outboard of the gun mount.

Millie got back to her feet, her battle helmet having taken the bulk of the blow when she hit the helm station. She heard the second volley of missiles explode the incoming battery, this time a little farther out.

Millie switched her phone to the interior circuit being used by the repair parties and heard havoc. *Let them have the time to do their jobs!* she reminded herself. Damage Control Central had hopped onto the 1MC and given some instructions and information on the ship wide circuit.

The call, "Missiles inbound!" on the bridge circuit broke her attention. "Fifteen of them!"

Dear God! Millie prayed. *Help us out of this!*

"The aft damage has sent the Sea Sparrows in the aft port cells into a reset mode!" the Ops Officer continued to update the captain via the speakers. "Two minutes until they're ready to launch!"

Millie grabbed her phone and reset to the CIC circuit. "We don't have two minutes!"

"Wait!" Dennis said. "There are American SM-2s moving in from the west!"

Millie moved to her combat radar screen. "Bunker Hill!" she screamed.

Twenty American missiles from her sister ship screamed over the LBJ at ten thousand feet elevation, moving at Mach Five. They slammed into the surely fatal barrage two miles away, filling the sky with fire and shrapnel.

"They're only three miles out!" Ops told his boss over the phone.

Millie scanned to the right of the PLAN destroyer, which was leaning heavily to its starboard, rapidly filling with water in the bow and sending her propellers into the air at the other end. A fireball erupted from Bunker Hill's five-inch cannon, exploding in the bridge of the sinking ship. The old-school cannon was firing rounds once every two seconds, moving to other targets as she smoked the enemy.

In the back of all of this was the wave. Millie had completely forgotten about it. She had run to the port side to scan for threats when the sight of the bows of enemy ships shooting skyward caught her attention. *South!* she remembered. *We need to—*"Turn!" she yelled with all that her voice would give. "Left full rudder! Sound the collision alarm!"

HUNTINGTON PARK, CALIFORNIA

THE CHAOS WAS UNBELIEVABLE. *WE'RE LIKE SALMON TRYING TO swim up a river!* Alex thought in a panic. He and Henry were both exhausted, having been carrying their feeble mother, weak from not eating her share for weeks. In the thirty-five minutes since a Chinese air-to-surface missile ripped their escort Humvee to shreds in a fiery explosion, the prospects of a violent and painful death had become a stark reality. They'd moved off the highway with nothing but their weapons and backpacks. The Guard members who'd been driving their trucks ordered their human cargo out in lieu of the ongoing invasion a mere forty-three seconds before the attack helicopter had made another pass and destroyed both military trucks.

The waves of paratroopers had been replaced with a fresh wave of tracked vehicles and giant loads of supplies hanging under triple-chutes, mostly just to the south in the Long Beach area. Counting elderly and children there were twenty-three tired and scared people in the group, which was starting to spread itself into a single column, with the strong and determined up front and the weaker being prodded along by Lauren and Jessie Duarte at the back. The streets were filled with Angelinos of both the dead and live persuasion. Most of the live ones were running east on foot, though many were using bikes. Moving cars of any variety were being targeted by aircraft, a lesson quickly learned by anyone who was still alive by that point. The smoke from the fires drifted in giant streams, obscuring the view of exclusively Chinese planes overhead. Any dogfights had already ended, the losers falling from the sky and joining the devastation of the fallen City of Angels below.

"There's a group of them three blocks up!" Micah called down to the rest through the throngs of screaming people pushing past them. "We're turning up Second Street!" They were traveling through an area dominated by stores and manufacturers. Every one of the smaller ones not surrounded by razor-wire-topped chain-link fences had been broken apart and looted in the preceding several days.

Nobody said anything. The group was following on pure instinct, thankful for the weapons that Lucky had provided. Alex was sure that was the only reason they still had the entire group alive and walking together. A few, like Roman and Ned, were also carrying their shotguns and bows slung to their backs. Even Alex's father was carrying a rifle, breaking a promise he'd made to himself when he left Vietnam. Still carrying his mother, Alex rounded the corner to turn north, seeing the collection of Chinese soldiers amassing at a rally point at a major intersection. He found himself wanting to shoot at them, knowing as soon as the invaders were organized, they'd kill any civilian with an open firearm. Just as he was getting ready to yell up to the front to speed up, something caught his eye. It had caught the foreign troops' attention, too.

A brown and frothy blob was rushing up Slauson Avenue hundreds of yards to the west, tossing cars and people aside. *Is that*—Alex thought in panic. "Ruuunnnn!!!!" he yelled as the realization hit him. The troops five hundred feet to the west were running, too, trying to find high ground. "Floooooddd!" Alex yelled. "Henry! Move! Grab dad!" He sprinted north along the confused 15th Street Posse's ranks. "Tsunami! We need to get on a building! Now!" He started scanning. Something or someone had triggered a massive rogue wave or tsunami which was marching its way miles into the L.A. area.

"Here!" Sassy Sasha called out, spying a rolling chain-link gate that wasn't locked. It led to the employee entry and parking area for a thirty-foot tall aluminum plant. She ran to it, trailed by Micah. The two youths pushed the tall obstruction open enough for people to pass through. The group began to bottleneck at it.

"Open it more!" Henry called from the back of the pack, trying to drag his father faster. The two youths moved the heavy gate a couple of more feet and then ran toward the extensive building's corner.

"Here!" Micah called out. "There's a ladder!" The tired, panting posse moved through the mostly empty parking area, finding a commercial roof access ladder and several semi-trucks on the loading dock side of the facility. At ten-feet off the ground, a circular fall-protective cage surrounded it the rest of the way up. But the first ten were an issue. A pair of locked, hinged flaps were covering the first ten rungs, meant to keep people off the ladder.

A couple of the group spewed angry tirades at the obstacle. Lauren and Jessie ran over to a six-foot-tall mobile dumpster near an employee entrance. "Help us!" Jessie called out as the two women began to push it. Roman Lopez and Philip Hogarty ran over and threw their body weight into it, getting the wheels moving.

Alex turned. *Anything?* He couldn't see anything due to the medical supply store across the street, but he could hear a noise unlike anything he'd ever imagined getting closer. "Hurry!" he called out, arms burning as he still carried his crying, frightened mother.

As the group parked the dumpster into place, Philip slammed the plastic lids shut and jumped up to the small metal shelf at the top where they were hinged. "Gimme your hand!" he yelled at Jessie. Lauren had already followed suit on the other end of the eight-foot-wide dumpster. First Philip, then Lauren, pulled a group member up and shoved on their butt to help boost them to the point they could grab onto the inside of the cage and hoist their feet to the first accessible rung. Ahn Ngo, Alex's mother's best friend, was the first to get up and start climbing. Next was Jessie Duarte. She prodded the elder neighborhood matron to hurry up the tall ladder. Ned Manners and Roman Lopez shoved Roman's kids up into waiting hands next, as people were fumbling with backpacks and rifles.

Sasha scanned a semi-truck and trailer about fifty feet away. "Alex!" she called. "Put your parents in there! And Ned's dog!"

She's right! They'll never make it up that ladder! he realized. "Henry!" Alex called as he ran to the cab of the big truck.

"The wave'll move this thing like it's a toy!" his brother argued.

"I think it'll just push it up against the building!" Alex countered. Though they were near a corner, the long building ran almost six-hundred feet away to the east.

Alex relented his argument and climbed up the steps into the passenger side of the cab. As he was handing his mother up to his brother, Alex called back, "Everyone! Throw your packs and rifles in here!" Ned had already started running toward the truck with Cisco, his mostly Labrador mutt.

Sasha caught on. "Yeah! They'll get stuck in that cage! Move it!" Those still on the ground ran over and started tossing their gear into the truck on the driver's side. Brown murky water, filled with sediment, trash, cars, broken phone poles, human bodies, and every other loose item in L.A., plowed its way east at the intersection they'd just left. Water took the path of least resistance and moved north along the road, filling all available spaces, as the water behind it continued to push. Group members were running back to the dumpster in a panic.

"Ba!" Henry called to his father to hurry into the truck cab as the wave entered the parking area. Over at the dumpster, people were screaming as they tried to get on. Lauren and Philip were pulling and shoving bodies up and into the ladder cage as quickly as they could.

Alex climbed up onto the big rig's first step, shoving his slow-moving father into the cab and following him. All four of the petite Nguyen family, along with several weapons and backpacks, were crammed uncomfortably into the truck. It shifted and wiggled as the water started to push on the tires and wheels.

"Go!" Philip yelled at Lauren, who started pushing Roman Lopez's feet as she was trying to squeeze herself up to the first rung. She grabbed onto the cage as the dumpster moved away by the water's force. Philip fell off it toward the building and was slammed by the large metal box into the building's concrete and metal wall. A sickening crunch rose to Lauren's ears.

"Philip!" she called out in horror, scanning, but not seeing him in the quickly rising murky water.

"Keep climbing!" Roman called out to her from above. "He's on his own!"

Alex watched the group finish ascending. The large truck started to get pushed along, slamming slowly into the side of the large building.

It came to rest at an odd up-angle a couple of hundred feet down from the ladder, part of a collection of trucks getting stuck at the loading dock. And though he wasn't aware of it at the moment, the wave had done better for their group than any of them could ever predict, as many enemies foreign and domestic failed to escape its unforgiving path.

CHAPTER 22

ACME RANCH
Southeast of Tucson, Arizona

"WHAT'RE YOU GUYS DOING?" KAREN ASKED IN DISBELIEF. Daniel just ignored her, continuing to load food, gear, and other supplies from the bunkhouse to the pickup truck.

"We're starting with this stuff," Fred Bowers explained.

"We're taking it to the cave since you don't seem to have a shred of common sense," his wife Pam added, practically spitting disdain as she did it. "I'm sorry your uncle died—but now is no time to freeze and not make a decision." She went back to carrying plastic tubs of spare medical supplies.

"Did you clear this with Donna?" Karen asked.

"She'll come to reason," Fred said. "We could use a hand at the cave unloading all this stuff." He looked at Daniel. "Maybe we should have them start taking the stuff from the house to the parking area... speed things up a bit."

Daniel set down two five-gallon buckets which contained mylar bags filled with water. He dodged his crony's suggestion, seeing an argument with Karen was building. "What?" he asked curtly, as she stared in awe.

"Donna and the others will be coming back up the trail shortly," she said as calmly as she could manage. Karen took a deep breath and then let it out slowly through her nostrils. The sounds of war mimicked thunder in the not-too-distant south. "We should pause, get our bearings... figure out if we should flee north instead of to a cave."

"Unsatisfactory," Daniel retorted. He strode past her back into the bunkhouse. Karen followed, trying to keep her cool. "The entire purpose of us all moving to this ranch was to stay and fight." He sounded annoyed that he had to explain it. "We can be a thorn in the Chinks' side when they roll through here."

"Chinks, huh?" Karen guffawed. "Real nice, Daniel." She moved back out of the bunkhouse and added, "Why am I not surprised that you're a bigot?"

"We gotta call 'em something!" he yelled after her.

Karen was getting ready to head back up the trail when the rumbling of heavy tires on gravel rapidly approached. An officer stepped out of the passenger side of a Humvee when it skidded to a halt near the house's front door. She jogged the hundred yards over, knowing that teens and children would be all he found in the house.

Seeing her, he turned and moved toward her, meeting by the corner of a corral. "Is the ranch owner here? We felt we needed to update you all on some issues." If the man's words tried to downplay the urgency, his face was betraying them.

"She'll be along shortly. But I'm the acting head of our group security. What's up?"

"Their magnetic flux and plasma weapons have been devastating our tanks! They've breached our lines outside both Nogales and Agua Prieta. We can no longer guarantee the safety of any civilians. The general is ordering all remaining civilians to evacuate."

"What are we talking, here?" Karen asked. "How many days?"

"Tomorrow," the man said bleakly. "Saturday if we're lucky. The mid-echelon units like our mobile artillery and combat engineers are retreating as we speak. The front may not hold through the night."

Karen gasped, instinctively putting her hands up to her mouth. *Those poor soldiers,* she thought. Once more for the day, her tears started to build. She heard the tractor moving up from the south and looked to see the rest of the group approaching the bunkhouse. She faced the young officer. "You can let them know that we've been told and will be bugging out as soon as we can gather ourselves."

SOUTHWEST OF BEATTY, NEVADA

LIEUTENANT COLONEL FREEMAN LOUIS 'SUPER BERT' Caldwell and his co-pilot, First Lieutenant Angela Skye 'Hot Dog' Knecht, walked around the C-17 Globemaster III conducting a thorough check. First Mate Rusty pulled at them from the end of his leash, anxious because of the noise and level of activity going on around him. He relieved himself on one of the tall port side tires. Despite being dusty and in dire need of a good scrubbing, the giant gray plane was performing well. The Marines had somehow arranged for a fuel delivery from the city of Pahrump seventy-two miles to the south. Travis had assumed responsibility for taking that on while Gray supervised the onboarding Marines.

There were only fifty-four total seats on the sides of the hold's hull, and slightly more Marines than that. Gray had a few of them help him retrieve enough of the snap-in frames of fabric seats from the lower hold to provide for the rest in the center of the hold. There was still plenty of room for their gear, weapons, parachutes, and breathing apparatus. And though the Globemaster had internal equipment that could easily be prepped for a static-line insertion of these special operations Marines, this mission would require a HALO insertion—High Altitude–Low Opening. The operators would be jumping as four different teams from a height of thirty-five thousand feet. They were supposed to pick up two F-16s from the Utah National guard as escorts on this impromptu operation to the northwest. *It'll do,* Lou thought, *but I sure wish they could cough up a couple of F-18s or F-35s from Top Gun at Fallon. They must all be in the fight in Cali and Arizona already.*

"Let's go, Hot Dog," Lou said as they finished their pre-flight inspection. Not that any negative findings would've much mattered. America was under open foreign invasion for the first time since the end of the War of 1812. *We will fly,* Lou knew. *No matter what.* Lou gave an informal wave to a small team of volunteer firefighters from the nearby town. They and a local deputy had come out upon learning that a bunch of Marines had helicoptered to the airstrip outside of town. Once the jumbo cargo plane had finished landing and taxiing, they offered to assist. Lou had them chock the wheels of the plane with a pair of fire truck chocks. They also kept the small amount of desert automobile traffic on the state highway moving along. The goal was to get off the ground before any critical details leaked on the airwaves.

He saw the firefighters head for the wheels. As he and Angie topped the ramp, they ran into Gray and Travis, who were discussing some details with five Marine officers. Lou had briefly met the major in charge of the op when they landed. "We'll be taxiing in three mikes, Major. Wheels up in six."

"Roger that, Colonel," Major Gregory Robertson acknowledged. "With your permission, sir, I'd like to provide some last-minute details to the crew before we're airborne."

Lou looked at his wristwatch. He handed Rusty's leash to Angie and said, "Lieutenant, go get us fired up and find out where our escorts are."

"Yes, sir."

"The floor is all yours, Major. Pardon us while we get the ramp up."

As Gray proceeded with raising the loading ramp, Major Robertson moved to the head of the cargo bay and took the center with command authority. "Raiders! Listen up!" With those three words, every conversation and preparatory activity in progress came to an immediate halt. It was one of the most impressive displays of discipline Lou could recall seeing in many years.

"We've gotten final confirmation of our orders and the last bit of intel I'll be able to provide. The northernmost units of the Army are still four hundred miles away and won't make it to the port city of Eureka until at least tomorrow. The local police and guard units are engaging the advance elements of paratroopers, but they're in over their heads. They will not be able to handle what is about to hit their shores. As a shipping port, there are seven docks and terminals capable of mooring and off-loading thousands of troops and hundreds of tanks. Our job is to ensure they don't succeed."

"Sir," one Marine called out as he raised his hand. "Wasn't that port destroyed in the big tsunami in November? Like everything in Oregon and Washington?"

"I had the same question, Hurm. I understand it was lightly damaged due to a large breakwater and kilometer wide peninsula that shields the bay. Any other questions?" The unit officers began handing out printed intelligence of the port and invading fleet for the Marines to study. The major continued. "One of the piers is a Chevron oil terminal, which means one less to worry about for the time being. Our four squads will try to disable the facilities at the primary four piers, followed by the other two. The company CO and XO will review the specifics with each of you when we're in the air. Oorah?"

"Oorah!" nearly sixty hardened warriors wearing camouflage paint on their faces all yelled from their gut in unison, sending shivers down Lou's spine. He nodded to the major and turned toward the cockpit. Stepping over Rusty, he saw that Travis had already strapped himself into place. Gray followed Lou into the pit and started securing himself. Before sitting, Lou saw one of the volunteer firefighters out front of the plane. He saw Lou looking at him and gave a big thumbs up sign.

Lou scanned the gauges as Angie finished the procedures for firing up the large engines. He strapped his small clipboard to his leg, checking for his startup checklist, post take-off checklist, and map to northern California. Slipping into his seat, he buckled himself and slipped his headset on.

"Sir, Tuskegee Flight is staged and topped off north of Hawthorne waiting for your orders," Hot Dog told him.

"Tuskegee flight," Lou repeated, knowing the honorific title probably meant both pilots were of black ancestry.

"They said we don't want anyone else covering our ass. Their words, sir."

"I believe 'em," Lou said. He saw the volunteer firefighter out front begin to assist him with two orange light-wands, waving one arm in a circle while pointing the direction he wanted Lou to turn. He needed to take off to the north to hit the wind, but they were already behind schedule. Lou taxied to the runway and applied his brakes. He killed their transponder, a small transmitter that made the craft visible to ground controllers via a unique signal. The enemy would need to use good old-fashioned radar to find them. He then powered up.

"We're not taking off north, sir?" Angie questioned.

"We're fairly light and have plenty of runway, Hot Dog," Lou answered. "And we're in a hurry. We'll overcome the seven-knot tail wind with plenty to spare." Checking his ailerons and rudder once more, he grabbed the finger slots on the master handle that applied power to all four of the Pratt and Whitney engines and pushed it all the way forward. The loud jets began to scream. *God, if you're there,* Lou thought, amused at how the events of the last few months had opened his mind to that possibility. *Please be with us tonight.* "Hang tight, team. We're about to earn our huge salaries," he said with a smirk as he released the brake. "Here's to hoping we get to land again..."

USS LYNDON B. JOHNSON DDG-1002

. . .

THE WAVE CREATED BY THE DETONATION OF THE HUNDREDS OF
warheads packed into USS El Paso nearly rivaled the similar wave
created by the nuclear torpedo that was the deathblow to the damaged
aircraft carrier USS Halsey. It was caused by the sudden evaporation of
almost a trillion gallons of seawater. With a giant void to fill, the
surrounding ocean crashed into the hole where all the energy met in
the center, shot skyward—and then rolled out in every direction. And
while the impact to California a mere one hundred fifty miles east
would be horrible, it was a last-ditch effort to use a non-nuclear
response to the coming invasion.

The lead vessels in the fleet—full of PLAN Army troops and equipment—received massive casualties. In all, there were seventy-eight
amphibious landing ships, built for a variety of purposes. The thirty-
three in the lead echelon of the invading swarm took massive damage,
with twenty-eight of them sinking outright. Ships farther west were
taking some battering, too, though a much smaller percentage were
sinking. Most of those were the smaller corvettes and patrol craft. The
end result was that the El Paso, combined with the sneak attacks by
Operation Flea Flicker, were heavily impacting the Dragon's blitz—but
it wasn't enough to stop it altogether.

After surviving the giant wave, second echelon helicopter landing
ships began to deploy medium range drones, capable of autonomous
flight for up to a week. With a range of two thousand miles, they
would be able to quietly chase any trailing Americans for their Chinese
programmers. Called 'clustering munitions', the drones would use
their satellite links and computer programming to seek and destroy the
correct targets not with missiles, but with laser-guided gravity bombs.
They hunted in packs, flying in formations and patterns that would
enable them to share data and cover a large area in a short time. Like
the fabled future 'terminator' cyborgs, they performed their jobs
without fear, without tiring, and without mercy.

Farther west than the launching drones, two U.S. Navy ships were preparing to mount and crest the wave. The USS Lyndon B. Johnson's hull was made for this. Its long sleek design was meant to pierce the pinnacle and guide the ship through the thinner water near the top before it could get flipped skyward. The USS Bunker Hill, however, was not so fortunate. The older Ticonderoga cruiser's sonar array, a bulbous sphere under the foremost bow, rode the giant wave to the very top. The terra-cotta red underbelly of the dome and the nearly two hundred feet of hull aft of it hovered over the far side of the ocean as the large swell pushed the ship up. It came crashing down the far side as the wave passed past the ship's midpoint, smashing the fiberglass housing over the sonar. People inside were thrown in every direction, bodies bashing into machinery, bulkheads, and each other. In the large gun magazines, the remaining five-inch artillery shells and powder casings were tossed around like pixie sticks, breaking the arms, legs, and necks of the sailors caught in the storm.

Millie Goldberg scanned her ally with her binoculars. "CIC, Bridge —get a report from Bunker Hill!" she ordered her Ops officer. She looked at their surface contacts screen, seeing something that drove her back and forth from the window once. Phone still in hand, she added, "CIC, are you seeing the targets to the south? I count at least seven destroyers and corvettes on a northerly heading, weaving in between the ones we've hit!"

"Copy, Captain. And there are six more approaching from the north! Radar is picking up probable drone activity from the east. And we've lost contact, but we know of two Ming class subs in the area!"

"Roger, CIC. We're coming around. Keep Mount One engaging south, and Two to the north. Make every shot count! And let me know if Bunker Hill requests assistance." She hung up the phone. "XO, come full right until we're bearing on two-four-zero. Get us within four hundred yards of Bunker Hill. She's about to get pounced on."

CHAPTER 23

"What?" Donna said upon hearing the news. Karen repeated everything the Army officer had told her to the best of her recollection. Most of the ranch group, including kids, were in the living room.

"Where's the Bowers?" Tracy asked. "Or Daniel, for that matter."

"They must've been gone by the time you all came back up the trail," Karen said. "They took the initiative to load the truck with all the supplies from the bunkhouse and head toward the valley with the cave." She looked at the wall clock. "Considering the Army has the roads jammed up and they have to drive over to the west access road, it'll probably take a while."

"They did what?" Donna asked. The way she ended her question was enough for her to be a 'Karen' momentarily, too.

"I didn't have it in me to argue," Karen said. "That guy and I will never see eye-to-eye."

Donna looked at Bob. "Go see if you can get them back here on the radio!" she ordered angrily. "Don't take no for an answer. You can make any threat you need to," she said to make sure Bob fully understood her position.

"Hooah," the old grunt said as he left the room.

"I sure wish Granger would get back," Donna sighed.

"He will," Karen said. "I can feel it. He knows we're in deep kimchee..." *He'll be here,* she added in her own thoughts, unsure about it, but not wanting to cause anyone else to lose confidence. "In the meantime, we need to all start loading rigs. Jerome, you and I will lead in the battered ranch SUV with Robin as the rear gunner. Bob will take all the kids in his suburban in the middle. We'll tow the cargo trailer with most of the supplies behind that. The older kids will have to be armed. Donna, can you take one of the all-wheel drive cars? And Tracy and Pedro will take the ranch truck as the rear guard."

"What about the three amigos?" Jerome asked.

"I don't really care what they do," Karen added. "With luck, they'll take their own truck and go another direction."

That comment got a few snickers. The group split up and started moving food and equipment out of the house, loading the trailer and the vehicles. Twenty minutes later, the ranch truck finally slid into the parking area and came to a stop. Karen and Jerome had been placing their rifles, spare magazines, radios, and packs into their lead rig. Daniel spotted her and made a beeline.

"What the hell is your problem, Kirkland?" he screamed.

Jerome stepped up and got between the two quarreling people. "You best step off," the muscular firefighter said.

"This doesn't involve you, Jerome," Daniel said a bit more calmly. Yelling at Karen once more, he challenged her. "Tell me you didn't go spread a bunch of lies and BS to Donna to get us back here! Tell me you didn't just endanger the entire group with your stupid arrogant decision!"

Donna and most of the rest had made their way to the SUV by then. "Daniel, come with me and cool off!" she insisted. He ignored her the first time. "Daniel!" she screeched in her angriest mom voice.

That made his head turn. There was a level of jealousy and rage in his eyes that was finally presenting his true self to her for the first time. "If you want to remain in this group, you'll take a walk with me—now!"

VERNON, CALIFORNIA

THE CURRENT WAS MOVING NORTH THROUGH THE CITY streets, just like Alex's eclectic group. Within minutes of surviving the flood, the water had started to recede back toward the ocean or any other path of least resistance. There was little natural ground in the state's second tiniest city—an amazing five miles south of downtown Los Angeles—for the water to drain into. What the small municipality did have going for the unnatural disaster, though, was a clear access to the famed L.A. River. The concrete trough moved through the area like a giant snake. The normally dry bowl, made famous by movies like Grease and Terminator 2, was a swift-moving body of ocean water in retreat back to its home, though not quite a torrent.

The other asset in the small city was manufacturing. Within the sight of a simple binocular survey on their haven rooftop, Micah had spotted a rubber goods factory. Lauren, Roman, Henry, and Ned had made hasty work of wading through the filth and returning seventy minutes later with pilfered recreational rubber rafts. It was approaching evening, and the former 15th Street Posse had hoped to make it past the Highway 101 corridor between Los Angeles and East L.A. before full nightfall. With the elderly and small children riding in rafts alongside the packs of supplies, the armed crew set out, pulling their family north through the filthy slosh.

"Ouch!" Henry proclaimed. "Something just got me!" The water was three feet deep, and the current was enough to move objects as it headed for the river basin. He pulled his leg up to reveal a hole in his left pant leg. Blood slowly discolored the tan wet pants.

"Into a raft!" Sissy Lopez ordered. "You need to stay out of this garbage!"

"I'll be alright," Henry argued. "Just let me have a few minutes to get it to stop bleeding."

"No, she's right," his father said. Lanh Nguyen moved himself over his raft's edge. "Trade places with me."

"Ba!" Henry started to protest.

"Stop," Alex said as he waded over. "You can make sure mom is sipping her water." Henry finally relented, allowing his father to take his place as a raft puller.

"But we do need to get past the river as fast as we can," Roman said. "The sooner we get out of this current, the better."

The children had finally stopped crying, dismayed at the sight of bodies amongst all the trash and other items floating by. Mostly it had been other citizens, but occasionally the body of an invading Chinese soldier was amongst the would-be jetsam. After the first time they'd seen this, Ned mentioned they'd lost an opportunity to find a potential piece of gear. They searched all the other enemy soldiers they came across. While they'd picked up two QBZ-95 battle rifles and a few hundred rounds of their unique 5.8-millimeter ammunition, the real score had been two night-vision devices and a CS/LR2 sniper rifle. It was a knockoff of the common Remington 700 platform and fired easily attainable ammo.

"I'll say this about World War Three," Micah joked. "Video games always made it seem like it'd be louder."

"It seems like most of their day one efforts were about securing the beaches and the port at Long Beach," said Ned Manners. The Coast Guard vet and plumber had been the group's most active purveyor of monitoring all news sources. "And the news the last several weeks described our military staging well east of here, along the axis of the central valley and desert. They're not going to go through and kill every American," he pointed out. "They still need to cling to some form of moral high-ground to justify this to the rest of the world."

"Then how come we're hearing firefights to the southwest?" Sassy Sasha asked.

"There's going to be some fighting," Ned theorized. "The Venom Spear soldiers and cops have been very active recently, right? There's still plenty of them in town. I was referring to the main Army that moved by train across the country the last couple of months."

"Dammit!" Sissy Lopez called out. "Our raft just got a hole popped in it by something floating by!"

"I can get out," her twelve-year-old daughter said.

"I think we all need to," Sissy said. "Help your little brother into Mrs. Ngo's raft." The elder matron was already sticking her hands out to welcome any children to her raft.

"This current is getting swift," Lauren said. "But it looks like it's down to calf-deep once we cross the bridge up ahead. Then we'll be going parallel where the river runs north for a bit."

Alex had been quietly taking in all the comments. *Things are going to be bleak when it gets dark,* he internalized. He had flashbacks to a bad dystopian movie that had come out in the mid-90s. Years later, he'd watched it as a teen. *Are we doing the right thing? Maybe we should try to escape from L.A.*

USS Lyndon B. Johnson DDG-1002

The two American ships were headed west, both damaged. Bunker Hill was limping along, her bow taking on water, slowly dragging the forecastle down. *I bet those sailors are fighting with everything they've got!* Millie thought emotionally as she scanned her wounded battle buddy with her binoculars. The sister ship had taken a shot directly to her Aegis fire control radars. Any more engagement for Bunker Hill would be point-shooting—something surface combatant ships had not been designed to do for a few decades. The pair of ships had engaged the southern attackers, destroying or slowing them. The six from the north had created a parallel course. Undamaged, they were advancing at a rate of over thirty knots. Millie had slowed LBJ to Bunker's speed, an agonizing twelve knots. They were slowly leaving behind all the carnage they'd caused the prior seventy minutes. *It's a matter of time,* Millie thought, before they attack. *A very short time.*

"Bridge, CIC!" Dennis Bates called on the speaker. "Radar is picking up odd signatures at eleven thousand feet. The computer thinks it is a cluster!"

Will it ever stop? Millie wondered in exasperation. "Roger." An idea was born at that moment. "Be ready to link with their system, Ops. We have eyes, but they still have claws. Bridge out." Millie relayed a message to the Quartermaster-of-the-Watch, who contacted one of his peers. *World War II technology saving the day,* Millie thought, triggering a slight smirk on the awful day.

Near the top of the ship, a quartermaster was using a signal light to send Morse code, speaking directly with a counterpart on the cruiser. Soon, both ships knew the plan. The older Aegis Combat System on the cruiser Bunker Hill was built exactly for this reason. It would link with the data being captured by LBJ as if it were its own. In a matter of moments, the two American vessels would absolutely need each other to survive. LBJ would see the drones—Bunker Hill would shoot them. And together they would both shoot the pending sea attack. Bunker would have the shooting-speed to keep pounding the enemy, while LBJ would have the high-energy weapons to sink their foes with one shot.

Millie closed her eyes just to get them moist again. She was startled by the warbling of her phone. She shook her head, eyes burning. *Did I just fall asleep?* Scanning her watch, it had been eight minutes since she talked to the Quartermaster, though it had felt like one. She picked up the phone. "Bridge."

"Check your radar, Ma'am," Dennis said. "I think they're setting up a picket, getting ready to cut us off to the west and come straight for us."

ACME RANCH
    Southeast of Tucson, Arizona

DANIEL AND DONNA WERE GONE FOR CLOSE TO TWENTY minutes. Karen had received a chilly vibe from Pam and Fred, something that ate at her inner psyche. *Just remember,* she thought in recollection of her last big talk with Claude before his heart attack, *they talk crap and spread lies out of jealousy and their own insecurities. Your sense of self-worth is completely independent of what idiots think or do.* She continued to help move long-term food storage, MREs, and bins of canned and boxed goods. She found some insulated grocery shopping bags and used those to hold things from the freezer that wouldn't fit in the coolers. She ensured that some of each commodity—food, water, ammo, gear, medical supplies—found its way into all vehicles, versus putting everything in the trailer.

Karen was monitoring the kids who had insisted on helping move stuff when Donna and Daniel approached. "Do you mind if we go have a little chat? To clear the air?" Daniel asked humbly.

Dude, you make my spidey sense tingle, as the kids say, she thought, sure that her resting bitch face was giving away her thoughts. "I guess, but it isn't going to change my decision about us getting out of here."

"I understand," he said as he looked around. He led her through the house, grabbing two glasses and filling them with room temp suntea from a pitcher on the breakfast counter. Karen opened the sliding door and led him out to a patio table by the pool. Daniel set his glass down and scooted out a chair. Seeing this, Karen sat on the opposite side of the table. Daniel then picked his glass back up and pulled the chair that was closer to her out and sat.

Karen let out an exasperated sigh. "Dude! Really?"

"I just want us to not have to yell across the table," he said calmly, with a smile that could sell vodka to a drunk Russian.

"You sure?" she asked with acid in her tone. "You're not afraid I'll try to grope you again?"

Daniel ignored the obvious callout of the even more obvious lie. "I know you're either Pedro's or Granger's gal, and all—" Karen said nothing, but the statement drew a frustrated laugh from her. "But some of us still have more practical experience in matters like this."

"Been through wars before this one, have ya?"

"That snotty attitude isn't helping, Karen," he said smoothly.

Karen set her un-sipped tea on the table and leaned forward. "Oh, you're a real smooth one, Monitor! You've done nothing but lie and undermine me from day one. You're a racist, a sexist, and a narcissistic mother fu—" She never finished her statement, as a glass of iced tea smashed against the side of her head with a violent crash!

Woozy and with her left temple bleeding, a short and powerful right hook to the same spot from Daniel nearly knocked Karen out entirely. He caught her as she started to fall forward onto the table. Looking at the lantern light drifting out to the patio from the house, he saw nobody. He wrapped his arms around her waist and stood her to her feet. She was full dead weight, so he had to move in close to keep her upright. As he dragged her backwards toward the pool, he nuzzled his nose through her dark hair and gave her neck a long sniff. He then twisted with all his might, throwing her into the pool.

CHAPTER 24

USS LYNDON B. JOHNSON DDG-1002

"FIRE AT WILL, CIC!" MILLIE YELLED INTO HER PHONE. IN THE previous three minutes, not only had a drone swarm started dropping bomblets at the pair of ships, but the line of PLAN destroyers that had built itself ahead had turned and were coming at the battered destroyer and cruiser. LBJ and BH were spaced a half-mile apart, while the six ships ahead were in a wedge formation three miles wide—four ships in the front echelon, followed by two. Bunker Hill had launched several missiles at the drone clusters to try to stop the attack.

Mount One shuddered as it let loose its first round at the ship closest to directly in front. It was eight miles ahead, and the round penetrated just to the port of centerline, ripping through the entire destroyer and coming out the back. Millie stared through her binoculars in awe, as nothing seemingly happened. The ship just kept coming. She was a second away from telling her CIC to hit it again when the sight of fire presented itself out the front hole. Four seconds later, the ship's forward engine room aflame from the ripped open fuel lines, smoke started billowing out of the ship. It got a round out of its forward gun before exploding. The round landed sixty yards to the port of LBJ and exploded, peppering that side with shrapnel and fire.

Millie moved to her port windows to see what was keeping Bunker Hill from opening fire. "The flooding must be affecting her forward gun!" Millie called out to nobody in particular. She could see the ship being navigated in an old-school zig-zag pattern, allowing the aft gun the angle needed to join the fight straight ahead. The net result, though, was a loss in forward distance gained. "Decrease speed to ten knots, XO!" she ordered. She watched as the other ship's aft gun mount opened fire. In the course of a minute, twenty rounds had been sent at two of the ships ahead, with twelve of them connecting. As Bunker Hill drew perilously close to LBJ, she began to turn the other direction.

Millie moved to the radar screen, seeing that the approach speed of the enemy was twenty-eight knots. They'd cut the distance to four miles. As Bunker started drifting south again, the aft gun mount was spinning around, preparing to fire off her starboard side. Several rounds came in from the three remaining ships. LBJ took a shot directly in the digits painted on her bow, but the fuse on the explosive projectile didn't operate. The ship shook from the impact and took structural damage to the anchor system, but no explosion occurred. *Thank you, Lord!* Millie thought in relief. Bunker Hill, however, was not so lucky.

The explosion of her ally, only five hundred yards away, shook Millie back to reality. She looked out in horror as she saw Bunker's aft end engulfed in flames, ripped open down to the waterline. Now flooding at both ends, the ship would not be traveling much farther. "Nooooo!" Millie called out. LBJ's Mount One fired again, missing the closest ship.

She yanked the phone out of its cradle. "CIC! Why isn't Mount Two firing?!"

"It's down again, Ma'am! They're working on it!"

"Bunker Hill just got hit!" Millie told him. "She's a sitting duck. Get both mounts firing on that one that is coming straight at her!" Millie watched as her forward mount engaged the target to their north, hitting it. The barrel began the slow transition to port, trying to match the rapidly approaching PLAN destroyer. It was aimed to pass between the two Americans. The PLAN destroyer shot a salvo at Bunker Hill, hitting the bridge in a thunder of light and flame, killing Captain Cooper and her team and most of those in the CIC, too. The enemy gun trained toward LBJ. To her bridge team, she ordered, "Flood the ballast tanks on the foc'stle, and start pumping them out on the fantail!" She wanted to sink the front end and lighten the other. "All ahead flank speed!"

Mount One spat a round that passed through the enemy's aft end, ripping it open below the helicopter deck. The intense friction and energy started a combustible fire in the aft end spaces, but it didn't ignite anything precious. The warship kept coming, poised to pass only three hundred yards away in just moments.

Mount One was recharging, and the Chinese cannon was aiming directly at LBJ. It fired. From point blank, the thunder was deafening and the fireball quite impressive. The round shot directly over the bow by a margin just a little more than the extra draft they'd taken on in their ballast tanks!

Millie grabbed her handset. "Fire!" she yelled.

Mount One shook, sending the heavy slug directly into the destroyer's gun magazine. The explosion of the powder room caused a cascading effect of subsequent explosions that would stick in Millie's mind forever. The heat and pressure coming off the PLAN ship as it ripped itself apart was enough to be felt through the bridge's heavy bullet-proof windows. Paint not already marred from nearly two hours of battle under the blood red sky began to boil. As LBJ picked up speed, it was plowing the waves heavily. "Pump the ballast tanks back out to thirty percent," she said. She had one more ship to annihilate before she could go start finding survivors of the sinking Bunker Hill.

"Bridge, CIC!" she heard a panicked and tired Dennis Bates call out on the speakers. "Torpedoes in the water!"

USS James L. Hunnicutt SSGN-93

"Range to the LBJ!" Carla Gingrey called out to her sonar team.

"Twenty-two thousand yards, Conn," came the tense reply. Somewhere between them were two Ming submarines hunting their surface cousin.

The starboard side-looking sonar had not reset properly after the concussion. As they moved northwest, the crew had figured out that the three-dimensional display was skewed. *Untrustworthy. Turn off the screens, Ma'am,* Darren had advised her almost thirty minutes earlier. *Old school.*

They weren't flying blind—they were now just as blind as their counterparts. Many of the younger sailors, including the junior officers, had not served on anything older than a Seawolf or Virginia class sub. Old school scared the snot out of them. Darren, however, was able to easily drift back to a place in his head. A place where staring at black and green operational panels in the hot, cramped space was the norm. He was taking a small liberty with passively assisting the XO in her stress, asking the questions and finding the data that she was forgetting in her very first command of a sub.

"Ma'am, the thermal is at three-seventy in this area," he said. The ocean was warmer near the surface. The temperature and salinity differences were enough to mask quieter submarine noises from the microphones on an enemy on the other side of the barrier. "Let's get under it and pop up... here," he advised as they looked at the Quartermaster chart.

"Another torpedo!" one of the sonar operators called excitedly. "A

Mark 46!" This told them all it was from an American surface ship rocket launched torpedo. LBJ was shooting back.

"Very well, COB. Make your depth six-fifty." As Darren relayed the instruction, she continued, "Verify that is a total of two torpedoes," she said to her team.

"Two, aye," the chief started to say. "Correction! That's now three!"

ACME RANCH
    Southeast of Tucson, Arizona

TRACY ROUNDED THE DARK CORNER AROUND THE OUTSIDE OF the main house. His broken arm and shoulder were still quite useless, bound in a composite splint and slung tightly to his body to prevent movement. He had caught sight of a fleeting motion as Daniel's legs passed through the door frame back into the house. He opened the wrought-iron gate for the fence and passed through it, making haste to get back into the house himself. Something was off with Daniel, and he couldn't quite put his finger on it. Then he saw it. Blood. He scanned, seeing that it wasn't an isolated drop, but an elongated splatter, one of several in a row.

"Help!" Tracy heard Daniel scream inside the house. The lantern wasn't that bright, but the blood trail went inside. "She attacked me!"

Tracy spun around, certain an illusion was afoot. He moved over to the poolside table with one glass of tea sitting on it. He saw a chair knocked over, then pieces of glass... and then...

"Karen!" he yelled, ignoring the yelling and commotion going on inside the house. Without thought, Tracy jumped into the pool feet first. He kicked with his feet and tried to swim with one arm, the wounded one feeling like an anchor. "Help!" he yelled as he approached her. The Navy vet was from the service's other, lesser-known special forces. Like SEALs, the SWCC boat operators went through an intense training, including a hell-week and being 'drown-proofed' in a deep pool. Tracy let himself sink the three feet down to the bottom and then kicked up, propelling himself to breach the surface. That gave him time to take a giant breath. He kicked, treading with just his legs, something that having his hands bound behind his back in the training pool had taught him. He reached under the face-up woman, trying to push her up under her back with his one good arm. "Help!" he screamed so loudly that it made his throat feel burnt.

A giant splash sent waves ripping through the pool as Pedro dove in like a human torpedo. He surfaced just a few feet away and swam over. Maneuvering to her far side, Pedro helped prop Karen's bleeding head up. The pair of men worked to get her to the side of the pool.

"Here!" Jerome yelled, followed closely by his wife who was wearing a headlamp and carrying a lantern. Jerome dropped to one knee and bent over, jamming his hands down into the water and scooping Karen under the armpits. With all his power, he hoisted the woman from the pool and dragged her onto the patio. He immediately assessed her airway and respirations. "She's still breathing!"

Robin knelt on the other side of Karen. "Roll her toward me!" she said. Karen started to cough and choke, trying to catch her breath.

Daniel, Donna, Bob, and the Bowers all came rushing out of the house.

"What the hell happened?" Pedro asked as he and Tracy moved to the shallow end to walk up the steps. He was eye-balling Daniel with white-hot intensity. Daniel was holding a blood-soaked towel to his forearm.

"I'll tell you what happened!" Daniel exclaimed as Karen continued to gasp and choke. "She broke a glass and cut my arm! I had to knock her into the pool in self-defense! She must've hit her head!"

Tracy stormed up the pool steps and stormed over to Daniel. He tried to swing the water-logged cast at Daniel, but the nylon swath kept it tethered to his body. He started a profane tirade that would make Samuel L. Jackson blush—it was second nature to the former sailor.

"Back off, Rogers!" Daniel yelled back. "It won't do anyone any good for you to get a beat down right now!" He stormed back into the house, still putting pressure on his sliced forearm with the towel.

Karen started to get up, and the Washingtons slowed her down. "Whoa, easy does it," Jerome said as he put a big pawl on her shoulder to keep her upright but sitting. "Take a couple o' minutes to clear your head first."

"I... I..." Karen mumbled.

"Just give it a minute, girlfriend," Robin said, examining the scalp wound on Karen's left temple.

"Dude said you attacked him," Jerome said.

"Uh-uh," Robin said, giving her husband a look. She told him with her eyes to look at the wound and then turned toward her medical kit to find tweezers.

Jerome saw the piece of glass stuck into the scalp about an inch beyond the hairline. His face shifted from concern to anger. "Donna!" he called the boss lady, who had been trying to pacify Tracy and Pedro from going to confront Daniel.

She walked over and looked at what Jerome was pointing at. Robin softly patted the wound with a piece of gauze once more, and then pulled it so that Donna could see. "I... I don't believe it!"

The sound of a quad starting up on the far side of the home sent Tracy and Pedro running into the house, with Jerome twenty feet behind.

Karen took the gauze from Robin. "Help me up! Please!" The two women each took a hand and helped Karen stand. A bit wobbly, she turned and let them hold on to her hands and elbows as she moved toward the house. "That SOB attacked me! I'm done with letting men get away with that!" The three women moved into and through the house, Karen's stability getting better with each step.

They went out the front door in time to hear yelling, followed by the quad engine revving up as it took off to the west. Upon entering the parking area, Karen saw a very pissed off Tracy and Pedro being calmed by a slightly less ticked Jerome. The Bowers had followed along, observing everything as quietly as church mice.

"Let him go," Donna advised. "We'll just take off and he'll be out there all alone, caught in a war."

"What?" Pedro said, upset.

"It's okay," Karen said. She walked up to Pedro and Tracy and grabbed each one of them around a neck and pulled them close to her. All three of them were still dripping and wet. "Thank you, my hermanos," she whispered.

"What'd I miss?" an overdue but welcomed voice said from the dark of the driveway.

They all spun to look, and Karen's heart skipped a beat. "Granger!"

CHAPTER 25

USS James L. Hunnicutt SSGN-93

"Twenty-seven degrees up-angle!" Darren said as he relayed the command to his pilots. He assisted them in watching the air gauges on the Hunny's ballast tanks. As the high-pressure cylinders pumped air into the large spaces, the voluminous ballast tanks' water levels decreased in proportion to the drop in pressure in the air tanks. The positive buoyancy, the up angles on the dive planes, and the speed all shot the submarine toward the surface. "Five-fifty!" he called out their depth. A few seconds later, "Four-fifty!" The tension was palpable.

As Darren called out three-fifty, the chief sonar operator yelled, "Contacts! Designate Uniform-zero-one! Range six hundred! Bearing two-zero-five! Depth two-ninety!" They'd popped up just ahead of and to the right of that enemy submarine. Without waiting to be told, Darren had the pilots level out their ascent.

Carla interrupted the chief. "Get a solution and launch tube two on that contact!" she yelled. As the sonar chief continued, they felt the ship shake. Another hunter had been added to the foray.

"Designate Uniform-zero-two! Range sixteen hundred! Bearing zero-one-four! Depth three-zero-five!"

"Launch tube one!" Carla ordered her fire control officer. "Where are those other three fish, Chief?!" The ship shuddered again.

"The 46 is going active on Uniform-zero-two," one of the junior operators announced. "ETA twelve seconds! They're turning away and diving!"

"Tango-one missed LBJ! It's coming back around at bearing zero-one-zero!"

"Fire tube three at Tango-One!" Another shwoosh as another armed killer entered the fray.

"Tango-two is going active at LBJ!" the third operator called out with stressed tension. "Range to target fifty-two hundred, ETA two minutes!"

"Impact on Uniform zero-two in three seconds," the chief announced as they pulled their headsets off for a moment.

"On speaker, Chief!" Carla said. They listened to the explosion of the destroyer's rocket launched torpedo, followed closely by the sounds of flooding. The active sounds of the torpedo chasing the LBJ could also be heard. Only two hundred yards from the sub to their rear port, the Hunny's torpedo went active, sending pulsating sonar to verify target Uniform-zero-one. It exploded midship along the PLAN sub's starboard side.

"Kill the speaker!" Carla said. "Increase speed to flank! Weapons, redirect our shot at zero-two toward the fish turning around on LBJ! Sonar, keep listening—verify both subs are sinking! COB!" she yelled at Darren, giving him a look of concern for the safety of the destroyer they were trying to protect. She was looking to her trusted mentor for guidance.

"We're at fifty-eight knots. We have the speed. You know what to do, XO," he said with a grave look that betrayed the calm in his voice. He thought of his wife and adult daughter back in Washington State. "I'm so proud of you, Carla."

One hundred twenty miles southeast of Eureka, California

An E-2 Hawkeye from Naval Air Station Fallon, designated as Sword-1 on the radio, had been airborne and monitoring all the dogfights and other military air travel in central California. They were circling northern Nevada and southeastern Oregon. One of the several radar control technicians on the craft had been assigned the sole responsibility of overseeing the Marine Raider insertion mission. Her only job was to monitor three craft—Tusk-1, Tusk-2 and Terrier-1, Lou's plane. She'd be ready to direct the Tusk flight F-16s toward any of the several Chinese carrier-launched fighters now patrolling western California should they detect and home in on Terrier-1. She would be the person they'd be begging for help if they were discovered.

Lou and Angie were holding course at 34,500 feet, due to hit south of Eureka and veer north just seconds before dropping the Raiders in four distinct groups. The piers and docks they were going to infiltrate and disable were a few miles apart and on both sides of the bay. There would be slight gaps between each group jumping. Lou had Terrier-1 maxed in speed at just over 500 knots, well above their normal cruise speed of 450. They would have to slow to an agonizing 120 for the drops and he wanted to be in the area as short a time as he possibly could. Their guardian angels were flying at 45,000 feet on a parallel course and speed eight miles to the east, ready to pounce, and praying for the opportunity to issue some payback.

"Ten minutes from depressurization," he announced on the cargo hold speaker. He cut the switch back to cockpit communication. "I need a favor, guys," he said to his two passengers.

"You name it, boss," Travis said.

"Monitor Rusty for me. Be ready to share your mask with him once we depressurize. I'm sure he'll be fine with a little air blowing on his nose if he starts to pass out."

"No sweat, colonel. He's one of us, now. We got his back!"

This made Lou finally say something that had been weighing heavily on his mind. "And to that end, fellas... and lady," he said as he looked over at Angie, "I'm sorry I dragged you all into this. But I'm glad you're here with me in the thick of it."

Before any of them could tell Lou to quit being such an emotional sap, their radio blared to life. "Tusk Flight, Sword-1! There are five, repeat five, bogies inbound on Terrier-1, bearing two-seven-two, speed eight-fifty! Range is eighty miles! Elevation 22,000 and climbing! They're on an intercept course!"

Lou and his crew knew immediately that they were already in range of the enemy planes' long-range missiles. "Terrier-1! You're clear for evasive!" She was giving them the clearance to move as needed— she would be ready to guide them back on mission.

Angie was already on the intercom. "We have enemy fighters inbound! Everyone, hold on!"

"They still need to jump from altitude! But we're not slowing down until the last minute! You guys mask up!" The three of them strapped the on-board pressurized air system masks that were staged within arm's reach onto their faces while Gray moved back to prep the hold for the jump evolution. Even though they could remain pressurized while the hold was open, this new threat was real and unpredictable. *Better to have it on before they shoot holes in us five miles up,* Lou thought.

Lou saw Tusk-1 and Tusk-2 scream west just ahead of them. They were still over 40,000 feet high, looking to keep the high air over the superior numbers rocketing toward them for a fight. All that the Terrier flight team could do was listen—and be ready to dive and bank if one of them got a shot off.

"Tusk-2," the flight leader said. "Hit them with the Deltas! You target the two to the north!" The AIM-120D was the latest variant of an advanced 'fire and forget' medium-range missile. The launching plane could send data updates in-flight, but the missile's ability to home-in on jamming emissions had been proven to be deadly accurate in conflicts around the world. Each of the Tusk flights carried two.

"Roger!" Tusk-2 replied. "Fox-three!" he called as he launched his two missiles a second apart.

"Fox-three!" Tusk-1 said, too. The two defenders had just launched four missiles.

Lou gave a quick scan, but the late afternoon sun angle made it difficult to see much of the long-range dogfight.

"Tusk flight!" Sword-1 called out. "Detecting four missile launches!"

"We got 'em!" Tusk-1 replied. Tusk-2 stayed two hundred yards off and slightly behind his flight leader as the pair of screaming Falcons began to target the incoming threats with their AIM-9 Sidewinders.

Lou tried to concentrate on his own job and not get lost in the worry of 'what if' should one of the inbound missiles sneak past their protectors. "Sword-1, ETA to our turn!" he called on the radio.

"At current speed, four minutes, Terrier..."

"Three minutes to depressurization!" he called to the teams in the hold. The Terrier team were all sweating bullets and holding their breath as they listened to the F-16s acknowledge they'd knocked down all four missiles. Three of the enemy had fallen victim to the F-16s' initial shots, leaving two fighters to find and destroy.

"Tusk-1!" they heard the other pilot call out. "That one from the south is getting around behind us!"

"Leave him, Robbie!" they heard the flight lead reply. "Let's stay on the J-31!"

"We need to start slowing, Colonel!" Angie called Lou back to their own world.

"You're right!" He pulled back on the jets' throttles and adjusted his control surfaces to account for the decreased thrust without losing altitude. The responsive plane started decelerating.

One tense minute later, they heard Tusk-1 get destroyed by the plane that had gotten past them. Tusk-2 had run himself down to one missile taking out the J-31. He was trying to hold on to it, which meant using his gun. That would require getting an excellent position behind or to the side of the evading but less-advanced J-20.

Lou scanned his heads-up display and saw that they were below two hundred knots in speed. "Commence depressurization," he announced. Angie began to depressurize the plane so that they could open the ramp.

"Terrier-1, start your turn to angle zero-one-zero in thirty seconds!" the nervous E-2 radar operator called.

"Roger!"

"Tusk-2, Sword-1!" he heard the radar plane call next. "Four more bogies inbound from the south, ETA eight minutes! I'm redirecting Seahawk-1 and Seahawk-2 to your position. ETA ten minutes!"

"Roger, Sword!" Tusk-2 screamed. "Terrier, this guy is coming right at ya! Gimme thirty seconds and I'll be on 'im!"

Lou ignored his guardian. *Don't have time to worry about something I can't control!* he screamed in his own mind. "Cabin is depressurized!" he called back to Gray, who powered on the ramp control panel. "One-minute to the first drop! We're looking at about twenty to thirty seconds between the greens!" In between each drop, he would switch the green 'jump' light back to red.

The big plane's attitude adjusted a bit as the ramp came down, revealing the sunny California coast below. Four fourteen-man Marine Raider Recon teams plus two regimental officers were all jocked up in their gear, breathing systems, weapons and parachutes, itching to go issue some pain and suffering.

Suddenly explosions began to sound off below the big gray plane, turning the air rough and choppy. Lou looked west toward the ocean. The lead destroyers in the invading fleet were only four miles away. "Sword-1, we're taking naval AA artillery!" he called into the radio. "It's a matter of time before they lob a SAM at us!" A surface-to-air missile would be the end of them, short of a miracle.

The shells were getting closer as they exploded, rocking the plane as they cruised slowly toward the drop zone. "These boys are gettin' thrown around pretty good, sir!" Gray called into the headset intercom from his station by the ramp control panel.

"Stand by!" Lou yelled into the hold speaker. "Ten seconds!" he said as he looked at his HUD, the digital displays, and the ground below them. He flipped the light switch from red to green.

In the hold, the first fourteen Raiders all ran toward the ramp as a pack, feet pulling up behind and almost over them as their helmeted heads began the drop to terminal velocity. Lou gave it ten seconds and switched the light back to red. The plane continued to be buffeted by the anti-aircraft explosions. He flipped the switch green again, and ten seconds later, the second quarter of their troops had disappeared toward the new war below. The low-opening drop was critical for the unorthodox daytime jump operation, enabling the Marines' parachutes to be exposed in the sky for only a few seconds before they landed in the softball fields and school grounds they'd picked for their LZs. Lou turned the light red once more.

A half-minute later and a slight planned course correction to get the next two teams on the west side of the bay, and he turned the light green once more. Just after the third team deployed, a shell exploded within a hundred feet of their left wing, rocking the plane sideways and sending a few cockpit alarms into panic mode. Instantly, Lou knew the Marines in the back had to have been thrown around like rag dolls. He scanned through his window. "We've got damage! I see smoke!" Another explosion rocked the plane, ripping holes into the underbelly.

"We've got wounded back here!" Gray announced. "That last one sent shrapnel up into us!"

"I'm on the way back!" Travis said, tying Rusty's leash to his chair handle as he opened the cockpit door and moved aft.

"We're losing fuel!" Angie announced. "And the landing gear is showing tire deflation alarms!"

"They've dialed-in on us! We're bugging out!" Lou called back to Gray as he banked hard to the starboard and pushed his throttles to the max, picking up speed. "Close the ramp!" he ordered Angie, who used the cockpit controls, not waiting for Gray to use his controls in the back.

"Good news, Terrier-1!" he heard Tusk-2 say. "I splashed the last bogey from the first wave with guns! I'm moving in to assess your damage!"

The C-17 was slow to respond as Lou continued to bank east. "Something's off," he told Angie. A fire alarm for both port side engines blared. Lou looked back out and saw that they were trailing black smoke. "Hit the extinguishers!" he ordered his co-pilot. As Angie turned on the onboard halon systems for both of those engines, Lou cut the throttle to them and started shutting down the fuel lines on that side.

"Terrier-1!" he heard Sword-1 yell. "I'm detecting a surface launched SAM!"

CHAPTER 26

"What neighborhood is that to the east?" Lauren asked Alex. As the sun settled in the west, the sounds of war on the beaches had been augmented with new sounds. Screams, gunfire, and the roaring of loud engines filled the air. The group was no longer carrying rifles slung on their backs—they were slung to their fronts, with a few people carrying them in a ready position. The water on the eastern side of the river was gone, and it was nearly gone on the western side, too, as best as they could tell visually. The basin itself was still several feet deep.

"I think it might be Boyle Heights," Alex said. "Which means the Arts District is over there on that side of the river."

"It is," Roman Lopez acknowledged from the left side of the group's front line. "It's largely Chicano. My cousin lives there."

"Should we go get him?" Jessie asked from the middle.

"No!" Sissy Lopez said before her husband could answer. She was shaking her head emphatically. "He's not a good person."

"She's right," Roman said as he continued to scan the river to their left. "He and his kind will be hurting good folks in that neighborhood tonight."

"Maybe we should try to cross back over," Alex suggested as the sounds of several guns shooting at each other suddenly flared up in the neighborhood just across the nearby highway.

"I don't think it will matter," Lauren said. "Evil will run in all areas from now on. But we do need to find a safe place to take a break. I'm sure the kids need to eat—and I need to go pee." People were growing beyond the social stigmas of announcing such things anymore. They were learning it is hard to fight or run for their lives with a full bladder —at least if the goal was to keep dry skivvies.

"Agreed!" Micah called out from the back. "Micah needs food," he announced in third person.

"Let's get across the First Street bridge," Ned suggested. "There's a fire station a couple of blocks over that I did a plumbing renovation in a couple of years ago. Might be a safe place to rest."

Gun fire erupted to their right, causing everyone to freeze and stare. "Everyone down!" Lauren yelled in recollection of their recent training by Lucky Charm. As she hit the dirty pavement, she flipped her rifle off safe and loosed two rounds at a muzzle flash. Incoming bullets were missing people by inches, some of them overhead, others ricocheting low off the ground. Roman was struck in the side of his chest and dropped before he could lower himself.

"Fire back!" Alex yelled as he picked one of the other four muzzle flashes and began to fire at it. "It's coming from those two buildings! Henry! Get them to the river!" Henry, Micah, and Sasha had been herding the older folks and kids near the back of the pack. He picked up his mother and started sprinting west down the short block to the fence meant to keep people out of the river.

Lauren picked herself up and ran toward a dumpster. She passed it and turned, kneeling, and continued firing. "Move!" she yelled.

Alex's ears were ringing, but he thought he heard a familiar command in the background. He got up and crouched, running as fast as he could while bent over. He got to Roman and tried to drag the big man, but Roman's eyes were nearly lifeless, chest ripped open by a large caliber round. Sissy Lopez was screaming as Ned dragged her towards the cover of the last commercial building corner between them and the fence. He let go of Cisco's leash, and the dog was staying right on his legs out of intense fear and confusion. Alex grabbed the two shocked children, his rifle barrel warm against his leg as it dangled in its sling.

At the fence, Henry was trying to remember who had packed the group's one pair of bolt cutters. "We need to make a hole!" he yelled out as he ran back toward the action to scoop up the slow-moving Mrs. Ngo. He froze in horror as he saw the old lady's head open violently from a bullet going through it. "Noooooo!" he yelled.

Alex planted himself next to Lauren and told the kids to run toward their mother at the fence. He and Lauren continued to fire at the muzzle flashes. Movement caught Alex's eyes. He shifted fire at the running human shapes, who were trying to flank them. "We need to get into the river! Go see what's holding them up!"

Lauren performed a magazine change as she sprinted toward her wife, who had just pulled her backpack off and removed the bolt cutters tethered to the back of them with small bungee cords. "Over here!" she called out three times as she spun and started firing again to cover them.

"Go through!" Jessie was yelling at the Lopez family, who were still wailing in disbelief that Roman had died right in front of them. Ned Manner pushed himself past them, guiding his lab mutt through the spread open hole with him. Once more, he released Cisco and turned back, pulling Serena Lopez and her little brother through.

"Get through there!" Jessie was yelling at Sissy.

Henry had recovered himself and was now trying to rush his parents along the fence toward the opening Jessie had made. The small team slowly made it through the opening and down the gentle incline. There was close to forty feet of distance down the concrete slope before they would find themselves in the murky flowing water. Lauren and Alex had finally made it through.

"What're the odds they'll follow us?" Alex hollered over his ringing ears.

"They may be glad we broke contact," Lauren said. "There are much easier targets out there for them to attack!"

Sissy and her children continued to wail in total shock. Alex's mother was screaming, too, having just witnessed the violent murder of her friend of over forty years.

"Listen!" Micah said. He started to run along the slope to the south. "It's an engine of some kind!"

Just then, around the angled turn in the aqueduct an odd sight sprang into view. A unique square and boxy boat with a roof and open-air seating was moving toward them. It was about forty feet long and painted in vibrant purple and yellow. 'Ride the Ducks!' was painted in orange artistic lettering on the side. There were four armed men and women sitting low in the vessel, heads and rifles sticking up only as much as necessary. Even against the river's flow, it was making good time toward the group.

"Everyone—hold your fire!" Lauren called when she saw Micah start to raise his rifle. He looked back, ready to argue, but relented and put his rifle back down to low-ready. The duck boat steered itself toward the bank, coming right for the group. A man as unique as the craft moved through what one might call the windshield frame. The plexi-glass screen itself was pushed down and flat onto the engine cover. He crawled, then stood on the flat bow of the boat and picked up a coiled mooring line.

You don't see this every day, Alex thought, still panting from escaping the near-death ambush. The man appeared to be in his late forties or early fifties. Aside from a round potbelly, the rest of him looked so skinny that his pants were about to fall off his butt-less frame. He was a skosh over six feet tall and had brownish hair on the sides that turned into a long ponytail. The top was clean of hair, as bald as an American eagle. He had a tie-dye shirt on under a brown leather vest that was adorned with pins representing various interests. Under his Fu-Manchu mustache was no beard and a giant toothy smile.

"Ahoy, maties!" the grinning man said, with a temperament that matched his golden hoop earrings. "You folks look like you could use a ride, considerin' the gunfight you were just in!"

"How do you know we're not the bad guys?" Micah asked sarcastically as the entire group and duck boat all converged on the same spot along the bank. The friendly man tossed the bow line to Ned, and the man operating the craft lowered the throttle to keep the props moving just enough to counter the current.

"Most gangs aren't multi-racial and have elderly!" the man answered, losing none of his fervor. He looked back at the adults in the group. The curious event had even caught the attention of those grieving enough to quiet them a bit. "Name's Hugh. But everyone calls me Star Bird!"

Alex and Lauren had both approached the boat, scanning it in awe. "How far you headed?" Alex asked.

"'Til the water runs out?" Lauren asked.

"We won't let that stop us," Star Bird said, still smiling. "This here duck boat can drive on land!"

"That's right," Ned said. "I went on a tour on one of these in Pearl Harbor once."

"You betcha!" Star Bird said. "I bought this one from a tour group in San Diego that was shutting down. That's who owns and operates these things anymore—tour businesses!" He scanned the bank above them. "Seriously! You all should probably hop on board with me if you're continuing north! You just don't know what you'll find around the next bend, but you're darn near guaranteed to find nothing but pain up there on the streets!"

ACME RANCH
Southeast of Tucson, Arizona

.   .   .

KAREN, TRACY, AND DONNA BROUGHT GRANGER UP TO SPEED on not only the night's events, but the history of subversive deception that Daniel had been slowly weaving. They finished by providing an update on the Army's advisement that they bug out... that the front lines would be shifting north past the ranch in the coming day or so. Karen was sitting at the edge of the garage in a camping chair while Robin wrapped her head with gauze and cling wrap.

"Yes, I've been privy to some of those updates. That's why VooDoo arranged to get me down here as quickly as possible. I have a place for us to go. It won't be as plush as this beautiful ranch," he said as he looked around. "But we'll be able to continue thriving and training to help repel Charlie. We're heading to a gun range about twenty miles east of Flagstaff. The I & I units are starting to gather there." Tracy gave a nod in understanding.

"The who?" Donna asked. "And isn't Charlie a derogatory word from Vietnam?" Bob just snorted as he hobbled by with some radio equipment.

"Oh—oops. The insurgents and irregulars. Fancy words for militia. But politics and the media and flabby idiots made it so we can't use that word anymore," Granger explained. "And Charlie is just the phonetic word for the letter C, right? C as in Cong, or Viet Cong. C as in Chinese. It's just shorthand, not meant to be insulting. People just apply that stigma out of ignorance. Just like the word militia," he added. "Anyhow, the camp is where we've been sending everyone. VooDoo heard there are others, too. Nevada. Texas. New Mexico. Even Kansas and a few other places." At that moment, they all felt the ground rumble, though there wasn't a corresponding explosion they could see or hear. "Uh-oh," Granger said.

"Uh-oh what?" Karen asked with a grave look.

"That can only mean Charlie has started a bombing campaign. Their hackers did a doozy on our own bombers and our more advanced fighters, I've heard. Dozens or more F-22s and F-35s driven into the ground through the hijacking of the plane's controls via malware."

"That's... just so hard to fathom," Tracy said, trying to pat dry his wet splint with a towel.

Granger scanned south, then walked to the western edge of the parking area. After taking a good hard look, he walked back over toward the gear he'd dropped on the ground when he arrived. He called Bob over. "Can we use the ATAK software?"

"I would need to fire up the generator to power the Wi-Fi, but sure. And I'll need to dig a tablet out of my gear. Why?"

"For comms. Karen and I are heading up to the top of the hill to make sure Daniel doesn't do something stupid." He was strapping on his battle belt and leg rig for his pistol. He stood and put on his coat and patrol pack. Finally, he picked up his rifle case. It contained his short-barreled rifle and a sniper rifle, which was the one he removed.

"Me?" Karen said, standing. "I—I'm not sure I'm up to it."

"You are," Granger said. "And you need to prove it to nobody but yourself. I have a special job for you. I'm counting on you," he said as he looked directly into her eyes. "Go grab your gear."

He then walked over to where Fred and Pam were loading one truck. "You two, too. Grab your stuff."

"Where are we headed?" Fred asked as he set a container in the back of the ranch pickup.

"Not 'we.' You. You two grab your stuff and take off. You're not coming with us." Granger's voice was as flat as an out-of-tune piano.

"Where—where are we supposed to go?" Pam stammered, fear crossing her face.

"Not my concern," Granger said as he turned to go meet Karen by the bunkhouse for their trip up the dark hill. "But you need to be heading there before I get back."

USS LYNDON B. JOHNSON DDG-1002

"ARE YOU SURE THEY'RE BOTH DESTROYED?" MILLIE GOLDBERG asked her operations officer on the phone.

"It's the Hunnicutt, skipper!" he replied excitedly. "Not only the subs, but they took out the torp that circled back around! There's only the one left!"

It was too much for the short redhead to bear. She ran back to CIC as fast as she could. "Range?" Millie asked with a strained yell.

"Five hundred yards!" the sonar operator called back. "Wait!" he added. Time froze in the dark tense space. "The Hunnicutt—she's slid in behind us!"

What? Millie thought in pleased exasperation. "Repeat that!" she commanded. The display projected an icon showing the ally U-boat pulling through the plane of the torpedo's path. All three vessels— destroyer, submarine, and enemy hunter—were cutting through the ocean at high rates of speed. LBJ, with her bow damage, was barely making thirty bone-rattling knots. Their submarine guardians were traveling nearly twice that. And the deadly torpedo was still twenty knots faster than that.

"Hunnicutt has passed through our wake!" The room was silent save for the sound of computer fans and bleeps for three seconds that felt like an hour. "The torpedo is following them!" the operator screamed with relief.

"Put it on the speaker!" Dennis Bates said to another sonar operator.

The sound of the torpedo's active sonar could be heard screaming in fast cycle. They heard the fizz-gurgling of chemical countermeasures start to erupt, like a giant Alka Seltzer.

"It went through the countermeasures!" the sonar operator called. "Range to Hunnicutt is one-hundred!" The sonar technician's voice transitioned from relief to terror. "Fifty!"

The room fell still as the explosion ripped through the speakers like a stake in their hearts. The explosion sent shock waves that rippled through the hull, but their submerged saviors had pulled the torpedo off course and toward themselves a couple of hundred yards to their port quarter. Several of the sailors gasped. Two cried out in horrified disbelief. The heroes had sacrificed themselves to save their surface sister crew, much like the USS Bunker Hill had done.

All of them listened in horror, like being stuck in a terrible nightmare, as the sounds of flooding compartments filled their ears. The submarine began to sink and break apart, slinking away into the cold abyss of the eastern Pacific waters below them. *Dear Lord!* Millie cried in her soul and mind. *Why?*

CHAPTER 27

"TUSK-2, THE BOGIES WILL BE ON YOU IN LESS THAN ONE minute!" the E-2 radar operator code named Sword-1 called over the air.

Ignoring her, the fighter pilot called out to Lou. "I've got one missile left, Terrier! Moving into position to take out your SAM!" After a tense ten seconds, "Fox-3!" he said to announce he'd fired. The fighter's last Sidewinder curved in ahead of the incoming ship-launched missile, which had quickly gained fifty-thousand feet of altitude to let gravity give it extended range. Tusk-2 continued to fly toward Lou's C-17, intent on protecting those he swore he would with his life, if necessary.

In the Globemaster, Gray, Travis, and the unwounded Marines were dealing with the continued loss of cabin pressure and shrapnel injuries. Lou was taking the craft down in altitude, not just for his crew and passengers, but to extend range from the rapidly approaching certain death. "Gonna need you to help me pull this out at ten-thousand!" he called tensely to Angie. He'd also had to overcome with the loss of both port engines by holding rudder at an angle with his pedals, which was going to be uncomfortable if they lived long enough.

"Where are we headed?" she asked relatively calmly, given their dire predicament.

"Reno!" Lou said. "Fallon, if we can make it," he added. "They'll be better prepped for us," he noted of the Naval Air Station.

"My sidewinder missed!" Tusk-2 announced. "I got about fifteen seconds to try something! Hold on tight!" On full afterburner, the pilot eyeballed the incoming SAM, praying God was blessing the timing on his near-sacrificial flight. He shot through the gap between the inbound spear and those he swore to protect, pumping out a continuous stream of flares. The SAM took the bait and curved just two seconds out from the C-17. It exploded with deadly force as its heat-seeking nose found a decoy flame.

More shrapnel peppered the tail of the battered Globemaster, tossing everyone around once more. "Wooohooo!" Lou called over the air as they marched toward the east at a turtle-like pace of three-hundred knots. "Tusk-2, you just saved our bacon!" He took a quick scan back at his pal and saw Rusty tucked in behind Angie's chair with a worried look.

Before their guardian could reply, four J-15s buzzed by. Their controller had not informed them of the two American planes' lower altitude. They split into two pairs and began to curve and dive for the easy prey.

"I'm going after the pair to the west!" Tusk-2 screamed into the mic, trying to pick up altitude and speed. "Sword-1, I'm on guns-only and low on fuel!"

"Copy, Tusk-2," the nervous controller said.

"This is Seahawk lead!" a new pilot called out. Two F-18s that had already been in combat to the south were almost on scene. "We're targeting the eastern pair with long-range! Still two minutes out! Fox-3!"

"Let's try to duck under those two looping around ahead of us!"

Lou told Angie. The duo turned to a northeasterly heading in an attempt to evade those enemies.

"It's getting hard to turn!" she called out. "I think that missile gave us a hydraulic leak!"

"I'm holding the yoke!" Lou said. "Switch over to the backup electrical motors!"

Angie flipped switches when one of the J-15s dove on them, guns blazing. The enemy strafed them with his thirty-millimeter cannon, sending rounds into the top of the hold and undamaged right wing before rocketing past them in a steep dive. The sound reverberated through the hold. *I bet that just killed some more of our Marines!* Lou thought. "Guys, gimme a report!"

"That was bad, sir!" Travis said. "Gray's down! Most everyone back here is wounded! A couple just got ripped to pieces by that!"

The two missiles from the Navy F-18s screamed overhead as they approached and killed one of the eastern pair of attackers. The other missile missed its mark.

"Seahawk, this is Tusk-2! I can't shake these guys!"

Lou tuned out the ongoing dialogue of the fighter jets. "Let's get headed east by southeast," he ordered.

Another cockpit alarm sounded off. "Fire in number one!" Angie said. Once more, she hit the extinguishers while Lou killed the throttle and fuel to that engine. Technically, they could fly on the one remaining engine, but it would be slow going in the best-case scenario.

After a minute, Angie said, "It feels like we're holding altitude!"

"For now," Lou said. "Look at the fuel! We'll be lucky to get to either airport!"

"A desert crash might be survivable if we can clear the mountains!" Angie said. "Should I check the landing gear?"

"Not yet!" Lou warned. "If they come down, they may not go up! We don't need the extra drag, and we may be better off landing on the belly if the ground is uneven."

"I think our rudder is stuck," Angie said. "Not much, maybe a half degree. But it feels like we're drifting to the right."

"I think you're right," Lou agreed. He pulled a map out of his seat pocket and started opening it up, looking at the contour and terrain. "We may not get much choice in where we land if we've lost steering."

USS LYNDON B. JOHNSON DDG-1002

"KEEP FIGHTING!" CARMEN YELLED AT HER NEW CREW members as they worked to shore up damaged bulkheads and seal the flooding from battle damage at both ends of the ship. Dusty, Carmen's fellow damage control specialist and co-survivor from the sunken carrier, had moved to the stern. She was in the bow. The two aircraft carrier firefighters, not yet assigned their permanent damage control stations on their temporary home, were desperate to motivate the crew to save the ship. "You do not want to let this ship sink!" *I can't live through that again!* she knew.

The ship's anchor windlass room had taken hull damage, but so had the space to the aft of it on the port side. That storage room's interior bulkhead was ripped open, as well, spilling cold and unforgiving seawater into the ship's main passageway at an alarming rate. The slender craft continued to bob and ply through the battle on the outside, as the fight for their lives raged on the inside.

Carmen ran back down the passage with two others, grabbing more four-by-four lumber from its stowage hooks on the bulkhead. They carried it back up through the flooding space under the flickering of the backup battle lanterns. The flooding had reached critical electrical cabinets that had to be shut down. Lighting and ventilation systems were down or at reduced capacity. The wall outlets in ships were wired differently than those civilians were used to in buildings. Each wire was hot and came from a different bus for exactly this reason—dewatering pumps and smoke removing blowers could be plugged-in nearby and still work. Lights and backup lanterns would still work, even if dimmer. Speakers could still pass critical data.

"Captain's pumping out the ballast tanks!" a voice on the 1MC called out. The flooding team was still establishing a sound-powered-line phone system for hard-wired two-way communication with Damage Control Central. Suddenly, the loud rumbling of compressed air bottles below the waterline and in the tanks erupted, sounding like a loud hiss, sending small vibrations through the steel decks. Nobody fighting the flooding could feel it, but the ship began to lift itself out of the water as it pumped seawater from the tanks. The unique destroyer's commanding officer had decided the tactical advantage to being lower in battle wasn't worth the additional risk of sinking sooner.

Carmen and the others laid their lumber on folding sawhorses that kept moving around in the torrent rushing past their legs. "Hold those!" the sailor with the handsaw yelled. He was calling off numbers to himself, trying to remember the instructions the repair party leader had called back. The crosscut saw had razor-sharp teeth, big ones. There were only four per inch on the old-school device, but they made quick work of the lumber. The pieces were passed up the chain and installed behind wood and composite patches over the holes. Metal grinders, powered by compressed air, had flattened the jagged metal edges down. The lumber was now being used to hold the patches in place, cut to just a few inches shorter than the span across the passageway to the opposite side. Wood wedges were driven in against the gap on the far bulkhead to hold the lumber in place.

The entire delicate system went through a process of continuous improvement even as the flooding had reduced itself to a fraction of what it had been. The closed off anchor equipment room was holding its seal at the watertight hatch access. The loss of the storage room they were sealing up was a nuisance when the alternative had been sinking. It was now just a matter of keeping the pumps moving and doing what they could to keep the patches firm.

Carmen breathed a sigh of relief. She caught the same look on the other sailors' faces. "Way to fight, Team LBJ," she said as she slapped another sailor on the back as he walked past her under the flickering lights. She realized she hadn't heard the big guns fire in several minutes. *Maybe we'll actually live through this day...*

WESTERN NEVADA

WITH TUSK-2 AND THE TWO JETS OF SEAHAWK FLIGHT covering the retreat, Lou and the crew were focused solely on staying in the air long enough to find a place to land. The area between them and northeast of Reno was filled with the Sierra Nevada Mountains. And though many times in Lou's life people had joked about him landing on a highway, he knew that doing so wasn't plausible. With a wingspan of just under one-hundred-seventy feet, the Globemaster was sure to clip signs, poles, trees, and anything else under the sun. Ripping their wings open while scraping down the road was a guaranteed way to end life in a ball of fire.

The sun was setting on the day America was invaded, visibility reducing to nil rapidly. "There's a dry lake out here that would be perfect," Lou said. "It's called Winnemucca. But we're clearly going to miss it with this tiny turn to right we're stuck on." Try as they may, the rudder was frozen. He and Angie were down to one jet, a sluggish ability to descend—which they dare not try until clear of the mountains—and landing gear that were flat at best. Fuel was leaking, and they had wounded and dead crew in the back. Next to punching out of his A-10 in Afghanistan at the beginning of his career, Lou couldn't remember a more stressful moment in his time as a pilot.

Angie was pouring through her own contoured map—the pair wouldn't dare fire up the electronic navigation at that point. The thought of being crashed by a hacker after surviving so much was incomprehensible. "The area north of Fernley looks like a giant field," she said. "Several miles in both directions."

God, don't you dare play with us, Lou thought. *Not like this.* "Is it in our arch?"

Angie scanned the fuel. "I think so. Not that it matters. Even if we can get some level of rudder response, this will be our one shot."

Lou looked out at the darkening forest mountains below. He tried to raise Travis on the comms but got no reply. He sent Angie back to check on the others and brief them to hold tight for a rough landing. He had Sword-1 contact the airfields at Reno and Fallon to let them know where they estimated they would be going down. They, in turn, notified the civil authorities of the small city of Fernley. Everyone in town was already on edge, knowing their country was under attack.

Fifteen minutes later, Angie pulled a snack out of her pocket and gave it to Rusty as she rubbed his head. After she reseated herself, Lou looked over, but it was dark—too dark to see the blood on her uniform that he could smell. "Let's start our descent."

As they approached the enormous field, they thought their eyes were deceiving them. "Are those... lights?" Angie vocalized.

"It looks like headlights," Lou said. There was a small town to Fernley's northwest. On the road that connected them, as well as on Interstate Highway 80 that headed east along the south edge of the open field, vehicles were lining the shoulder of the road, their headlights pointed in toward the field. Lou flipped on every exterior light he could on the plane, as well as the transponder he'd shut off for the insertion mission. "God bless Americans," he said with wistful hope.

"At least it tells us where the perimeter is," Angie said with a choke in her voice as she cinched her seat harness as tightly as she could. She grabbed the yoke once more. "I've got it for a minute, Lou." Without hydraulics, the beast had become a tiring burden to keep on an acceptable glide slope.

Lou pulled his hands off and gave them and his forearms a good stretch. He cinched his own harness and keyed up the cargo hold speakers. "About ninety seconds, gents." He looked at his co-pilot, her face illuminated by the electronic gauges. "I'll take the throttle. You hold the rudder and work the ailerons. There's no telling what will happen when we hit the ground. Forget the wheels, our belly is so flat I think that's the way to go." He put his left hand on the yoke and started to power down engine number two, which was pushing them at a measly one-hundred eighty knots. According to the maps, the elevation of the town was at just under 4200 feet. They'd barely cleared the mountains and were approaching the ground more rapidly than Lou would've preferred. He tried his best to feather the craft down, sweating as he worried about stalling out too high off the darkened field. The partners were flying on faith.

The headlights a few hundred yards to their right seemed to raise in the illusion of loss of altitude. "We're at forty-three hundred!" Angie called out nervously.

Lou watched the air speed start to tank. "Flaps to two-thirds!" he ordered, as he pushed the throttle back up on the remaining jet. He was trying to keep the plane's attitude with just a slight up-angle on the nose. As they settled toward Earth, he felt the nose pick up. The added drag of the control surfaces on the wings helped add a bit of loft, which pushed the nose up like Lou wanted. The added thrust was just enough to correct their pitch as they settled over the dark field full of scrub, dirt, and grass. There was an odd sense of quiet for the last three seconds. Then they settled.

The C-17's shape kept the wounded craft's wings and rudder well above the field, even without the landing gear deployed. The plane shook and rumbled violently as they started scraping the pasture. Lou killed the last of the engine's thrust and shut down all fuel lines, while Angie fired off the remaining wing fire extinguishing systems on both sides. Dirt flew up. The cockpit windows started being pelted by rocks, sod, grass, brush, and cow manure.

Outside the craft, each town had sent as many volunteers as they could muster with virtually no notice. Two fire apparatuses designed for off-roading, called brush trucks, drove into the field and chased the descending plane. Civilians in big pickups followed suit, eager to do their part for the American heroes ahead of them. The sound of engine two reverberated off the field, slowly being replaced with the sound of metal grating on rock. As the jet engine slowly whined itself down, the craft stopped sliding, followed shortly by the rest of the churned-up dirt and pebbles falling back to gravity's pull. Terrier-1 was down.

CHAPTER 28

CYPRESS PARK
Los Angeles, California

THE THREE-HUNDRED-FIFTY CUBIC-INCH CHEVY SMALL BLOCK continued to idle as Star Bird's son, Pierre, went about a few post-waterborne tasks. He pulled the plugs on the hull and disengaged the two driveshafts from their differential boxes. Finally, he used a couple of wrenches to remove the propellers, knowing they would be as valuable as platinum if they were to be lost or damaged. The motley crew had exited the river, having traveled the previous three miles purely on the six tires. The flood waters that remained were well south, and they were approaching the point in which the famed river reverted to its natural state instead of the concrete one.

Star Bird's brother-in-law and sister were the other two members of the odd-duck's party. They had stepped out onto Riverside Drive to guard the rest once Star Bird had parked the beast on the west side of the river. It was dark, and the Santa Monica Mountains not only glowed a dull orange reflecting the fires below, they also reverberated the sounds of a society lost. Los Angeles was at war—with gangs, with the Chinese army... with itself.

"We need to get rolling," Star Bird's sister, Babs, warned. "I got a case of the hinky jinkies!" Though not quite as extravagantly 'hippie' as her older brother, Alex had gotten the feeling that she marched to her own drummer, too. Short and round, the gruff woman seemed to be graying prematurely and wasn't nearly as jovial as her brother.

"All set," the skinny, extra-tall Pierre said as he moved out from under the duck-like craft's rear end. "We're going to need gas soon. We had to have burned through most of it already."

"I think our allies can offer you some when we get there," Alex told Star Bird.

The hippie was watching his family re-board their craft so he could start driving again. When they were all seated, he stated, "I'd appreciate it if you all can keep an eye out for gorillas, ghouls, and aliens!" He winked at Alex as he nodded and moved back to the driver's seat. "Whatever you all can provide, we'd appreciate. But we were already headed this way, so it didn't cost us anything. In fact—you helped me erase some past bad karma, right?"

"I guess," Alex said, not sure how he was prepared to deal with such a... 'big' personality. *I grew up in a crowded and uptight Asian home, mister,* he thought. *My mom woulda killed you if you were her kid.* He scanned back at his mother, who was leaning against his brother and trying to sleep. There were several rows of benches in the large tour boat. On another, the two Lopez children were wrapped in each other's arms, trying to sleep after the nightmare that had claimed their father. On the floor at their feet was a cage with a pair of chinchillas. Pierre Stevens had let the kids hold them for a while to help them cope with their grief. "I don't know if we'd be alive if you hadn't come along," Alex told Star Bird.

"Like I said, brother! Karma! We should be able to follow Riverside Drive all the way to Griffith Park. Did you say you're headed to the old zoo?" he asked in confusion. "That... might be just a bit dangerous at night."

"Our allies are the kind of people dangerous people should be afraid of," Alex said without even thinking about the context.

"That's twice," Star Bird said, assuming he didn't need to have the rest of the conversation. He'd already had it in his head and was just waiting for Alex to catch up.

"Uh... What?"

"That's the second time you've used the word 'allies' instead of friends."

"Well, they're part of... that is to say, I've only met them—you know what? It doesn't matter. The place was rendered a safety zone by a joint civilian and military op. And we've been invited."

Star Bird proceeded along the winding road at no more than fifteen miles-per-hour, ready to react to any kind of attack or emergency. After they'd traveled another twenty minutes in silence, Alex said, "Did you and your family need to take a rest there? I'm sure it'll be okay."

"We'll see," Star Bird answered as he kept scanning the road on the drive. "I don't really sleep, anyhow—I drop acid. But they may want to nap..."

Alex had just started taking a long pull of water out of the bladder from his backpack. Hearing that made him exhale half of it through his nose. He started coughing and gagging. "You—you what?"

"Oh, don't worry," Star Bird said. He turned his head and with the most deadpan stare Alex had ever witnessed, added, "I haven't hit a tab in like a half-hour..." After five long seconds of not looking at the road, he finally smiled and winked at the young hotel owner. He looked back at their path. "I think we're about there," he announced as he crossed Los Feliz Boulevard. The road they'd been on converted itself to Crystal Springs Drive. It split, with two lanes headed north and two south, divided by a wide greenbelt barrier that resembled the hills to the left. As they slowly moved around a slight curve to the right, a series of floodlights came on.

There was a vehicle trap made out of sandbags that the duck boat was going to have a difficult time maneuvering through. Star Bird pulled over. "This might be about it for the Stevens clan," he announced.

The spotlights turned back off after three seconds, on just long enough to tell visitors they needed to proceed with caution. Alex stood and moved back to where Jessie was sleeping against Lauren's shoulder. "Pssst. Lauren."

The former correction officer shook her head and tried to peel her eyes open. "Why are we stopped?" she asked, trying to wake herself in case there was trouble.

"We're here," Alex told her. "Some kind of roadblock. I'm heading out. Catch up when you can."

The tall blonde stretched and yawned, trying not to disturb her wife and best friend. "Be right there."

Alex grabbed one of their procured night-vision sets and exited the stairs attached to the rear of the duck boat, hitting the pavement on the right side when he was done. Leaving his rifle hanging low, he proceeded up to the people and vehicles a hundred yards to his north. He had a sense that he was under the scrutiny of one or more snipers. He was a bit nervous about making sudden movements. There was a quarter moon out, and as he approached the location, the shapes of sandbags, trucks, and armed people started to present themselves.

"Park's closed," a gruff man's voice announced calmly. "But I have to admit—the fact you made it here alive in a duck boat has my curiosity piqued."

"Name's Alex," he announced. Lauren stepped up next to her shorter battle buddy. "We're part of Rampart Edge."

"Never heard of it," the voice in the dark said.

"What about Dacso? The tan dragon? Heard of him?" Lauren asked.

"And your name?" the voice asked.

"Lauren."

There was a long pause. "Wait here. And don't make unnecessary chit chat." Three other visible silhouettes continued to guard the entry point while the one that had been talking moved farther into the dark.

The sound of bike tires on gravel made its way back to their ears as an electric bike took off and up the hill. *Makes sense,* Alex thought. *Using a radio is probably a bad idea now that the Chinese seem to own the air.* Lauren took a seat right where she stood and yawned, finally settling on laying down right in the road. Alex sat next to her.

It took a full twenty minutes to hear tires coming back down the hill. After the electric bike parked, footsteps approached the gate, causing Lauren and Alex to get back to their feet. "Well?" Lauren asked.

"Whut teck you so long to geet here?" a welcome and familiar Hungarian accent asked in the dark.

USS Lyndon B. Johnson DDG-1002

THE LONG SLENDER SHIP HAD MOVED WEST PAST THE LAST OF their enemy's raiding fleet. The explosion that sank the USS James L. Hunnicutt had sent a concussion and air pocket hard enough to cause a bad shimmy in their port propeller. They were moving along at fifteen knots, utilizing a zig-zag steering tactic to slowly get west— much farther west than she'd thought possible. There were a pair of lost American non-combatant ships that needed aid—and an abandoned place off the ocean's 'beaten path' to hide.

She sat in her bridge chair, too pumped to sleep. She'd ordered the crew back to modified General Quarters. They needed half to try to catch naps, but she was still worried a stray submarine would sneak up on them. Millie closed her eyes, and instantly her thoughts went to her family, hoping she wouldn't accidentally drift off to sleep and have a nightmare about them.

ACME RANCH
Southeast of Tucson, Arizona

THE LIGHT FROM THE EXPLOSIONS OF CHINESE BOMBS, artillery, and missiles in and around the small towns north of the Nogales border crossing danced off the high clouds that had formed up that evening. They were rhythmic like the lights of a discotheque sans the music. The rumbling off in the distance and the vibrations in the ground Granger was lying on added to the sensation that war truly was beating at their doorstep. His time in the Recon Marines was half his life ago, but the events of the last few months had made it feel as if he'd been fighting for years, the time in uniform as if it had been yesterday.

He scanned through the night vision scope on his rifle, barrel elevated on the stock's bipod. He'd not bothered with building a sniping hide or laying out a recon mat to lie on—the goal here was just to provide overwatch for the busy bees loading trucks and a trailer down below. He laid but a few feet from the old mesquite branches covering the observation post that had been occupied almost non-stop since they'd all moved to the ranch. Behind him was the quad and his pack, positioned to head back down the trail when he received word from Bob via the ATAK app that they were ready to roll out.

The ride up had been slow and methodical, stopping to scan for signs of Daniel and dropping off Karen so that she could provide a sort-of overwatch, too. Not daring to turn on a light, the movement of the desert dust could be smelled easily enough but finding usable tracks to hunt for Daniel would have to wait for morning light. *And with any luck, we'll be a hundred or more miles north by then,* the scarred firefighter thought.

The consistent rumbles were growing in intensity, reminding

Granger that hundreds if not thousands of Americans were dying in tanks and foxholes, unprotected from the air at a level not seen by troops since the Pacific Theater. It also masked the slight rustle of dirt and grass, as a shape—almost a mere shadow—of a man crested the hill to the southwest. He knelt, stopping to look and keep bearings. Slowly, the phantom crept, repeating the process of checking for its prey's alertness every few moments. Daniel Monitor was slowly gaining on Granger from behind.

Daniel waited for a fresh rumbling, pausing under the eerie glow off the clouds at the quad. He slowly slid a six-inch fixed-blade knife out of a Kydex sheath and waited. While tempted to poke the sidewall of the quad's left-rear tire with the knife during the next big sounds from the war, he instead reached with a hand. He unscrewed the valve-stem cover and patiently let the air out, taking the full two minutes for the tire to be effectively flat. The entire time he scanned all around, surprised that the supposed super-Marine ahead of him had not done the same.

Daniel got onto his belly and began to crawl, keeping the knife in his dominant hand. He froze about thirty feet away from Granger when the scout did a quick check of a comms app on a dimly lit screen. Giving it a few seconds, his slow hunt in the loose dirt began once more. As he moved through the sandy terrain, his knees, toes, and elbows continued to push down to gain traction. The dark was perpetually flashing from the strobe of war, and the vile man failed to notice the lump of sand next to the small path he was on.

After he'd passed it, a creature not unlike one of the scorpions that constantly invaded the ranch's overwatch hole only feet away started to un-burrow itself. Sand and dirt slid off silently as a second predator began her stalk. Karen rolled over off her back and pulled the child's pool snorkel out of her mouth, sand and dirt sticking to her sweaty face. She got up to one knee. She waited for another bright flash off the clouds. Then it came...

Karen ran for eight feet and jumped with a sprawl shape through the air. As she came down on Daniel, she let loose the war cry of a wounded Banshee. The soft dirt cushioned her knees as they landed on each side of Daniel's thighs at the moment the startled man was trying to decipher what that horrible screech was. Both hands on the Kabar's hilt, she plunged the seven-inch blade down between the predator's shoulder blades.

"Yeeeiiiaaaarrrrrrggghhhh!" she screamed. Granger rolled over, pulling the pistol that had been laying under his propped-up chest with him. There was no need. Karen pulled the dagger out of the screaming man and plunged it again. And again. Years of torment, buried under the psyche of abuse both in adolescence and at the hands of her ex-husband flooded to the surface. She began to cry, her body's way of dealing with the intense anger and raw emotion.

Granger had gotten to his knees, then to just one as he scooted another step to the side. Daniel had made it to within one body-length away from the willing bait. He made a sickening gasp and gurgle. The first plunge had all but guaranteed success as it severed his spinal cord. The rest had only served oddly merciful to him, the pain a tradeoff for a quicker death by hypovolemic shock. "Karen..." Granger said calmly. He repeated the passive command three more times as he walked over slowly and knelt. He held his hand out.

Karen looked at him sobbing, the flashes off the clouds occasionally showing the blood splatter up and down her face from the repeated overhead thrusts down into the last page of the painful chapter that had been her life. She looked at her friend's eyes and then down to his open and waiting hand. She dropped the Kabar in the dirt. She placed her hand in his, and the sobbing joined the tears. Her emotions were full and frail, having spanned the enormous gaps between fear and courage... rage and relief... and hate and inner calm, all in a matter of moments.

Granger just held the hand, letting the woman he had started to truly admire retain control through the rapid grieving process. *She's not grieving his death,* he knew. *But rather the death of her own innocence.* After several moments, Karen retracted her hand. Granger pulled a bandana out of his cargo pocket and gave it to her. He retrieved her knife and wiped it on the back of the dying man's pants to clean it. He patiently collected his gear, donned his coat, and gathered his rifle while Karen collected only her calm and composure.

She walked over to a piece of scrub brush and found her own gear, putting it on. Granger moved to her and then looked back at where the past lay unburied. No flash of light bounced off the clouds for the last look. "You'll never have to go through that again," he told her.

She glanced into the black as well. "Killing? I'm not so sure about that..."

"Oh—you'll most assuredly have to kill again." He sighed. "But there's only one first time." With that, he put his hand out once more. She took it, and side-by-side the pair slowly made their way back down the trail toward the ranch house.

CHAPTER 29

NAVAL AIR STATION FALLON
Fallon, Nevada

LOU TOOK RUSTY OUTSIDE TO RELIEVE HIMSELF AFTER sheltering inside most of the night. In the week since the crash landing, he and the rest from his plane had been recovering at the Branch Medical Clinic and barracks. The least injured included himself and Angie, mainly just stiffness from the jarred landing they rode out strapped into chairs. Out of those in the back, four had perished from wounds received from the strafing run, including crew member Gray Saylors. Three more Marines were recovering from surgery. Mechanic Travis White had been banged up, but was expected to fully recover with more rest, as were the remaining eight Marine Raiders.

The base had come under a cruise missile attack the night prior. Though it had only lasted moments, the secondary explosions of hangars and the fuel manifolds that led to the underground storage were still happening. The blue sky was obscured by black, oily plumes in several locations, giving a burnt smell to the air. *Everything feels slimy,* Lou thought, thinking it might be unburnt aviation gas droplets resettling to Earth. The war had finally come to Nevada, and everywhere he looked he saw fear on people's faces.

The enlisted Marine Raiders had been granted space to recover and wait in the same officer's barracks as Lou and Angie. As Lou took a worried Rusty off the sidewalk and to the nearest pecan tree, he saw the eight men finishing up a jog back from the base gym. The young officer in charge of the remainder of his squad headed over to Lou when he saw him. He knelt and petted Rusty, who started to lick his face.

"Mornin', Colonel," First Lieutenant Jonathan Patrick said.

The sound of yet another civilian fire engine roared by to assist the military's fire units, led by a base police car. Lou waited until the sirens made it past to respond. "The base half explodes all night, and you guys go hit the gym? I'm starting to figure out why they call y'all 'jarheads'."

The young man stood and laughed. "It's not all fun and games, sir. I received a message at 0330 this morning that we've been assigned to augment a local EOD unit. They've been given a mission here in Nevada, and they're short-handed."

Lou tugged on the leash and started a slow mosey through the grass back to the sidewalk. "I guess that's good. Waiting sucks." He scanned the young man's face. "But I guess you've probably been in the Corps long enough to know that."

"What about you and your team, sir? Any news?"

"'Fraid not," Lou said. "We were on a special assignment. The plane is from Ohio. Angie and Travis are both part of a reserve unit there. They headed back last night before the attack hit. Like I told you a couple of days ago, I work directly for General Montgomery and what's left of his staff. I think the front line along the spine of California and Oregon has rightfully captured their attention, though."

"Yes, sir, the thing where you were organizing civil defense groups..."

"Exactly," Lou continued. "Anyhow... I've spent my days trying and failing to track down my number two, who I last knew to be in the L.A. area." Lou's face perked up. "A leatherneck, like yourself. Someone, I'm ashamed to admit, I've grown quite fond of."

The pair grew silent after Jon's courtesy laugh at the last quip. He reached the door to the barrack before Lou but held the door shut. He turned to face Lou again, his expression deep in thought. "Listen, sir. I still need to talk to EOD. But if you can score a small plane, I think we could use you—and not just to fly."

"Where are you headed?" Lou asked. The Marine had piqued his curiosity.

"Hawthorne," Jon said. "It's the nation's largest weapons depot, and it's just sitting there, waiting for Charlie to grab it."

JOHNSTON ATOLL
    Pacific Ocean

MILLIE WATCHED THE ACTIVITY BELOW ON THE PIER, COVERED in gull droppings and tufts of tropical vegetation growing from nearly every crack and crevice. Hours earlier, teams of Combat Controllers, part of the special forces community in the Air Force, had parachuted onto the island. Their mission was twofold—ensure the runway was up to par and help a trio of Navy ships secure themselves to the piers without the aid of a tugboat. It had been a long and stressful week of limping south since the big battle.

Almost nine hundred miles southwest of Hawaii, the tiny atoll had been beefed up with dredging after World War II, not unlike the Chinese military bases in the sea lanes connecting the Pacific and

Indian Oceans. The four islands had grown to just over three thousand acres. The nearly rectangular largest island had two delta shaped piers on its southern long side. In the last three decades, the only activities had been seasonal use by the United States Fish and Wildlife Service, other than the occasional medevac of a wounded sailor to a waiting plane. After the Cold War, the high-heat incinerator made use of its time burning up the nastiest chemical and germ weapons known to humans. That, and its older history of testing nuclear and bio weapons, had left the place hazardous to stay on for long durations. Nature had slowly started to heal mankind's sins.

The solution to pollution is dilution, Millie thought somewhat cynically as she scanned her crew's refuge. *I guess licking our wounds here is the best bad choice, though.* The Air Force CCTs had set up heavy rubber bumpers to keep the ship from banging the pier too badly. After handling the lines and helping rig a light aluminum brow to send over for the crew to cross, they went back to help their comrades with removing debris and patching holes on the runway and taxiway that bisected the long slender atoll.

Hawaii was under siege, as the assigned military was entrenched in a fierce fight against their invaders. Millie feared it might be months or years before one side would win. The Chinese were in a position to resupply troops and equipment. And they'd done substantial damage to the American military with their advanced weapons and asymmetrical tactics. But the American military had a one-hundred-year head start on the pros and cons of operating there.

At the larger delta pier on the island's east end, Millie saw the two non-commissioned ships pulling to the pier. Staffed by civilians, the merchant vessels served the Navy's battle groups. The USNS Guadalupe was a replenishment oiler and the only reason Millie's destroyer had been able to travel to the atoll haven. The USNS Charles Drew was a dry-good ship. Both had escaped the sinking of several combatant ships in the South China sea via space-based weapons. Millie felt it had probably been Divine Providence that the ships found each other after her battle.

She left the bridge, which was quieting down. She'd ordered a 'skeleton' team to continue staffing the CIC around the clock, though they were being selective with their use of radar and electronic communications. There was a good chance China was ignoring the abandoned atoll, and she didn't want the overzealous use of her gear to give them away. After making one last trip to her cabin to change into a fresh uniform, she proceeded down to the hangar bay.

"Everything in order, XO?" she asked her second-in-command. They were staring at their remaining Chinese POWs, still in the two cages.

"Ready to transport when you give the word, Captain," Agwe Bailey confirmed. His usual smile still showed no sign of returning.

"Air Force expects they'll be landing the first C-5s sometime tonight," Millie informed him. "We'll have these prisoners staged and waiting to take off as soon as they're ready. Right now, I'm heading ashore with the chief engineer. The fleet operations—what's left of them, that is—have been transferred to Norfolk. The attacks on Pearl and San Diego have left us against the ropes. They want a SitRep on the state of the facilities here."

"Speaking of San Diego," Agwe said. "The crew has been asking how bad it is. What the status of our families is…"

"I know, XO. I'm still trying to decide how to address this. I think an all-hands face-to-face tonight after chow might be the way to proceed. We've lost our homeport. The entire west coast is under Chinese control right now, which includes our families." Her face turned grave. "We may not know for a very long time if they're alive or not."

NORTH OF CAMP LONGHORN
    Coconino County, Arizona

. . .

THE WEATHER IN NORTHERN ARIZONA HAD JUST BEEN TOO tough for Jerome and Karen to handle in the vehicle with no front and back windscreens, even with winter gear and goggles on. They abandoned the shot-up ranch truck on the south side of Flagstaff, using the parking area of a gas station near the airport to transfer people and goods to the other five vehicles in their procession. Granger had talked them into spreading themselves a bit thinner for just such an unplanned issue. They all used some of the metal green and red 'Jerry' cans to top off the rigs, those being the limiting factor on leaving ranch fuel back in the larger above ground tanks.

The convoy moved to Interstate Highway 40 and started to head east when they encountered snow. There were four inches on the ground by the time they exited at Winona Ranch Road twenty-one miles later. They stopped once more. Granger gathered the adults at the lead vehicle after all of them had made the exit and large loop back to the west onto the paved road. "The road turns to dirt when we turn onto the forest service access," he said. "There'll be enough of the larger group's vehicle traffic down past those houses a mile up," he said as he pointed southwest, "that we should still be okay without chains. They know we're coming."

"Who all will be here, again?" Donna asked.

"Some military. Guys like VooDoo. But mostly folks like us. Civilians and veterans of every flavor."

"If anyone thinks they're losing traction, flash your lights and honk," Karen suggested.

"Good call," Granger said. With that, the group checked their tires and loaded back into their vehicles, proceeding the eight slightly winding miles to what used to be the Northern Arizona Shooting Range. The facility had become the gathering spot for the Rampart Edge teams being assembled in Arizona. As soon as they turned onto the dirt forest service road, they encountered a manned checkpoint.

Though Granger presented the correct pass phrase, his unique burns and reputation easily identified him as one of the Road Runners. Since they'd been involved in the border shootout weeks earlier, the Road Runners had developed a certain notoriety.

They moved past the two trucks and four people on duty. Camp Longhorn was the only facility down the long road. The lane ran four hundred yards south and east of the winding Walnut Creek, on a roughly parallel course. The creek was only wet during the first weeks of spring and during the heavy rains of July and August. Similar to the famous canyon seventy miles northwest, it had been carved over many centuries and was almost fifty feet from the desert's surface to the creek bed, which provided an excellent northern natural barrier.

The facility was blanketed in snow. There were two square and neatly detailed traditional ranges that both pointed toward clean tall berms on the east. To the west and south sides were compact gravel parking areas, and well south down the continuing road were trap, skeet, and archery ranges. The parking areas and desert on all sides were filled with campers and tents. A virtual city had sprung up. Several tractors and one bulldozer had found their way up in the preceding weeks, which contributed to building not one but three different gravity-fed septic systems and fields. An existing well was augmented with rain collection off any roof surface. To the west, a solar farm was growing, and the first small shed had been built to contain the batteries and electronics. Pumps down in the creek basin, which was part of a protected national monument, were filling large plastic holding tanks with water by night, and the system was recharging by day.

Greenhouses of several sizes had sprung up, and there were shipping containers for which people could store the food and ammunition they donated to the cause. Antennas were displayed near several tents and trailers. There was an aerial work platform staged in the field to the west, its telescoping boom played up to ninety feet. In the basket at the top was a weatherproof box containing two remotely zoomable cameras pointed toward the highway miles to the north. One looked toward Flagstaff, the other toward New Mexico. Also mounted to the device was a weather data unit and additional radio antennas. The other three cardinal directions were nothing but desert and low mountains.

The group found places in the larger south parking area to stop and get out. As they did, Donna and Robin gathered the kids and made for the restroom and shower house. Most of the rest began to stretch and discuss the nuts and bolts of where to establish their tents in and amongst the nearly three hundred people already at Camp Longhorn.

"Jerome," Granger said. "Why don't you organize our basecamp in that direction? I'll go find a couple of the leaders and bring them over."

"You got it, brother."

Granger made his way off toward the office, while Karen and Tracy just looked at each other and started to smirk for no reason. They'd both caught some long overdue sleep on the trip north to their home for the foreseeable future.

"I guess I'm just glad he found us a place to stay," Karen admitted as she looked around.

"I knew he would," Tracy said. "It's his nature. He's always thinking. Always working on a backup plan, just in case the current backup plan becomes the main plan."

Karen turned, her boots crushing gravel as she spun to see the man she was falling for walk away. "That he does." She began to help Pedro and Jerome haul tents and tarps out of the trailer and take them east through the tent city. They each gave cordial greetings to the variety of men and women they encountered, receiving polite glances and smiles in return. As they started to erect a large Army surplus tent, Granger showed back up with one familiar face and one new one.

"Hello again, Road Runners," Delta operator Mikkel 'VooDoo' Hudson said. As they returned the salutation, the fresh face stepped up to introduce himself.

"So, you all are the Road Runners," he said with an almost fanboy mesmerized tone.

"Kind of," Bob said. He pointed to Tracy. "The guy with the broken wing and I are originals. Most everyone else here has been in one or two shootouts with the cartel or gangs in Tucson."

Granger gave a slight grunt of a laugh, about the most he was known for. "They're all Road Runners," he announced, as if his word were final. "Two of our plank-owners are on permanent watch at the border and a third is laid to rest at our ranch." The middle-aged man nodded in understanding, not having to be told Granger was referring to Mick and Dave, who had perished at the hands of the human traffickers they were fighting. "Everyone gather 'round!" Granger called out to those that were working. "Vince, why don't you go ahead and tell everyone what's happening here," he suggested to the stranger.

"Right-o," he said in his usual concurrence. The man stood out in a worn and dirty white cowboy hat. He wore a faded denim coat with a white wool liner on the cuffs and collar, jeans, and cowboy boots. His hair was as white as the snow on the ground. His face and hands were tan with the sunspots and wrinkles of a man that had spent too many years handling horses or golf clubs—or both. He had caramel-colored eyes that looked like they were made of Italian marble. The striking older man was tall and lean for his sixty-one years. "I'm Vince Delaney."

"Why does that name ring a bell...?" Bob said.

"You probably know it from the news. I'm known by my first name in Phoenix. Senator Elwin Delaney. Everyone calls me Vince, though."

"You're a state senator, right?" Tracy said in recognition.

"Was," Vince said. "For the senate district that covers Coconino County here. I retired four years ago after my wife had an accident." Most of the rest nodded or gave looks of approval.

"Was Camp Longhorn your idea?" Karen asked as she eyed the cowboy hat.

"Not exactly," he grinned. "But if you used to follow state politics, you'll know I was one of the more outspoken members of the House and then the Senate in support of limited government and pro individual liberties. So much so that they tried to brand me as some kind of whack-job. As if supporting American ideals was some sort of fringe activity. So, my name was in the Phoenix New Times anytime they wanted to smear Republicans."

"You're the one that orated for thirty hours straight during a filibuster, aren't ya?" Bob asked as he walked over to shake the man's hand.

"Right-o," Vince said as he took the handshake. "Not that it did any good!" he laughed. "They still passed that damn bill!"

"Why don't you tell them a bit about what you have planned, Vince?" VooDoo nudged.

He looked at the Army soldier and nodded. "Right-o. So first off, welcome. The layout is straightforward. This used to be our local blue-sky range. I've spent a bit more time out here since I left office. I still have plenty of contacts in Phoenix, which vicariously means I also have some contacts in what's left of Washington D.C., too. I got wind of the program to build the civilian irregular forces up. I knew you all would need a place not too close to the border, but also not too far. If we're going to defeat Charlie, we need to have a secluded place to live and train."

"Aren't they just going to see us on satellite or plane recon photos?" Jerome asked.

"It's possible, sure," Vince said. "But unlikely. We've been taking out their satellites with hacking and physical attacks even more than they've been doing it to us. And if we're going to make P.S. work, we need to organize and train. 'Well organized' some might say. It's almost as if I read that in a document somewhere..."

"P.S.?" Karen asked.

"Oof! The op we're planning. We want to fill in the gaps wherever the line stabilizes after their initial push past the border. Stuff the holes with anyone willing to fight for America. We're calling it the Patriot Shield." Vince spent another five minutes giving them the updates he'd heard for the day. He finished with an invitation for them to all tune-in to Radio Free America on a variety of shortwave bands at seven each evening. Then he and VooDoo parted so that the new arrivals could get themselves oriented.

"Granger, can you show me where the ladies' room is?" Karen asked once the group was working on their tents again.

After they'd walked fifty feet down the snowy path, he asked, "If this is about you not having a tent, don't sweat it. You can have mine. I'll bunk with—"

"No," she said. "I know where I'll be sleeping tonight. I'm set." She patted the Kabar on her hip. "First, I wanted to know if you want this back. I inherited Claude's stuff, so I have more gear now..."

"Well," he began, "if my daughters lived here instead of North Carolina... maybe. But I'm not big on sentimental value. That served me in the Corps. It has mostly sat in a box since then." He stopped walking toward the field restroom so she would face him. "Besides, that's truly yours. In old warrior cultures, that knife owns part of your soul now. And you, part of its soul."

Karen laughed and smiled. She decided not to ask how a knife could have a soul when she saw how serious he was being. "Okayyyy. Second thing." She reached up and pulled his scarred head to hers, planting her lips deeply onto his, squeezing around his neck. She felt his arms wrap around her waist. When they finally broke the lip-lock, she retreated her face enough to make eye contact. "Just making sure you know you belong to me now. I'll kill any ho that tries to make a move on you!"

Granger busted his gut laughing in an uncharacteristic manner. "Marking your territory, huh?" he smiled.

"Absolutely. Last thing. It'll take me a long time to make peace with what I had to do. But I will. Thank you."

"You did it. I just showed you the path. You're the one who walked it. Don't forget that," he said.

"I won't." She gave him one more passionate kiss. When they pulled apart to walk again, Granger looked up.

"It stopped snowing," he said. "Maybe that's a good sign."

"Maybe," she said as she took his hand in hers while they moved down the snowy path. *Maybe not,* she thought. *But as long as the Patriot Shield has something they love to fight for... to fight beside... then there will always be a break in the clouds just around the corner to give us hope.*

The End.

I COULD USE YOUR HELP...

Three things.

One. *Please go leave an honest review* at your purchase platform, whether my website or Amazon or any of the other retailers. And if you truly enjoyed it, tell a friend (or six!)

Two. <u>Need the next book in this series? Or the next series?!</u> Please check out my website at authoraustinchambers.com. I direct sell most books and audiobooks there, the exceptions being any e-books that are currently enrolled in the Kindle Select program.

Three. Please consider joining my newsletter on my website. Starting May of 2023, I'll be providing a Free e-copy of <u>Tahoma's Hammer</u> to anyone that signs up for it. It is the best way for me to keep you up-to-date on my coming works, cover reveals, and what inspires me to write disaster and war thrillers. Thank you.

ABOUT THE AUTHOR

Navy veteran Austin Chambers spends his days concocting ways to drive his kids and grandkids crazy with new and untested "dad jokes." After multiple novels, he's finally getting comfortable with the thought of pursuing writing full-time. The former DOD Shipyard manager and his family live near the Hood Canal of Western Washington and long for the day that God needs them to move somewhere warmer and drier. Until then, they garden and enjoy the few sunny days outside watching Combat Kitty kill moles and squirrels.

Made in the USA
Monee, IL
30 December 2023

50828180R00184